Sniper Shot

Barry Ozeroff

ibooks
Habent Sua Fata Libelli

ibooks
1230 Park Avenue
New York, New York 10128
Tel: 212-427-7139
bricktower@aol.com • www.BrickTowerPress.com

Library of Congress Cataloging-in-Publication Data

Ozeroff, Barry.
Sniper Shot

p. cm.
1. Fiction. 2. Thriller—Fiction—
Fiction, I. Title.

ISBN-13: 978-1-59687-956-0, Trade Paper
Former ISBN-13: 978-1-59687-150-4, Mass Market

January 2013

Sniper Shot

Barry Ozeroff

www.ozeroffbooks.com

Author's Note:

   The characters in this book are not modeled on anyone who actually exists. Rather, they are combinations of various people I've known and the product of my own somewhat bizarre imagination. With very few exceptions, any resemblance to actual people or events is unintentional and coincidental. All errors, technical and otherwise, are my own.

I wish to give my sincerest thanks to the following people:

To my wife Cyndi and my children Sarah, Rebecca, Leah, Jordan, Barry Jr., and Andrew—I'm sorry for the unrecoverable lost time, I really am. You deserved more from me. To my mother Sheila Ozeroff (whom I have placed on a pedestal so high I can no longer see her), thank you for your unending enthusiasm and support, which actually kept me going when I gave thought to throwing in the towel. To my brother and fellow author Mark Ozeroff, thanks for all your invaluable input, editorial suggestions, and other help. To my other brother, Captain David F. Ozeroff, USN: You were manning your post all the while, and I salute you.

To Randy Bulger—teacher, mentor, physician, inspiration, critic, and, above all, friend. Also, my provider of good diversions, good music, and good fellowship. To my publishing team—my agent John Talbot, my publisher Roger Cooper, my editor Anne Greenberg, and my webmaster, Bill Parker. You da bomb.

And to the many others along the way, each of whom has been uniquely helpful, though you are too numerous to list, I send you my sincerest thanks. I hope to pay it forward.

Dedication

For the late Dr. Leonard N. Ozeroff

This book is dedicated to America's domestic warriors; men and women who, though they wear different uniforms and patches, are all still part of the same army. These are the heroes who run toward the sound of gunfire; the officers, deputies, and troopers who man our country's internal front lines against an ever growing tide of homegrown evil. Every day they push a sled around the worst areas of town, going head to head with and taking crap they don't need from people everyone else is afraid of. Too often they must see and do things that should be asked of no human, and only occasionally do they get to do things that make it all seem worthwhile. How is it that I always hear them say, "Can you believe they actually pay us to do this?" You stay safe out there, all of you.

Also by Barry Ozeroff
RETURN FIRE, the sequel to SNIPER SHOT

Prologue

THE POLICE LIGHTS, sliced into neat red and blue ribbons by the window blinds, flash ominously off the terrified faces of my hostages. Sticking to the shadows with my back to the wall, I creep to the window and risk another glance between the slats.

The officer is still as I left him, facedown on the porch near the front door where he fell. The two cops who had been hiding behind their cars are now gone. The abandoned cars remain, their overheads flashing brightly against the backdrop of dark clouds. It stopped raining about the time I shot the officer; fifteen, maybe twenty minutes ago.

The weather is typical for the Pacific Northwest in mid-December, and I'm glad I'm indoors. It's a small comfort.

Since I can no longer see the cops, I figure the SERT team is here. I can't see them, but they are here, I can feel it in my bones. Hiding. Watching. Preparing. I understand that my time in the house is limited. I'm okay with that.

The police cars and their incessantly flashing lights are the only visible sign that we're not alone, my hostages and I. And as if to response to that thought, a trail of angry red sparks arcs in front of my window. The source, a gray canister slightly larger than a pop can, was tossed from the corner of the house, out of my view.

The sparks leave a brief trail of diminishing lighted arches as the canister bounces on the ground and rolls to a stop between the fallen officer and the house. Moments later, the sparks give way to thick, dark smoke the color of the pregnant clouds.

A gentle breeze blows lazy curtains of smoke across my window, fully obscuring my view of the downed officer. Whoever threw that thing has very good aim. Through the smoke, I see more sparks and another canister, and the smoke doubles in thickness.

Three minutes and a third canister later, I hear noises. Through the drifting smoke I see fleeting images of shadowy, black-clad figures bearing guns and shields. There are several of them, materializing and disappearing like ghosts who can't decide whether or not to haunt me. Something's happening behind them, but I can't see what.

I have no illusions about what will happen if they see me. I slowly withdraw from the window and move to the back of the room.

The assault I'm expecting never comes, and in moments, the officers' ethereal images are just gone.

A few minutes later, the smoke stops and the air clears. The downed officer is no longer there.

"Okay," I say to those in the room, my quavering voice betraying my nerves, "Everyone circle around me." Reluctantly, my little group of hostages—a man, a woman, and their two children—gather close to me as I position myself in the corner of the room farthest from the door. The pistol in my hand urges them on. The deer rifle I'd found in the couple's bedroom... Well, that's for the police.

My stomach rumbles, and I take a look at my watch. One-fifteen p.m. I've been here less than a half-hour, though it seems like an entire day. Winding up here with these good people wasn't exactly in my plans when I got up this morning, but here I am.

Feeling suddenly ravenous, I say to the woman, "Anything good in the fridge?"

At 2:40, the living room window crashes inward, causing us all to jump. I'm thinking the end is at hand and tense my grip on the rifle. Come on in, boys.

But instead of black-clad men bristling with weapons and testosterone, a gray plastic box flies through the broken window and skids to a stop on the carpet among knifelike shards of glass. I stare at it dumbly, half wondering if it's going to explode. My hostages and I make a curious little audience. We look at it with anticipation, expecting something of it, and it doesn't disappoint. Seconds after its unheralded arrival, it begins to ring.

I have the little girl fetch the box and bring it to me. A thick, shielded cable trails along behind it. I open the box to reveal a simple telephone handset, and pick it up.

"Uh, hello?" I say stupidly, as if a friend of mine might be calling to invite me over to watch a game.

"Hey there," says a cheery, crystal clear voice. "This is Bo Pinter, of the Stratton Police Department. Who am I talking to?"

I hang it up and close my eyes. I'm not going to do this.

It rings again.

Come on, I think, exasperated. I pick it up again.

"Hi. This is Bo again. I think we got cut off. Hey, is this Ben? Ben Geller? I'd like to make sure you're okay in there; maybe see if you need anything, or if anyone needs, like, a doctor or something. You guys all okay in there?"

He sounds so damn cheery. He's no doubt sitting in a warm room somewhere, probably drinking a latte and listening to the stereo. His life isn't in jeopardy, his freedom gone. He's not in any danger whatsoever. And he knows my name. He probably knows a hell of a lot more than that. Basically, I'm screwed.

"Bo," I say, exasperated, rubbing the sore spot between my eyes. "Don't call me again. Okay? If you call me again, I'm going to kill the little girl. Do you understand that? Do *not* call me again!" I slam the phone down in an effort to scare him into thinking I'm a dangerous killer. Inside, I wonder what I'll do if he calls back.

He doesn't. Score one for the bad guy.

By four, the sun is going down behind the house. The room I'm in faces east, so it's now deep in shadow. I send the girl to the window to raise the blinds for me. I know there's no way anyone out there squinting into the sun can possibly see into the back of the room. Just to make sure, though, I don't move for fifteen solid minutes, until the light is too poor to read by. Now it's time to show them exactly who they're messing with.

I pick up the hunting rifle. They—police, SERT, sharpshooters—they're out here, and I'm pretty sure I can find them. Let the festivities begin.

I take a seat on a dining room chair and balance the rifle on the back of another chair I place in front of me. It makes for a good support. This is a nice rifle, and it has a pretty good scope. I scan under the porch of the house across the street first, but don't see anything interesting. Then under cars, at the base of trees, in the windows of nearby houses, but still nothing. They're good. Must be SERT. I shift my magnified gaze to the roof of the house across the street. Nothing looks out of place, but still, something about the chimney structure bothers me. As I stare, I finally get it. There, at the base of the chimney, is something that doesn't belong on a roof. The light is fading fast, and it takes my eye a second to adjust, but then I get it. It's like one of those random-pattern mosaic posters they used to sell in the malls—if you look at it long enough, you eventually see the image your eye can't at first distinguish.

At the base of the chimney, silhouetted against the darkening sky, is a head. A head, which after I stare at it for a moment, becomes a head behind a scoped rifle. Both are covered with a tarp, and the rifle is pointed right at me.

Nope. Not today. In less than five seconds I zero in on the head and my rifle does the rest.

The shot is so loud in the closed room that it scares even me, and my little group of hostages scream in unison. The male, an off-duty police officer with whom I work on graveyard shift, recovers first. He smiles, and says, "You get him, Ben?"

"Oh yeah."

"He's gonna shit, you know."

"Carlos!" admonishes his wife. "The children!" Their two kids, eight and nine years old, giggle.

"I know," I say. "I don't think I'm very high on Slater's favorite person list as it is, *without* beating him to the shot."

I pluck the portable radio from my back pocket and push the transmit button. "Geller to command post, you just lost your side-one sniper. One-two-zero yards off the one-one-two window, on the roof of the house north of the target."

"CP to Geller, copy. CP to SERT, pack it in. Everyone meet up at the front door to debrief." My hostages begin filing out of the room, the kids chattering excitedly and Carlos Vega making jokes about Bob Slater, the sniper I'd bested.

I pause to look out the window before emptying the rifle of the three remaining blank .308 cartridges in its magazine well. Men hitherto invisible begin materializing from bushes and shadows all around the house, listlessly slinging assault rifles, 37-mm cannons, gas masks, shotguns, the heavy iron ramrod known as "the key," and other SERT gear, and began moseying toward the house. I watch Slater clamber angrily off the roof clutching his Steyr Mannlicher custom-built sniper rifle, his tanned skin and sharp-featured face darker than the clouds in the dusky half-light.

As Slater approaches the house, some comedian from the immediate reaction team, or IRT, which had performed the downed officer rescue, utters, "Dead man walking." Knowing Slater, I can imagine how pissed off he is at me right now.

I have to admit, a part of me loves it. Slater is what I refer to in police vernacular as an Adam Henry—an asshole—and it feels good to one-up him. There has never been any love lost between us. He can take his dapper good looks, his perfectly trimmed mustache, and his always-on-the-golf-course suntan, and piss on himself for all I care. He's the only cop in my department I don't like, and the feeling is clearly mutual.

Slater doesn't like me because I'm the primary sniper on Stratton, Oregon's Special Emergency Response Team, and he's the secondary. He thinks that that because he's the better shot, he should be the primary sniper, and doesn't hesitate to make that opinion known to anyone who'll listen.

The position is mine, not just because I'm senior to him on the team, but also because he's just not disciplined enough to take the more difficult, primary spot. Everyone knows I'll never shoot half as well as Bob Slater. We're about the same age, but that's where the similarities end.

I am a former Portland tax attorney who decided I'd rather chase crack addicts through back alleys and bust whores in Rockledge than save corporate clients tens of thousands of dollars exploiting loopholes in the law. Slater is an ex-Recon marine, a world-class competition long-range shooter. I'm a family man with a wife and daughter, and he's a loner without a steady girlfriend.

Last year, at the National High-Powered Rifle Competition at Camp Perry, Ohio, Slater placed third in the country in long-distance shooting. Only two people in the United States are better shots than Slater, and I'm definitely not one of them. I'm smart enough to realize that once Slater overcomes his poor attitude and gets some discipline and SERT experience under his belt, Lieutenant Capelko will move him into the primary position. I figure when that happens, I'll just as quietly retire from the team.

Slater glares at me with ill-concealed contempt as I join the rest of the team for the post-training debrief. I try to glare back, but I admit I'm the first to look away.

"Okay, everyone, listen up," says Capelko. "This is why we have training, so this stuff can happen here, not in the field. Let's find out what went wrong. Reid?"

Steven Reid, a member of the inner perimeter containment unit, says, "I could hear him more than I could see him. The blinds went up, and all I could see was some kind of motion in the back of the one-one-two window, so I reported it."

"Good enough," said Capelko. "Slater?"

Slater is clearly pissed. He's a pretty big guy, six one, two hundred, maybe two-ten, but he seems to compact like a black hole when the spotlight turns on him. He manages to keep his voice cool when he answers.

"Well, there was nothing for the first couple of hours. Then Reid reports movement in the one-one-two. I focus in on it, but all the movement's lost in the shadows in the back of the room. I knew we were under a shot of opportunity, but I couldn't establish that it was Geller, so I couldn't shoot. Basically, that's it. Then I see a flash, and I realize it's a scope reflection. I was just starting to back off the roof into my alternate position when I heard the shot and you called the scenario over."

"Okay," Capelko said. "Of course, by then you were dead. Did you remember the pre-scenario briefing, when I told you there was a hunting rifle in the house?"

"Yeah, Vince, I remembered. That's why I started backing out of there," Slater snaps, his brows pushing his eyes into narrow black slits.

"Right, well, just think about it. Geller?"

"You said you wanted this scenario to run like a real callout as much as possible," I say. "You said it was mostly for the inner perimeter guys, and to start training Slater as the secondary sniper. Well, being a sniper myself, I know that nothing ever happens right away and complacency always sets in. So, I didn't do anything for the first few hours. I wanted to ratchet up the tension for the team, so I decided not to negotiate. Once it started getting dark, I just hung back in the shadows with the rifle, surrounded by hostages. I set the rifle up on the back of a chair and started scanning the obvious places a sniper might be."

"Where'd you look first?"

"First, I scanned under the porch of the house across the street. That's where *I* would have gone. It was so dark under there, I knew I'd never see anyone camo'ed out and in that position, so I figured that's where Slater would probably be."

I probably shouldn't bait Slater, but this is a little more fun than I anticipated.

"I was going to spend two or three hours just watching under the porch if I had to," I continue. "Knowing what it's like to sit that long in one position, I figured he'd eventually *have* to move, and then I'd nail him.

"But then, while scanning the whole area looking for the perimeter guys, I happened to check the roof."

I shift my gaze to Slater's eyes. It pains me to put him in the spotlight, but it's my duty. Well, not really. Actually, this is fun. "Bob, you were totally silhouetted on that roof. I looked at the chimney, and at first, I didn't see you. But then you moved your head around the base, and I could see you plain as day. Camouflage makeup doesn't make you invisible if you're highlighted against a lighter sky. So, I took you out."

All eyes are on him. He isn't very good at hiding his emotions, and he looks as if he wants to answer me with a fist in the face.

Capelko turns to him and says, "Okay, Bob. You screwed up and got spotted. You know what that means. The rest of you take thirty and grab a bite. We'll do another scenario after dinner. Meet back here at eighteen hundred."

I dawdle just a moment, screwing unnecessarily with my gear. "Shit, Vince," Slater says to Capelko. "We're adults here. We're cops, not grunts in basic training. I got the friggin' point."

"You wanted to be on SERT, Bob. Just do your pushups and don't complain about it."

Slater gets down and begins doing pushups. Fifty is nothing for a guy in his physical condition, but his attitude is that of a spoiled kid who got grounded from video games.

Afterward, Slater sits apart from everyone, eating his dinner by himself. I decide to have a word with him in private.

"Bob, this kind of thing is the reason why you didn't get the primary sniper position. Hell, everyone knows you can outshoot me, but that's really just the smallest part of the job. You have to be able to out *think* the other guy. I might be retiring off SERT in a year or two, and when I do, you'll become the primary sniper. But Vince won't put you there if he doesn't think you're ready for it. I know under that porch it's dirty and nasty, and there are spiders, but you should have gone there anyway. Don't take the easy way out. You gotta think like a *sniper*, not just a shooter. Find the best position available with concealment, and once you're there, don't frigging move around so much. It was hard for me to learn, and I'm still working on

it myself. Hell, you already know that from the Marines. No offense man,"
I say sincerely, offering my hand. "Just a friendly word of advice, that's all."

Slater glances around. No one else is within earshot. "Get lost," he
says, slapping my hand away. "You and Capelko think this team is some
tough-ass unit. Let me tell you something. In recon, I've seen shit and done
shit and been places you can't even have nightmares about. This team? It's
okay considering it's made up of civilians, but you compare it to the worst
recon platoon, and you'd see what a Mickey Mouse outfit it really is. So, I
don't need a fieldcraft lesson from *you*."

"Just letting you know, Bob. Mickey Mouse or not, we've got
standards, and Capelko runs the team as tight as he can. You don't get dirt
under your fingernails every now and then, you aren't going to go very far,
Marine or not."

His reply is a cordial, "Fuck you very much for your advice. I'll take it
under consideration and give you my report in the morning."

Shaking my head, I turn to walk away. As I do, I hear him mutter,
"Asshole." I take this to mean that Bob Slater isn't in the mood to reconcile,
let alone get any friendly advice from me.

This is the first time his animosity has come out so blatantly, but I
know it will not be not the last. He's not really as scary as I thought. He
wants to be a dick, that's fine with me. I can go the distance with him, and
we'll see how it all shakes out in the end.

1

TODAY IS OUR anniversary. We've waited months in eager anticipation of this night, and Sharon, my wife, is waving her hands back and forth, her eyes closed in rapt attention, threatening to burn down the world with a cigarette lighter. Twenty thousand people around us are doing the same thing. Elton John, the center of all the attention, sits alone at a white grand piano a hundred and twenty yards downrange and forty or fifty feet below me, belting out the words to *"B-B-B-B-Benny and the Jets."* Halfway up the nosebleed section; that's the best eighty-five bucks could get me in the Portland Rose Garden arena.

It's more accurate to say that *Sharon* has waited for tonight in eager anticipation. To me, the waiting was more like counting down to a date with a dentist for some unanesthetized root canal. I can't stand Elton John. Hearing one of his songs never fails to conjure in my mind his ridiculous seventies appearance, with orange hair and big yellow sunglasses. Tonight, he just looks like somebody's mother. How pitiful.

After stuttering his way through Benny, Elton does *"Saturday Night's Alright for Fighting,"* the one song of his I don't mind too much. Then, somehow, he segues into *"Candle in the Wind '97,"* and tears begin coursing down Sharon's cheeks.

I want to make some snide crack like, "Come on, honey, you and the princess barely knew each other," but after twenty years of marriage, I know better

As Sharon mourns the loss of a royal she barely knew existed in life, I mentally calculate the scope adjustments I would have to make in order to score a perfect kill shot on Sir Elton. My eyes automatically do that nowadays: see everything in terms of range, wind, barometric pressure, and elevation.

I've been on SERT for five years. We're the police the police call when they can't handle a situation. The SERT tactical unit is composed of three elements; entry, inner perimeter, and snipers. There are other elements associated with SERT, such as EDU, or explosives disposal unit, and HNT, the hostage negotiating team, but the only thing I'm interested in is the tactical unit.

I started on the inner perimeter containment unit, or IP for short. They're the ones responsible for surrounding a target location and making sure nothing goes in or out. If the bad guy or a hostage tries to sneak out a window to escape, the guys on IP handle it. They report everything they hear, see, smell, or otherwise perceive. They are also responsible for the delivery of chemical munitions such as tear gas or smoke grenades when needed.

I loved that job and never really had the desire to change positions unless a sniper spot opened up. Most guys on the team aspire to move up to the entry team. Entry, as they are known, are arguably the elite of any SWAT team. My department prefers SERT over SWAT, incidentally, because here on the Left Coast, we don't like to sound too overbearing or offensive. I mean, we might offend someone camped out in a tree, protecting a spotted owl, dude.

Anyway, entry is comprised of the best of the best. They go in when all else has failed, and rescue the hostage, take the bad guy into custody, or take care of him in a more permanent way. The amount of training and experience necessary to be a good entry team member is phenomenal. When most people think of SWAT, they're thinking of the entry team.

Me, I always wanted to be a sniper. One shot, one kill. A good sniper can deliver a surgically precise shot on a moving target shielded by hostages from a great distance that will effectively—and permanently—neutralize the threat. In the politically correct world of the twenty-first century, we use euphemisms like "neutralize the threat" instead of "take the motherfucker out," and "shoot to stop" instead of "kill the bastard." It just sounds better that way. Can you dig it, dude?

Of course, the end result is the same. If you happen to be a threat, and a match grade 168-grain boat-tailed hollow point .308 caliber bullet, with a muzzle velocity of 2,600 supersonic feet per second, enters that little divot between your nose and your upper lip and shears your brain stem from your spinal cord before exiting the back of your skull with seventy or eighty percent of your head, I'd say you've been effectively neutralized, wouldn't you? I've never been a sadist, and I've certainly never shot anyone, but to me, the fact that I *can* do that is awe-inspiring. And to be able to say that I'm a sniper is pretty bitchin', too.

After I'd been on the team for two years, our secondary sniper, a great guy who thought with the little head instead of the big one, got caught diddling a seventeen-year-old police explorer, and was fired. Not a good thing to do when you're thirty-five and have a wife and a twelve-year-old kid. Anyway, five guys; two from entry and three from IP, applied for the job, but I'm the one who got it.

The police department sent me to Virginia for a two-week U.S. Army Special Forces Police Sniper School, then saw to it that I put five hundred rounds downrange with Hank Venegall, our primary sniper. Then, bingo, I became the team's secondary sniper. A year after that, in 2004, Hank retired from the team, and I was promoted to primary. That's when Bob Slater got on SERT and became the secondary sniper. It was about six months ago, during his first day of sniper training, that he and I cemented our enmity with the scenario in which I countersniped him on the roof. He still hates my guts for it, even though we're sniper partners and are supposed to be working together.

The difference between primary and a secondary snipers is basically the part of the target building he covers. SERT numbers the sides of a building one through four, going clockwise, starting at the side facing the street. Floors are numbered vertically—the basement is simply called the basement, level one is the ground floor, level two the second story, and on up. Windows and doors are numbered from the left side of the building to the right, so a ground-floor street-facing first window on the left would be side one, level one, window one, or simply the one-one-one window. The primary sniper covers side one, or the front of a target, and the secondary sniper gets side three, the back.

Side one is where the action usually is, which is why it goes to the more experienced sniper. The "action" generally consists of delivery of food or medicine, negotiated release of hostages, the surrender of the suspect, the introduction of the entry team, and the like. Usually, but not always. Anything can happen on any side at any time.

Generally, the only deciding difference between primary and secondary snipers is seniority within the unit. I've been on longer than Slater, so I am primary, even though he's such a better shot. I figure that our team commander, Lieutenant Vince Capelko, will eventually bump Slater up to primary simply because he's a world-class shooter, but so far, there's no indication it will be soon. It's probably because Capelko realizes that Slater hasn't achieved the disciplined attitude it takes to keep a cool head. Simply put, he doesn't play well with others.

Anyway, back to the moment. I'm starting to doze off in the middle of Elton John's cornball tribute to the late princess when my pager goes off.

Glad for the reprieve, I pull it out and try to illuminate the display. I've had this particular pager for three years, but I have yet to figure out how to get the damn thing to light up. There are only three buttons on it, but when it goes off, I am either too excited, too tired, or too *something* to figure it out.

I'm guessing it's the babysitter wanting to know if Leah can stay up to watch cartoons or have candy or something. I begin pressing buttons randomly as I always do, and the light eventually comes on, as it always does.

When the message finally pops up on the screen, it sure as hell isn't the babysitter.

SERT callout. Shots fired, officer down. Armed suspect holding 2 hostages. Command post Chevron gas station, 12th and Main.

Officer down? Raw adrenalin floods my veins, and my mind goes blank. It's like one of those fleeting power losses; a brownout that puts my brain temporarily out of service. My hands and feet begin to shake.

I take a moment to calm myself, and the power comes back on. In my fifteen years with the department, Stratton has never had an officer go down. I've been to my share of police funerals, but thank God none of them had been for anyone I knew very well. I am a friend of everyone in the department, except for Slater, and I can't imagine one of us going down.

I check the time: 2130, or 9:30 p.m. That means swing shift is out on patrol. It's Friday night, which means it is Andrea Fellotino's first day back to work after her days off.

My heart hits another speed bump. It really could be her. Stratton generally fields about ten officers on swing shift, so there's a ten percent chance she is dead or dying right now. Andrea and I are close, too damn close. I hope to God it's not her, but even if it isn't, it is someone else who I count as a brother.

The song comes to an end, and I frantically begin packing our stuff. Sharon opens her eyes and immediately gets angry with me.

"What do you think you're doing?"

I try to calm myself, but my voice is an octave or two higher than usual. "Honey, we have to go. There's a SERT callout. An officer's down, and the suspect is holding hostages."

"Ben, we've waited *months* for this concert," she argues. "It's *Elton John!*"

I let the expression on my face tell her how stupid I think that statement is, then resume packing our things. She resorts to a personal attack. "Oh, wait, let me guess. Your girlfriend Andrea's working tonight, isn't she?"

My heart speeds up again, and I wonder exactly how much Sharon suspects.

I had been Andrea's first training officer two years ago when she first hired on. I was instantly attracted to her chestnut brown hair, green eyes that wouldn't have looked out of place on a Persian cat, and her firm and shapely tennis player's physique. For some strange reason I have yet to discover, the attraction was mutual, and despite the eight-year age difference and the fact that I am at least somewhat happily married, the sexual tension in the car after her first week as my trainee was palpable.

I had never before even contemplated the idea of cheating on my wife. When I was growing up, the idea of infidelity was incomprehensible to my folks and their circle of friends. Stuff like that only happened to other people whom I neither knew nor cared about. But there I was, not even forty years old, and suddenly the prospect of risking the happy life and family I had so arduously worked for seemed reasonable. Andrea revealed in me a weakness I didn't even know existed.

Sharon and I are the same age; forty. She carries an extra fifteen to twenty pounds she doesn't need, and mentally balances our checkbook on the rare occasions we make love. I can't say when our marriage first began to stagnate. It's not that we don't love each other; we do, but I can't even remember what it was like to be glued together all the time like we were in high school.

Andrea, on the other hand, is rejuvenating in so many ways. The complete opposite of Sharon, she is thirty-two, divorced, and at five foot six and one thirty, firm, tanned, and gorgeous. She has a killer sense of humor, loves classic rock, and actually pays attention to me. From the first day she got into my patrol car, we both had to resist the unspoken temptation to hold hands. I very nearly passed her on to a different field training officer, which would have been the right thing to do.

After two weeks, she went to a different officer anyway, which was the established training protocol. On our last day together, we worked a domestic violence case in which the suspect broke his wife's jaw and blackened both her eyes. The husband had previously moved out of the house to an unknown location and had already left by the time we got there, but the wife told us from her hospital bed it was a sure bet we could find him at a Rockledge titty bar called Shaky Bob's in about two hours.

Detectives couldn't do the stakeout because of prior considerations, so our sergeant authorized the overtime for us to do it ourselves. Andrea and I sat in an unmarked van in the parking lot for an hour-and-a-half waiting for him to show. We ended up killing the time in each other's arms, which made me feel guilty as hell, but flamed my passion out of control.

We arrested our man and completed the paperwork by ten, but I'd already told Sharon not to expect me before one or two in the morning. Needless to say, I wound up at Andrea's apartment for the duration.

At first, I was very remorseful about what I'd done. But Andrea and I both felt as if we were made for each other, and I was powerless to stop it. By this time, adultery was no longer restricted to people I didn't know, as was the case when I was a child. The various conquests of more than one married man were openly discussed in the locker room and over coffee, and to them, the idea of infidelity wasn't looked upon as taboo. The way they figured, if their wives never found out about it, it never happened. Even the members of Stratton's God Squad, the close-knit group of outspoken Christian cops, only shook their heads in disapproval when the subject came up.

Well, the fact remains that I became a quiet practitioner of that particular taboo. Andrea wasn't interested in seeing anyone else, and our once-every-couple-of-weeks liaisons seemed good enough for her. I couldn't understand that, since she was attractive on so many levels and every unmarried cop on the department, as well as half the married ones, wanted to be with her. But the arrangement has worked ever since, and we carry it on with great anticipation and excitement. It still bothers me that I've so badly compromised my morals, and I feel like a real shit, because I'm having my cake and eating it too. I realize this comes at both Andrea's and Sharon's expense, but it doesn't bother Andrea, and of course Sharon is completely in the dark. Andrea's quite satisfied with the arrangement, and though we run the serious risk of falling in love, I have to admit I'm happy with it myself.

When you get to where I am, you begin justifying yourself to yourself. I have done this incrementally. At first, it was wrong simply to have the attraction. Then I decided it was okay to have the attraction, but it would be wrong to discuss it with her. Once our conversations steered themselves to our attraction for each other, that became okay, but it would be wrong for us to take action on it. After we kissed and felt each other up for an hour and a half in the stakeout van, that became understandable, but it would certainly be wrong to have real sex. Then our one-time sexual liaison seemed to be understandable, but it would be wrong to continue the affair. Of course the next step, seeing each other every couple of weeks, became acceptable as long as we were careful not to fall in love, at which point I would have to contemplate leaving Sharon and our six-year-old daughter, Leah.

Now that we're just about at the "L-word" stage, I guess everything's okay, and the only sinful thing would be if I were to actually leave Sharon and Leah.

I'm such a lowlife.

So, anyway, Sharon obviously knows *something's* up. I'm not really surprised. I snap at her, "Jesus Christ, Sharon. Gimme a break, I have a little more on my mind right now than your petty suspicions, okay? For Christ's sake!"

"Well, you spend more time with her than you do with me. Out of all the cops, why do you have to be best buds with her?"

As we are having this conversation, one of my brothers is fighting a bullet for his life, and my fear of Sharon's suspicions gives way to genuine anger. "Sharon! Someone I work with took a bullet tonight. I don't know who it is, and I don't know if they're dead or alive. Goddamn it, it might *be* Andrea. But if it was me lying facedown in a pool of blood, would you want SERT to respond, or would you rather they waited until the goddamn Elton John concert was over before dragging my ass out of the line of fire?"

My little diatribe serves to calm Sharon down and focus her attention on the immediate problem. Right now, that means getting us the hell out of the concert venue and back to Stratton, some eighteen miles east, before the SERT van leaves.

We stuff all our concert gear into backpacks and make our way to the stadium's garage. Fortunately for me, the motorcycle parking is just off the elevator, right at the entrance to the street. In no time, we have our helmets on and are on the road.

Sharon knows it will be a wild ride, and I don't disappoint her. I blow red lights and stop signs as if I'm driving a black-and-white in hot pursuit, and there are no cops around to stop me. Once we hit the freeway, I settle my custom Road King into a nice cruising speed of about eighty. You can hardly tell you're moving on that bike.

I hear the inter-helmet microphone break squelch, and Sharon's voice fills my ears. "I'm sorry about giving you a hard time at the concert, Ben. I hope whoever it is isn't really hurt bad."

"Me, too," I radioed, feeling a bit gutsier now. "But why is it that because Andrea was my trainee and now we're friends, that means we're sleeping with each other?" I want, but don't want, to talk about this.

"Come on, Ben, don't play stupid. You think I don't know that—"

Before she can finish, my pager vibrates again. "Another page, Shar. Grab it, will you?" I interrupt, glad for the reprieve. I guess I've heard enough.

She pulls the pager from my belt and seems to have no trouble figuring out how to turn on the light.

"'More shots fired. Downed officer Hollister en route OHSU, condition unknown.' Oh my God, Ben, it's Dan," she says, her voice cracking.

My stomach goes queasy. *I* know his condition. It's bad. The Oregon Health Sciences University Hospital is one of Portland's two major trauma centers. Had he been taken to Stratton Regional Medical Center, also known as Stratton Dog and Cat to the cops, it would have indicated that his wounds weren't life-threatening. But the fact that he's going twenty-five miles away to a trauma center means he's in bad shape.

"Not Dan," she whimpers. "Oh honey, I'm sorry I gave you a hard time. Please, God, let him be okay." She begins crying for real now.

"Shit," I mutter. Dan and I are pretty good friends. We get together with some other guys to watch the Blazers every spring, and his wife, Sue, is a Mary Kay customer of Sharon's. They have two little kids. We get together with them once a month or so. I fervently hope he'll pull through.

Stratton hasn't had what I would refer to as a heavy callout since I joined the team. Probably the biggest one we'd had was when a gang member shot and killed another gang member, then holed up in an apartment refusing to come out. This happened in Rockledge, a crappy neighborhood on Stratton's west side, which is our "other" side of the tracks. The gangbanger taunted the hostage negotiating team, telling them that he was going to kill the first cop who came in to get him.

He said there were little kids in there with him, but we found out later that he was lying. HNT negotiated with the guy for over ten hours, and the talks went nowhere. It really looked as if we were going to have to kill him. It was only the second time I had been on the gun, and I was pumped. Well, to make a long story short, Lieutenant Capelko finally decided we couldn't negotiate this guy out and that it was time to go in and get him. The guy was wanted for murder, and after an entire day of him telling us to go to hell, Capelko sent the entry guys in.

It turned out that our suspect was a teenage wannabe poser. He had been pressured into the shooting in the first place by his homies, and when we finally went in, he shit himself. So much for the *Surrano Trece*, Stratton's toughest street gang.

As a comparison, in the five years since I'd been on the team, Portland SERT had had about three times as many applications as us and had been involved in four shootings, all of which resulted in dead bad guys, and one of which also involved the wounding of an entry team member. Now *that's* what I would refer to as a heavy callout.

We all know it's only a matter of time until it's our turn. Riding into the office from the Elton John concert, I feel the sharp edge of fear. A cop has been shot. What did the bad guy have to lose by going for more? His life? Hell, even in Oregon a cop killer will get the needle.

Neither Sharon nor I feel like talking much after she reads the last page. Just as I get off the freeway, only a few blocks from the office, the next page comes in.

"The van's leaving in five minutes, babe. You gonna be all right?"

"Yeah," I say absently. She's still sniffling, and I feel a little sorry for her. "I'm really sorry about the concert, Sharon. But at least you got to hear that Marilyn Monroe song."

She jabs me in the ribs. It's about Princess Diana, you idiot."

I already know that.

"Seriously though," I say, "I'm sorry we had to take off. I know how badly you wanted to see it."

"Ben, don't. Dan needs you. And I'll go right over to the hospital to be with Sue. Ben, I… You think this might be the one?"

She didn't have to explain; I know what she's talking about. We've often talked abut what it might be like for me if I ever have to take somebody out. Even the snipers in the Evil Empire to the west (Portland) had never taken anyone out. That job always seems to fall to entry.

There are some major differences, though, between a shooting by the entry team and a sniper shooting. When entry kills someone, it's not that different from an officer-involved shooting at the street patrol level. It's combat; fast, furious, close, and unpredictable. You kill him or he kills you.

But it's essentially the opposite for a sniper. If *I* have to drop the hammer on someone, it's not like combat at all. He's not a personal threat to me in the slightest. It's cold, calculated, and more like premeditated murder than anything else. I mean, I'm between one and two hundred yards away from the guy; he can't see me and doesn't even know I'm there. He may be actively engaged in threatening someone else's life, and then again, he may not be.

I've had the guy in my crosshairs for the entire time; hours, maybe, and if my radio says "shot of opportunity," my finger pulls the trigger. He might be threatening someone with a gun, and then again, he might be standing at the toilet taking a leak. I don't get to hide behind the 'it was either him or me' excuse. I can't think about his wife and kids, or his parents, or how his death is going to affect those who love him come shooting time, though I'll have plenty of time for it later. I can't be concerned about whether he's some demented homicidal sociopath, or a mental who has no clue what he's doing, or simply a halfway decent guy who's just made a terrible mistake. Not at the moment of pulling the trigger, anyway.

Quite possibly, I won't even get the opportunity to make the decision. The decision for him to live or die will probably rest on someone else's shoulders. If they decide he dies, they just tell me when. In that case, I'm just the executioner.

But every sniper who has to assume that role gets plenty of opportunity to think about it later. From what I hear, the act of pulling that trigger lasts a hell of a lot longer than the eighth of a second it takes the gun to fire. From what I hear, that trigger pull lasts for years and years and years.

When I was in sniper school, they talked about guys who had passed all the psych tests and had gone over the possibility of a cold, calculated shot until they were absolutely confident that they could do the job, but then, *after* the fact, they found out that they couldn't really handle it. They talked about the nightmares that wouldn't go away, about the drinking, the failed marriages, and the ended police careers. They also talked about at least one police sniper who ate his gun three months after dropping the hammer.

So, Sharon and I went to counseling together at the behest of the department when I got the position. We both know that I won't be a sniper forever, and that Stratton had never had a heavy callout, and that the chances are a thousand to one that I'll ever have to take a shot. We also know that even if I do, I'll be as prepared for it as a man could be. Further, I'm pretty sure I know myself well enough to know that I'll be able to handle it.

But now, as I pull into the parking lot of the Stratton police and fire departments, and ride over to the fire bay that holds the SERT van, a little voice of doubt begins whispering in my ear.

This call is different. Sharon and I both think that this night might hold that one-in-a-thousand chance. As I command the annoying little whisper to silence, I hope I know myself as well as I think I do.

Deep down inside, at the business end of my subconscious, I know I'm not designed to kill people. Thus far, I have never really expected to be placed in that situation, even though I am a police sniper, but I've always known that if that were ever to change, it would be on a callout such as this.

The bottom line is this. I don't really know what will happen if worst comes to worst tonight, and I fervently hope I won't have to find out.

2

I GIVE SHARON a quick kiss and hop off the bike. She slides forward, tells me she's off to the hospital, then speeds away.

The SERT van, a thirty-foot box truck painted midnight blue, has already been pulled out of its berth in the fire department, and is on the tarmac, its generator running and powering its internal systems. The van functions as a mobile command post, weapons locker, and communications center. Every square inch of it is packed with sophisticated equipment and tactical gear. The front passenger seat area, affectionately known as the hot seat, is where most of the comms and computer systems are. This is usually where Lieutenant Vince Capelko, the team commander, can be found on a callout. Immediately behind it are numerous storage areas, shelves containing tactical gear, and a large, climate-controlled weapons locker that is barrel-keyed for extra security. Inside is an impressive array of weapons, including HK MP5 and MP10 submachine guns, HK53 fully-automatic carbines, my Remington 700 sniper rifle, Slater's Steyr, five sawed-off Remington automatic shotguns, and a couple of silenced Ruger Mini-14 22-caliber rifles, which are used for taking out street lights and dogs. There is also a peg rack on which we have twenty Sig Sauer P226 .40-caliber pistols.

In bins below the gun racks are other storage compartments that can be accessed from the outside. These are where we keep the fun stuff—smoke grenades, antiriot stingball grenades, a couple of L-8 37-mm repeater cannons, and flashbang stun grenades, which are some of our most commonly used munitions. The latter emit a blindingly brilliant flash, an ear-shattering report, and a stunning concussion. The combined effect is the temporary immobilization of everyone near the detonation. Our techie gurus are always finding and ordering new gizmos for these compartments.

Other tools, such as bomb blankets, telescoping pole-mounted cameras, pry bars, and the key, etc., are stored in compartments accessible from either inside or outside. In the case of heavily reinforced doors, we

just cheat and have the bomb guys blow them for us, a task they are almost
too eager to perform.

The interior of the SERT van is bathed in red night-vision-preserving
light. Men in various stages of undress are suiting up, gathering and
preparing gear, and loading weapons. The basic rules of safety that apply to
cops everywhere are often ignored on the SERT team. No weapon can fire
unless someone pulls the trigger, so we rely on trigger control and discipline
for safety. Men loading weapons inside the SERT van without pointing
them into a safety barrel is not even thought of as out of place.

I enter through the rear door and can immediately feel the difference
in the atmosphere for this callout. An officer's been shot. Though we live
with the possibility every day, the reality of it is damn near
incomprehensible.

"What's the situation?" I ask, joining the melee inside.

"I just came from the scene," says Peter Pepperidge, an entry team
member who is changing out of a patrol uniform. "Dan Hollister got
popped while on a family beef call. He took one under the left panel of his
vest and one in the neck. Andrea Fellotino was his cover. Apparently, the guy
threatened to kill his baby, and holed himself up in a back bedroom with
it. Holly was negotiating with him through the door when the guy just
opens fire, shooting through the door. Andrea said the guy is some kind of
schizo-defective whatever religious nut, and he's been on a two-day trip
where God has been telling him he's got to sacrifice their kid or some shit
like that. She said the wife says he's been doing meth for a while, too."

All activity temporarily stops while Pepperidge continues his rundown.
"Holly said something like, 'Just let me make sure the baby's okay,' and
that's when the dude opens fire. They think he's got a .357 from the sound
of it, but the woman said she's never known her husband to have a gun
before. Holly took the first two rounds and went down in the hallway.
Andrea had to pull him out. She laid down her own cover fire while
dragging Holly's big ass down the hallway."

My mind is reeling while listening to Pepperidge. So Andrea was
involved after all. I hope to God she's okay. We've kept the affair to ourselves,
so nobody really knows about it, but everyone knows we're close. The bad
part about it is that I have to listen to half the guys talk dirty about her in
the locker room all the time.

"Holly's no small guy, so you can imagine how hard it was for her to get him out of the kill zone. Halfway down the hall, she got center punched by a round, right in the strike plate of her vest, but she still managed to get Holly out of the line of fire and put a couple rounds into the room. She said she shot high so as not to hit the kid. Once she got around the corner into the kitchen, she screamed for cover, then pulled Holly's big ass all the way out into the driveway behind a van."

"I heard her put that cover call out," said a voice from the front of the van. "Scared the living shit out of me, man. You know, the panic in her voice."

"Me, too," said Pepperidge. "Anyway," he continues, "like, twenty cars from three different agencies responded. Andrea starts cutting Holly's vest off, and guess what dipshit's fuckin' wife does? She runs back into the house and joins her husband in the baby's room! So, now we got *two* hostages for the price of one! Of course, the wife hasn't been seen or heard from since. You believe that shit?"

"Wh-what happened to Andrea?" I stutter, hoping I don't sound as personally involved to the others as I do to myself.

Pepperidge continues as if he hasn't heard me. "Anyway, me, Davidson and a two-man county car arrived first. We formed a four-man rescue team and pulled Holly and Andrea out of the driveway. They were using a minivan for cover, so it was pretty easy. Andrea had stripped her shirt off and was using it to staunch the flow in Holly's neck wound, which the paramedics said saved his life. Once we got outside behind hard cover I checked her for wounds while the county guys worked on Holly."

"So how's she doing?" I ask again.

"She's got massive bruising right in the center of her chest, but nothing looked fractured, and there was no puncture."

I visibly deflate. Nobody seems to notice.

"You got to see Fellatio's hoots? You dog!" says a young, immature inner perimeter officer named Mike Piccone. Nobody laughs, and Piccone quickly shuts up. My blood comes to an instant boil. I hate it when I hear people call her that.

"Lay off, Nosepick," I snap. "She saved Holly's bacon out there, and took a round while doing it. She's a fucking hero, asshole, unlike you'll ever be!"

Just then, Bob Slater steps aboard. "Did I just hear the pot calling the kettle black?" he asks.

I roll my eyes and turn away.

"What's the scoop?" Slater says to no one in particular.

Pepperidge answers, "Holly took two rounds during a family beef, and Andrea Fellotino dragged him out of the line of fire. She took one in the vest on the way out, but she's okay. Nobody knows how Holly's doing."

"Christ. Well, hell, looks like we're gonna finally get to grease someone." Then he looks right at me. "Listen, Helen, no offense, man, but maybe I should be primary on this one. I mean, we might actually have to shoot somebody tonight. If we do, it'll look a whole lot better if we hit him. What do you say?"

Just being around Slater is enough to raise my blood pressure. Hearing him call me Helen makes it that much worse. I hate my nickname, which, in truth, is the goal of the team when assigning one. It stems from a day on the sniper range when I couldn't shoot consistently for love or money. My first shot, which is known as a cold bore, done without the benefit of recent practice or a warm barrel, was dead-on. But after that, my rounds struck all over the target.

Slater began calling me Helen Geller, because my target looked as if a blind person had been shooting at it. It was later determined that the scope mounting on my rifle had come loose, but the name stuck. Privately, I've always suspected Slater had intentionally loosened the mountings, but I could never prove it, so I've kept my suspicions to myself.

Before I can address Slater's remark, Hugh Wilkes, the newest member of the team, twists in the driver's seat and shouts, "Hang on, we're taking off!"

Slater grabs his crotch and says, "Hang onto *this*, Baby Hughie."

Maybe it's of tension due to the nature of the callout, but Slater is getting on my nerves more than usual. Two officers had been shot, and one is in surgery at the moment. Is he so really so tasteless as to think this is a setting for making jokes? Pissed, I say, "Nobody wants to hear about your stupid little prick, you stupid little prick, so why don't you just shut up?" Immediately, I regret saying it.

The van grows very quiet, and Slater shoots me a look that can freeze saltwater. My heart flutters for a second the way it used to before a fight in high school. It looks like he might come after me right here.

I'm tensing up when Slater smiles and says, "Yeah? That's funny, 'cause your wife didn't complain last night when I shoved it up her ass. She came so hard she damn near pinched it off. Nothing like that little kosher weenie she's used to."

That's it. I don't have to take that kind of crap from Slater, crazy look or no. I start up the aisle, my fists balled and my face red with rage, when Stan Hauser, the tactical team leader, steps between us.

"You guys are acting like little kids. Two cops have been shot, so cut out the shit and save it for the bad guy. We got work to do. You guys are supposed to be snipers, for crying out loud. You're supposed to be a team. Screw with each other after we're done, but not now. You get it?"

I get it. I turn away just as Wilkes hits the gas.

An open rack of stingball grenades spills over Hauser, who lets loose a string of curses that would embarrass a drunken sailor. Everybody is thrown backward into a writhing pig pile as the van accelerates out of the parking lot.

Ablaze with intensely strobing red and blue lights, not to mention the bright high-powered floodlights on all sides, the van looks like a moving Las Vegas marquee when rolling code. It must make one hell of a show. I glance out the back door and see the armored car and the SERT truck falling in behind us. Then the chase cars fall into formation, one in front and one behind the line, as we collectively pull onto Eastwood Parkway.

Almost immediately, the car behind the line jumps ahead, rocketing toward the first intersection, its siren screaming like a banshee. The lead car is doing the same. They will proceed ahead of the train to the first intersection and block the cross street, holding traffic back with lights and sirens until we clear the intersection. Then they will speed ahead to the next intersection, riding shotgun like jet fighters escorting a flight of bombers, as we leapfrog our way to the scene.

"Left turn coming up!" yells Wilkes, just a little too late. The van leans sickeningly into the turn, throwing half-naked men onto me, and crushing me against the weapons locker doors.

Normally on the ride to a callout, the van would be filled with animated conversations and shouted war stories, but today, everyone dresses and readies their gear in solemn silence. Each of us is intently focused on the task at hand. I'm sure that, to a man, we are geared more toward avenging the shooting of Dan and Andrea than peacefully resolving the incident.

Dan and Andrea are the first Stratton officers ever to get shot. The chances of the suspect's surviving our response tonight are slim to none.

For me, the moment is particularly intense. I am the primary sniper, and though we'd never before gone to the highest rule of engagement, I think that's about to change. I feel pretty confident that tonight I'll hear those three little words come over the radio.

Shot of opportunity.

No matter how hard I have trained for taking a shot on a living, breathing, human being, no matter how much I have contemplated it, and that's a lot, actually facing the prospect of it is a different story. The specter of liability begins to shadow my thoughts like an unexpected storm on an otherwise sunny day.

Regardless of the rules of engagement, no matter what my orders might be as a sniper, the ultimate liability—moral, civil, and criminal—of either taking the shot, or *not* taking the shot, rests solely with me. The same holds true for the consequences of whatever follows my decision. The I-was-merely-following-orders defense won't work for me in a civil lawsuit or criminal trial any better than it did for the Nazis at Nuremberg.

My equipment begins slipping as my palms moisten. All the confidence I thought I had is melting away. In all my training, and on all the actual SERT callouts I've worked, I've never actually thought I might have to do it. But tonight is different. Sometime in the next few hours, I will very likely have to shoot a man. My stomach begins to heave, and I have to consciously calm myself.

Can I really do it if I have to? If I do, how will I be afterward?

As I wrestle with unexpected doubt, I begin to think of Dan and Andrea. Suddenly, the doubt is replaced with confidence, and I begin to feel better. Good, this is good. I force myself to think of what a nice family Dan has, and how his wife and daughter will react to the news he's been shot. I make myself think of Andrea, in our most intimate moments, then think of how this man coldly shot her as she struggled to pull Dan's limp body out of the line of fire.

Now the hate begins to build. In my mind, I can picture him dead, even though I don't even know what he looks like yet.

This is how I have to feel, not like some wishy-washy puss.

Trying to be inconspicuous, I pull my key ring out of my pocket, and for the millionth time, I gaze at the quarter hanging between the handcuff key and the key to my sniper rifle case. The ring is threaded through a perfectly round .308 caliber hole dead smack in the middle of George Washington's head. I shot the quarter on the last day of sniper school from a distance of two hundred yards with my initial cold-bore shot of the day. But it wasn't until I successfully passed the school's final exercise that I was allowed to hang it proudly on my key ring for the world to see. In the intervening years, it had become a talisman of sorts.

Fingering the quarter gives me comfort and strength. I close my eyes and try to picture Andrea as a police officer; a hero exchanging shots and getting hit while dragging the body of her limp and bleeding comrade out of the line of fire. But it is hard to view her as a hero, let alone even as a cop. All I see was a beautiful woman, one about whom I care very deeply.

It is then that a revelation slaps me hard in the face. Somewhere along the way, that which I have feared most had come to pass. Somehow, the lines have blurred, and my feelings for Andrea have changed. Somewhere along the line, I've fallen in love with her. I thought I'd had myself convinced myself that we were both just in it for the sex. I've always tried my hardest to avoid falling in love with her, because if that ever happened, it would throw everything off balance. My family, my job, my future... Everything. I'd have to look at it all in an entirely different way, and that's always been too scary for me to contemplate.

I think of Sharon and realize, to my relief, that I have not fallen completely out of love with her. How in God's name have I gotten myself into such a mess?

I force myself to put these thoughts on the back burner and concentrate on the situation at hand. Grabbing my palette of camouflage makeup, I begin darkening the naturally light areas of my face and lightening the dark areas. I cover my ears and neck with black grease, and angle tiger stripes of forest green and black across my face. Satisfied with the job, I pull a hunter's woodland camouflage net over my boonie hat and put on matching gloves.

Whoever this dirtbag is, he wounded Holly and shot Andrea, and now I am ready to kill him for it. The trepidation I had been feeling is gone, replaced with a new sort of excitement.

Don't worry, baby, I think, trying to transmit my feelings telepathically to Andrea, I'm gonna to take care of it for you.

I surf my way through the final preparations. I want to be done before the van arrives. As snipers, Slater and I are expected to be ready before anyone else.

It is our job to get into position first. That way, we can get vital information out to the rest of the team as they get into position. If, for example, an officer has to cross an open space in back of the house in order to get into a position, and I can see the suspect in a front room, then I can let him know it's safe for him to move. Otherwise, he would have to risk being spotted, or just stay where he is.

That sort of real-time intelligence gathering is ninety percent of our job as snipers. If a light goes on in a back bedroom, we report it to the command post.

In reality, that's all we've ever done—report movement in such-and-such a window, whether a blind was open or shut, or let the CP know when someone was peeking out this door or that window. On some callouts, the suspect remains underground the entire time, and there is nothing to report. It can get pretty boring staring at a house through a rifle scope and a pair of binoculars for fifteen hours without seeing any movement.

Nonetheless, observing and reporting is what we do. In Stratton, Oregon, it's *all* we do. But in order to do it right, we have to be the first ones there, scanning with advanced optics while everyone else is waiting for the briefing or still changing into their SERT gear.

Wilkes shuts the siren down, and the van's relative quiet becomes loud. The chase cars fall into position in front and behind us, and the whole train slows down.

The exhilarating ride is over, and business of preparing to kill begins.

3

I AM READY at the back door when the van comes to a stop. We're in the parking lot of a gas station around the corner from the scene. There are police cars everywhere, and I notice a Channel 8 Action News van in the parking lot. Its crew is gathered around a cameraman who is intently filming the arrival of our team.

I am the first out of the van, with Slater hot on my six. There is a cooling between us now. We have work to do, and our petty bickering can wait.

I lay my drag bag on the ground and unzip it, carefully extracting my rifle. My hands caress its stock and barrel lovingly as it comes out of the bag. With reverence, I lift and pull back the bolt.

It is a beauty, this rifle. And like the most beautiful of snakes, it is also very, very deadly. An artificial sun bathes me in white light as I unfold the forward-mounted spring-loaded bipod, and set the rifle on the ground next to the van. Ignoring the TV camera, I remove a box of Remington match grade .308 rounds from the bag. I always keep a couple of boxes of new match-grade rounds with me. I shoot the old ones at training, and replace them with new ones when I'm done. That way, I'll never find myself out of rounds when I need them, the sniper's worst nightmare.

Pulling out the first cartridge, I carefully examine the bullet's smooth coppery surface for burrs or deformities that might alter its trajectory. Finding none, I snap it into the rifle's magazine. This I repeat four more times with four more rounds, not that I'll ever need them. Really, all I will ever need is two, the second in case the first is a misfire.

One shot, one kill.

The real beauty of this weapon is its optics. Somehow, we were able to convince the department of our need for night vision scopes. After much persuasion, the department coughed up the bucks for two Generation II Dedal DN-530 Variable Power DayVision/NightVision rifle scopes, at three grand apiece. We got them at a savings of just over a thousand dollars, due to a deal Slater worked out with the manufacturer that involved some promotional advertising capitalizing on his status as a world-champion shooter.

These beauties have interchangeable battery-powered eyepiece receivers for night vision, and give a remarkably clear sight picture without altering the rifle's zero point. They can be changed very simply in the field under no-light conditions, and switched to day use when the sun comes up. They are magnificent optics, with a 3.5 magnification under no- or low-light conditions. Since we got them, we've never had to request floodlights.

I remove the night vision receiver from its padded case and place it on my scope just as Lieutenant Capelko comes out of the command post looking for his snipers.

"Geller, Slater, are you guys ready to go?" he asks, the impatience evident in his voice.

"Yep," I answer with confidence. "What kind of suspect info do we have?"

Capelko shoots the TV camera an ugly look and says, "Come into the front of the van."

Once we are safely out of camera range, he says, "Our man is Hugo Route. He's twenty-eight years old, paranoid schizophrenic, and on a two-day meth binge. He was raised in a fire-and-brimstone Pentecostal family in the South, and as of early this morning, was heard by neighbors ranting and raving about God telling him things. He's never been known to have a gun, but somehow, he got his hands on a .357 Magnum revolver."

I start to ask for a description when Slater interrupts me by saying, "I need to know what he looks like."

"Good idea, Bob," Capelko says. "Why didn't I think of that?"

Slater was clearly trying to make an impression on Capelko. I just hope the lieutenant can see him for what he is.

"According to his driver's license, he's five eleven, one eighty-five, with sandy blond hair and blue eyes. Here's a blowup of the picture," Capelko says, handing us a color photo of a very normal-looking man. "The neighbor says his hair is a lot longer now. About shoulder length."

"Do we know what he's wearing?" I ask, "And other than the family, do we know if there's anyone else in there with him?

"No, and as for anyone else inside, not that we know of. Just the wife and baby."

Slater pipes up "Do we have any plates from cars in the driveway?" He's still trying to impress Capelko, and now it's becoming obvious. Vince must have seen it, too.

"You guys are the snipers, Bob. You tell me when you're in position. Isn't that what I'm paying you for?"

Yeah, score one for me.

Capelko continues, "The wife's name is Pammi and the kid is Chastity. She's maybe two years old. That's all we know. Now you guys move out. Enrique here is familiar with the best way into the target area, so he'll lead you in. Slater, there's a house not more than seventy-five yards off the three side. You should have no problem finding a spot back there. Geller, there's no cover or concealment in the front yard, so you'll probably have to be on the other side of Tenth, pretty far off. You still ought to be within one fifty, one seventy-five yards, anyway. Is that gonna be a problem?"

"No sweat, Ell-tee," I say confidently. Though we train at distances much greater than that, and I feel comfortable taking a surgical shot anywhere up to two hundred yards, and a minute-of-angle shot up to three hundred, the fact remains that most police sniper applications are made at a range of less than one hundred yards. That's where I would rather be. I'd rarely deploy more than a hundred yards out, and there must have been something in my voice that reflected my hesitation.

"Good," says Capelko. "'Cause if you don't like it, I can always switch you and Slater out."

Oops, score one for Slater. Tie game, my error.

"Not necessary, Vince. Anything else? If not, I'm ready to go."

"Fine," he says. "Now get your asses moving. Remember, people are—"

"I know, people are *dyin'* out there," I finish for him. It is the team motto. We've even had "Because people are *dyin'* out there" T-shirts made for us.

I shoulder my pack and sling the drag bag containing my rifle across my back, then follow Enrique Sandoval, one of the Multnomah County deputies who had rescued Andrea and Dan, into the night.

Patrol officers had closed NE Tenth Street five blocks east and west of number 415, the address of Hugo Route and his family. We make our way across the street about a block west of the location, then head into the backyards.

"You got three fences to cross, and then you'll be in the backyard of the house across the street from the target," Enrique says. "You can't miss it. It's green with white trim, there's a blue shot-up minivan in the driveway, and the house has the number four-fifteen right above the front door. All the houses have been evacuated on this side, so nobody should bug you. One of your guys is on the corner of the house you'll be going to."

Sandoval's a good cop, one of the Multnomah County Sheriff's Department's best. "Thanks, Enrique. So when are you gonna go from green to blue and become a real cop? We're hiring, and our standards are low enough that you might qualify."

"Wha, ju need a token Mexican to meet federal standards or something?" he asks in an exaggerated Cheech and Chong accent. "Ju jus' wan me so ju can make jur quota, vato."

"Yeah, man, we need someone to keep the precinct clean, you know? Mow the lawn, wash the police cars, that kind of thing."

"Odale'! Lemme talk to my parole officer, homes."

We share a laugh; my first since the SERT page. "Thanks for showing me the way, Sandy."

"Later, bro. Happy hunting."

Happy hunting. Somehow, that seems appropriate.

The first fence I come to is a three-foot chain link, which I have no problem going over. The second is a rickety wood fence, which I don't want to climb. As nearly all of them do, this one has a loose board, which flies into the yard on the second kick. A dog cowers in the yard close to the fence, and I'm glad to see he's timid. I carry a silenced .22 pistol for those who aren't, but I don't want to have to go through all the bureaucratic bullshit that happens when some kid wakes up and finds Snoopy lying in a pool of blood with a hole in his head in the backyard. I can understand it; I'd be pissed too if someone kicked through my fence and shot my dog after ordering me to leave my house.

The last fence is a six-foot chain link. I hate climbing fences with all this gear on. This one is wobbly and rusty. Screw it, I think, pulling a pair of wire cutters from my backpack. Four minutes later, I silently approach Kevin Anderson, a swing shift traffic cop, at the one-four corner of the house. I stand there unmoving, two feet away from him.

His back is to me, and I hold my breath so he can't detect my presence. After a moment, he turns around and sees me, half jumping half out of his Nazi-looking motor boots.

"Christ, you scared the shit out of me! That you under all that paint, Ben?"

I remain silent, staring hard and unblinking into his eyes.

"Ben? What's up? You're creeping me out, man."

I hold my sniper rifle out in front of me, and in a menacing, monotone voice, asked, "Do you know what this is?"

"Yeah, your rifle. Why, what's it supposed to—"

"Wrong! It's an extension," I say slowly and deliberately. "An extension of the hand of God."

He looks at me a second longer, probably trying to decide whether or not I am kidding. "Uh, roger that. I think you've been on SERT a little too long, man."

I relax and indicate the house across the street with a nod. "What's going on over there?"

"Absolutely nothing. It's almost like nobody's home. Seriously, Ben, this is a bad one. I hope you get to waste this motherfucker."

"From your mouth to God's ear," I reply. "Go ahead and back on out of here now, Kevin. Stick to the backyards. Fences are open for three yards west of here, and don't worry about the dog next door."

"You shoot him?" he asked hopefully.

"Naw, didn't have to. He's a weenie. I'm saving it for the bad guy."

"I hear ya. Good hunting," he says, creeping off to the back of the house.

Good hunting.

I peek around the corner of the house from under the shrubbery. There, nearly two hundred yards away, is 415 NE Tenth Street. A powder blue Ford Aerostar with a shattered right front window sits in the driveway. Behind the left rear tire I can see discarded bandage wrappers and an orange plastic medical kit, no doubt left in haste by Sandoval and his partner. Next to it is a good sized pool of blood. Dan Hollister's blood.

I scout out the front yard of my location, and find a spot that looks promising in some shrubs growing around the base of a tree. It will put me in a better position to cover the front door, which is my main objective. To get there, I'll have to belly crawl twenty yards, during which time the front picket fence should block the view from the target house. My current spot will be a good backup position if I need to change later on

Crawling across the yard, I feel a spider web pull taut across my nose, then break, which gives me the heebie-jeebies. I'm glad it's dark so I can't see the bugs. For a guy who lies among them, I absolutely hate bugs.

I think of Bob Slater, mimicking my movements on the other side of the target location. I can't imagine him going too far out of his way to stay covert. He probably sounds like a herd of elephants getting into position. For a Recon marine, the guy is a train wreck as a police sniper.

Once safely ensconced in the bushes, I use binoculars to scan the target house, and see that despite the angle (I am roughly directly across the street from the target's one-one-one window), I have as good a view into the front door as I can hope for. I also have a good view of the three windows on either side of the front door, although two of them are obscured by venetian blinds.

Before setting up my rifle, I take a long, hard look at the dark pool by the tire of the van. The discarded medical trash next to it is a silent reminder of what recently happened there. An involuntary chill sweeps through me. Andrea did some heroic things there. She reacted under fire, exchanging shots with Route, taking a round herself, and still managed to pull Hollister out. Then she had the presence of mind to begin first aid and probably saved Hollister's life in the process. She'd been in the shit and had done the right thing. Nothing told the story like the mute reminders behind the dead minivan.

Would I have been able to do it? I think so, but you never really know until after the fact. If you don't react fast enough, you may never even know it at all.

Blinking my way back to the here and now, I pull the rifle from the drag bag and set it up in front of me. Using my wire cutters as pruning shears, I make a little hole in the shrubs though which I can extend the barrel and maintain a clear line of sight for the scope. Without needing to, I nurse the bolt open, making sure a round is chambered, then thumb the selector switch from OFF to FIRE.

I estimate my range to the front door at about a hundred and ninety yards. I've been meaning to buy myself a digital range finder, I haven't gotten around to it yet. Fortunately, I am good at estimating range. I check the sight picture and adjust the elevation, zeroing the scope for the approximate two-hundred-yard distance.

I wet my finger and hold it aloft for twenty seconds. Detecting no breeze whatsoever, I take a long, hard look at the leaves of the trees across the street. After a moment, I can detect a bit of movement, but so little I can't even determine the wind direction, let alone velocity, and decide that I won't need to make any windage adjustments. Satisfied that I am ready, I push the transmit button Velcroed to my left index finger and say, "Geller to CP."

"Go ahead."

"In position, one nine zero yards off the one-one-one, in the shrubs at the base of a tree off the four-one corner of the house across the street. Break."

"Copy. Go ahead."

"Three openings on side one. Window one-one-one looks like a bedroom, blinds closed, no lights. Then the front door, which is closed. Window one-one-two, closed with no blinds. This is the living room, and there are some background lights in the hallway. I can see through to what looks like a kitchen window on the three side. There's a lot of living room furniture, and the television's on. Break."

After a moment to allow for priority radio traffic, during which I know they are writing down everything I've said, Capelko's voice came back. "Go ahead."

"Last window, one-one-three, another bedroom, blinds are down and no lights are on. No movement anywhere. That's it."

"Copy. We're setting the perimeter now. Scouts'll be going out in a minute."

"Copy."

For lack of a better target, I zero the crosshairs a foot above the doorknob on the front door and scan the front of the house, alternating between my naked eye and a pair of high-powered binoculars. From my angle, I can also see a number-two-side window, but I decide not to mention it, leaving it to for IP guys assigned to that side. I'll watch it, too, though, just in case.

My eye keeps straying back to the pool of Dan Hollister's blood on the driveway. It glows eerily green in the night vision optics. I have to force myself back onto target more than once.

Now comes the tough part. Time to hurry up and wait. I bide my time by scanning the entire house through binoculars.

After a moment, my radio goes off. "Slater to CP, in position."

"Go ahead."

"In high grass, seventy yards from the rear slider. I got a good view of three-one-one, rear slider; three-one-two, which is the kitchen; and three-one-three, a bedroom closed off with blinds. No movement. Hallway light's on in the center of the house. Nothing else."

"Copy. Scouts are out, and IP's getting set."

I watch the members of the inner perimeter find their spots. Like ghosts, they emerge from the blackness, visible to me only because I know what to look for and where to look. One materializes snakelike next to a garbage can in a ditch off to my right; another magically shows up behind a car in the driveway one house east of the target; another slides octopus-like out over the fence into the backyard. If I have to take a shot, it will pass close to another one now crouching next to the pool of Holly's blood in Andrea's old position behind the Aerostar.

It is hard for me to stay focused on the callout while thinking of Andrea. I have to forcefully drive a fantasy out of my mind. In it, Andrea and I are together after the callout, lying naked in bed, my head on her ample chest, talking about what she did. The excitement of it has increased our ardor, and our lovemaking is more intimate than ever.

Something about that quick little fantasy bothers me, and at first I cant put my finger on it. Then it comes to me. Sex with Andrea has always been on the wild and passionate side, but recently it has become less wild and more intimate. Lots of kissing and half-murmured 'I love yous.' This only confirms my worst fears—that I really am falling in love with her. Through it all, though, I am so damn proud of her for what she had accomplished here tonight.

Twenty minutes goes by, and the light in the hallway snaps off. I press my transmit button, but Slater beats me to the transmission.

"Slater to CP. Interior hallway light just went out."

"Copy."

A few minutes later, I see Stan Hauser and Brian Pole, our two scouts, making their way around the house, silently documenting which way the doors swing, what type of windows there are, locating and documenting the electric, water, and phone connections. Not only are these guys experts at moving silently, they are also experts at deciphering accurate floor plans from nothing more than windows, roof vents, laundry vents, cable TV connections, chimneys, and anything else they can use as references. They will catalog their observations, and from them they will draw up the entry plan, an alternate entry plan, gas assault plans, downed-officer rescue plans, and all other possible contingencies. Their movements are so stealthy it is hard even for me to see them.

They are making their way across the yard by the number four side of the house when a light snaps on in the window closest to them. A figure appears at the blinds. Before I can say anything, he splits the louvers and begins peering intently into the direction of the scouts.

4

"GELLER TO SCOUTS!" I yell into the mike, trying not to sound like a scared twelve-year-old girl. "One-one-three, light on in the room!" Hauser and Pole immediately freeze as motionless as two statues. "Stan, it's the one-four corner, right where you guys are."

The blinds are down and closed in that room, but they are the translucent type that allow a fair amount of light to pass through. All I can see is a human silhouette. He is holding something at waist level, and I am unable tell what it is. My throat becomes dry and dusty, my breathing shallow and rapid. Hauser and Pole are caught in the open with no cover and only their black fatigues and discipline of movement for concealment. Both are lying facedown in the grass now, less than fifteen feet from the window, fully exposed to fire from within. I am their only protection, and right now, both their lives are in my hands. Because they are facedown and can't move, they have no way of knowing if the bad guy has a gun on them or not. It is up to me.

Unfortunately, I can't tell, either.

I don't move a muscle. The blood rushing through my ears sounds like the rotors of an inbound assault helicopter. Beads of sweat form on my nose and run down in irritating, itchy rivulets. Way back in my mind is an unformed premonition, sticky and black. The kind you can't get away from for the rest of your life.

A bright light shines through the separation between two louvers where he peeks out from behind them. I don't need to look at the photo Capelko gave me to confirm that it is Hugo Route.

The moment freezes in time. Right now I am closer to killing a man than I have ever been in my life. Although the time is bad for life-altering revelations, I suddenly realize that I desperately don't want to do it. What a time to learn this about myself.

As I place the intersection of the crosshairs on Hugo Route's nose, I remind myself that this man shot Dan Hollister in cold blood, and then put one dead center in Andrea's chest as she dragged Dan out of the killing zone. My body defaults to the rage I had nursed to life earlier, and the doubt loses this round. Confidence floods me, and my trigger finger is ready to curl. If he even begins to make a threatening move, he will get some.

Unconsciously, my grip tightens on the rifle until I have about three pounds of pressure on the trigger. Route is peering in the direction of the men lying outside his window. My crosshairs cut his nose into neat little quadrangles. And then, his left arm begins coming up, still silhouetted behind the blinds. I can see this only fuzzily, but he is clearly holding something in his hand. It has to be the revolver.

My mind takes me through the fire procedures the same way a pilot goes through a pre-takeoff checklist. Control your breathing. Do not hyperventilate. It's a five-and-a-half-pound trigger pull. Safety's off. Wait till his hand is at shoulder level, then don't jerk the trigger. Just a gentle squeeze with the whole hand...

I can't hear the radio asking for an update, so I don't answer. Running completely on autopilot, I focus my entire concentration on the object in Hugo's hand. The pressure on my trigger increases at the same rate as Hugo's hand elevates. In about a second-and-a-half, it will reach shoulder level—aiming level—and at the same time, my trigger pull will reach five-and-a-half pounds, and Hugo Route will disappear.

I have fired this weapon thousands of times and I know the exact amount of pressure needed to make it do what I want. Together, we work as if we are one.

Just when the irreversible is about to take place, after I have breathed my final breath as a man who has yet to kill, Route's right hand goes to the object in his left and begins dialing.

I deflate monumentally. A telephone. I nearly killed a man over a goddamn telephone. Route moves away from the window, and the light snaps off.

Inhaling half the atmosphere, I force myself to relax, settle into a position from which I can still watch the house, and depress the transmit button.

"Geller to Hauser. Suspect gone from the one-one-three, and the light's out. No sign of him now. Hold your position 'til we get eyes on him again. And CP, FYI, he's on the phone." The voice I hear is certainly steadier than the man behind it.

"Got ya, Ben. And thanks," comes the reply from Hauser, with no movement visible from either scout.

Seven minutes later, Bob Slater reports from side three that Route is now in the kitchen opening the refrigerator. This I can see clearly through the living room window, but the kitchen is Slater's side of the house, so I let him report it. Now that they knew where Route is, the scouts are free to resume their mission, certain that he can't be watching them from the shadows.

Finally, Hauser reports they are done scouting and are headed back to the van. I figure it won't be long until they have the entry plans, gas plans, rescue plans, and any other necessary plans completed. Once all that is done, the rules of engagement will change.

A short time later, Capelko breaks the long radio silence and says, "Command post to SERT, the rules of engagement have been elevated to compromised authority. Roll call copy."

"Geller, copy."

"Slater, copy."

"Reid, copy." Each man answered in turn.

The elevation of the rules of engagement is standard procedure at this point. When essential elements of intelligence and planning are in place, the rules are always elevated, giving the snipers, entry team, or inner perimeter the unfettered authority to take any immediately necessary action without asking.

Under all the rules of engagement, a SERT member can take lethal action only to prevent immediate loss of life, which is no different than the way any cop in the field has to act. Under standard rules of engagement—the lowest level at a SERT callout—if that were to happen, the scene is frozen until SERT command can come up with a safe plan to enter and do whatever is necessary; a process which can conceivably take hours.

But under compromised authority, the next step up, every member of the entry team is prepared to immediately execute the assault plans drawn up from the scouting mission; thus, the team has a freer hand to deal with any emergency situation. If, for example, I have to take a shot without warning, rather than freeze the scene until a plan can be made to safely enter, the entry team will immediately conduct a hot entry, according to the plans they've drawn up. Nobody has to check with the command post; they just go, and everyone knows what to do.

The highest, rule of engagement is a shot of opportunity. Those words are a license—a *duty*—to kill the suspect at the first possible opportunity. Such an elevation of the rules would be nightmarish for a man in my position.

You don't think about why you have to kill him. You don't think about whether he's a threat to you or not. You don't think about his wife or kids. You don't think about what he'll look like splashed over the walls and dripping from the ceiling. You simply kill him, as fast and efficiently as possible. Unlike any other kind of police shooting, it is cold and calculated; more like a preplanned execution than anything else.

But even under a shot of opportunity, when the fat lady finally sings, the decision to shoot, or not to shoot, and the liability that goes with it, rests solely upon the sniper. If I take the suspect out, they'll sue me for blindly following orders when it wasn't really necessary to kill him. If I decide not to take the shot when I have it, and the suspect later harms or kills someone, they'll sue me for not doing it when I had the opportunity. It's a damned-if-you-do, damned-if-you-don't situation.

In Stratton, the joke has always been that under the department's current administration, a bad guy could be shooting up a convent full of pregnant nuns and they wouldn't elevate to a shot of opportunity. There was nothing this administration feared more than a lawsuit or bad press. Somehow the joke doesn't seem as funny on this callout, though. This guy had shot a cop.

With that in mind, I recheck to make sure the fire selector switch is on FIRE, and go over everything one more time. Then, snuggling the gun in the bizarrely intimate way snipers do, I settle in to wait.

Several hours go by with nothing happening at all, which is typical. It is possible, even likely, that Route has fallen asleep. Capelko takes advantage of the inactivity to offer breaks to members of the team. People rarely take them, and none do tonight. Everybody wants to be on station when it goes down on this one.

About an hour before dawn, Hauser and Pole detach themselves from the entry team and deliver doughnuts and orange juice to the IP. I gladly accept mine.

"Need a bathroom break or anything?" Pole asks.

"Nope. Thanks for the OJ."

"Just make sure you're awake enough to kill this prick when the time comes," Hauser says. "Much as I'd like the honor, I think this one's gonna go to you."

"It'll be my pleasure," I lie.

"I bet, after what he did to Andrea." Then, with a slap on my ass, they disappear into the darkness.

After a moment, I realize that Hauser didn't say "after what he did to Hollister," who was still fighting for his life in the operating room, according to a broadcast by the CP an hour earlier. He'd said "after what he did to *Andrea*." Is our relationship that obvious?

The command post has been giving us little updates about the progress—or lack of it—of the negotiations. The bottom line is that Route believes his infant daughter is possessed by Satan, and that he is acting upon orders from God to kill her before daybreak. The CP has reported no real progress thus far.

Based on that, HNT does not think they can negotiate an end to the standoff, which means it will likely end with either a sniper shot or a hot entry. So far, the suspect has not been afraid to show himself. I've always joked around with the negotiators about having them talk a bad guy into a window. I always tell them to say, 'The officers outside don't believe you have a weapon. Go to the window and show them your gun.'

Up until tonight, it's always been a joke. Now it's a distinct possibility.

I find myself wishing Slater *had* taken the primary position tonight. How ironic. I imagine he is champing at the bit to drop the hammer on Route. After all, whoever gets to kill him can claim bragging rights forever and will no doubt be lauded as a hero.

I just know that for me, if push finally comes to shove, after all the congratulations have been offered, and all the slaps on the back have been delivered, I will eventually have to sleep, and that's when the demons will come. Now that I am this close to actually having to take Route out, it is easy to envision how I might be haunted by self-doubt afterward. I've been with other officers after a shooting. You don't just eat your hot dog and mutter something witty like Dirty Harry. The emotional trauma can wring a man dry, leaving him an empty husk.

I wasn't going soft on Hugo Route, not by a long shot. I *want* his mind to be on the living room wall, as callous as that sounds. It could have just as easily been Andrea instead of Dan fighting for her life on the operating table. Hell, it could have been me if it wasn't our anniversary and I'd taken the available swing shift OT instead of going to the concert with Sharon.

Like the father of a rape victim who wants to see the perp executed, but doesn't want to pull the switch himself, I want to see Route dead for what he did to Dan and Andrea, I'm just not so sure I want to be the one to paint his living room red and gray when the time comes. There is a tremendous difference between knowing the deed has been done, and actually doing it yourself.

I've seen probably a hundred and fifty gunshot wounds and bullet-riddled bodies in my career, and have never been grossed out by any of them. But then again, I hadn't created any of them, either. One thing is for sure. If I do have to shoot tonight, I won't be taking a look in the house afterward.

As I ponder this, Capelko's tinny voice sounds in my head, breaking my concentration. "CP to SERT. HNT reports the suspect hung up on them. They say things are heating up in there. HNT's gonna try reestablishing contact. Keep sharp, people."

From this distance, I can barely hear the phone ring. This it does twice, and a great deal of yelling ensues. For the first time, I can hear Route's voice. I can't tell what was being said, but clearly the exchange isn't very positive.

The yelling ceases, and a moment later, Capelko speaks up. "CP to SERT. HNT advises Route is refusing to negotiate. If they can't keep him talking, they're afraid he's going to harm the baby. Apparently, things are getting steadily worse as it gets lighter outside. This isn't going to last much longer, people. Keep yourselves sharp, but for now, the rules have not changed. Entry, wake up and get ready to go without warning. IP and snipers, we are maintaining compromised authority for now, but that could change real soon. Snipers, acknowledge."

We both do.

The phone begins ringing in the house. It rings twice before a tremendous crash cleaves the predawn silence like an unexpected clap of thunder. The phone, trailing several feet of cord, comes flying out the living room window amidst a constellation of twinkling glass. It lands ten feet from the window on the front yard, its bell giving a final clang before everything returns to silence.

"Damn," I mutter into the mike, now sounding as scared as I feel. "Uh, I mean, Geller to command post, side one, level one, window two... Ah, telephone out the window."

"Say again, Helen?"

"You heard me. Out the one-one-two," I say, a forced calmness now audible in my voice, "a *telephone* came flying out the window. It's sitting on the front lawn. Must've been Whiner on the other end."

"Whiner" is the nickname given to our lead hostage negotiator, Bo Pinter.

My remark is actually met with some laughter on the radio. Making jokes serves to help quiet the tiny voice which constantly reminds me that I must be nuts for doing this.

A moment later, Hugo Route makes an encore appearance in my scope, shouting out the now-broken living room window.

"You bastards! Get the hell out of here! This has nothing to do with you. It's spiritual warfare, don't you understand that? It's between The Lord, and that thing that used to be my daughter! You're guns cannot help! No weapon formed against me shall prosper, sayeth the Lord! So get thee the *fuck* behind me, Satan!"

"Side one, level one, window two, suspect at the window yelling for us to leave," I report, sounding nonchalant now. Inside, it is a different story. The greenish sight picture in my night scope is quivering about a hundred and twenty times a minute to the beat of my racing heart. If we were under a shot of opportunity, as we probably should be now, Hugo Route would already be dead. The reality of taking a shot is so utterly different from the pretense of training that I can't imagine making that one tiny index finger contraction that will change the lives of so many people forever. Especially *my* life.

I don't need to remind myself that I've already come incredibly close to shooting this man, and that the callout is by no means over. That the *real* fun and games, in fact, are probably only moments ahead.

Keeping the crosshairs centered on Route's less-than-attractive face, I concentrate on a mental image of this man firing rounds into my friend Dan; into my lover Andrea. With those images in mind, doubt vanishes, and I know I can do anything I needed to. I am now once again prepared to kill. The back-and-forth is creating so much stress that I feel as if I am aging decades on this callout.

"Copy that," Capelko says. "Ben, remember—we are still at compromised authority."

"I copy, Vince. And I'm off target now. I can't tell where the suspect went after he left the window."

"Slater to CP. He's in the three-four bedroom."

"Copy that. CP to entry. Stand by to deliver the throw-phone."

"Entry, copy. We're ready anytime you want."

"Okay, HNT says the throw-phone is a last-ditch effort. They say Route is adamant that the baby must die before sunrise. That's less than an hour away, folks. Stan, put that phone in the one-one-two ASAP."

"Copy, we're moving now."

I dial the magnification on my scope out to encompass the entire front of the house. My eye will remain pasted to the scope from now until the reaction team arrives safely back at the jump-off point.

The four-man IRT, or immediate reaction team, detaches itself from entry and comes sneaking around the one-side of the house next door to the objective. With MP5 submachine guns at the ready, they advance on the target. They move in unison, quickly but with precision. Three of them have guns trained on all openings of the house, and the fourth, remaining behind and shielded by the others, carries the phone.

After what had happened on the front yard with the scouts, and with the way this callout has been going, I'm not looking forward to the delivery of the phone, which will no doubt set Route off. I've never experienced feelings such as these on a callout before, and I am completely unable to shake a premonition of dread.

They move closer to the house. When they are within six feet of the broken one-one-two window, Carlos Vega, the entry guy carrying the phone, steps forward, and, like an athlete throwing a discus, he pitches the phone through the hole in the living room window. In the same motion, the team withdraws in formation, disappearing around the corner to the jump-off point in less than five seconds.

"Entry to CP, the phone has been delivered."

"Copy. HNT trying for contact."

From this distance, I can clearly hear the electronic buzz of the throw-phone. It is cut off in mid-ring by the earsplitting blast of a gunshot. A very large-caliber gunshot.

"Shots fired!" I yelled into the mike. I've never heard the sound of a gunshot on a real callout before, and despite my best efforts, I am unable to keep my voice at a normal, conversational tone. "One shot, unknown target!"

"CP copy. Roll call. Slater."

"Code four."

"Reid."

"Code four."

"Nosepick."

"Code four."

After every team member had been polled to make sure there were no SERT casualties as a result of the shot, Slater speaks up.

"Slater to CP. Requesting rules of engagement elevation."

I have to admit, I agree with him.

"CP to SERT. Stand by."

I feel my extremities turn to ice. They are going to do it. We are going to elevate to a shot of opportunity. What choice do they really have? Even though I know the rules of engagement change is necessary, I very much do not want to hear those words. More than anything, I want to watch the entry team go in, and then sit back and listen to a magazine or two being emptied into Hugo Route.

But with Hugo as willing as he is to show himself, I know it will fall to me to do it. I have trained for years just to be lying in these bushes with this man in front of me on this mild summer morning. This is why I am here—to take the shot. To save that baby.

To pay him back for what he did to Dan Hollister. *To avenge Andrea.*

Nonetheless, I'm not some third party that you read about who had to take a sniper shot in the field somewhere. I am Benjamin Geller, a Jewish tax attorney who wanted some excitement in his life, so he threw away his education and joined the cops. But somehow along the way, I've gotten myself in over my head.

Perhaps Slater can do it, I think. Slater *wants* to shoot him. He's probably praying the shot will present itself on his side.

"CP to SERT..."

Ashamed and confused by my doubt and conflicted feelings, I close my eyes and prepare for the three words I do not want to hear.

But they do not come. Not just yet.

"HNT reports Route shot the throw-phone. No rules of engagement change at this time. We remain at compromised authority for now. Snipers, acknowledge."

"Geller, copy," I said in a voice that somehow remains neutral.

"Slater copies." The note of disappointment in Slater's voice comes through loud and clear. But Capelko's order does carry a caveat, doesn't it? Rules unchanged *for now*?

I look to the east and see a noticeable lightening in the sky. In half an hour it will be light, and in forty-five minutes the sun will peek out from the north side of the now-visible Mt. Hood.

What will my life be like an hour from now? He shot the throw-phone. Jesus Christ.

Somehow, Capelko's words are of little comfort to me.

5

SOMETHING FALLS OVER in the house and crashes, startling me again. The woman and the baby begin screaming and crying. There are more sounds of a struggle. This activity can only bring the standoff closer to a forced end—a sniper shot, most likely—and I find it to be terribly unnerving. I wish it will all just end soon.

By now the house is visible to the naked eye but still too lost in shadows for me to make out any details. My night vision scope keeps things discernible. Through the broken living room window, I can see movement, but I am unable to tell if it was the man or the woman.

"Geller to CP, I have movement in the living room. I can't tell… Stand by…"

The figure turns to face me. It is the woman, and she is carrying the baby. Before I can say anything, Hugo comes into view, grabbing at the child. My heart is an engine running at a disturbingly high rpm, and it takes everything I have in me to keep the rifle under control. A tiny movement will translate to inches at this range, and I don't have inches.

"CP to Geller, update!"

Hugo is holding his wife by the back of her shirt, but she twists free and runs out of my view. He follows hot on her heels. I briefly see the gun in his hand as he disappears from my view. They have been struggling so closely, and the situation has unfolded so quickly, that even if we were under a shot of opportunity, I wouldn't have had a shot.

"They were fighting over the baby in the living room, but they just went out of my view toward the one-one-one. Off target!"

"CP copy. HNT reports—"

Another gunshot cuts through Capelko's words, silencing him. Before its echoes die away in the lightening neighborhood, Stan Hauser screams into the radio, "*Compromise! Compromise! Compromise!* Entry, we are moving!" They are stacked around the corner, and I see the last man in line start the tap up. Hauser is at the head of the line, and when the tap gets to him, the team will go in. I breathe a sigh of relief. It will be them, not me, after all.

Just as the tap reached Hauser, Capelko yells, "CP to entry, stand down! I repeat, stand down!"

"Vince, they're compromised in there!"

"Not my choice, Stan. I said stand down, damn it!"

Hauser's silence says it all. I feel my bile rise. I can hear Pammi crying, but no sound of the baby. He shot the baby. I am certain of it.

"Slater to CP—" There was no urgency in his voice.

"Stand by!" Capelko cut him off, angry and stressed, and I could only imagine what must be going on in the command post.

Pammi's weeping becomes fainter and fainter, then quiets altogether. A moment later, the most wonderful sound I've ever heard in my life comes drifting across the front yard and the quiet road; the baby crying.

I deflate like a silk sheet spread over a mattress.

"CP to SERT. We will remain at compromised authority. No shot of opportunity. This is coming from the highest level, despite my on-the-record objections. Geller and Slater, acknowledge."

"Geller copies." I am sure I sound relieved.

"Stand by while he shoots the baby; copy that!" says Slater.

The highest level. So, it's out of Capelko's hands, and Chief Moody is running the show. Or is it the mayor? Regardless, it is another first. I can envision Capelko making his case, and Moody shooting him down. Route should have been dead by a sniper shot by now, and absent that, entry should be inside killing him right now. If nothing else, we should be at a shot of opportunity. Route is going to kill his baby, and when he does, Moody will have to explain his position to a very unforgiving public.

I can hear another flurry of movement from within the house, and then Pammi Route, still carrying the baby, runs into the living room. I have no time to get on the radio. Hugo is right behind her.

She grabs a vacuum cleaner and throws it into her husband's path. Hugo picks it up and swings it at her, but succeeds only in hitting the light fixture on the ceiling, plunging the room into black shadows. This makes no difference to me. My starlight scope gives me a front row seat to all the action in sickly, ghostvision green.

Clearly visible in Hugo's right hand is a large-frame revolver, probably a Smith & Wesson. From the way it glows so brightly in the scope, it looks as if it is either stainless or nickel plated.

Pammi makes it to the number-three-side slider—the back door—and that's where Hugo catches her. The relief I feel is palpable. They are at the back, which means they now fall within Slater's purview.

Still, I try to maintain target acquisition on Route. My new job with respect to the killing of Hugo Route is to be a good witness. Slater has mere seconds to take Route out before he dominates his wife and seizes the baby.

Pammi is being crushed against the glass doors, trying desperately to unlock them and get out. Hugo is behind her, with his back to me, trying to turn her around.

Dimly, I am aware of someone screaming into the radio, but I have no idea who it is or what he is saying. Route succeeds in getting his wife spun halfway around. He makes a grab for the baby and gets one of her little arms free.

For the first time, I get a clear look at her. She is tiny, only about six months old, and is screaming. He has her by one arm, and Pammi has her by the other. She is caught up in a deadly game of tug-of-war.

The baby becomes taut between them, held by outstretched arms; her head lolling to one side and her legs dangling like a tiny Christ. Her diaper, soaked yellow and heavy, hangs halfway off. Like my own daughter Leah at that age, she is bald except for a layer of soft, blonde down on top.

Hugo has the gun in his right hand, which faces Slater. I can see it glint in the night scope. Slater will have a much better view than me. He is perhaps a hundred yards closer than I am, he has the same optics, and Hugo is pressed against the glass door facing him. Perhaps he can see something that I can't, for he surely should have fired by now. Even under standard rules of engagement, this is already well past a shoot situation.

My own crosshairs come to rest on Route's head, but Pammi twists, and now they are on her. She and Hugo have now traded positions, and he is against the slider. I see Hugo's right hand come slowly up, reaching over Pammi, and then the muzzle of the revolver kisses the back of the baby's neck.

I know Hugo's head is about to explode, and I silently urge Slater to hurry and get on with it. Fractions of a second pass, seeming to take hours, but still, no shot comes. What is taking Slater so long? Another fraction of a second or so, and it will be too late.

Slater does not shoot. Pammi has a hand on the gun, trying to misdirect the muzzle from the baby, but Hugo is stronger. As they struggle, they twist, and my crosshairs go from Hugo back to Pammi.

Slowly, painfully, I put them back on Hugo's forehead, but Pammi is now between us. Where the fuck is Slater? Hugo is facing him and he must have a perfect shot. If I have to do it, Pammi will be in the way. Not that it matters. Her life is unimportant compared to the baby's, at least to me.

Then time does something weird. Like an old movie at the end of the reel, the action slows. The epic struggle over the baby separates into single frames, flipping from one, to the next, to the next. Each image remains on the screen of my mind longer than the one before it as the clock slowly winds down. Her agonized face. The baby's skin as it is pulled in opposite directions, so taught I think it might split. Their two hands, each trying to redirect the muzzle of the gun in a different direction.

I have a flash realization during all this. I suddenly understand that Slater isn't going to shoot. That *I* will have to do it. That I don't have time to do it right. That if I wait for good target acquisition, the bullet will not get there before Route pulls the trigger.

I'm not about to watch a .357 muzzle blast rip that baby's head off. If I have to watch that, I will never be clean again.

The frames have just about stopped flipping now. Time is practically at a standstill. The current frame shows the muzzle of the revolver making solid contact at the base of the baby's skull.

One last frame. The hammer on Route's gun, previously forward, is now cocked back.

The clock runs out.

The rifle jumps in my hands, its sharp, cracking blast reverberating inside my head and chest. My hands work the bolt reflexively, chambering another round, and I hear myself screaming into the radio.

"Sniper shot out! Side three slider! Compromise, compromise, compromise!"

The window pops back into my scope as I fight the rifle for control. Broken glass; vertical louvers hanging askew; nothing but darkness within. The wonderful sound of the baby screaming fills my ears.

Running men cut in front of the window, heading for the door. At the same time, I can hear somebody yelling "Code Red! Code Red!" It is a warning not to fire, that good guys are now in the house.

I close my eyes and sag. I am strangely empty inside, and feel nothing. Come what may, I have done my job. The act of pulling the trigger, now done, can never be undone. I have killed a man. Now I will have to deal with it. I keep my mind free, realizing that I have the rest of my life to second-guess and armchair quarterback the act I have just undertaken.

I roll off scope onto my back, and rub my eyes. Now, all I want to do is relax, but I don't get the chance. Hauser's voice, still calm somehow, breaks squelch and fills my head.

"Suspect down, but get me code three medical in the house, and you better start LifeFlight. I got a female adult gunshot victim in here, with arterial bleeding."

"CP copy. Can you be more specific?"

My head lightens, and I become nauseous as realization dawns on me.

"Geller's shot hit the woman before it got Route. Brachial artery. And you better have them step on it. She's bleeding out fast."

6

I PUSH THE rifle away from me as if it has become red-hot. I shot *an innocent person.* I stare at my hands as if trying to figure out why they have done what they have just done.

Helium fills my head, and my eyelids flutter. Never in my life have I felt as much a failure as much as right now. The vast majority of police snipers will go their entire careers without ever having to take a shot, but when they do, their shots are almost always perfect. I trained years for this, and when my moment finally came, I blew it.

I think of Pammi Route, knowing the police are out there, trusting that we will save her and her baby, and then feeling a bullet tearing through her body.

My stomach heaves, and I barely have enough time to roll over before vomiting. I turn off my radio and lie there with my eyes closed for five solid minutes. When I finally look up, Lieutenant Capelko is standing over me.

"Vince," I say, my voice cracking, "I hit the woman. I shot the *wrong person.*"

"Ben, don't think about that. Hugo Route is dead, and that baby is alive." He gives this a moment to sink in, but it means nothing to me. "Did you hear what I said? *The baby is alive.*"

That should mean something, but I can't get past the fact that I shot a hostage.

Several members of the inner perimeter unit have gathered around me. At my glance, they turn away and tried to look as if they had come for some other reason than to gawk at the sniper who had shot a hostage.

Feeling like a schoolboy who'd had an accident in his pants, I wipe my nose on my shirtsleeve, and allow Capelko to walk me to a waiting car.

As I get in, I turn and see a sergeant securing my rifle. Another SERT member is cordoning it off with yellow POLICE LINE tape. My sniper position has now become a crime scene.

Lieutenant Capelko drives me directly to the Stratton police station. There are reporters waiting, and I have to run the gauntlet in order to get into the building. As I get out, I look skyward toward the *whop-whop-whop* of the LifeFlight helicopter's rotors as it nears NE Tenth Street to pick up Pammi Route. When I look back down, microphones have been shoved in my face.

"Are you the sniper that shot the woman?"

"Was the shot accidental?"

"How does it feel to shoot a hostage?"

Capelko actually knocks one persistent reporter to the ground, and then we are in the building. He leads me to the detective bureau and places me in an isolated interview room. A moment later, Sharon walks in.

"Ben…"

"Shar."

Nothing more is said, and we sit there hugging each other until I begin to settle down. During this time, another person enters the room. Ross Chamberlain, the president of the Stratton Police Officers Association. My union rep.

You need a union rep when you do something wrong.

I'm together enough to realize I have some serious legal problems on my hands. That my shot had saved the day, that it had saved little Chastity from certain death, will play a distant second to the fact that I shot a hostage. Although her baby is alive, Pammi Route will probably sue the department for everything she can get. If she doesn't die first. She had turned to the police for help, and we shot her.

I shot her.

"I'm in a world of shit, aren't I, Ross," I ask.

"No, you're not," he answers immediately. "Don't even think about that now, Ben. Right now, just try to relax. You've had a hell of a night, and now it's time to go home."

The worst part about all this, I think, is that it wasn't my shot. Everything had happened on side three, in the rear slider. It was *Slater's* territory; it was supposed to be *his* shot. I only took it because *he* didn't.

"I didn't do anything wrong, Ross," I hear myself saying. "This was just a horrible, unavoidable thing. Slater never took his shot, and I had to do it for him. If *he* had done his job, *I* wouldn't be here right now."

"Look, Ben, you did what you felt you had to do. Nobody's gonna hang you for that."

Everyone is treating me as if *I* had made a mistake, not Bob Slater, This scares me more than it pisses me off. "Ross," I say pleadingly, "He was going to kill the baby. I waited until the last possible second for Slater to take him out, but he never did. Slater fucked this one up, not me. Do you see that? Will *anyone* see that?"

"Ben, you're putting too much thought into this. Just look at it this way. Hugo Route is dead, and his baby is alive. So is his wife, for that matter. Being a hostage sucks. You need to focus on that fact, and let the chips fall where they may. Hell, in my book, you're a hero."

His words are of little comfort. Finally, it all catches up to me, and I feel like I'm going to pass out. I've been up for over twenty-four hours, and under the stress of being on scope for nearly half of them.

"I'm tired, Ross. I'm really, really tired. All I want to do right now is go home."

"And that's exactly what you're going to do. Listen, Ben. You're on paid leave of absence, just as a matter of routine. You understand this isn't any kind of discipline or anything like that, right?"

"I know."

"Good. Call me tomorrow sometime in the afternoon, or whenever you're ready to, and we'll talk more about it. In the meantime, don't talk to anyone about this. Not a soul, except for your wife. You can talk to her about it all you want. Got it?"

I get it. Conversations between spouses are constitutionally protected. She can't be forced to testify against me in court. Jesus.

Everyone manages to avoid looking at me as we make our way out of the office. Sharon drives me home, and we crawl into bed. Leah is at Sharon's mother's house for the duration.

Tired as I am, I am unable to go to sleep. We talk for about an hour, and finally I begin to doze. Sometime later I wake up with a start, a feeling of doom and dread gripping me. I am freezing, soaked in sweat, breathing hard. It is the middle of the night, and I feel utterly alone, but as my eyes adjust, I see a figure looming over me in the dark. It is my wife. She is wide awake, sitting up, her eyes steady on me. She strokes my forehead. She's been here with me all along, and foregoing sleep, has chosen to watch over me instead. Her hand slides down my face and cups my chin, her eyes tired, but bright. She is my sentinel, my guardian angel, awake and on duty at this ungodly hour.

I feel safe and protected under her guard in a way I could never feel on my own, and I love her for this; maybe more than I ever have in my life. I tell her exactly that, and she wipes tears from my eyes. It is a truly foreign experience.

She lays down next to me and cuddles me. Slowly, my anxiety dissipates, and I begin to feel comforted. Her breathing speeds up, and her hand alights on my stomach. Then, for the first time in perhaps a year, Sharon makes an attempt at initiating sex. She burrows under the covers and tries to arouse me orally. To my horror, nothing happens. I try, but all I can do is relive the moment when Hauser described my round passing through Pammi Route on its way to killing her husband.

"Honey, I'm sorry... I can't..."

"Shhhh, shhhh," she soothes, emerging and covering my face with kisses of a different sort.

We remain isolated in the house all day long. I sleep until five. Sharon was resourceful enough to turn the ringer off when we got home, and now there are eight messages waiting.

We plan on watching a movie tonight, but instead, I fall asleep at eight and don't wake up until morning. Now there are fifteen messages on the recorder, the machine's limit. Ignoring them, I go out to get the paper. I half expect a media mob to be outside, but thankfully, there is nothing. And then I see the headlines.

"Botched Sniper Shot Hits Innocent Hostage."

Nothing about saving the life of a baby, and certainly nothing on the order of "Side-Three Sniper Fails to Do His Job."

The main story continues on page two. In it is a long expose´ on the events leading up to the "near-deadly mistake."

Mistake?

I dismiss as much of the article as I can until I get to the part about Hollister's medical condition. I'm hoping for something I don't already know, but all they say is that he has suffered two serious gunshot wounds and is in critical condition.

I am unable to function all day. I can't take my mind off the incident. Specifically, those last few seconds, when the Routes fought over the baby at the rear slider.

Slater *had* to have been in a perfect position to take the shot. Neither Pammi Route nor the baby would have blocked his line of fire after they twisted around, and Slater would have had a perfect line of sight to Route's gun hand. So, why hadn't he taken the shot?

I can think of no good reason. Lack of confidence in his abilities? Not likely. Cowardice? Perhaps. Uncertainty and inexperience, since we were not at a shot of opportunity? Most likely. Not that it matters. I want to talk to him, to find out why he didn't shoot, and then again, I want to beat the shit out of him.

I also want desperately to talk with Andrea. None of the messages on my machine are from her. She would never call the house.

I check my department Nextel and find three text messages and two voice mails from her, all saying she wants to see me. In her voice mails, she says she wishes she we could get away for a few days to the beach or something, just to deal with what we've gone through and lie in bed without getting up.

I think of Sharon keeping a silent vigil over me the night before as I slept, and her attempt at lovemaking. How long had she sat like that and watched me?

Then my mind flips back to Andrea, how I am falling in love with her. I know what an asshole I am, and become increasingly depressed. It seems I have fucked up just about all the important areas of my life.

Sharon's mother, who has been watching Leah since the shooting, brings her home at two. I've never been happier to see my little daughter. In the way small children do, she realizes something is wrong; that for the moment, *she* must be strong, and I am the weak one. We snuggle together on the couch while she watches a cartoon in which millions of years of animated dinosaurs get wiped from the face of the earth in one terrible meteor storm. Before their extinction is complete, I fall asleep with her on my chest.

I speak with Ross Chamberlain later in the day, and am greatly relieved when I hang up. He says the police department and the district attorney's office intend to back me a hundred percent, and that Chief Moody wants me to know that he is proud of what I have done. Everyone acknowledges that the shot was incredibly difficult with the fight that was going on at the door, and they all understand the difficult choice that I had in taking it.

Chamberlain never mentions Bob Slater, or why he didn't take the shot, so I ask him point-blank.

"Ben," he says seriously, "Slater's not talking. He asked for a union rep when Moody and Phil asked him what happened."

Phil is Detective Sergeant Philip Mahoney, lead investigator for the Multnomah County Major Crimes Team, which handles all officer-involved shootings. "Eric Cullberg is representing him," he continues, "To tell you the God's truth, I don't have a clue what Slater's doing. He's acting as if he committed a crime. I can tell you this, though—he's refusing to make any statements right now and has submitted a formal request for a union attorney."

"Jesus Christ, Ross, what's that mean?"

"I don't know, but Eric and I have already agreed that due to a potential conflict of interest, we won't collaborate with each other. I'm sure Slater realizes he dropped the ball and bears some liability with regard to Pammi Route's, uh, injuries."

That was the best news of the day. "Doesn't that indicate Slater knows he should have taken the shot? Isn't that good news for me?"

He hesitates, and says, "Yes, *if* that's what's motivating him. We just don't know, because he hasn't even talked to Eric yet, and we don't know what he's going to say. Just be thankful that you have the department on your side. And with the DA supporting you, you probably won't have a problem with the grand jury, either."

I already know that all officer-involved shootings go to grand jury as a matter of course. I don't believe there has ever been a case in Multnomah County's history that didn't come down on the side of the officer.

Chamberlain tells me that Dan Hollister is still in critical condition, and that there have been members of police departments from around the state maintaining vigil at the hospital. He suggests that Sharon and I go down there when we can and mingle with other Stratton officers. He only cautions me not to talk about any of the details of the shooting with anyone.

We decide to do just that, and at six thirty, we drop Leah off with Sharon's mother again and head off to OHSU Medical Center in Portland.

Hospitals, by their nature, have a tendency to portend more bad news than good. Sometimes it comes in ways you don't expect.

7

THE PARKING LOT of the hospital looks more like a precinct substation than anything else, given the number of police cars parked there. Sharon and I make our way inside and are instantly greeted by officers from departments all around the Pacific Northwest who are there to support Dan and his wife Sue.

The rank and file are wholly in support of me, and I am pleased to hear several people grumbling about Slater's inaction at the callout. I hope that's the way the administration feels, too. So far, so good.

Sharon and Sue are fairly close, and Sharon's presence really seems to give Sue comfort.

"He's still in a coma," Sue tells us, "But I believe that God's taking care of him. I also believe that Danny knows what's going on and can hear what you say. Go on in, Ben. Talk to him; I know it does him good when people talk to him."

As ready to see Dan as I think I am, I am still shocked at the sight of him lying there, unmoving, with tubes in his mouth, nose, and arms, hooked up to so many machines. One of them appears to be breathing for him, and the realization that he might not make it hits me hard.

Sue introduces us to Dan's parents, who are staying in a motel close to the hospital for the duration. "Mom, Dad, this is Ben Geller. He's the sniper who killed the man who—"

"I'm goddamn pleased to meet you, Ben," interrupts the father, holding out his hand. "I'm very sorry about what happened to that man's wife, but from what I hear, there was no way around it. I'm just glad you got that sumbitch and saved me from having to do it myself."

I shake his hand, and then Dan's mother, a tiny little thing with a face white from powder and a back like a question mark from scoliosis, unselfconsciously pulls me down to her level and plants a big wet kiss on my cheek. "You have our gratitude, son. I just hope you don't have any problems of your own to deal with. I understand that you saved that baby's life. You should be proud of yourself."

I am. I want to say thank you to them, but I don't trust my voice. Sharon says, "I bet Ben would like a moment with Dan alone," and everyone nods and files out.

I try not to stare at Dan, and am glad to see that his eyes are closed. I hope he can hear me, but I don't want him to know how uncomfortable and scared I am. He looks awful, pasty and lifeless, and I don't want him to see my reaction to his appearance.

Hesitantly, gingerly, I take his hand in my own. It feels very awkward. "Dan? Dan, it's me. Ben Geller."

I don't know what to say. I want to thank him for placing his life on the line out there, but that sounds pretty lame coming from one who does the same thing every day. That kind of thing should come from a civilian, not another cop.

"Dan, I'm, uh, I'm pulling for you. We all are. I hope to see you back at work soon."

This is all wrong. It sounds forced, contrived. I don't think he can possibly hear me. Hell, he didn't even look *alive*, let alone able to hear.

Then I think, what if he dies? What if he really *can* hear me, and this is the last opportunity I have to speak with him? Suddenly, talking to him doesn't seem so hard.

"Dan," I said conspiratorially. "I want you to know I got the bastard that shot you. I took him out with a .308, right between the fuckin' eyes. I just want you to know that. He was going to kill the baby. He *tried* to kill her. But that was just my excuse, Dan. What I really shot him for is what he did to you, and Andrea.

"Did you know that after you got shot, Andrea dragged you out of the line of fire? As she was doing it, he shot her, too, only she wasn't hurt too bad because she took it in the vest. But I killed him, Dan. I killed him for you, and I killed him for Andrea. We shouldn't have to arrest guys who shoot cops, I really believe that. I *hate* it when I read that a guy shot a cop, and was taken into custody 'without incident.' Well, not this time.

"The only thing that went wrong was that my shot hit Route's wife in the arm before blowing his fucking head off. She's gonna live, but I don't know about the arm. I really feel bad about that, but *she* placed herself there. It was her *choice* to go back in there. Being a hostage is a shitty job, isn't it?

She'll sue the crap out of the department and me, but I don't care. She was stupid. She shouldn't have been there. And by the way, I saved her baby's life. Think she ever thanked us for that? Hell no.

"And, I'll tell you another thing, just between us. Bob Slater fucked this up. The job of killing Hugo Route was his, because everything happened at the three-side slider, but Slater chickened out. The wife would never have gotten shot if Slater had done his job. When you're out of here, we'll talk more about it, bud. Right now, you need to rest."

I give his hand another hard squeeze, then turn and leave the room.

We remain in the hallway for the next hour, talking with officers about the SERT callout and the shooting of Hugo Route. I am careful to stick to generalities and avoid details, which seems fine with the other cops. To a person, they all support me. I am surprised and buoyed at how many express disdain for Slater for not taking the shot.

"Hey, Ben, you got a sec?" asks Rodney McNamara, a Stratton detective. McNamara is on the Major Crimes Team. He is also a golfing partner of Slater's and perhaps Slater's best friend on the department.

"Sure, what's up?"

McNamara leads me down a corridor to an unoccupied nurse's station, the only place where there are no other cops. We haven't worked together in the three years since he'd made detective, but were pretty good friends before then.

"Look, Ben, I'm going to tell you something, but this is strictly fifty-one info, okay?"

Code 10-51 in our department means for authorized ears only. If a dispatcher says it, it means get away from the bad guy so he can't hear what she's about to tell you.

"Okay, strictly fifty-one. What's up?"

"I have it on good authority that Slater's gonna say Route had no gun when you shot him. That he didn't take the shot because there was no need to. That—"

"That's bullshit, Rod! He knows goddamn well there was a gun. He had to have seen it. I mean, that thing practically *glowed* in our starlight scopes!"

"Ben, just listen to me, okay? Don't shoot the messenger for the message. He's going to say that you shot prematurely, that there was no real danger to the baby or anyone else, and that from a sniper's perspective, it was a bad shot, because they were fighting too hard, moving around too much."

"How can he say that? The entry team found the gun right by Route's body, for Christ's sake."

"Look, obviously I'm not supposed to even be talking about this, and neither are you. So this conversation never took place. But yes and no to the gun. It was found in the hallway, almost eight feet from the body. That's consistent with him dropping it as he got shot, but it's also consistent with him dropping it as he chased his wife, or just leaving it in the hallway without taking it with him when he chased her. So, even after the investigation is complete, it could still boil down to his word against yours."

"Yeah, but Route's wife'll confirm that Route had the gun and was about to use it on the baby, so I'm fine, and Slater's gonna be in a world of shit when she says he's lying."

"That's just the thing, Ben. We don't know what she's going to say. She lawyered up the moment we said we want to talk to her."

"What? Hell, that doesn't make any sense. Why would she do that?"

"That's what worries me."

"Well, I'm not worried about Slater. He's a slimy little shit, and the only reason he would say something like that would be to cover his ass for chickening out when it was time for *him* to kill Route."

"Yeah, well, there might be another reason. Slater was seen talking with Pammi Route here at the hospital when she was brought in after you… After she got injured. Personally, and mind you, this is just my own opinion, but I think they may have made a deal—they agree on their story about Hugo not having the gun, in exchange for Slater getting a piece of whatever settlement she might get in a lawsuit."

"You're shitting me! Slater's slimy, but he's not *that* slimy. Is he?"

"I don't know, Ben. But I've never fully trusted that guy. You be careful around him, you hear me?"

"Yeah, man. Thanks."

Just then, my wife catches my eye, and zombie-like, I leave Rod to see what she wants. I decide for the moment not to tell her what he just told me. Not yet, anyway. I'm getting a really bad feeling about all this. Slater might just be slimy enough to pull something like that, and apart from Rod's theory, I can think of no other reason why he would refuse to make a statement to investigators and ask for a lawyer.

Since Slater's not looking at any criminal charges, the department can order him to make a statement, but that doesn't help me out at all. If he's going to say there was no gun, it will probably boil down to my word against his, and if he has Pammi Route in his pocket, then that's two against one and I'm screwed.

Sharon is hungry and suggests we go to the cafeteria for a bite. As we head downstairs, I feel as if I am living in a dream world. Even apart from what McNamara said, seeing Dan unconscious and looking so lifeless has affected me intensely.

"I don't know how Sue's coping so well," Sharon tells me as we find a booth and sit down. "I can't imagine what I would do if anything ever happened to you."

I take her hand, and her eyes well up. "Sue said they had a fight before he left for work that afternoon. Something about him going fishing the next day, which would have been yesterday. She said they didn't get it resolved, and she refused to kiss him good-bye. She was mad at him."

"Honey, you know that doesn't mean anything. If Dan is still kicking under there, he knows how much she loves him, and he probably doesn't even remember a stupid little argument like that. Dan would probably get mad if he found out she was worried about it."

"Oh, I know, but can't you imagine it from her point of view? It's tearing her up inside."

Then Sharon does something she hasn't done in years. She moves over to my side of the booth and takes my hand. "Promise me you'll never leave me," she says, leaning her head against my shoulder.

Thoughts of Andrea flit through my head like little birds. I see us talking, then kissing, then making love, and then me falling in love with her. I put my head down on Sharon's thick brown hair, but feel and smell Andrea's silky chestnut hair instead.

"Of course I'll never leave you," I say, forcing Andrea from my mind. I don't *really* love her. It's nothing more than a juvenile infatuation. Andrea wouldn't have kept vigil over me like Sharon did while I slept, would she? That was an act of maturity and deep love that's completely beyond anything Andrea is capable of.

Sharon leaves the majority of her food untouched and leans up against me while I eat. We both drew comfort from the contact.

After dinner, I head to the bathroom before going back up to see Dan. As I turn the corner by the restrooms, I run smack into Andrea coming out of the ladies room.

"Ben! Oh my God, I've wanted so badly to call you, but I was afraid to! I'm so glad to see you!" She throws her arms around me in what is much more tender than a friendly embrace.

This is the first I've seen her since the incident, and the fact that she'd nearly been killed overwhelms me. As close as I feel to Sharon, she would never be able to understand the bond that Andrea and I have as police officers, let alone the whole boy-girl thing. Sharon will never really understand from first-hand experience what it's like to be in the position of having to kill another human being, but Andrea does.

Andrea and her scent have always been enough to make me forget that I'm married. She's the only woman I've ever cheated with. Here she is, in my arms, just moments after I thought I could never love anyone other than Sharon. Her hair—silky, clean, and fragrant—is in my face, and I inhaled deeply, taking several strands in my mouth in a stolen moment of intimacy only I am aware of. She cradles the back of my head in her hand the tender way she does when we make love. Despite our surroundings, I feel myself becoming aroused, and gently nuzzle her neck.

I relish the fleeting moment, then open my eyes and begin to disengage. There, standing directly in front of me, is Sharon. She is staring at us in open-mouthed disbelief.

"Honey," I say, fairly pushing Andrea away from me, and knowing I sound as guilty as I look. "You remember Andrea Fellotino, right? She's the one who saved Dan's life. And Route shot her, too."

I sound like I am trying to make Sharon less angry by attempting to build sympathy for Andrea, which is exactly what I am doing. Clearly, I am failing miserably, and I know it. Sharon gives me a look of intense hurt, disappointment, and anger all at the same time. To her credit, she does not make a scene.

"I'm going back upstairs," she says woodenly, then shows us her back and walks away.

"Shit," I tell Andrea. "Listen, I gotta go with her. I'll call you as soon as I can, okay?"

"Go, Ben. Christ, I'm so sorry. Are you going to be okay?"

"I'll be fine. I wish we could talk right now, but I really have to take off."

"Okay. Ben… I, uh, I think I love you."

"Huh?" I said, pretending not to hear her.

"Nothing. Go to her Ben. You still have to live with her."

Thankful just to get out of there, I turn to leave. As I round the corner, she adds, barely loud enough for me to hear, "For now, anyway."

8

I AM TOLD I will remain on administrative leave until the case goes before the grand jury. The DA's office will do this as quickly as possible, most likely next week. Randy Bulger, my union attorney, reminds me that the bottom line of a grand jury is to gather evidence to determine if a crime had been committed. If so, the DA's office, will prosecute the case.

My testimony to the grand jury is entirely optional. Since they might find that I committed a crime, even negligently, by shooting Pammi Route, I cannot be not be compelled to testify against myself. If I choose not to testify, they will have to go on the statements of all the other witnesses in making their decision, which will include Bob Slater. If I choose to testify, then at least they will have my side of the story.

To me, I have no real choice but to testify. The grand jury needs to know exactly what was going on in my mind at the time I took the shot. Randy wholeheartedly agrees with me.

The only problem is the potential damage Bob Slater can do to the case. Randy thinks the worst he can do is to get the jury to believe I had negligently shot the Routes (God, how I hated that it was plural) because there was no tactical need to do so. He doesn't think the jury will go so far as to determine that any such negligence rose to the level of being criminal.

The problem, of course, is that grand jurors are just plain people. Portland people; of the type who like to keep Portland weird. And many Portland people who like to keep Portland weird hate the police. So you never really can predict exactly what will happen with grand juries.

To me, the shooting was clearly righteous. And I'm not about to let Bob Slater get his side of the story in without the opportunity to let the jurors know exactly what the truth is. I am going to testify. Period.

The days between the incident and the grand jury hearing are a living nightmare for me. I feel alone and unprepared, even though I've spent several hours a day going over my testimony with my lawyer.

Sharon knows I want to contact Andrea, and we've argued about it twice since she caught us hugging in the hospital. I tried telling her that we are just friends, and there are issues we should discuss since she'd been shot and I'd killed the man who shot her. She didn't buy it, and still doesn't. I've learned that it is better just to not to bring it up any more.

In the meantime, our phone rings incessantly. I take calls from SWAT snipers I know throughout the state, and receive uncounted messages of support from Stratton cops. Reporters also call, but I just give them a terse "no comment" and hang up. Sharon maintains a weird state of limbo between being sympathetic to me and freezing me out because of her suspicions regarding Andrea. I find myself wishing I'd never met Andrea. Or that my moral fiber was stronger than it is. Well, if nothing else, that I had been more discreet with her.

As if all that isn't enough, I am under orders to stay away from the police department, which is nothing more than standard procedure. They will call me when they want me. It's ironic; everyone there is talking about me, the public information officer is dealing full time with the press about me, the entire detective division is tied up in an investigation about me, I am the topic of conversation on everyone's lips, and I have to stay away. I hate that.

I arrive at the courthouse dressed in my best suit by eight o'clock on the morning of the grand jury hearing. I know I probably won't get to testify today, but I have to be here nonetheless. Sharon is with me the whole time, either showing support for me, or keeping her eye on me. Probably both.

We sit on a bench down the hall from the grand jury room on the seventh floor of the Multnomah County Courthouse in downtown Portland. The other witnesses take a few minutes to mumble a few words of encouragement, but for the most part they leave us alone, following unwritten rules of courthouse protocol.

Rebecca Allison, the county's most senior assistant district attorney, is assigned to the case. Before the proceedings get under way, she tells me I shouldn't have anything to worry about, that despite there being a question in the mind of one of the officers involved, she feels the facts of the case fully support the shooting. She cautions me, however, that this is only her opinion, and she is referring only to the criminal aspect of the case.

I don't need her to remind me that there is also a civil aspect to it; that I am no doubt going to get my ass sued off by Pammi Route and a bevy of attorneys waiting like vultures in the wake of the grand jury ruling.

One thing at a time. The first hurdle is being cleared of criminal charges.

On the first day of testimony, Allison starts with Andrea Fellotino, who testifies about the radio call, the shooting of Dan Hollister, and getting shot herself. Then Pammi Route testifies. The day closes with the testimony of Bo Pinter and some other members of the hostage negotiating team.

Nobody says anything to me about the proceedings, which is standard procedure. Most, however, give me a nod and a smile after they come out of the hearing room. I am glad for the support of all the people around me.

On the second day of testimony, the DA calls Lieutenant Capelko and Chief Moody. They are followed by Roland Hogue, the IP guy closest to the rear slider. After Roland, Bob Slater testifies. Slater is in there for two hours, and I try to get his eye on his way out, but he avoids me and looks down as he leaves. He doesn't talk to anyone, and immediately leaves the building.

At two thirty on the second day of testifying, the door to the little room labeled Grand Jury A opens, and Allison comes out. "Ben, they're ready for you," she said. I don't know what my expression is, but she winks at me as I head in.

I have testified before the grand jury hundreds of times in my police career, and I am always somewhat surprised at their appearance. An Oregon grand jury is made of seven people, chosen from the general jury pool, which is comprised of registered voters. A jury of my peers.

My peers, in this case, are quite a mix. From left to right is a wizened old black man in his seventies who seems to have some difficulty staying awake, an overweight housewife in a threadbare cotton shift, and a man about my own age in a business suit who has the smug look of one who thinks he controls everything. Then there is a small gap and a person with the sign Grand Jury Foreperson on the desk in front of him. This is a long-haired guy in his late twenties with lines in his face that tell the story of a hard life. He is the type I would be tempted to stop if I found him walking down a nice residential street after dark. Next to him is a conservative looking college kid, a large but attractive Asian woman, and a woman of indeterminable age in a wheelchair.

After looking each member in the eye, I am more apprehensive than ever about the outcome of the case. The foreperson returns my gaze and says, "Raise your right hand, please. Do you swear to tell the truth, the whole truth, and nothing but the truth, under penalty of perjury?"

"I do," I say solemnly, then take my seat in the chair that faces them. The grand jury is arranged in a semicircle around the witness, making him feel as if he is sitting in some sort of hot seat. In this case, I am.

Allison takes me through the standard stuff—my name, my job, and my position as a sniper on the SERT team. Next, she has me go through a detailed explanation of my training and experience as a sniper, and then we move into the facts as I knew them about the Route callout.

She takes me through the progression of the callout, my understanding of the rules of engagement, and finally, the sequence of events that took place at the rear slider.

"Officer Geller, did you perceive a danger to any persons in the Route household in the minutes prior to the confrontation between Pammi and Hugo Route at the glass door in the back of the house?"

"Yes, I did. First of all, throughout the callout we had been given consistent updates from the hostage negotiators that Hugo Route intended to kill the baby before dawn. It was getting closer and closer to dawn, and was, in fact, past first light."

"Based on these updates, did you believe that either Pammi or the baby was in danger?"

"Yes, both of them. The hostage negotiators had been in contact with Route by phone at several points throughout the standoff. Their updates were quite clear in stating that they believed Route intended to carry out his threats to kill the baby. He had a gun, and in fact, fired it several times during the siege. Pammi clearly wanted to get it away from him and was trying to do so. Plus, Route had already shot two police officers prior to all this."

"And in the moments preceding the confrontation at the back door, were there any other indicators to you that the situation might be changing?"

"Yes. I had several indications that the situation was deteriorating."

"By 'deteriorating,' what, specifically, do you mean?"

"That Route was becoming less inclined to negotiate a settlement, and that he was getting closer and closer to killing his baby."

"And how did you determine this?"

"Well, first he cut off negotiations by throwing his telephone out the window. Then the SERT team delivered what we call a throw-phone into the house, kind of as a last resort to keep the negotiations open."

"I see," says Allison, as if she is perhaps hearing the story for the first time. "And how did Hugo Route respond to the introduction of the throw-phone?"

"He shot it."

"What do you mean, 'he shot it'?"

"He literally shot the device, with his .357 Magnum revolver."

"What happened next?"

"There were sounds of a struggle in the house, and the woman and baby began screaming. Even from my position a hundred and ninety yards away, I could hear things getting knocked over and crashing in the house. It all sounded very violent."

"Go on," she urges.

"They came into my view in the living room for a few seconds. They were fighting wildly, and they immediately left my field of view. A moment later, there was another gunshot in the house. At that point, I believed that Route had made good on his threats and shot the baby, but after a second or two of silence, the baby started crying."

"And was there any change of the rules of engagement at that time?"

"Well, I was certain that after two gunshots, the rules would be elevated to a shot of opportunity, but that didn't happen. Lieutenant Capelko came on the radio and made sure that the other sniper, Bob Slater, and I acknowledged that we were still under compromised authority."

"Was there, to your knowledge, any controversy about those orders?"

"Yes. At one point, Officer Slater had requested that we elevate to a shot of opportunity. I concurred, and still feel that way. And Lieutenant Capelko told us over the radio that he was in favor of elevating to a shot of opportunity, but that the order to remain at compromised authority had come straight from 'the highest level,' which I took to be the chief of police."

"So, you were ordered to remain at compromised authority, but you and at least several other team members, including the tactical team commander, thought the situation should have been elevated to the highest level, a shot of opportunity, is that right?"

"That's correct."

"Okay, continue, please."

"Well, right after Capelko said that, Pammi ran through the living room, carrying the baby. Hugo was chasing her, and was right behind her. They were throwing things at each other, and the overhead light got knocked out, making it very dark inside."

"Could you still see what was happening?"

"Yes, I was using a starlight scope... Uh, that's a night vision scope, on my rifle. I could still see everything in clear detail, although I lost the ability to distinguish colors. Everything appears in various shades of green or black in the night scope."

"Please describe Hugo Route as you saw him chasing Pammi through the living room."

"He kept reaching out for her, but she was running away from him. I saw a revolver in Hugo's right hand. In my night scope, it was glowing very brightly, and I remember thinking it was either stainless steel or nickel plated."

"Are you certain it was a revolver? Might it have been anything else?"

"Yes, I am certain it was a revolver. I could see it in quite good detail. It was not cocked, and Route had his finger in the trigger guard, on the trigger. And no, it could not have been anything else."

"Had you earlier seen anything else in Route's hand?"

"Yes, as I said earlier, when the scouts were out, I saw him with a phone in his hand."

"Might it have been a phone this time?"

"Absolutely not. It was definitely a revolver."

"And he was chasing her, and his finger was on the trigger of a revolver. Is that right?"

"Yes."

"And he had several times earlier threatened to shoot the baby?"

"Yes."

"When did he say he was going to shoot the baby?"

"At dawn. Or by dawn, I think it was."

"And what was the state of the morning when you saw Hugo chasing his wife and baby through the living room with his finger on the trigger of a revolver?"

"It was well past first light. It was just about light enough outside to read by, and you could clearly see things around you in the existing light. Dawn was perhaps ten or fifteen minutes away."

"And Hugo Route had previously shot this weapon in the house on at least two occasions while you were there?"

"Correct."

"Okay. What happened next?"

"Pammi made it to the sliding glass door in the back of the house and tried to get out, but she couldn't get the door open. Hugo grabbed the baby and tried to pull her from Pammi. This was all going on at very high speed, and the whole confrontation took less than thirty seconds. They each had the baby by an arm and were engaged in a tug-of-war-type match with her."

"And did Hugo still have the gun?"

"Yes, he reached up and around Pammi and brought the gun up against the baby's head."

"What happened next?"

"Well, there was no doubt that this was a shoot situation. I fully expected—"

"Excuse me, Officer Geller, but can you define the term 'shoot situation'?"

"Yeah, it's a situation that calls for an officer to shoot the suspect. In this case, that response would be to save the life of the baby. It was clear that Hugo Route had the intention and the means to shoot his baby, and was in fact, in the process of doing so."

"So, believing that it was, as you defined, a shooting situation, did you intend to shoot Hugo Route?"

"No, not at first."

"Why not?"

"Because this action was going on at the back of the house, where we had another police sniper. Hugo and Pammi were directly up against the back door, which was made of glass, and I knew that the other sniper would take the shot."

"And did he in fact take the shot?"

"No, he didn't. I didn't understand why he didn't, and still don't, but the fact remains that he did not take the shot. Therefore, either I would shoot Hugo, or Hugo would kill the baby. *That* was my choice."

"Why did you believe that?"

I know Allison is questioning me this way for the sake of the jury, but still, I can't keep the exasperation out of my voice. "Because he put a loaded handgun to her head after telling us he was going to shoot her at dawn, and the day was dawning!"

"And what did you do?"

"There was no time left. As a matter of fact, I wasn't sure I had time to shoot Route before he shot the baby. I'd been trying for good target acquisition the entire time they were in my view, but the way they were fighting at the door, they kept turning around, and it was impossible to keep Hugo in my sights."

"Officer Geller, if you were not under a shot of opportunity, why were you trying to keep Hugo Route in your sights?"

"Because I knew at any time the situation might call for a shot. Like I said earlier, we were at compromised authority, which meant that if anyone were compromised and a team member had to shoot the suspect, the entry plans and everything were already complete, and the team could make an immediate entry. Well, there was no doubt that the baby was compromised. I mean, he was putting a loaded handgun to her head with the stated intent of killing her."

"Okay, then continue, please."

"Well, I tried to get a good, clean shot on Hugo, but the way they were fighting, it was impossible. Like I said, I had to do this because the other sniper wasn't. He should have taken the shot by now, but since he didn't, it fell to me. At the moment Route put the gun to the baby's head, they were kind of sideways toward me. Pammi kept getting in and out of the way of my shot on Hugo's head. Well, he put the barrel to the back of the baby's neck, and he pulled the trigger. I remember the hammer coming back, and then my gun jumped. I had taken the shot."

"Did you have a clear target at Hugo?"

"To be honest, I didn't really know at the time. It definitely wasn't a clean shot. Pammi kept getting in the way, and there was no way to say whether she was actually in the way at that moment or not. I just knew that if I didn't take the shot when I did, he would have killed the baby. In fact, I remember thinking that I valued her life, the baby's I mean, higher than Pammi's. I don't even remember taking the shot."

"And what did you find out later about your shot?"

"That I had killed Hugo Route but that the bullet passed through Pammi's arm on the way."

"And how do you feel about that?

"I feel like I saved the baby's life. It came at the price of wounding Pammi Route, but it was well worth it. I feel horrible about wounding her, but I take great satisfaction that, because of me, the baby is still alive."

"Thank you, Officer Geller. Are there any questions from the members of the jury?"

"Yeah," says the long-haired foreman. "Officer, was it possible to shoot to wound the suspect?"

"Under those circumstances, no. That's because anything other than a shot that separates the brain stem from the spinal cord would have left open the possibility for a reflexive spasm or muscle contraction to cause him to pull the trigger, which would have resulted in the baby's death."

"Officer Geller," says the old black man, opening his eyes for maybe the first time during my testimony. "If you were in the same predicament right now, tell me. What would you do?"

"I'd still pull the trigger. There's no way I could live with myself knowing that I had to watch him blow that baby's head off in my scope because I didn't do my job. I was that kid's only hope."

"I would, too," said the old man. The other jurors nodded their heads, and I knew I'd come out of this intact.

9

"BEN, IT WAS a total sweep. They voted "no true bill" all the way down the line. And to a person, the members of the grand jury all commended you on your actions and even called you a hero. Congratulations on that." It is Chief Moody on the phone, the day following the grand jury.

I exhale lungful of air I didn't know I was holding. "Thank God," I say. "So, what happens next?"

"We'll be concluding our own investigation. I'm ordering you to come in and make a statement to Phil Mahoney today at two. Can you do that?"

"Yeah, Chief, it's not like I have anything else going on right now."

"Good. We'll make sure you have a union rep there."

"I don't care. I just want to get it done and over with. What happens after the interviews?"

"Tomorrow night, we're doing the shooting reconstruction. I'm also ordering you to be there, at 415 NE Tenth Street, at midnight, ready to cooperate fully with the reconstruction. It's going to go all night long. Any problems with that?"

"Nope. Looking forward to it."

"Fine. After that, we'll have a department meeting over the results, and you'll be notified of our decision with regards to the internal affairs investigation. We hope to have it all completed in a couple of days."

"And after that?"

"You meet with the department shrink, and as long as you're cleared in the IA investigation, which, off the record, you will be, then it's back to work. We want you back on the street in a week. How's that sound to you?"

"Chief, that's about the best news I've heard since the shooting. I can't wait to put it all behind me."

"Well, that might not happen for a long time. Pammi Route's still not cooperating with us, and we expect that she'll be suing the department. You do know that, right?"

"Yeah, but I'll take that as it comes. Right now, I'm looking forward to getting cleared and restored to duty."

"There's no rush to get you back on the street, Ben. If you need time, even after you're cleared internally, take all you want. I encourage you to take advantage of counseling available through the Employee Assistance Program."

"Thanks, Chief. I'll probably do that."

I tell Sharon that my statement will likely last most of the afternoon, although I don't believe it will take much longer than an hour.

It doesn't. Because I am no longer looking at criminal charges, the department can order me to answer questions, but they certainly don't need to. I am more than willing to do so on my own, and I have the blessing of Ross Chamberlain, my union rep. I am confident, and the statement lasts only about forty-five minutes. It covers nothing more than my grand jury testimony had, but isn't nearly as detailed. When I am done, they tell me I have nothing to worry about. I get in my car and immediately call Andrea on my department cell phone.

Since the Route incident, I've gone from being in love with Andrea to wishing I never knew her. At the same time, I've gone from thinking I was through with Sharon to falling in love with her all over again. The bottom line is I want my wife, but Andrea has been filling a need that Sharon has been unable to fill. And during the course of our relationship, we've formed an incredibly close bond.

As I drive across the Columbia River toward Andrea's Vancouver apartment, I think about what a jerk I've been to Sharon. I love her, but the problem is, I am connected to Andrea too, and Andrea and I need some time to discuss all that has happened with the Route incident. Her getting shot. Me killing Route. Dan Hollister. Pammi Route. Bob Slater.

I finally feel like I'm getting my priorities straight. Andrea is a minx; the most sexual person I have ever met. But the bottom line is, after the way Sharon has taken care of me since the shooting, I can see that the thing with Andrea really is purely physical. With her, it's just sex. Good sex. Great sex even, but still, just sex. Sharon and I, on the other hand, have a life together. A history since high school. Common likes and dislikes. Judaism. And above all, we have Leah. In fact, we have everything *but* the physical.

I have jeopardized it all for good sex, and I don't want to continue doing that. I know I must break it off with Andrea, and I resolve that tonight, after we talk out the Route incident, I will do just that.

Sharon's reaction to me after the shooting was the convincing factor. She saw my uncertainty, my vulnerability, and my fear, and through it all, she was the strong one; the one I leaned upon for support. Since then, I've come to see my wife in a new light. Now I can look behind the extra lines in her face, past the wrinkles in her stomach, beyond the sag of her breasts. Now I can see the love behind the irritation we feel around each other. Sharon has a heart of gold, and she is my wife. She is my *wife*.

Like it or not, it is time to put Andrea behind me, once and for all. I conjure up Sharon's image and decide I will come clean with her after I break it off with Andrea. I will put both the shooting and my affair behind me in one fell swoop.

I feel as if Sharon is with me as I approach Andrea's door. We will do this together.

I raise my fist to knock, but never get the chance. Andrea has been waiting for me and opens the door the moment I step onto the porch. She pulls me inside and wraps her arms around me.

"Oh, Ben, I didn't think I'd ever get a chance to be with you after everything that's happened," she says, and immediately lays her head on my chest.

"Andrea..."

"Shhhh, just let me hold you. I've felt so *alone* since the shooting. Everyone's telling me what a good job I've done, but Dan is still lying in that hospital in a coma. Oh Ben, what if he doesn't wake up? I don't need to hear what a good job I did. I need someone to *listen* to me, to hear what's inside me, and I don't have anyone like that. Anyone other than you." She begins crying in earnest now, and I feel my own emotions beginning to rise.

"Ben, what if I did something wrong?" she says. Her eyes are wide and wet. I can tell this has been killing her. It's been bottled up inside her since the incident because I am the only one she can talk to about it. "He was in so much agony, and there was so much blood! There was so little I could do. Oh Ben, I'm afraid he's going to die, and it'll be my fault."

She is really sobbing now. I have never seen her like this, and it is a little unnerving. I tighten my hold on her and make little soothing sounds. Sharon would understand this. She's a big girl, and not without a heart, either.

I lead Andrea to the couch and we sit down. Her tears wet the front of my shirt, and I begin crying, too. It suddenly occurs to me that I haven't done enough of that.

I don't know how long we remain seated there sobbing, but it is enormously cathartic. We cling to one another, and draw strength from each other. It turns out I have tons of feelings and emotions about the shooting that haven't come out yet. I find my self drawing strength from her as much as I am giving strength to her.

After some time we quiet. She turns to me and buries her face in my neck. I close my eyes, partly because I know I have to break up with her, and partly because the gamut of emotions and feelings I'm experiencing are now making me insanely aroused. The war that is fought within me is short and not too keenly contested. The arousal wins, hands down. Thoughts of Sharon flee from my mind like animals from a burning forest, and suddenly, it is just Andrea and me.

Andrea begins sucking my neck and moves atop me. She adjusts herself so that my erection is between her legs, and that's all it takes. Sharon is by now entirely gone from my thoughts.

My hands find their way under Andrea's shirt before I am aware of what they are doing, and our mutual sorrow and pain turns into a lust so hungry and intense it is a physical presence, demanding to be sated.

As in any other hunger, we both feel the need to use our mouths, and our kisses are more consumptive than erotic. I can't get enough of her, and she's the same way. I want to envelop her with my mouth. I can't imagine a sexual release that can satisfy what I need, and I don't really know how to go about trying.

Somehow, our clothes come off. This consumptive physical need has by now progressed to the entire body, and we do things I've never even considered, let alone would have thought of as sexually satisfying. But this level of lovemaking is entirely out my realm of experience. When we finish, I am exhausted.

We begin to talk about the original Route call. She tells me she heard the first shot and saw Dan take a step backward. She thought he was just trying to get away from the shooter, but then she saw his hand go to his abdomen. Before she could react, there was a second shot and he went down, spurting blood from his neck.

She never got the chance to think, she just started dragging him out of there. She says she was almost paralyzed with fear when she heard additional shots coming from the room, and didn't know if she should continue dragging him out, or if she should return fire. She felt inadequate; too inexperienced to make the right decision, too weak and small to drag Dan out of the line of fire. She chose to return fire, and only after her second shot did she remember there was a baby in the room and angle her shots high.

She was terrified at the massive amount of arterial spurting from Dan's neck, and sickened by the heat of the blood splashing across her. She stopped to cover the wound with her hand, and that's when she took a round in the chest.

I run my hands across the horrible purple and greenish mass centered between her lovely breasts, mindful not to mar the mood with any sexuality in my touch.

She confesses that the impact of the shot caused her to release her bladder, but everyone was considerate enough not to mention it. I tell her nobody has said anything, and I'm sure no one even knows about it. She sighs heavily and says, "Thank God." This comes as a huge relief to her.

She doesn't remember much after being shot. She has no recollection of dragging Dan out of the house and into the driveway. The only thing she remembers about being outside is Dan's eyes flying open and bulging inhumanly from his head as every muscle in his body tensed. He yelled, "Sue!" and then just lay there, his neck arched with veins bulging and his mouth open and silent. Crying, she confesses she was sure he was dying at that point

When she is done with her story, I soothe her and reassure her that she gave Dan his only hope, that she did everything just right. It's as though she needed to hear this from me, and she makes me promise I'm not lying to her. I do, and then I begin talking about the shot I'd had to take. I struggle, and find myself fighting unexpected tears as I recount the fear and trepidation I felt at the thought of killing a man. I reaffirm that I too have a great deal of unshed tears inside me that Sharon has yet to coax out of me. I don't think she can. I think only another cop can truly understand what I had to do. Only a cop who has been through it.

Only Andrea.

When I get to the part about the fight at the back door, my anguish turns to anger. Anger at Bob Slater.

She listens, which is exactly what I need. I can tell that she shares my anger, and believes that Slater was at fault for what happened to Pammi by not taking the shot.

Then, I go out on a limb and tell her my suspicions about the collusion between Slater and Pammi Route. She understands this, and warns me to be careful around him.

Talking it out has a cleansing effect on me. When I am done, I am tired, but I feel weightless. We both fall asleep. When I wake, it is almost seven in the evening. Andrea is sprawled naked across the bed. She looks absolutely lovely, and I burn the sight of her, and the knowledge of what we have just shared, into my brain to draw upon whenever I need it.

I slowly untwine myself from her and begin to dress. I want to stay with her, to fall asleep with her, and wake up with her in the morning. But even though I know I can't stay, I nevertheless feel *intact*, really intact, for the first time since the shooting.

Without waking her, I kiss her tenderly, then leave and drive home to my wife.

10

THE SHOOTING RECONSTRUCTION is a major event. It comprises the majority of the internal affairs investigation, and the department will draw heavily from it in deciding whether I violated any Stratton policies, procedures, or general orders.

I've never been involved in a reconstruction of this magnitude before, and I am amazed at the lengths to which the department is willing to go to replicate as closely as possible the conditions at the time of the shooting.

It has to be directed—choreographed really—much the same as a theater production. The department supplies as many "actors" as people who were involved in the actual incident, plus the exact same equipment that was used that night. Fortunately, the weather conditions are just like they were the night of the shooting, as are the lighting conditions.

Timing is also critical, because the fatigue factor has to be replicated as well. If the reconstruction is to be of any value, it must be done correctly. The shooting occurred at 4:27 a.m., after the team had been in place all night long. We will be conducting the reconstruction at approximately the same time. The neighbors have all been notified what was going on.

In addition to me, the "actors" include Vince Capelko from SERT command, Stan Hauser, Bob Slater, an inner perimeter guy named Roland Hogue, and me, since we were the three individuals closest to the action that night and the only ones within sight of the rear slider.

Also included are Liz Dittman, a records clerk who is approximately the same size as Pammi Route, and Detective Louis Beau, a persons crimes investigator who is a fairly close physical match to the late Hugo Route. The fire department's infant CPR training doll has been cast for the role of Chastity Route. The team's former sniper, Hank Venegall, and Portland SERT's primary sniper, Chuck Castor, are present to serve as technical advisors and to render their expert opinions on questionable matters that might arise. Venegall has kept current as a backup sniper, training with the team regularly since stepping down a couple of years ago, although he hasn't responded to any callouts since then.

Several other support people will also be present in a wide variety of functions, from setting up the scene exactly as it was the night of the shooting, to recording the reenactment and subsequent tests on video.

I show up at the appointed time, ready to get all this behind me. Most everyone is already present when I arrive.

The Stratton Vehicular Crimes team has already created a to-scale diagram of the incident, using the laser-guided transit equipment they use to document fatal car crash scenes. This was done after I had left the scene the night of the shooting. Using this diagram, we are able to place everyone and everything in the exact same spot they were on the night of the shooting. Mahoney has checked my rifle out of the evidence room to be set up exactly as it had been. Even my ground tarp has been cleaned of vomit and brought to the scene.

Setup and recording the logistics of the scene eats up the first several hours. Detectives measure the exact distance from the rifle barrel to the broken pane of window glass the bullet struck on its way into Pammi Route's arm. They make their best guess as to the distance between that pane of glass and Pammi herself. Angles, such as the trajectory of the bullet from barrel to glass, then from glass to target, are measured and recorded.

The scene is photographed from numerous angles, and detailed drawings are painstakingly made. It takes a team of four crime scene specialists from the Major Crimes Team two hours just to finish the scene documentation. Part of their work requires the actors to be in place so the team can get the proper perspective and scale in both photos and drawings. Since the reconstruction is expected to last well into the morning, arrangements had been made for a catered breakfast to be brought to the scene at six a.m.

Finally, we are all told to get into our respective positions exactly as we had been that night. The only thing that seems to be missing is a director yelling, "Action!"

Phil Mahoney fills that role in his capacity as lead investigator. The reenactment will begin with the shooting of the throw-phone, meaning it will be a very short play. Only two minutes had elapsed between that shot and mine.

It takes several iterations to accurately replicate the struggle at the window, but finally the tactical team members agree that it is a good representation of the way things had actually unfolded. Neither Dittman, Beau, nor the doll are likely to receive an Oscar nomination, but I think they all do a hell of a good job.

We go through several versions of the scenario in speeds varying from slow motion to full speed. When all is said and done, the results are both interesting and ambiguous. For example, the investigators determine that from his point of view, Slater would have had a perfect view of the gun and a much better shot than me. With the action happening the way I say it did, which is the way it actually occurred, neither Pammi nor the baby would have been in Slater's line of fire at any time. And Slater would have had to have his eyes closed to miss the gun in Hugo's hand.

Both our sniper consultants get behind Slater's rifle, and both see the revolver in the suspect's hand. Then Slater himself takes up the position he had that night, and he sees the gun and takes the shot. When he does, I realize McNamara had been right. He is going to say there was no gun. Butterflies of fear begin flapping around in my gut when Slater takes the shot in the reconstruction that he hadn't taken during the actual callout.

Everyone, Slater included, agrees that it is a shoot situation, and no shot of opportunity order is necessary. Slater even says that not to take the shot would have been, in his words, "opening the sniper up to both criminal and civil liability."

At this point, I am nearly shaking with rage. He is setting the stage to nail me, bad. The problem with all this, he says, is that Route did not have the gun when he and Pammi fought at the slider.

Despite being prepared for it, I can't believe what I am hearing. Slater is throwing me under the bus alright. What motivation can he possibly have, other than a deal for a cut of Pammi's lawsuit? Slater might hate my guts, but that certainly isn't reason enough for a supposedly sane man to risk his career, and possibly even a prison sentence.

He won't elaborate, other than to say that he specifically watched Route's hands, looking for a gun, and that he was prepared to shoot him if he so much as picked one up. I know now that he will cooperate with the department when he is questioned. He'll give a detailed statement saying that Route had no gun, which is why he never took the shot.

I am so pissed off I want to shoot Slater right here and now, and Capelko has to take me off to the side to calm me down so we can continue the reconstruction scenarios, this time with an unarmed suspect.

We do several replays without the gun, and in every case, we find that if Route did not have a gun, it *may* have been a shoot situation, but because of the way they were fighting, it wasn't a clear-cut shoot situation. Taking the shot from my angle at when I did would have been justified, but would have demonstrated poor judgment due to the fact that it wasn't a clear shot and there was no weapon involved. Nonetheless, shooting Route would not have amounted to a criminal action.

The tests show that, from where I was situated that night, the lack of a gun in Hugo's hand would have been plainly obvious. They also show that Hugo's hand could not have been construed to be holding a gun if, in fact, it was empty.

Further, both Venegall and Castor come to the same end result I had with respect to taking an "iffy" shot on Hugo, given Pammi's and the baby's proximity and the degree to which they were struggling. Under the circumstances in the gun scenario, both agree that they would have shot Hugo Route exactly when I did, clear shot or no, and hope for the best. Other than that, the sniper would have to watch that baby die, and that simply wasn't going to happen.

If there had been a gun.

The reconstruction lasts until 9:30 a.m. When it's over, we are all exhausted. Despite Slater's lying and treachery, I am pleased with the results, because I know the truth. I it buoys me to know that two unbiased, seasoned SWAT snipers whom I respect had arrived at the same conclusion I had, and had both stated that they would have done the exact same thing at the exact same time as I had. The burden that affirmation lifts from me is equal to that of the grand jury's clearing me of criminal charges, and I know I will sleep easier now.

But the confirmation that Slater is lying about the gun, and the specter of a coordinated lawsuit by him and Pammi Route… That haunts me like an evil spirit.

The more I think about it, the angrier I became.

11

THE DAY AFTER the reconstruction, Chief Moody calls me into his office. He tells me I am being restored to duty, but not yet released to the street. The rest of the internal affairs investigation is expected to take three days to a week, during which time I have the option of being reinstated to a light-duty position in the office or remain off work on vacation. I choose to stay on leave.

I opt to take a week's vacation instead. It will be good to get away and spend some time with Leah, whom I had been neglecting with everything going on.

I reserve a condo for the week in Sunriver, Oregon, using our timeshare. I'd like to go to the coast, or maybe even Vegas, but Sharon wants to see her aunt in Bend, and Sunriver is only about fifteen miles from there.

The night before we leave, Sharon heads off to the store to buy groceries for the trip. I take advantage of the opportunity and decide to call Andrea. My plan is to tell her that I'm so torn between my increasing feelings for her and my commitment and love for my family that I'm going crazy, and that I think it's time we call off the affair. Regardless of what happened last time, I know this is the right thing to do.

Of course, once I get her on the phone, it's a different story. Not only can I not tell her what I want, I find myself briefly wishing Sharon would just find out about us and leave me so I can be with Andrea. Just the sound of her voice is enough to do this to me.

She tells me that she would probably be in the nuthouse if it wasn't for me getting her through the Route incident, and in return, I tell her how Sharon is unable to fully understand what I've gone through after I killed Route. I say something about how inadequate it is for me to talk to Sharon about it compared to talking to Andrea. I tell her that holding her in my arms and talked it out the other day was the real beginning of my healing, and that it's just not the same when I try to do that with Sharon. I wind up telling her that the Sunriver trip is Sharon's idea, and make it sound as though I don't want to go.

Some of what I tell her is the truth, but most of it is exaggerated. Why men feel the need to tell women what they want to hear at times like this is beyond me. The actual truth is, I feel so guilty about what happened the last time I tried to break it off with Andrea that I'm really looking forward to this trip to re-bond with Sharon. But I can't tell Andrea this right now, with her feeling so fragile after what happened during the Route callout.

An hour into the drive to Sunriver, Leah asks, "Daddy, do you feel bad about killing that man?"

"Well, that sure is a stupid question, Princess. You need to understand something, Leah. That twisted fuck signed his own death warrant the moment he shot two cops. You want to know how Daddy feels about it? Well, it was an honor to remove that slimy cocksucker from the gene pool. You'll understand when you're a little older, baby."

Of course, I don't really say that, but it *does* flash through my mind.

"Of course I feel bad, honey. That's the worst thing a policeman could ever have to do in his whole life."

"Then why did you do it?"

"Well, sweetie, there was something wrong inside his brain. Something that made his thoughts go all crazy and made him think that he had to hurt the people around him. Then he shot two police officers who were there to help him, and when he was done doing that, he was going to shoot the other people who were with him. The other people with him were a woman and a little baby. We just couldn't let him hurt those nice people."

"But did you have to *shoot* him? Lana told me her mommy said the police should never have to shoot anybody."

"Lana's mommy isn't a police officer, is she, sweet thing?"

"No, silly." She laughs. "Lana's mommy is the janitor at school!"

"Okay then. I'll tell you what. I won't tell Lana's mommy how to mop the floor, and she won't tell me how to be a policeman, okay?"

"Okay. But *did* you have to shoot that man?"

"Well, I'm sorry to say, I did have to. You see, we tried talking to him and giving him other choices, like coming out and getting some help, and stuff like that. But this sickness that he had in his brain, the one that made his thoughts go all crazy, wouldn't let him listen. He wouldn't let that lady and the baby leave the house when they wanted to. And he was going to shoot them. So, just when he was about to shoot them, I had to shoot *him* instead. It's a very sad thing."

She digests that for a moment. "Was the little baby his child?" she asks.

"Yes, Punkin. The woman was his wife, and the baby was his daughter."

In the rearview mirror, I see her face screw up in thought. After a moment, she says, "He must have had something really wrong in his brain. Daddy, what would happen if something went wrong in your brain? Would you kill Mommy and me?"

"That could never, *ever* happen, honey. What that man had wrong in his brain only happens to about one person out of millions and billions and *cajillions* and *bajillions* of people, and will probably never ever happen again. It could never happen to us or anyone else around here. You don't have anything to worry about."

She brightens. "Good. Daddy?"

"Yes, baby?"

"If he was gonna kill his wife and their little baby, and you had to kill him first to stop him, then you saved his wife and the baby, didn't you?"

"That's right, dear. As bad as it was to have to kill that man, I had to do it so they would live."

"Well, I think you're a hero, then."

I smile. "Yeah, I guess I am."

"I can't wait to tell Lana. Her mommy may be a janitor, but my daddy's a *hero*."

Sharon has been moody since before we left, and barely speaks two sentences in the car. As much as I want to heal my marriage, I think the affair with Andrea has been too costly. I don't know what Sharon knows or suspects, but our relationship is strained from the moment we arrive at the condo. We never seem to get beyond the Andrea wall I've put up between us. Leah, probably sensing our tension, is edgy and whiny.

She loves miniature golf, but Sharon and I fight our way through the course, ruining the first six holes for her, and we end up leaving before the game is over. Leah and I sit in the hot tub while Sharon goes on a bike ride by herself. When she comes back, I take Leah on a bike ride, pulling her on a rented pony bike behind my own, while Sharon takes her turn in the hot tub.

Leah watches cartoons all evening while Sharon and I either argue or stay away from each other. I don't like the way this is going and suspect that we are on final approach to a major blowout. The timing couldn't be worse, with the Route shooting still so fresh, the vacation, and my pending return to work. I just don't need the added stress.

The morning of our second day, we ride into the village for breakfast, but it turns into a disaster. Sharon starts crying for no apparent reason in the middle of it. Leah becomes upset and begins crying as well. Finally, amid the stares of those around us, we have leave our breakfast untouched and ride back to the condo in silence.

As soon as the door is closed, I make the mistake of asking Sharon what the hell the problem is, and that's when she goes all Mount St. Helens on me. Leah runs and hides in her room as Sharon lets me have it with both barrels.

"What's the problem? Oh, there's not much of a problem, Ben. Only that you're having an affair! We've been married for *twenty years,* and suddenly, none of that is good enough for you. Look at me, Ben! I'm forty years old. I've got lines in my face. I'm twenty pounds overweight. My boobs are sagging. You want to know why that is? *Because I'm forty fucking years old, that's why!* But you know what? Your little honey Andrea will be forty someday, too! What are you gonna do then, leave her in the dust and start fucking someone Leah's age?"

"Sharon, listen—"

"Listen? *Listen?* What am I going to listen to? Your denial that you're fucking her? Please, don't even go there! I'm not stupid, you know. And you're not so smart, either. I came back in the house before I went to the store the other night, and I sat outside the bedroom door and listened to your little lovey-dovey conversation with her. 'Oh, baby, nobody can understand me like you! Sharon just doesn't get it. I started healing in *your* arms, Andrea. I don't want to go to Sunriver with *my wife and my own goddamn daughter*, I'd rather spend the time with you, my little fucktoy Andrea!' Goddamn it, Ben, how could you do this to us? How *could* you?" She dissolves into heartfelt sobbing.

"Sharon, I… I…"

Looking up at me with the most hurt, angry expression I have ever seen, she says, "You what? You have an explanation? You're sorry? You promise me it will never happen again? You *what*, Ben?"

I sit down on the bed, overwhelmed with my failures. I feel like the scum of the earth and bury my face in my hands. "I'm sorry," I say. I mean it from the bottom of my heart, but the words are utterly inadequate.

"Go to hell, Ben," she spits, and storms out of the room. I hear her collect Leah, and then the door closes. The condo becomes silent.

Half an hour later, I look outside. Her bike and Leah's pony bike are gone. It's nine a.m., and we've been here less than twenty-four hours.

At ten, Sharon's aunt calls. Leah and Sharon are at her house and intend to stay there for the rest of the vacation. She has a message from Sharon. I can either stay in Sunriver, go home, or go be with Andrea, it doesn't matter anymore.

I do nothing all day long, and then at eight that evening, miserable, I go to bed.

The following day I call Sharon's aunt, but Sharon won't talk to me. The aunt tells me not to call back. I want to talk to Leah, but the aunt says she's out with Sharon. I didn't believe her, but I'm not up to the fight.

It's a beautiful day, and there is so much to do in the area. I sit alone inside with the drapes shut all day long.

That night, the phone rings. It's Leah.

"Daddy, are you and Mommy going to stay married?" she asks, getting right to the point as she so often does.

"I really hope so, honey."

"What happened?"

"It's very complicated, honey. I don't know if you'd understand."

"Is your brain getting sick?"

It takes me a moment to understand what she's referring to. "Oh, no, Leah. It's just that Daddy's made mommy very mad and very hurt, honey. And I'm so sorry about it. Mommy and I just have to have some time to cool off, and then we can talk about it, that's all."

"And then everything will be better again?"

"I hope so, Princess."

"Did I do something wrong, Daddy?"

"Oh, no, baby. None of this is your fault at all. *I* did something wrong. And, I have to show Mommy that I'm sorry."

"What did you do wrong?"

"Don't you worry about it, Punkin. No matter what happens, though, you're always going to be our little girl, and we're always going to be your mommy and daddy. We're always going to be a family, sweetheart."

"Do you promise?"

"I promise," I say, hoping now that it's the truth. We hang up, and for the first time, I really weigh my options. Now that this is all out in the open, I *can* go to Vancouver to be with Andrea. I can leave my family and be with her forever. I know that's what Andrea wants.

But in light of everything, and with the ability to actually do it before me, I suddenly get things in proper perspective.

My relationship with Andrea is not deep, and it never really had the potential to be anything but superficial. In fact, it's never gone past surface-level connections. She was hot, and I was horny. I'm some kind of father figure/male role model to her; the attractive, slightly out-of-reach older guy. In reality, we don't really have much in common past that, other than the fact that we're both cops and we've each been put through the wringer at work recently.

They say boys and girls can't be good friends without there being some sexual element to it. They, in this case at least, are right.

And now I've done that which I've always scoffed at others for doing. I've jeopardized the biggest thing in my life—my family—for the sake of a little pussy. How utterly shallow of me.

The conversation with Leah has served to bring it all into perspective. I feel ashamed of myself. As of this moment, the relationship with Andrea is no more, and I will see to it that she understands that, too. Even if Sharon were to leave me, which is a real possibility, I can no more have a relationship with Andrea now than I could with my own sister. I could simply never enjoy it knowing the price I've paid for it.

I can't believe what a prick I'd been, to *both* of them.

I call Sharon at her aunt's and leave a message that I am going to make everything all right, and that I love her and Leah too much to risk anything further. I tell her that I can't stand being away from them and asked her to call me at the Sunriver condo when she wants to talk. I tell her I'll be waiting for her to call, and I hope we can go back to Stratton together.

When I hang up, it's time to call Andrea. I won't even let her down easy. I will come right out and tell her that regardless of whether Sharon takes me back, our relationship is over. There's just no other way. I dial her cell, and she answers on the first ring.

"Andrea? It's Ben."

"Ben," she sobs, crying into the phone.

"Andrea, what is it? What's wrong?"

"Oh God, Ben, it's Dan. I'm at the hospital. I'm with Sue. A bunch of us were in his room when he just—he just... Went away. Not fifteen minutes ago. He's dead! Oh Ben he's dead!"

12

SHARON AND I return to Stratton together that night. We talk all night long, and I promise her it's entirely over between Andrea and me. I call Andrea the next day with Sharon by my side and make sure she understands that it's over between us. She doesn't say much, and I know it will be rough the next time we see each other, but I'm not worried about that now. Sharon and I spend the remainder of the time tentatively trying to see if our shattered marriage can be salvaged.

On the morning of Dan Hollister's funeral, we go together as a married couple. Dan had been raised in Newport, along the central Oregon coast. His folks still live there, and Dan and Sue own a beach house there, so that's where he's to be buried.

The procession of police cars, all with lights flashing mournfully, stretches for nearly a mile along the winding, hilly road. I drive the fifth car back from the front. Another officer is in the front seat and my wife and Leah are in the backseat. Andrea, with three other officers in her car, is in the car behind me. Eighty-three other police cars from thirty jurisdictions in four states are represented in the procession, all snaking their way slowly down the coast.

An Oregon State Police helicopter leads the way, flying slowly above the hearse at a height of five hundred feet. Almost two hundred officers have turned out for the funeral of Dan Hollister, the first Stratton police officer to be killed in the line of duty.

"He had the guy eating out of his hands," the officer next to me says, reminiscing. "Even though he invoked his Miranda rights, Dan got him to confess by simply talking to him, so his statements couldn't really be called into question in court. 'I gotta charge you with assault,' he told him. 'And even though I don't want to, I gotta charge you with vandalism, 'cause the cue stick you broke over that guy's head belonged to the bar.' The dude looked at him with an open mouth and said, 'I didn't bust no bar's cue stick on that dude's head, that was my *own* cue, so you can't charge me with vandalism.' Bingo, Dan had a confession, and off the guy went to the slammer!"

Sharon doesn't find anything amusing about the story. I laugh, but my laughter peters out, replaced by silence with the thought that Dan would never entertain anyone with his unique sense of humor again. Slowly, we enter the cemetery, and I pull to the side of the road near the open grave.

We get out and pause to watch a lone piper pacing the lawn adjacent to the large open tent that has been erected graveside. The mournful tones emanating from the richly uniformed officer's pipes sound unearthly in the otherwise quiet atmosphere. I cannot tell you how much I hate funerals.

The tent and the surrounding areas are quickly packed to capacity, and my family and I stand a few rows back from the small podium. The front row consists mostly of people I have never seen before, all wearing black. The only two I know are Dan's parents. As for the others, I assume they are his brothers and sisters and their families. A skinny, long-haired boy, wearing black denim pants, a Metallica T-shirt, and a black sport jacket several sizes too big for him, sits in the front row fidgeting. The kid has a small, battery-operated video game, which plays an annoying, repetitive tune. I want to wring the little bastard's neck.

Just beyond the podium is the flag-draped casket. Flanking it on either end are two members of the Stratton Honor Guard, standing casket watch with heads bowed respectfully. They are replaced in a ceremonial changing of the guard every ten minutes. Two large photographs of Dan have been propped up behind the casket, One is a portrait of him in his dress uniform, and the other depicts a smiling Dan standing outside a patrol car, and had obviously been taken from a distance without his knowledge.

Russell Moody, our chief of police, steps to the podium and says in his deep baritone voice, "This is a day I have feared since the moment, twenty-seven years ago, when I first put on a Stratton Police uniform. We're not a large department, which means that we're more like a family than a group of people who work together. Every person on the force knows every other person, and good friendships abound. Dan Hollister—"

Chief Moody's voice cracks, and an uncomfortable moment passes before he can continue. "Dan Hollister was a personal friend of mine. I was his sergeant fourteen years ago when he was a scared rookie. I was his lieutenant, when, as a detective, Dan almost single-handedly cracked a double homicide/robbery case that had plagued this department for eight long months. That arrest, by the way, cleared a string of three similar robbery/homicides back in north Georgia, where the suspect had lived prior to moving to Oregon. Three years ago, as his chief, I proudly pinned the Departmental Medal of Valor to Dan's chest for bravery above and beyond the call of duty when he was forced to take a life in order to save one of his fellow officers during the notorious Rodriguez shooting incident."

I shiver as a cold, white fog rolls across the hillside from the ocean a half-mile away. The effect seems appropriate. "Dan Hollister was a cop's cop," Moody continues. "His influence on this department will be a lasting tribute to his years of service here, and his humor, his amiable way, and likable personality will be long remembered.

"But beyond all that, Dan was a friend of mine. He was a guest in my home not three weeks ago, and we... And we... Moody sniffs and turns from the crowd, wiping his eyes with a handkerchief. There is an uncomfortable moment of silence in which the hot sting of tears burns my eyes, then he turns back to the crowd, his dark face now blotchy and wet.

"I will miss him sorely," Moody says, obviously cutting his eulogy short. "I would like everyone to take a moment of silence in remembrance of Officer Daniel J. Hollister."

The bagpipes, which had maintained their steady funereal keening through Moody's speech, suddenly stop. The silence, combined with the somber mood, becomes oppressive.

Thirty seconds into it, a member of the honor guard raises a bugle to his lips, and the mournful strains of taps drift across the grassy expanse, driving home the fact of Dan's death in a way that emphasizes the permanence of his passing. Everyone breaks down and weeps openly at the haunting sound.

At some point, the bugle quiets, and there is no sound other than soft weeping. Then a police radio, turned up high, pierces the silence. The dispatcher's voice is clearly strained, and I can tell she is trying to hold it together for the broadcast.

"Unit one twelve." One twelve was Dan's unit designator. Of course there is no reply. The weeping grows louder.

"Unit one twelve, come in." A brief delay. "Unit one twelve, Officer Hollister?"

Why must they always do this? None of us can handle it, but I've rarely been to a police funeral in which it hasn't been done in some form or another.

Sharon is clearly conflicted. I can see her emotions bouncing around from wanting to comfort me and wanting to give me the cold shoulder, which she's been doing ever since Sunriver. And around it all is her grief and sorrow for Dan and Sue.

The dispatcher's voice continues, "Swing shift roll call for missing officer... Unit one ten?"

Eddie Kowalski, quivering, raises the radio to his lips. "Code four," he chokes.

"One eleven?"

"Code four," answers Peter Pepperidge steadily.

"One thirteen?"

Andrea raises her radio but can't speak the words. Finally, she just clicks the transmit key, causing the radio to squelch, then returns it to the holder on her belt.

"One fourteen?" Mike Moffler, a very tall, muscular officer, raises his radio to his mouth but breaks at the last second, broadcasting a loud sob. Cyndi Blair, standing next to him, puts her arms around his shoulders and grabs his radio when it looked as if he might drop it. "He's code four," she says, her own voice showing emotion.

"Unit one fifteen?" And so the roll call goes. After polling the entire swing shift, the dispatcher comes back to Dan's number.

"One twelve, Officer Hollister?" When there is no reply, she says, "Unit one twelve, Officer Daniel J. Hollister. Ten seventy-nine, end of watch. Officer Hollister, you may be gone, sir, but you are certainly not forgotten."

A hundred men and women sob as one. It's as if I am in a bad dream. I just can't believe that Dan has been shot and killed. And I still haven't had a chance to get a real grip on my own feelings about his death because of the tragedy of my own shooting. Right now I am glad I shot Route. I'm fucking *proud* of it.

Just then two helicopters, one from the Oregon State Police, the other from the Seattle Police Department, race side by side over the gravesite at low altitude, heading west. At a point directly overhead, the Seattle PD chopper breaks right and screams away to the north, disappearing beyond a hill in a classic missing-man formation.

Shortly after the fly-by, the Honor Guard members ceremoniously fold the flag that had been draped over the coffin and formally present it to Dan's parents. The casket is then lowered into the ground, and seven smartly uniformed honor guard members from various departments take up rifles.

The detail commander steps rigidly up to the group. He stands statue-still before them, eyes wet but unblinking, and draws a gleaming sword. He raises it in salute and barks a command. "Ready!"

Seven bolts are opened, drawn back, and slammed home in unison. "Aim!"

Seven rifles are shouldered and aimed at a high angle in a perfect row.

"Fire!" As one, the rifles discharge loudly. We all jump at the shots.

The commands are given a second time. Seven more shots, and everyone jumps again. Between the second and third volley, there is a commotion at the front of the tent as Dan's frail little mother collapses. Her husband and two other women guide her into a chair. The long-haired kid looks on sullenly, but doesn't make a move to help her.

"Fire!"

My breathing comes in hitches, and I can no longer hold the tears back. I would have been embarrassed, but everyone else is reacting the same way.

I look up, and the squad of riflemen is no longer standing at attention in a perfect row. Four of them still are, but one is bent over shielding his eyes, another has turned to blow his nose, while the last man holds both their rifles.

"Squad... dismissed!"

After a moment, we all get up to leave.

13

ANDREA AND I haven't said a word to each other since my phone call to her with Sharon, and I purposely avoid her now. But not so with Bob Slater. The funeral is also the first time I've seen him since the reconstruction, and I am gunning for a confrontation.

I waylay him at his car, which is parked near the mausoleum buildings. "We need to talk," I say without preamble.

"No we don't. You're under orders not to talk to me, Helen. So, go away." He starts getting in, but I slam the door, narrowly missing his hand.

"I said, we need to talk. You're not going to worm your way out of this one, Slater. I want to know why. Why didn't you shoot him, and why are you lying about the gun?"

Slater looks around and says, "Not here. Over there." He indicates the mausoleums thirty yards distant. There are several of them, little buildings standing in neat rows.

He walks behind the farthest one and waits there for me. I am right on his heels. I know why he chose this spot.

"What were you doing, Bob? Sleeping?" I ask. "Jerking off? Or were you just too afraid to take the shot?"

Slater's face clouds over—a hint of an approaching storm. "Look, I feel sorry for you, Helen," he says. "You're not a very good shot, and you hit the bitch. Too bad. Live with it. But you'd better be real careful about who you accuse of being a coward. You gettin' my point, *partner?*"

I am enraged. "Coward? *Coward?* Funny you chose that particular word, Bob. Because it's the same word that I've heard mentioned by some of the guys on the team about *your* failure to shoot Route. 'Coward' and 'chickenshit pussy' were the exact words, as I recall."

Slater's face contorts into an ugly grimace. This is getting nastier by the second. That's fine by me; I'm pissed off enough that I'll welcome the fight.

"Watch your fuckin' mouth, cheesedick," Slater snarls. "What happened the other night comes down to bad fuckin' luck, that's all.

Nothing more, nothing less. You've always been a thirteen sixty-nine, Helen, but that's your problem, not mine, so leave me the hell out of it."

Thirteen-sixty-nine is a play on words, or numbers in this case. It is supposed to sound like a police code, but all it really means is "unlucky cocksucker."

"Now, do yourself a favor," he continues. "Walk away from this. Take your fuckin' lumps, and let it go." He backs off on his threatening tone just a bit and almost smiles at me.

"Hell, milk it into a stress retirement and live the good life for all I care, but keep me the fuck out of it. You're a lousy sniper, Ben. *You* fucked up, not me. Don't come looking to me to unfuck you, 'cause it ain't about to happen. Now run along and cry to your pretty little wife over there. Better yet, go find Fellatio and let her show you why we call her that. Lots of guys say she's a squirrel in the rack—"

My fist catches him square in the chin and sends him reeling into the bushes. Slater recovers immediately and flies at me like a man possessed. The fight goes immediately to the ground.

Being larger than me, Slater has the natural advantage, but I have a hell of a lot of rage in me. Plus, I don't like to fight and am into it for only one reason. To win.

He lands a good one on my face, and from the shock and the sting, I know I'll have a hell of a shiner for the next couple of weeks. I clench up on him, locking his body in next to mine, and bring my knee up into his midsection. I hear the wind go out of him and press my advantage.

I knee him again, this time in the balls. He doubles over, and I feel his hold relax. Pushing him aside, I give him an elbow in the face so we'll at least carry matching shiners, and I disengage.

I stand up, which he is unable to do at the moment. Wiping blood off my nice clothes, I say, "See you at work, Bob," and walk back to my car.

Three days after the funeral, I am released to patrol duty. The internal investigation is closed, and I am fully cleared.

Slater's contention that there had been no gun in Hugo Route's hand remains an enigma to the department. The official party line regarding the discrepancy is that there exists a point-of-view perception difference, despite the obvious contradiction to the conclusions drawn at the reconstruction.

If there had been a gun, Slater would have seen it, and if there had not been, there's no way I could have misconstrued Route to be in possession of one.

Despite the discrepancies in our respective points of view, the circumstances surrounding the shooting are justification enough for it, regardless of the rules of engagement. Even if there had been no gun, he had still repeatedly threatened to kill the baby at dawn. It was dawn, and he was literally pulling her from her mother's grip. He didn't say *how* he would kill her, just that he would kill her at dawn. The fact that he was tearing her from her mother's arms demonstrated sufficient intent for any officer present to shoot him, gun or no.

I understand that this outcome should make me happy, but Slater has managed to color the Rout shooting with a lingering shroud of doubt, and smear my reputation at the same time. To me, this is unacceptable.

The police department is unequally divided—about eighty percent on my side, and twenty percent on Slater's side. Those on Slater's side tend to keep their opinion to themselves, but those on my side are vociferous in their support of me, which I deeply appreciate. The discrepancy in our stories is hot gossip around the office. Not a day passes in the week after the reenactment in which I don't hear people talking about Slater's lie. Occasionally, though, it's me they're talking about. I hate the specter of doubt as to my integrity. Those who fall in with Slater believe that I am lying about the gun to cover my eagerness to take a sniper shot.

Most of the department just believes Slater is flat-out lying, most likely to cover some unforeseen cowardice he'd encountered when it came time to actually shoot Route. In my opinion, this is the only explanation. World-class shooter, ex recon marine, SERT sniper, none of it matters. When the shit finally hit the fan, Bob Slater was a coward, pure and simple.

Gossip intensifies when I return to graveyard patrol with a black eye, making jokes about Sharon keeping me in line and remaining silent about the fight with Slater. Slater took a week off after the fight, but enough people saw him in the days following the funeral that his broken nose and black eyes became common knowledge. The standard joke is that Sharon kicked *both* our asses.

Chief Moody calls me into his office the day I go back to work and gives me a personal order to stay away from Slater until further notice. I am only too happy to comply, and I hope Slater will reciprocate. I do not relish the idea of another fight. I'm just getting too damn old to act like a kid on the school playground. Besides, fighting hurts.

Slater owns a modest home in east Portland about a mile outside the Stratton city limits. I take to driving past his house two or three times per night. There's never anything to see, but the man occupies so much of my energy and thoughts these days that I feel compelled to do so. I also drive past Pammi Route's house a lot. I suppose my line of thought is that I might see Slater's car parked at her house, or vice versa, although I hope I never will. The possible collusion between them weighs heavily on my mind.

Whenever I see a vehicle parked in front of either house, I run the plate and make a record of the registered owner's name and address. This I do in a separate, personal notebook. Over the course of a couple weeks, this happens only three times at Slater's house, and not at all at Pammi Route's.

Slater's first two guests are women, and both stay until the wee hours. Slater often boasts that he is quite the swordsman, and from my surveillance of his house, it appears he's not exaggerating.

In the third case the vehicle is a pickup truck registered to a man named Timothy J. Connors. I write the information in my notebook, fearing that Connors is an ambulance chaser. Attorneys like that make my stomach churn.

Rather than engage in my nightly hunt for drunken drivers, I go back to the office and run Connors. He's not in our law enforcement data banks. I Google him, and the only entry I find is a white pages listing, which shows the same address on his truck registration. I come up with nothing that indicates he is an attorney.

Connors' truck was parked at Slater's house at about 1:00 a.m. I go back a half-hour later, after looking him up at the office, and it is now gone. I figure he's just a friend of Slater's, but I would have liked to take a covert peek in the cab. I don't know what I hoped I would or wouldn't see; a briefcase, maybe, or legal papers.

Before dropping the whole thing, I take a drive past Connors' address, but the truck isn't there, either. Finally, I figure my paranoia is beginning to spiral out of control, and I back off the surveillance. Eventually, I drop the whole thing.

Slater returns to day shift patrol, and we occasionally see each other in the locker room when I am getting off duty and he is suiting up. We keep our distance, but as our bruises fade, so to some degree does our animosity.

One day, we both happen to be in the report room when another officer brings a drunk driver into the interview room, which is behind a large two-way mirror. The suspect sits down on the bench and proceeds to vomit all over the floor. As everyone is laughing at her, Slater tells the story of a drunk passenger in a car he had stopped a couple of years ago who puked all over herself. I had been his cover officer and remember the incident well.

At some point prior to the contact she had peed herself, and to our amazement, she wiggled out of her soiled dress and panties right there in the middle of the street, and just stood there, completely naked. As her friend scrambled to put a jacket around her, Slater took a photograph of her with his department Polaroid, and it still hangs in his locker.

Slater and I share a hesitant laugh over the incident. It is almost a first step toward some sort of reconciliation between us.

We will never be friends, and I will never trust him enough to work the same shift as he, but I want to at least try to get along with him professionally. Apparently, he is willing to do the same.

The first time we are scheduled to work together again is the upcoming SERT training, three weeks after I am restored to duty. It's one thing to laugh over an old war story, but a whole other animal to work together all day long. Friendly or not, I'm convinced he's working a deal with Pammi Route in a potential lawsuit, and this is as hard to ignore as a pile of stinking garbage.

The shift before training is a slow one. Around one o'clock a.m., a patrol officer comes to a stop at a changing traffic light and gets struck from behind at low speed by a pickup truck. I volunteer to take the report, hoping to arrest another drunk driver.

When I arrive on the scene, the officer points out the vehicle that hit him. It's a green pickup with a load of dirt and shovels in the back. The truck hit the officer at less than ten miles per hour. There's no damage to either vehicle, and neither driver is injured.

"The guy's sitting in his truck," the officer tells me. "I think he's got some alcohol onboard, but I don't think he's deuce."

I get the guy's license and say, "Why don't you tell me what happened, Mr., uh, Connors,"

"I don't know. I guess I was looking away when the light changed, because I looked up and the officer had stopped. I hit the brakes, but there wasn't enough room to stop. We barely hit. Nobody's injured, and there's no damage to either vehicle. I'm really sorry, officer."

Tim Connors. The name is familiar but not the face. I rarely forget someone I meet, and it baffles me that I can't remember this guy.

"Have I ever arrested you?" I ask. "Because I remember your name, but not your—"

A warbling alert tone from the radio cuts me off. The emergency alert is used to warn officers that a high-priority call is about to be broadcast.

"One sixteen, one fifteen, and any unit in the area. Hot-prowl burglary in progress, 203 SE Marwood Drive. Female complainant woke to the sound of glass breaking and saw a white male in the adjoining bedroom. She's hiding in a closet, and we're keeping her on the line till officers arrive."

I throw the license back at Connors, and the other officer tells him to forget about it. We both hop into our cars and take off toward Marwood, which is only about fifteen blocks away. We park a few houses away from the victim's and head in together.

"Units responding to Marwood, the victim says he found her in the closet and jumped out the back window. I'm trying for a description now."

"This way," I say, heading into the backyard of the house next to the victim's.

As soon as we get into the yard, a dog starts barking one yard over, which is two houses away from the victim's. I climb a wooden fence and look over just in time to see the suspect going over a back fence into the yard of a house one street to the east.

"One sixteen, I have the suspect jumping a fence into a yard on, I think it's Wainwood, one street to the east! White male, five ten or so, maybe one eighty. All dark clothes!"

Just as the suspect disappears into the yard, I make it over the fence he'd just hopped. He is at the corner of the house when I draw down on him and hit him with my flashlight.

"Police! Get on the ground!"

The guy looks at me, startled. He hesitates for a moment, and I know he's going to rabbit.

"Get on the ground, motherfucker! Do it now!"

He turns and flees, disappearing around the corner of the house.

"Foot pursuit," I yell into the radio, kicking in the afterburners and heading toward the house. "South side of the house, around the corner! Heading around to the front!"

I am going full speed when I round the corner of the house, and begin to slow down at the last second, realizing my mistake. Slowing down is probably what saves my life. I don't know how many times I've drummed it into rookies *not* to charge around blind corners, because so many officers are killed by suspects who lie in wait to ambush them on the other side. This is just such a scenario.

I am of the fortunate ones. Rather than a gun, this suspect has armed himself with a small shovel he's found in the yard. Because I realize what I am doing and hit the brakes at the last moment, I have just enough time to get my hands up to block the shovel swinging toward my face.

The blow damn near breaks two fingers on my gun hand and sends my Sig Sauer flying into the darkness. It also fillets my forehead open like the belly of a rainbow trout. I am on my ass in the wet grass before I can figure out what has happened.

Rolling away, I manage to get my backup .380 out of my vest holster. It is very dark in the yard, and I have also lost my flashlight. I can't tell if the bad guy is still here or not, and right about then I notice I am lightheaded and woozy. It isn't a good scenario.

The next thing I know, flashlights are all over me, and several cops swarm me. The cavalry has arrived.

"One fifteen, I found him. He's down and bleeding from the head, start me code three medical! It doesn't look like a gunshot wound, but I can't be sure."

That's when I realize I'm not hearing anything on the radio, and feel for my earpiece. It is nowhere to be found.

"I'm okay," I say, pointing. "He went through the front yards that way." My voice is shaky, and so is my hand.

I find my earpiece, and as I get it in my ear, I hear our canine unit say, "I've got a good track northbound through the front yards from 210 Southeast Wainwood!"

I tell everyone to take off so we could get a perimeter around the area. I want this guy more than bad.

Units quickly cordon off a two-block perimeter. Sergeant Leonard Norman stays with me until paramedics arrive. Against his advice, I insist on getting up and walking to the front yard to meet them. Leonard finds my weapon on the way.

"K-9 six," whispers the canine officer over the air, "The dog tracked right up to the front door of 318 Wainwood. The glass in the front door is broken and the door is ajar. I need the perimeter sealed around this house *now!*"

As units tighten the perimeter to this specific house, someone runs the plates in the driveway. The registered owners are a male and female, both in their late thirties. Someone else advises there are children's toys in the yard. At this hour, the family will certainly be home. Records comes back with a phone number to the house, taken from a theft report from a year ago.

Once the perimeter is tightly locked down, Leonard calls the house from a cell phone while paramedics close my head wound with four butterfly bandages. My uniform shirt, soaked with blood, is toast, but at least I don't feel as though I am in imminent danger of dying. I quickly sign the refusal of treatment form to get rid of the paramedics.

I listen to Leonard's brief conversation. "Hi, is this Dr. Zieroff? I'm sorry to wake you at this hour, but this is Sergeant Norman from Stratton PD. We, uh, found your door ajar and just wanted to make sure everything—"

He blinks and lowers the phone. "I got cut off."

Just then, there is a scream from inside the house, and the door slams shut.

Norman gets on the radio immediately. "Thirty one-Sam, activate Stratton SERT. Hostage situation at my location. Have 'em stage at… Make it the intersection of Sunnybrook and Chevelle Drive."

Here we go again, I think. Best kind of training available.

14

LESS THAN A minute after Norman calls out SERT, my pager goes off with the call. Norman and I make our way to the intersection. When we get there, I give him the best description I can of the bad guy.

Not more than fifteen minutes after the page, Lieutenant Capelko shows up wearing Bermuda shorts and a T-shirt. Norman gives him the rundown, adding that two patrol units are at the original complainant's house trying to get further information.

After he's been briefed, Capelko turns to me. "You look like shit, Ben. You need to be in the hospital, not here."

"Baloney. I'm ready to go," I lie. In truth, I am seated because I'm afraid I'll pass out if I stand up.

Capelko looks at me, then says, "Do you even know where you are Ben?
You don't look like you could shoot a rubber band, let alone your rifle. I'm ordering you to go to the hospital."

"Come on, Vince. Okay, I've felt better. Granted, I can't be on the gun tonight. But I'm not going to a hospital, Vince. Not now. Let me stay here, help out however I can at the command post. I need to be here when we get this guy. He looked right at me, then pasted me with that shovel."

Capelko thinks about it for a second, then says, "Okay, fine. Just hang out here, and we'll find something for you to do."

I know Capelko will forget about me the instant the SERT van arrives. He'll sit down in the hot seat, the office he'd had wired into the passenger side of the SERT van, and forget about anything that's not directly involved with running the operation.

From the hot seat, Capelko has access to everything coming in from HNT, two outside phone lines, a computer with wireless Internet access, a police mobile data terminal, a Portland Police Data Systems terminal giving him access to every law enforcement data system in the county, and communications on every police frequency in the county. Once he gets settled there on a callout, Capelko rarely comes out.

My pager goes off again. "Van is leaving."

"One twelve," says my radio, "a bedroom light upstairs just went on. The blinds are drawn, but the light went on."

It is a dispatcher who answered. "Uh, copy, a light went on upstairs. All non emergency traffic switch to Stratton tac-one. A dispatcher is there to handle it. Thirty-one Sam, do you want me to have the county pick up calls in Stratton?"

"A-firm," says Norman. "I'm having our office call out day shift early. Until then, only priority ones and twos, and have them go to the county."

"Copy. Nine ten Sam, did you copy?"

"Affirm, anything we can do to help," says the county sergeant.

"One twelve, I got a guy yelling out of the southeast corner window, telling the police to go away or he's going to kill the family. Sarge, I can probably talk to this guy. You want me to respond to him?"

Norman grabs the radio. "Is he asking for a response?"

"Negative, it was just, like an ultimatum. We either leave, or he kills the family."

"Then no, don't initiate any communications. Bill, you're a CIT officer, aren't you?"

"Yeah, Sarge."

"Okay, you stay by that window, but keep behind cover. If he wants to talk, get me on the radio, and if HNT isn't here yet, you'll be our talker."

"Copy that."

I can hear the eagerness in Bill Kelton's voice. He's a crisis intervention team officer, which means he'd had a forty-hour training course in dealing with mentally ill people. I'm pretty sure he's an HNT wannabe, thought I can't imagine why.

Twenty-five minutes after the initial page, the van arrives with about half the team. Several members had already arrived by car. I get out of the sergeant's car just as the van's back door opens. Bob Slater is the first man out. He is completely dressed out and carrying his rifle.

Stan Hauser, the tactical team leader, is right behind him. Capelko brings them over to my location for a briefing. One of the officers who contacted the original victim is there as well.

"The first victim never saw a weapon, but she doesn't know if the guy's armed," he says. "She heard glass breaking, then saw him in the next bedroom over. She hid in the closet with the phone, and after a few minutes, he came in and saw her. He yanked the phone cord, then ran out."

"That's when I got here," I say. "I ended up chasing the guy over some fences and into the yard of the house behind hers. He ran around the front, and like an idiot, I chased him around the corner. That's when he tagged me with the shovel."

Hal Andrews, the canine officer, picks up the story from there. "Schmeisser got a good track on him from that yard. He went straight to the target house, where I found a broken front-door window and the door ajar. According to neighbors, the Zieroff family lives. Father Leo, mother Sheila, and sons David and Mark, both of whom are elementary school age. That's the last we've heard."

"Any updates from the house?" asked Hauser."

"Yeah, one. The guy came to the one-two-one window maybe ten minutes ago, telling police to leave or he'll kill the family."

"What's the suspect description?" asks Slater.

"Ben, you were the last to see him," says Norman.

"I didn't get a good look at him, but five ten, one eighty, sandy medium-length hair, all dark clothes. Age could be anywhere from twenty to forty. Sorry, but that's it. Hell of a baseball swing, if that helps."

"Yeah," Slater says. "Glad it was a shovel and not a pick. Then we'd have to call you Pick Nose, and I'd keep confusing you and Nosepick. Hell, I confuse you two enough as it is. Vince, I'm all ready to go. Side one, I assume?"

"Yeah, Bob, you get side one tonight. You know where the house is?"

"I think I can find it. And don't worry, I won't shoot any hostages," Slater gives me a little wink as he says this, and my blood pressure rises. My wound actually started oozing again, but I keep my mouth shut.

"Okay, take off then," Capelko says. As Slater gets up to leave, Capelko adds, "Oh, Bob, one more thing."

Slater pauses, looking at him. Capelko gives me a sly little wink and says, "If it comes down to a shot, I want you to fuckin' take it this time."

Glaring at him, Slater heads off.

I catch Capelko's eye as he heads off to brief the rest of the team. "Shut up, Helen," he said, the corners of his mouth turning up a bit. "If you want to make yourself useful, then brief HNT when they get here."

Feeling pretty good about myself, and understanding I'm actually lucky to be alive, I sit back and relax, waiting for HNT to arrive. The look on Slater's face as he headed out was a Kodak moment if I ever saw one. Apparently, there's little love lost between Slater and Capelko. I'd heard Slater badmouth him a few times in the past, so I know Slater doesn't care for him. Slater's one of those guys who just doesn't have it in him to play well with others.

The hostage negotiating team arrives in their converted motor home ten minutes later. Bo Pinter, aka Whiner, is the HNT primary negotiator. I give him a rundown, and he tells me I'm welcome to hang around if I want. One of the HNT techies hadn't arrived yet, so I assist them with setting their gear up.

My first job is to run a connection from the bat phone, which is what they call the primary negotiating telephone, to Capelko's hot seat. Next, following the directions of one of the negotiators, I connect three five-hundred-foot spools of cable together. Then I connect the lead to a smaller spool, which is attached to the throw-phone. The cable on this smaller spool is heavily shielded with tough nylon netting so protect the cable as the phone goes through through windows and the like.

I plug the end of the third spool into the proper outlet on the motor home. Pinter flips a switch and a generator kicks in. In addition to the generator, the motorhome can also run on shore power, and, as a last resort, it is equipped with a bank of the biggest batteries I have ever seen, which can run the whole thing for days. I am duly impressed.

Back inside the motorhome, the negotiators are testing the throw-phone. This is the only piece of HNT equipment with which I am familiar, and the reason is because the back of the headset is painted with an infrared dot that can be seen through our starlight scopes. That way, if we are under a shot of opportunity, HNT can get the suspect on the phone, and all the snipers have to do is follow the bouncing ball.

I look at the intel officer's station, and see a live picture of myself on his HD monitor. I'm befuddled, until someone points to the throw-phone, which is sitting on the counter a couple feet away from me. It turns out the thing is dripping with hidden cameras and microphones. No wonder HNT loves it so much.

Once the motorhome is ready, I head off to the SERT van. Capelko is standing at a marker board, where he's drawn a rough diagram of the target house and surrounding area. An X marks Slater's position inside the garage of the house across the street, and others marked the location of the perimeter guys who have checked in so far.

Outside the van, Hauser and the entry team are huddled together, drawing up a gas plan. There are no babies, elderly people, or infirm inside, so the use of flashbang grenades and gas has been approved. The plan thus far is to gas side three level two first, beginning with the bathroom, which is window two. The suspect will invariably run to avoid the gas, so we use it to put him where we want him. Generally, that would be outside the house, but it doesn't always work that way.

Bathrooms are the first places bad guys usually go to escape the gas. Fortunately, this one has a window in the shower. Several rounds can easily be placed in there to encourage him that the best place he can be is outside the house. You can run, asshole, but you can't hide.

In this case, if he doesn't come right out, the plan is to drive him downstairs to whatever room has the one-one-five window, in the northeast corner of the house. That's an easy walk from the front door, which was the primary point of entry. If the entry team has to use the secondary point, which is the back door, it's still about the same distance. Only if they have to make a covert entry will that room be at a distance. A covert entry will, if necessary, be made through the two-one-one window, which looks like a bedroom.

A covert entry is a silent, stealthy entry, and the intention is to take the bad guy completely by surprise from inside, once the entry team has been fully inserted into the house. The technique is difficult and risky, but highly efficient. It can also be used to spirit hostages away while the bad guy is tied up talking to HNT.

A public information officer is in the process of briefing the two reporters already on scene. He will remain busy until long after the callout is over. Watching him for a moment, I am glad I never put in for PIO. I wouldn't have much patience for dealing with the press.

Capelko looks too busy to interrupt. He is talking with Pinter, and I hear him tell the negotiator to try calling the house as soon as they can the phone company to change the phone number and block all outgoing calls. That way, nobody can call the house but us.

It's about time, I think to myself. Things ought to start happening now.

15

I FOLLOW PINTER back into the HNT van. "We have the phones isolated yet?" he asks no one in particular.

"Yeah, just got that done. They have two lines, and we got 'em both," says Timmy Van Buren, one of five other HNT members. "No calls in or out, except to us."

"What are you going to use as positives," asks someone else.

"We don't have much," Pinter admits. "Basically, he hasn't done anything serious yet, so they'll go nice and easy on him. That's about all I can think of."

"Bo," I said, "Did you get hit in the face with a shovel or something? Even here in The People's Republic of Multnomah County, they're going to take a giant shit on this guy. Burg one times two, attempted murder of a police officer, assault one, kidnap one times three… Every one of those is a measure eleven crime. Minimum sentencing guidelines'll put this guy down for forty-eight, fifty years. Even *here*, for God's sake. Go easy on him? I don't think so."

Pinter rolls his eyes. "Ben, we're not talking about the real world, just what we'll tell *him*. A positive is something we tell the bad guy to give him a reason to come out. You know, using intel on him, his favorite pet, or something. We find out what we can about the bad guy, then use it against him in negotiations. Like, 'who's gonna feed Fluffy if you eat your barrel?' All we have positive for this dude is, it's not murder unless someone dies, and the officer is going to be okay. And, you haven't hurt those people in there, or done anything *really* bad yet, so they won't come down on you like a ton of bricks."

"Well, what if he *had* killed someone in there?"

"Then we couldn't use that," Pinter says like a teacher trying to instruct an abysmally stupid child.

A phone buzzes quietly, and one of the negotiators picks it up.

"Capelko says someone just closed all the windows," he announced.

"That's a sign he won't negotiate," says Pinter. "I bet we don't get an answer."

"We're ready if you are," says a voice from the back of the motorhome.

Pinter sits down at a long desk that occupies part of one wall of the motorhome and puts on a headset. Van Buren sits next to him. Spread out between them are a yellow legal pad, a telephone log, and several laminated cards containing various abnormal personality disorders. The cards have information on each disorder, and negotiating suggestions for that type. The ones I can see are 'paranoid', 'borderline', and 'schizotypal.' There are several others I can't see. An open notebook contains suggested active listening keywords and open-ended questions.

"Dialing the primary number," says Pinter, and Van Buren makes a note on the log. He dons a headset and poises his pen over the legal pad. Pinter dials the number, and they both sit there with intent expressions on their faces.

After about a minute, Pinter disconnects the line. "Bet he yanked this phone out like he did that other lady's," he said. "But I'll betcha he didn't know about the other line. Dialing the secondary number now."

This time, after only about ten seconds, he says, "Hello? Hello? Hey, this is Officer Pinter of the Stratton Police Department. Who am I talking to?"

Van Buren writes "Les" on the paper.

One of the other HNT guys offers me a headset and shows me where to plug it in. I do, and the conversation comes right into my ears.

"What do you do for the police department? Are you the chief?"

"No, Les, I'm just a cop, but they use me to talk to people who might need help. Is there anything I can do to help you?"

"What do you want to help me do, Bo? Die?"

"Nobody's talking about dying, Les. Quite the opposite, actually. I want to help you live. Listen, do you need anything in there? Anything I can get you?"

"No. And I don't want to talk to you. I know you guys want to kill me for hitting that cop, so don't lie to me."

"Les, I do what I do 'cause I *don't* lie."

"Look, don't give me any of your we-just-want-to- talk-to-you crap. I'm not stupid. And I *don't* want to talk."

Van Buren scribbles something across the page. All I can make out is the word "positives."

"The thing is, Les, that you haven't done anything really bad yet. The cop you hit with the shovel is fine, I just talked to him. And you haven't hurt anyone in there yet, either. At least not that we know of."

"Goddamn it of course I haven't hurt anyone. That's not what I do. And I'm not stupid. I broke into a house, man. That's burglary, and that's a felony."

"Les, do you really think the DA's gonna give a shit about a couple of pissy breaking and enterings? This is Multnomah County. All they care about is big stuff—rape, murder, you know. Hey, I'm not saying you get off with nothing. I mean, you did a burg and you hit a cop. You're not gonna just skate. But what they really look at is, did you really harm anyone, or are you just committing a property crime? And now that we're at this level, they're gonna want to know how you handled yourself with us. Did you cooperate, or did you make things worse? If I tell him you cooperated, they're going to look at your property crimes in a little different light. Six months, a year, max. Hell, maybe they'll even just let you go with probation. It ain't too late, man."

"You must think I'm an idiot. I'm holding *hostages,* dude. That's *kidnapping* or something. You're trying to snow me, and that makes me not trust you."

"Look, Les, I want you to trust me, okay? Now let me ask you something. Do you want me to lie to you, or do you want me to tell you the truth?"

"You already tried lying, so why don't you try the truth now?"

"Okay man, you want it, you got it. You're gonna get arrested. You're gonna get charged with everything they can charge you with. But what I said is true. The DA is gonna look at how you handled yourself right now, at this time. When it's still time for talk, and not action. And they're gonna look at what I have to say about you. In fact, I'm going to get called to testify about your attitude, whether you cooperated, or whether you didn't. You're in a position to help yourself, and I'm in a position to help you."

"Why would you want to help me?"

"Because if I help you, I end this thing faster, which means I get to go home earlier. Plus, that makes me look good. Besides, do you think I like being up at this hour?"

"Okay, at least I know you're not bullshitting me now."

"Look, Les. You don't want to hurt anyone at this stage. It's not in your better interest."

"I'm not a violent guy. I don't want to hurt no one. I just want to get the hell out of here. But I'm not about to fuck myself by just walking out. I ain't that stupid, man."

"Well, you know we can't just let you go. So, I'm back to my original question. What *can* we do for you? Call someone? A wife? Your mother, maybe?"

"You leave my mother out of this, asshole! She didn't do shit, and she doesn't need to know about this. You got that? Now I need time to think, *so gimme a freakin' break!*"

The line goes dead, and we all take our headsets off at the same time.

"You catch that reaction when you mentioned his mother?" asks Van Buren.

"Yeah," muses Pinter, deep in thought. Drumming his fingers and staring off into space, Pinter says, "His mother's the key. Find out who he is, and you find out who mom is. And once we've got her, we've got him."

Van Buren turns, grabs a phone, and calls the office. I hear him asking someone to run a check on all people named Les in our computer database and find out how many have been in trouble before.

Everyone in HNT seems to have something to do when they're off-line with the suspect, so I mosey out the door in search of something with which to occupy myself.

A county transit bus has arrived and is slowly filling up with the neighbors who've been evacuated by SERT. It isn't much for folks roused from their beds in the middle of the night who are supposed to get up and head off to work in a couple of hours.

I go into the SERT van, but Capelko and Hauser are locked in conversation. At the moment, they are the only two occupants. I study the board with the perimeter diagram. Where would I be if I hadn't been injured?

Slater has chosen a position in the garage of the house across the street, a distance of only about sixty yards. That's probably a smart choice, though it puts him within range of the house. I try to find fault with it, but I have to admit it's probably where I'd have ended up, as well.

Well, Slater has his wish. He's the side one sniper tonight. Capelko hasn't fielded anyone on side three. Tonight, that will be up to IP to handle. We just don't have enough people cross-trained, and Capelko must not have wanted to call Venegall out.

I'd been trying to talk Capelko into adding at least two more qualified snipers so we could field two sniper/observer teams of two men apiece. That way, we could stay on the gun indefinitely, rotating in shifts as snipers and observers on an as-needed basis, even allowing one person to sleep if the call went on for days. I was told the budget wouldn't allow it.

As always, my mind returns to the last callout. Why hadn't Slater taken the shot? Was he just plain afraid? Had he been sleeping? How I would love to sneak into the garage he was in right now and just watch him. He has no patience for this kind of thing when there's no action going on. Maybe he didn't really have the stomach for taking a guy out. All the ability in the world won't do you any good if you don't have the intestinal fortitude to actually do the job when the time comes.

That reminds me of Capelko's little parting shot, and I smile to myself. At least Vince believes me.

Back at the HNT van, Pinter is talking with someone on the phone, and Van Buren looks lost in thought. "You guys develop any intel on him?" I ask.

"No. There are over two hundred people named Leslie or Lester in PPDS. Searching only the white males between twenty and forty, we were able to narrow it down to about thirty or so, and of all those, two are dead and the rest are in the system for a variety of things; crime victims, witnesses, accident victims, and reporting parties. Five have been arrested before, two of whom are in prison. The other three are a shoplifter, a drunk driver, and some guy Salmon Creek PD busted for drinking in a public park. Basically, we got nothing."

"Too bad."

"Bo just tried calling back. He told us not to call again and hung up. I think he may have ripped the phone out of the wall. If so, we'll try the throw-phone later, but we're gonna let him cool down some now. Vince says maybe in an hour or two if nothing happens."

My head is ringing like a church bell on Sunday morning, so I take a seat on one of the benches in HNT motorhome to rest for a while. I really should go to the hospital to get checked out, but I don't want to leave now.

I look at my watch—5:10 a.m. It's been over two hours since I got tagged with the shovel.

I pick up a phone and dial my house. Maybe the fact that I got injured would help Sharon get her mind off Andrea.

It does. Sharon makes me promise to call her the moment the callout is over, and she'll pick me up and take me to get checked out. I hear nothing but real concern in her voice, and she tells me quite sincerely that she still loves me and that she thanks God I am alive. Personally, if it is God that kept me alive, I'm just a little pissed at Him for not reminding me sooner about what a stupid idea it is to chase bad guys around blind corners. But I could forgive Him that as long as He keeps Sharon from staying angry at me. Hearing the kindness and compassion in her voice is the best healing there is for me now, and I'm not about to blow it. Despite my head injury, I feel as if I am thinking clearly for the first time since I started seeing Andrea.

Clear thinking lasts for about ten minutes. That's when my department cell phone rings. It's Andrea, of course. Someone has called her at home and told her what happened. She won't tell me who.

The conversation starts out with her concern for my welfare, but of course, it degenerates into how much she still cares for me. Maybe I'm still just a little woozy, but I say something to the effect of I still care for her, too. Oddly enough, it's Andrea's call that really turns things around for the callout.

"Anyway," she says toward the end of our conversation, "I just wanted to hear your voice to make sure you're okay. Promise me you'll go to the hospital, okay, Ben?"

"I will. 'Night, Andrea."

"'Night, Ben. By the way, are you sure that guy said his name was Les? Because I had a friend in third grade named Lassiter, and we all called him Las. Anyway, I'm just going to say it. I love you. Bye!" She hangs up before I have the chance to reply.

16

I GO DIRECTLY to the SERT van. "Vince, you mind if I use your PPDS terminal for a few?"

"Have at it, Ben. I want to change out of this Hawaiian outfit anyway."

I sit down in the hot seat and begin typing, doing a PPDS search using the name Lassiter. I come up with five people with that last name. Three of them were females, and of the other two, one is eighty years old, and the other is a transvestite that Oregon City PD had busted in a men's room stall with another guy.

On a whim, I try Las, and get nothing. Frustrated, I type in Laszlo, the name of a debating star I knew in college, and come up with a hit.

Bingo! Laszlo Duval Bowman, busted in 1998 at age twenty-two for masturbating in the Stratton K-Mart. Busted in 2001 for Sex Abuse II, a case in which he fondled a thirteen-year-old girl at a bus stop. A suspect in February of this year of a first-degree burglary at the home of his mother's best friend, where the victim awoke to find a naked male staring at her in the middle of the night. Last contact was a traffic ticket in Portland, listing a Stratton address.

Mother is Eleanor Bowman, with an address in Boring, Oregon.

Laszlo's physical description is five eleven, one ninety, with blond hair over green eyes.

I get on the phone and call Clackamas County Sheriff's Office, requesting that they get a car out to the mother's house in Boring right away to gather all the info they can. I tell them to make it a priority.

Fifteen minutes later, I call Vince and tell him to meet me in HNT right away.

"Our guy is Laszlo Duval Bowman, and he's a rapist in the making," I say confidently. I give Capelko and HNT a rundown on Bowman's arrest record, and then say, "And you were right about the mother, Bo. Bowman's mother is dying of cancer. According to the docs, she's only got six months. And here's the kicker. Bowman hasn't seen her for three weeks. According to his sister, who has no way of getting in touch with Laszlo, Mom just went in the hospital two days ago. *There's* your positive for him."

Everyone looks at me like I have the ear of God or something. I smile painfully, and make a crack about how getting pasted in the face with a shovel must have put my brain back where it belongs, and credit Capelko's hot seat. After congratulating me, HNT breaks into a flurry of activity.

I feel like shit for not giving credit where credit is due, but there's enough talk already about Andrea and me, and I don't want to fuel that particular fire.

Things move quite quickly from this point on. Capelko gets Pinter suited up and has the reaction team escort him to within megaphone range of the target house. We can all hear his amplified voice.

"Las. Laszlo Bowman, we need to talk to you."

After a moment he tries again.

"Laszlo! I've got some bad news for you regarding your mother's health. She's in the hospital, Las. They say the cancer's spreading. They found it in her uterus. She's not doing too well, and you better think about taking this opportunity to see her one last time."

Nothing.

"Las! Help me help you see your mother before she dies. I lost my own mother two years ago; I know how important this is."

A moment passes, then Slater's voice comes over the radio. "Slater to CP, front door opening! White male, all dark clothes, sandy hair coming out with hands up!"

"Entry, we got him!"

From a block-and-a-half away, I can hear Hauser yelling at Bowman to get down on the ground and put his hands out to his sides. A moment later, he broadcasts that the suspect is in custody.

Slater puts out a code red, indicating that entry has gone inside to clear the house, and two minutes after that comes the code four from Hauser. The tactical mission is over. It is almost seven o'clock, nearly four hours since the callout got under way.

I round the corner and see Pinter talking with Bowman, who is now seated in the back of a patrol car. I want to go up to him and gloat, but after all the excitement, I barely have the strength.

Sharon arrives and takes me to the emergency room at Emanuel. They remove the butterfly bandages and replace them with six stitches. I am made to undergo a CAT scan, which reveals a minor concussion, and am given a prescription for Percodan. The doctor tells me to return for a follow-up visit in a week, and if I am doing okay by then, I might be allowed to return to duty.

My phone rings while I am in the hospital. Fortunately for me, it is set on vibrate. I surreptitiously check the number. Just as I suspect, it is Andrea's cell. I elect not to call her back.

Four days later, I get called into the office at 3:30 p.m. Chief Moody wants to talk to me.

"I just thought you should know this, Ben," he says. "The city attorney's office was just notified this afternoon by the Law Offices of Samuel Rosenberg that Pammi Route has filed an Intent to Sue the department about her shooting. It lists you as a codefendant and states that you 'recklessly and without justifiable reason caused the death of her husband Hugo, a mentally ill person who had voluntarily surrendered his weapon; you recklessly endangered the life of and caused grievous injury, mental anguish, loss of income, and pain and suffering, to the person of Pammi Route; and endangered the life of and caused severe mental trauma, pain, and suffering, to the person of infant Chastity Route,' blah blah blah. It's for five million dollars, plus punitive damages."

"What should I do?"

"Nothing. You're welcome to hire your own lawyer if you want, but you're covered by the city's attorneys."

"Are we going to defend it ourselves or go with an outside firm?"

"If it ever comes to court, we'll probably contract with an outside firm. That's what they usually do."

"Okay, then for now, I'll save the thirty thousand dollars and go with the city's defense attorney."

"That's what I'd say. Look, Ben, I just want you to know that the city is standing behind you. I've gone over the results of the shooting reconstruction, and it's my belief that Slater's... Well, let's just say that he misperceived things. But before we ever see the inside of a courtroom, I'm going to order the two of you to undergo a polygraph. Are you going to have a problem with that?"

"Chief, that's the best thing you can do for me, and the worst you can do for Slater. I bet he refuses to take it."

"Let him try. His job will depend on it. We're going to get to the bottom of all this, sooner or later."

"Thanks, Chief."

Swing shift roll call is just getting out, and I wait by the back door as officers head to their cars. When Andrea comes out, I walk past her and whisper, "The Lariat." She nods, and I get in my car and leave.

Twenty minutes later, Andrea and I are seated in the Lariat grill in Salmon Creek, a mile outside Stratton city limits.

I have been ignoring her, and I know that it's hurt her. I've already let her go, but I feel she at least deserves an explanation.

"Andrea, I'm just going to be honest with you, and you can do what you want with what I'm going to tell you. I'm a prick and I'm a bastard. I know this, but there's not much I can do to change.

"I've been married for twenty years. Sharon and I tried and tried to have a baby, and it took us fourteen years to do it. The docs say it's a miracle that she got pregnant at all. It would seem that I have a low sperm count. Anyway, Leah's my miracle kid, and I love her more than anything in the world. What I'm trying to say is, I just can't give up my family. Not even for you."

The expression on her face confuses me as I chug my way though this. I expected her to be crestfallen, but bemused is maybe a better word. Like she knows what I will end up doing as opposed what I *want* to do. Even if I don't yet know it myself. This little talk of mine doesn't appear to be much of a surprise to her.

"Go on," she urges.

"But, when I'm with you, I think I've made the biggest mistake in the world being with Sharon. You're everything she's not. I can't get enough of you, and I don't know what to do. I want to have my cake and eat it too, but I can't. That doesn't work for any of us. All I know is, it's not fair to you to keep you tied up with some married guy who won't leave his wife, and it's not fair to Sharon to throw away everything we've got invested over the last twenty years, and it certainly isn't fair to Leah to risk breaking her family apart."

"So, what are you saying?" she asks with just a hint of amusement. "That you want to break it off? You've already done that."

"Yes. No… I don't know! More than anything, I wish we could be alone for a while without any chance of getting caught. But if I do that, I'll want to walk away from Sharon, which would mean losing Leah, too. So yeah, I want to break it off."

"You're lucky I'm in uniform, Officer Geller, or I'd be jumping your bones right here and now. You're so cute when you get upset! Ben, listen to me. You go work it out with Sharon, and I'll wait for you, in case it doesn't work. I'll even stay with you knowing that you'll never leave Sharon. I'll sleep with you knowing that you'll sleep with her later that same day. Hell, I'll sleep with you both at the same time! God, Ben, don't you understand? I've fallen head over heels in love with you. I don't care if I'm being an idiot or not. I fell for a married guy, and I can accept that. Maybe I won't feel this way in five years, or maybe not even in one year, but for now, this is what I want. A stolen moment, *whenever* we can grab one."

My head is spinning. This isn't supposed to happen. She is supposed to cry, then get angry, and then come to the realization that it is for the best. This is supposed to be hard for me to say, but then I'm supposed to feel really good after having finally broken it off.

What she isn't supposed to do is let me have my cake and eat it too. Somehow or another, Andrea knows this will work for me. And she's right. What she saying *should* make things worse, but instead it sets me at ease. I think it's what I was looking for when I came here, although I didn't know it. It's almost creepy that she knows me so well.

I clasp her hand under the table, and the contact is electrifying. She can't resist, and comes over to my side, where she kisses me long and hard. I kiss her back, then make her go back to her side of the table.

"Look," she says a moment later. "I've got something for you."

She reaches into her uniform pocket and pulls out two round plastic cases, each containing a bright silver coin. "These are actual U.S. currency one-dollar coins. I ordered them from the Mint. They're proof sets, which means they've never been touched by human hands. Here," she says, handing me one, "Take a look at it."

It is a commemorative coin honoring police officers killed in the line of duty. It's beautiful.

"I want you to have it, and keep it in your uniform pocket as a reminder of Dan. And as a reminder of me. Every time I touch mine, I'll think of you."

"It's beautiful, honey," I say, taking one. "I'll carry it with me every day in the field. It'll be a constant reminder of you. But I gotta tell you, I don't need a coin to think of you. Or of Dan. Thanks, Andrea."

"I don't know where we're going to end up, Ben," she says, "But call me if you want when you can get away for a few hours. You need to quit thinking so much about all the what-ifs and start thinking more about plowin' the back forty."

She once told me that watching herself ride me in the mirror in her bedroom makes her think of the way the guy bounced up and down on his tractor on *Green Acres,* and it has been our euphemism for making love ever since.

After looking at her, smelling her, feeling her tongue in my mouth, and imagining us plowin' the back forty, how am I supposed to think of anything else?

Later that night, I have Leah on my lap, watching *Finding Nemo.* Sharon is next to us on the couch when the phone rings. She takes it in the bedroom and is gone for a long time. Halfway through the movie, she calls me in.

She is near tears. "That was Linda. Remember her sister Lydia? The fat one, from the Christmas party last year?"

"Yeah. Why?"

"No you don't. She lost eighty pounds and looks very different. She's a waitress at the Lariat. Ben, *how could you?*"

17

GOING BACK TO work has been good for me. It takes my mind off the fact that I am living in a friend's fifth-wheel in his backyard. Sharon still won't talk to me, and though Leah pages me once or twice a day, I've only seen her a few times. Yet again, it has become painfully clear just how shallow a relationship based only on sex and not love can be. I have been avoiding Andrea, but that's not getting me any closer to moving back home. Now that I am finally free to see Andrea all I want, I don't want to see her at all. All I want is to be with my family, but they don't want to be with me. How ironic.

I've seen Slater only once since hearing about the lawsuit, and that was a couple days ago. I told him about the lawsuit, and he said he didn't care. He said he'd heard about it, but wasn't worried since he wasn't named as a codefendant. He was so smug that I let it slip that Moody was going to order us polygraphed. This revelation earned me a brief, but satisfying oh-shit look. Once it was gone, he said, "Oh well, it won't matter by then anyway," as if he wanted me to guess what he meant by that. What an asshole.

It is just after 10:00 a.m. on the last day of my weekend, and I will have to go back to work at eleven tonight. Days off can be hard on graveyard shift. To sleep or not to sleep during the day. It doesn't matter today, I can't sleep anyway. I just miss my family so much. I am sitting at the foldout kitchen table, looking at some old family pictures of Leah as an infant when my pager goes off again.

Andrea is working an overtime shift today, and has paged me so often I'm beginning to feel like the guy in the movie where his girlfriend cooks his daughter's rabbit. I hit the button, expecting to see her number yet again, but this time, it's not her.

SERT callout. Shots fired. Suspect barricaded with hostages and automatic weapons. Command post Oregon Trails Medical Plaza, Logan and Burnsdale. Approach from the north only.

A *third* callout? We normally only get about three callouts per year, and now we're getting a third in what? A month? All back-to-back hostage situations, too. It is unprecedented.

I grab my SERT bag, change into my BDUs, and gear up in record time. I'm out the door and in the car four minutes after the initial page.

I call the office on the way to the police department. "Geller checking in," I tell the records clerk who answers the phone. "What can you tell me about it?"

"I don't know, it all happened so fast. It's the grand opening of some business, and there were, like, a bunch of famous people there or something. Some guy went in with a machine gun and shot the place up, and that's, like, the last anyone's seen of anyone."

"Damn. How many suspects?"

"We don't know. At least one, but who knows?"

"Okay, well, I'll be there before the van leaves."

I am the first one at the van. I let myself in, de-activated the alarm, and retrieve the keys from the ashtray. I have the van out of its bay in the fire department and running on internal power before anyone else arrives.

Within minutes several SERT members arrive. Roland Hogue comes in from the scene to change, and briefs everyone present.

"The place is called Northwest Healing," he says. "It's that new building they've been renovating on the corner of Burnsdale and Logan. It's some kind of charity organization, an aid-for-homeless clearinghouse where they store blankets or something. Anyway, today is their grand opening, so they have famous people there. They've got a really famous concert pianist there, and Loretta Epstein, the actress who ran around screwing all the cops in that movie *Ventura Freeway* is the guest speaker."

Everyone knows of Loretta Epstein. She is the daughter of Pio Cantelli, a rich business owner rumored to be heavily tied to the mob. Cantelli is the founder of the Night Out chain of movie theater/restaurants, which he'd recently sold for close to a hundred million. Loretta, his only child, is a hometown girl who recently got a big Hollywood break. She was nominated for an Academy Award for her role as the drug-addicted wife of a street cop the previous year in a sleeper movie that unexpectedly hit it big.

"So," continues Hogue, "they're having this big celebration with speeches and everything, when some psycho runs in with an AK-47 and opened up on full-auto. One guy made it out, but nobody else has been heard of since it got started, which was"—he consulted his watch—"only about twenty-five minutes ago."

"Jesus," somebody says. It seemed appropriate.

"There's more," Hogue announced solemnly. "It couldn't have happened at a worse time. Everyone was tied up on a perimeter in Rockledge. Everyone except Andrea. She'd just gone '61 with a shoplifter at the Freddy's just down the street from this Northwest Healing place. Of course she bails on the shoplifter and goes to the shooting, and is the first to arrive on scene. When I got there only about two or three minutes later, I found her car idling in the lot, but no Andrea. She never answered up on the radio, and hasn't been seen since."

I sit down heavily. The van becomes as busy as an anthill as people change and ready their gear around me. "Ben," says Hogue, sitting down next to me. "I know you and Andrea are, uh, tight. If she's in there, we'll get her out."

I look at him without really seeing him, then get up and begin checking my weapon.

Like the last time I was in this van, this callout lacks the fun and jocular atmosphere of a normal SERT activation. On the Route callout, Andrea was the hero. Now, at Northwest Healing, she's a hostage. Either that, or she's already dead.

I don't remember much about the ride over. Somehow I manage to get fully prepared, and when the van comes to a stop in the parking lot of a medical office building, I am the first one out. Slater's still not here, but he arrives shortly after we do. He shoulders his way into the back, past the outflowing tide of fully armed and ready SERT members.

Capelko is, as usual, already on scene, and takes me off to the side. "Ben, look, it's hard to keep secrets in this outfit. Now, I'm not saying anything, but are you certain you want to go out on this call? I mean, given the fact that Andrea is probably in there?"

"Yeah, Vince. I'm sure. Don't sweat it."

"Well, you were invaluable as an intel officer on the last callout. I think I'd like to use you in that same capacity now. I have more than enough for you to do in the van, and we can let Slater take side one, just for this one. I promise. Just for this one."

"Come on, Vince, don't take me off the gun. Not tonight. Not on this one. If we need to take a shot on this guy, I don't want Slater to fumble the ball."

Just then, Slater came out of the van. Capelko says, "I think it's best, Ben. Just for tonight."

"What's just for tonight?" asks Slater.

"Bob, I'm going to put you out as primary tonight, and—"

"No! I mean, Ben's always been primary, and I don't want to take that away from him. Not on this one, anyway."

I turn to face him, stunned into silence. Slater has been vying for side one since the day he was accepted onto the team. He'd been primary on the Bowman callout, and he'd done nothing but gloat about it ever since. And now he'd just refused side one, out of concern for *me*? I don't think so.

"What?" I ask, incredulous.

Slater seems to recover from something. "Shit, Helen," he says smugly. "Everyone knows you're fucking Andrea. Even I don't want to take this one from you. And besides, I bet we get side three action tonight. Vince, let him take primary. He'll wet his pants if he doesn't get it."

Capelko looks a little baffled but then acquiesces. "Okay, Slater, you got side three. Geller, you're primary. We got nothing on the bad guy, but anything we find out, you'll be the first to know. Now, both of you get the hell out there. I need eyes on that place yesterday."

We move out to find decent sniper positions, Slater on the back and me on the front. The building is situated just east of the corner, facing Burnsdale. It is set maybe fifty yards back from the street with nothing in front but a parking lot. The closest side-one sniper spot will be across Burnsdale, where there are a few buildings that look promising.

Directly across the street is another plaza, this one facing north toward Northwest Healing. It looks as though I'll be another long-distance shot, close to two hundred yards, but the plaza is the only place I can find concealment, so I head over there.

Once behind the plaza, I work my way to the east end, to a point directly across the street from the target. The temperature is already in the mid-seventies, and will probably peak out in the low-nineties, which isn't uncommon for Stratton in early August.

By the time I reach the end of the building I am soaked through with sweat. A skateboard shop occupies the end of the building almost directly across from the target, and the roof look perfect for a sniper blind.

The roof is crenellated, with a decorative cinder-block wall approximately two feet high running along the perimeter of the roof. Every couple of feet along the bottom of the wall a cinder block is missing, giving the roof a fortress-like appearance. The missing blocks are perfect for my purpose.

Patrol officers are in the process of evacuating the plaza, and the skateboard shop has already been closed. I break out a ground-floor window in the back and hoist myself through with my gear. I plop down hard on the floor, causing a wave of pain to go through my still-swollen pinkie and ring finger. From here I find the roof hatch in the back office area and climb up the access ladder.

Predictably, the hatch is locked, and I have to use bolt cutters to remove the padlock. A moment later, I climb out onto the roof.

I belly crawl to the front, where I set my rifle up on its bipod, careful to ensure that the barrel doesn't extend through the gap in the cinderblocks.

My view of Northwest Healing is excellent, and I set up my gear. My range is close to two hundred fifty yards, but I already know I can make an accurate shot at this range. It's a bit windy on the roof, and the five-to-seven knot breeze is steady enough that I make a scope adjustment to compensate. I make sure my elevation is set for this range, then hit the transmit key.

"Geller to CP."

"CP, go ahead."

"In position on the roof of the skateboard shop across from the number one side, range about two-forty or so yards. View is good into the front windows. The whole side one is made of glass. There's no sign of people, but the place does look pretty shot up. There are ceiling tiles down everywhere, and at least one shattered windowpane. No blood that I can see. Break."

I have a lot to say, but don't want to hog the air if anyone else needs it. When no one else speaks up, I resume. "Continuing, there are numerous cars in the lot. Are you clear for plates?"

"Go ahead."

I proceed to recite the twenty license plates I can see. When I am done, it's Slater's turn.

"Slater to CP. In position, about one-two-zero yards off the three-four corner in a small grassy depression with trees behind me. Good view of all of side three, including the loading dock overhead doors. Everything's closed, and there is no movement."

He goes on to give another two or three plates that are parked back there.

It irks me to no end that Slater and I are back in our old positions as number one- and number two-side snipers, as if nothing had happened on the Route callout. How could Capelko keep him after his failure to take the shot, or his obvious lying about it afterward? What had he really been doing?

A half-hour passes, during which I marinate in my irritation. Finally, I can stand it no longer. I roll off scope, pick up a pair of binoculars, and begin scanning the terrain visible to me off the three-four corner behind the building, looking for Slater's position. I can't see him from behind my gun, but by moving about three yards to my right, I finally locate him.

Slater is sitting in a shallow canyon in a lightly wooded are directly off the three side, next to a concrete sewer pylon. He is surrounded by high grass, and from where I am situated it doesn't look as if he could possibly see the target through the grass. His rifle is set up, but I am shocked beyond words to see he isn't even lying behind it. Instead, he's sitting up, actually talking on a phone.

I can't comprehend, and don't understand what I'm seeing. There's a barricaded suspect with an automatic weapon inside, holding hostages, and a fellow police officer is likely among them. And Bob Slater, the three-side sniper, isn't even on his gun. To make it even more bizarre, the device he's on isn't an ordinary cell phone, either. In fact, it looks like a regular landline telephone handset, complete with a cord that disappears somewhere underneath him.

I scan the area to see if another IP guy might be in a position to see him, but he's at least seventy-five yards behind the inner perimeter, so he he's pretty much on his own.

Seeing Slater screwing off on a callout is too much. Wishing I had a camera, I make a mental note to fill Capelko in on his behavior. Up until now, I had actually assumed he had at least been ready to take the shot on Hugo Route. I just figured he didn't because shooting a man is so different from shooting a paper target. Now, however, I see I might be wrong. He may have been on the phone and not even looking at the target.

I'll tell Capelko about this, oh yeah. And Moody, and the city attorney, and Pammi Route's lawyer, and everyone else I can think of. I go back to my own rifle satisfied that, if nothing else, Bob Slater will be kicked off SERT in disgrace, and I will be wholly exonerated in the Route shooting.

It takes nearly an hour for the inner perimeter to get set. Once everyone is in place, I sneak another quick peek at Slater. He's put the phone down, and is now up walking around in front of his rifle, clearing away the tall grass with as much stealthy conservation of movement as a guy chopping his way through a jungle with a machete. He might as well advertise his position to the any bad guys watching from the three side with flashing neon lights.

When he's done, Slater finally gets behind the rifle and settles in. I'm sure he'll be intently peering through his scope when the scouts happen upon him as they make their rounds. I am absolutely furious.

Only then does it occur to me that I am doing the exact same thing he is. Twice now I've been off target myself, for a total of at least three or four minutes, watching *him*, while Andrea is being held hostage in the building I'm supposed to be watching. I must be obsessed with Slater. Disciplining myself, I make it a point to get back to the task at hand, which is keeping an eye on Northwest Healing, without distractions. As for Slater, he's signed his own death warrant, at least as far as SERT goes. If I have any input beyond reporting what I've seen, he'll lose his job as well.

There is no sign of anything going on in Northwest Healing from my vantage point; the place looks like a ghost town. But it's not. Andrea is inside there somewhere, and I am going to do everything in my power to get her out.

18

I GLANCE AT Slater twice during the next couple of hours. The first time, he's on his rifle, and the second time he's just sitting, staring off blankly into space. I can't believe he is such a malignant goof-off.

Just before one p.m., we get our first situational update.

"CP to SERT, HNT reports that this is an act of domestic terrorism. The suspect, or suspects, have planned this out and are demanding a ransom of fifteen million dollars. If the demand is not granted by fifteen hundred hours, they say they will kill a hostage. After they get the money, they'll give us instructions on how they intend to leave.

"That's just a little over two hours, people, so keep sharp. HNT is working on getting an extension. We don't know how many suspects there are, and we have no suspect descriptions, so we are remaining at compromised authority. That's all the info I have now. We'll try to get you more before the deadline. CP out."

In sniper school, they showed us video footage of a callout just like this one. Asian gang members had taken customers hostage at an electronics store in California and lined them up on the floor, bound and gagged. When it finally came to taking a shot, the sniper's round first hit a glass door, which deflected it enough so that it missed the target. The suspects, realizing that the end was at hand, proceeded to calmly walk down the row of hostages, shooting each in the head.

I pray this callout will not result in another shooting. I'd thought I was ready for anything, but not this. Not another shooting, so close to the last one. Why hadn't I let Slater take side one?

Then I remembered that Slater had insisted that *I* take side one. He must have foreseen that this one would go bad. I wish my instincts were that good. He'd insisted on side three so he could be lazy and dick off, ignoring the rifle and the callout while I do all the work. In other words, he's managed to double-crossed me again.

Now I'm afraid of what might happen in the next two hours.

Capelko gives us the fifteen-minute warning at 2:45. He says HNT has not been able to reach anyone in the building since the suspect issued the ultimatum.

I can't resist the urge to have another glance at Slater, just to document what he's doing now that the deadline is at hand. I know I shouldn't hazard a glance, because if something bad happens, I will need a relatively long time—seconds—to get back on scope.

But I look anyway. I slide out of position, which feels good to my cramping muscles, and use my binoculars to scan Slater's little corner of the woods by the sewer pylon.

I half expect him to be off scope again, but to my surprise, he isn't there. At first I assume he must have moved to a secondary position, but if one of us has to make a move like that, we have to inform the command post. We would at least have to tell the CP we were off scope.

Of course, Slater had been off scope for a long time at least twice so far today, and he'd made no references to doing so at all. Scrutinizing the area, I see his rifle set up at the base of the concrete manhole. Where was he? Taking a leak?

Just then, the radio pipes up. "Baker to CP, movement in side one!"

Cursing myself for not being on scope, I quickly slide behind my rifle and re-acquire the target. A door against the back wall has opened, but it is too dark inside to see what is behind it, or who had opened it.

"Geller to CP, an interior door to a back area has opened. No one visible. Door's just standing open… Wait, movement inside!" I squint as hard as I can, but I am unable to make out any details in the dark interior. Even if I were to see someone, I would have no way of knowing if the person is a good guy or a bad guy, armed or unarmed. It isn't beyond reason that someone who had thought this out so thoroughly would put an unloaded weapon in the hands of a hostage to "give to the police," just to see if the cops are under a shot of opportunity. And that's *not* going to happen to me.

"HNT to SERT," comes the voice of the HNT intelligence officer. "Stand by for the imminent release of two hostages!" Their intel guy has authority to get on out tactical net if he has information that's too important to wait for it to go from HNT to the command post and from there, to be broadcast to the team..

A woman holding something comes to the doorway. I can't tell what she has in her hands. The only thing I know about the hostage taker, or takers, is that the one HNT has been speaking with is male. We don't know if there are more than one, or if any of them are female. Hell, half the "hostages" could be his accomplices for all I know. Not knowing is the most frustrating part.

"I have a woman in the inside door, side one," I say, trying to sound calm. "Unknown object in her hands."

Please be Andrea, I think to myself, squinting. I can't tell; it's just too dark inside.

"Reaction team holding on the four-one," says Hauser. I can't see them because I have my magnification dialed in to maximum to watch the woman, but I know they've moved right up to the corner and are prepared to intercept.

The woman steps into the light of the front foyer. It's not Andrea, and I can see what she has in her arms. It's an infant. This is the second baby I have seen in my scope recently. A vision of Hugo's gun with the hammer back and the muzzle touching baby Chastity's neck pops into my head.

"A baby! She's holding a baby," I yell, forgetting to sound disinterested. "She's approaching the front door. Interior door to the back room is still open."

Now, I concentrate with everything I have on the black space behind the open door to the back. If I see a bad guy with a gun, he's going to get some.

The woman maneuvers around downed ceiling tiles and shattered glass, then gingerly opens the front door and steps outside. As she comes out, I realize she's only a teenager.

I dial out the magnification a little, but keep concentrating on the open door to the interior. In my peripheral vision, I see Hauser and his team call her to the left, toward the four-one corner. When she gets past the front windows, they rush her, snatching the baby from her arms and pulling her around the corner. Though I can't see it, I knew that both she and the baby are being searched.

The door closes, and at the same time, Hauser advises that they have the girl and the baby in custody. Just like that, the action is over. The scene becomes as stationary as it has been for the past several hours.

I hazard a glance at my watch, and see that it is now 2:55 p.m. Five minutes until the deadline.

I want to take a look at Slater's position again, but there's no way I'm going to risk getting off the gun again, even for a minute. I hate Slater for goofing off on scope, and blame him for the fact that *I* hadn't been doing what I was supposed to be doing when the hostage came out.

"CP to SERT. HNT reports the suspect hung up when they asked for an extension on the deadline. Everyone keep sharp."

Two fifty-nine p.m. One minute to go.

The next sixty seconds are right up there with the worst of my life. I just know I'll hear a gunshot and a body will be dragged into the parking lot by an hysterical hostage. I am also quite certain now that this will end up in a shot of opportunity, and I will have to kill again. I desperately don't want to do that. Not again. Not ever again.

Three o'clock comes and goes, and nothing happens. By 3:15, I am more than a little relieved. The fact that the suspect has given us an irrefutable deadline that has been refuted is a very good sign.

It speaks well of our negotiators, but even more, it tells me that the perpetrators haven't thought the whole thing out well enough. Maybe they're "allowing" us to have more time, which in fact means that *they* need more time to figure out what to do now that their bluff has been called. Perhaps now they will try to bargain for good terms of surrender.

In any event, the expired deadline signals a tenuous, but definite, shifting of authority. The person or people inside Northwest Healing with automatic weapons are no longer in complete charge of the way things will go from this point forward.

I feel good about this, and see it as a very positive development—the first step toward a resolution of the crisis. That's just fine for me, because I've decided I am not going to shoot anyone else in my life if I can possibly avoid it. As of this moment, at exactly 3:16 p.m., I make the decision that this will be my last callout. I am going to quit the team. In fact, I decide to rethink the idea of even staying on the police department. I am, after all, an Oregon bar-certified attorney. That's how much I don't want to have to kill again.

"CP to SERT, HNT update. Stand by for the release of another hostage."

I dial right into the front doors, hoping against hope that this one will be Andrea, and not ten seconds later, the interior door opens again.

A middle-aged, potbellied man appears in the doorway. He is clearly scared, glancing furtively back and forth like a deer that inadvertently stepped out of the woods onto a busy city street.

"White male, beige shirt and tan pants coming out," I say calmly.

"Reaction team, copy."

Slowly, the man comes though the interior door to the front doors, then steps outside.

I can see him sigh as he steps into the afternoon sunshine. In my peripheral view, I see members of the reaction team beginning to call him to the one-four corner. He starts walking toward them.

I peer intently into the still-open interior door, but as was the case the last time, I can see nothing but blackness. I dial the magnification out a bit as the distance between the hostage and the reaction team begins to close.

There is a flash from the blackness beyond the interior door. Simultaneously, a puff of red mist blows toward me in the breeze from the man's head. His legs give way, and he crumples to the ground. A fraction of a second later, the crack of a high-powered rifle shot reaches my ears.

The interior door closes, and I hear my own voice make a unrecognizable, high-pitched noise.

I zero in on the hostage as multiple voices try to get on the air at the same time. He is positioned basically on his stomach, his legs folded unnaturally beneath him, and his head intact with the exception of the top quarter, which is missing. A pool of thick, gelatinous dark red blood of a type I've come to associate only with gunshot wounds to the head gathers slowly around his face.

A wave of sorrow passes over me; not so much for this unfortunate hostage, I hate to admit, but for myself. I want to cry, but I can't. Briefly, I try to, but nothing happens. Once again, I blame Slater. He refused to take side one on this callout, and now I have to watch this, and will no doubt have to kill the man responsible.

It is amazing how strongly I do not want to be on the gun any more; how, since I have just resigned from the team in my mind, I want to secure my rifle, abandon my position, and go home and wrap my arms around my daughter. The need to do this is physically pulling at my stomach, and I think I might be sick if I don't.

But I can't, and I know it, so I function on autopilot, doing what I've been trained to do, and unsuccessfully reminding myself that I am a hard-ass cop who is unfazed by such things as watching innocent people being executed in front of me.

When the air clears, I report that the shot had come from the open interior door, and that I had been unable to see anything but the door closing afterward.

"CP to SERT. HNT reports the suspect says the hostage just bought us another six hours. That's 2100 hours for those of you who can't count. Same consequences apply for our failure to deliver the ransom at that time. After that it will be a hostage every ten minutes. Reaction team, rejoin entry. Hauser, meet me at the van. CP out."

The reaction team rejoins the rest of entry around the corner, and Hauser marches off to the command post. The radio grows quiet and nothing moves. The body of the dead hostage lies baking in the hot August sunshine.

I think of Andrea, still being held captive inside Northwest Healing. The last time we'd made love, her bruises were still visible, but just barely. And now, she is in there, one of those waiting to see if they will be next. She must have heard the shot. If hostages hadn't been told what was going on, they must certainly have figured it out by now.

After ten or fifteen minutes of quiet, the urge to see what Slater is doing becomes overpowering. He'd better be glued to the rifle now, knowing that we are under a deadline with a stone-cold killer inside promising to kill again.

I don't want to get off scope myself to check, but I decide if I want a good, detailed report for Capelko I had better. Briefly rolling off scope, I move to where I can see his position. Slater is lying behind his rifle, not looking through the scope but apparently not goofing off, either. Scanning with the naked eye is acceptable and essential to avoiding the eyestrain of peering through magnification optics for hours at a time.

Just as I am about to move away, I notice something very odd. The manhole cover has been removed from the concrete pylon, and is now leaning up against it.

Why the hell would he remove the manhole cover? Those things are incredibly heavy. This behavior of his has me totally baffled. Bizarre stuff like this on such an intense callout, on *any* callout, is way beyond unacceptable.

I tear a page out of my shooting log and began making notes about Slater's behavior. I am going to make goddamn certain there is an internal affairs investigation about this. Slater's days on the team are over, and I hope his days with the department are numbered. Slacking off when a fellow officer is being held hostage is a career ender in my book, and knowing Chief Moody as I do, I bet it is in his, too. Moody can be pretty slimy at times, but he came up from the ranks, and at least somewhat of a "troops" kind of guy.

Less than a minute later, I am back on scope myself, furious but functioning.

One of the dead man's eyes had been obliterated with the top of his skull. The one he has left is staring right at me, sightlessly scrutinizing my every move.

19

THE DECISION WAS made two hours ago to leave the body where it lies rather than risk officers to recover it. In the meantime, absolutely nothing has happened. The rules of engagement have not changed. We can't be at a shot of opportunity if we don't know what the suspect looks like. Plus, since there's a good chance there are multiple suspects, what good will it do to kill one, then have to deal with the other afterward? Normally, if there were two suspects, we would try for a simultaneous shot on both at the same time. Slater and I have trained on countdown shots enough that I know we can do it. At least, before the Route callout, that is.

The radio is preternaturally quiet. Nobody has anything to report. The only update we've had from HNT in the past two hours said all attempts to contact the hostage takers were being ignored.

Since we are clearly here for the long haul on this one, I figure arrangements are probably being made with the Portland SERT team to relieve us. On protracted callouts, we usually rotate in shifts with Portland SERT, per a reciprocal agreement made years ago.

At 5:45, Capelko gets on the radio with an unprecedented announcement an that both shocks and surprises me. "CP to SERT. The suspect has been in contact with the families of the celebrity hostages by cell phone, and has made arrangements with them for delivery of the ransom. This was not our idea, but we are going to comply with their wishes. We are arranging for a peaceful solution to the situation that will allow for them to escape for now. We are also developing intelligence that we will be able to use to track them down afterward.

"Now for the good news. The suspect is telling us that Andrea is alive and uninjured. Our agreement to the suspect's demands is contingent upon this. More will follow as it becomes available as to how the suspects will be allowed to leave, etcetera. Until then, scouts will be coming around to all perimeter positions to provide relief if needed. CP out."

A tremendous burden is lifted from me at the news about Andrea. Anything, even capitulation to terrorist demands, is worth hearing that. For the first time since getting the initial page, I feel that I might just be able to get out of this without having to shoot anyone.

At the same time, the paying of the ransom is unheard of. And the idea that we will let the suspects go? Absolutely unprecedented. I don't believe it for a moment. Capelko wouldn't stand for that, although I suspect it's something the chief might be open to.

Nonetheless, I am glad to hear it. It means two things. One, Andrea will remain safe and will likely be released unharmed. And two, I won't have to shoot anyone. The more I think about it, the better I feel about it.

A short time after Capelko's announcement, the scouts find their way to my position.

"Ben, you need anything?" asks Carlos Vega.

"Yeah, I need to pee. Keep an eye on the place for me for a sec?" Vega takes up my binoculars, and I rolled off scope, grateful for a stretch and a pee.

I belly crawl to the roof hatch, go down, and find a bathroom. I am so elated at the thought of Andrea coming out of there safely that I feel energized. On the way back to my position, I check on Slater. I am relieved to see that he is peering intently into his scope, finally acting the way a sniper is supposed to act.

When I get back on scope a moment later, Vega says, "Now for the good news. Capelko made that last broadcast specifically to butter the suspect up. HNT thinks it's likely that he, or they, are listening to the SERT operation on Andrea's radio. From now on, we will assume that our communications have been compromised, even that we're being watched."

"They think they're that sophisticated?"

"Short answer? Hell yes. Whoever is doing this is smart."

"So, are we really getting the ransom?"

"Oh yeah, that part's true. The only thing that isn't like he said is this. There's no way these bastards are getting out of here after what they've done. We're going to promise them the moon and give them the money, but when push comes to shove, we're going to end it with a shot. You're gonna earn your pay again today, Ben."

So much for my relief at not having to take a shot. I manage to keep my voice level, and say, "What's the plan?"

"We think they're going to use a covered pile to try to make it to a getaway vehicle."

A covered pile is when the bad guy surrounds himself with hostages and leaves the location under a tarp or a blanket of some sort, denying the police (specifically the sniper) a target. The tactic to counter it is to rush the pile with as many men as possible, pull the cover, then locate and shoot the bad guy with a contact wound to the head. The actual shooting of the bad guy is generally done by a member of the team that rushes the pile as opposed to the sniper, unless, of course, the pile isn't covered. Then, the sniper is the one to take the shot.

We've trained in the maneuver numerous times. In a covered pile situation, it is the sniper who controls the action, calling the team in if he doesn't have a shot, before the pile reaches its destination, giving them whatever intel he can get.

"Okay," I say, nodding. "That makes sense. But let me run this by you. We don't know what this guy looks like. He's obviously prepared for this quite well. What if he gives everyone in the pile a gun and a black suitcase or whatever the money comes in? How will we know who to shoot?"

"How am I supposed to know? But here's the deal. Vince says that whatever conveyance he demands for his escape *will not move,* regardless of how many hostages he takes. Your orders are simple. If the pile makes it to a chopper or a bus or whatever without a shot on the bad guy, you are to disable the vehicle however you have to. Understand? That comes directly from Capelko, who got it directly from Moody, who got it directly from the mayor, who got it from the governor. Nothing about this will go over the air except the word shoot. When you hear that word, take it out. And if the pile makes it there, you *will* get the order, so be prepared. If it's a chopper, we'll try to get you some kind of target to shoot. But no matter what, that thing is *not* to take off. Just do whatever you have to in order to prevent it from leaving. If it's a vehicle. take out the tires, the engine block, whatever. As many shots as it takes. Just listen for a cease-fire, because entry will be right on top of it to finish the job. Understand?"

Feeling a little sick to my stomach, I said, "Yeah. Jesus Christ."

"Damn straight. Now I gotta go tell Slater the same thing. Incidentally, Vince will do everything in his power to see to it that this is done on side one. We do not want to leave this up to Slater."

"Thanks," I say, even though I'd rather see it the other way around.

"Lastly, take this." He gives me a Nextel phone. "This is a direct line to Capelko in the hot seat. Slater gets one, too. We know the bad guy can't tap into that."

He moves on to go tell Slater, then everyone else, of the plan.

I should have known better than to think I could get out of this nightmarish scenario so easily. Now not only might I have to locate and shoot a moving suspect surrounded by a group of innocents, but I might have to figure out how to shoot an idling helicopter full of hostages without somehow blowing it up.

Right about now, the prospect of a simple shot of opportunity on the suspect, without the likelihood of inflicting casualties on hostages, sounds pretty damn inviting.

At 2008 hours, my Nextel buzzes. "Ben? You there?"

"Yeah. Go ahead, Vince."

"Okay, this is the deal. The money is on the way, in an armored car. Two suitcases, both black pull-along types. Entry will deliver them into the foyer area, and a hostage will be dispatched to bring them into the building. Andrea will be made to open them in case they are booby-trapped, and the suspect will want some time to count the money. After that, he will give us specific instructions regarding his getaway. He's also asked for a twenty-four by twenty-four-foot blue plastic tarp, so, we're probably looking at a large covered pile."

"Copy. Any word on his method of escape?"

"Just getting to that. He's demanded a six-passenger Bell Jet Ranger with fully fueled tanks to be waiting with the money. He's agreed to a police pilot. So, that's the arrangement. Obviously, we'll do a covered pile assault if at all possible. But if he makes it to the chopper, you *will* get the command to shoot."

"Damn," I said, not really knowing what else to say. "Okay, well, can you get at least get the pilot to recommend a target for me?"

"That's already been taken care of. Don't shoot anywhere near the engine, which is located directly beneath the center of the rotor. The pilot is an Oregon State Police pilot, and he's going to land it in such a manner that you can get one under the rotor and through the windscreen from the right rear through the center of the front. Got that? Right rear to center front, right between the seats. The pilot will be seated in the left seat, and someone else will probably be in the right seat. The chopper is being rigged with false engine failure alarms, which the pilot will activate on your signal. When he hits that switch, it will set also off teargas canisters rigged on both skids. At first, the bad guy will think it's smoke from the engine, and by the time he realizes what's going on, it'll be raining flashbangs and entry will be using hostage rescue tactics. That's the plan, anyway."

"Jesus Christ, this is unbelievable."

"Believe it, because it's all going to happen real goddamn soon. You're going to be in for quite a show. All you have to do is shoot out the windshield to convince him it's real and get him to duck. Entry'll take it from there. You understand?"

"Yeah, I understand."

"Okay. The money will be here thirty minutes before the deadline, and they're working on the chopper now. It should get here at around the same time as the money. I'm gonna need you at a hundred percent, Ben. Are you?"

"I'm fine. Anyway, do I have a choice?" I ask back, just as sincerely.

"Nope. That's why we pay you the big bucks. I'll be in touch."

At 8:18 p.m., my Nextel chirps again. It's Capelko, telling me the money has arrived at the command post. Fifteen million dollars in cash, in two large, black suitcases delivered by armored car. Pio Cantelli had to do little more than snap his fingers to get it. Incredible.

"Ben," Capelko says, "everything is going to depend on what you say. If it's a covered pile, then we go on your command. If you have a shot, then take it. If for any reason they get to the chopper, don't wait for my command to fire. Put one right through the windshield the moment the last person gets on. That last person may be our bad guy, and we don't want him running loose while we're trying to kill him, so make sure the last guy gets aboard, then do it."

"Got it, Vince."

A few minutes later, at 8:22 p.m., the whop-whop-whop of an approaching helicopter breaks the evening stillness. In moments, the bird is overhead, and then it makes a sideways approach into the wind and sets down in an empty area of the parking lot about eighty yards away from me.

The pilot has done an outstanding job. The chopper is facing Northwest Healing, with the cockpit situated at my two o'clock and the tail at my eight. From this angle, I have plenty of room to get my round under the rotor disc and through the center of the cockpit between the front seats with a foot to spare on either side. I should easily be able pull off such a shot, even considering the rotor wash effect on the bullet. Plus, the pilot has put it down in such a manner that the pile will have to traverse my field of fire on its way to the chopper.

Capelko has reduced the perimeter to one man per side. Everyone else is ordered to join entry in a delivery truck, which will be used to deliver the assault team to the pile from around the side of the building. The team will make the assault when the pile is approximately halfway between the building and the helicopter. Canines from surrounding agencies have filled the gap in case the bad guy, or guys, make a break for it.

In the end, we're going to have to play it by ear, and everything will to depend on what I say and do.

Eight fifty-five p.m.

"Command post to SERT. Entry will be delivering the money in one minute. Keep sharp. We still have no suspect description, so we are still at compromised authority. We want this to go smoothly, to get Andrea and the other hostages back. Hauser, is your team ready?"

"Affirm."

"Okay. Make the delivery."

"Entry, copy. We're moving."

Through wide magnification, I watch the team advance on the front doors. Four shooters lead the way, forming a deadly shield for the two money handlers. Both of them pull heavy, bulging black suitcases behind them with one hand and have pistols at the ready in the other.

My eye is automatically drawn to the suitcases. Each holds seven-point-five million dollars in paper currency. It's mind boggling. And they say crime doesn't pay.

I expect no trouble whatsoever at this stage of the game. For the moment, we're marching to the tune of the suspect's drum. But knowing Vince Capelko, I wouldn't be surprised if he'd wanted to put Vega and McKenzie, our two smallest guys, in the suitcases to jump out with guns blazing in a Trojan Suitcase attack from within.

No matter what the arguments, the bottom line is the suitcases contain nothing but cold, hard cash, and no there are surprises with respect to the delivery. Andrea will open them to ensure there are no booby traps, and once that's done, she will be released. The suspect will count the money, and then give us further instructions.

On the suspect's command, the pilot will start the engine and spool it up to full power so they can take off immediately, and then the pile will come out. According to Capelko's last Nextel conversation with me, the suspects say if they think an assault is underway, they will mow down his hostages in a suicidal rampage, then go after SERT members until they all "fall in battle." Capelko tells me he's been using the plural since negotiations began.

It has already occurred to me that this might be a group effort, and the "hostages" might really *all* be bad guys. We wouldn't know until the last shot's been fired.

Regardless, I know what my role will be in all of this. How the hell are we supposed to pull off this kind of stunt without civilian casualties? I can see me shooting at the windshield, and the next thing I know, the whole chopper explodes, killing ten innocent people.

The delivery team makes it to the front doors, actually stepping around the fallen hostage. It is getting dark now, and pre-erected lights have been switched on to illuminate the building. I keep my scope on daylight setting.

One of the shooters holds the door, and one by one, the two draggers heave their heavy loads into the foyer. The team then makes an orderly retreat, walking backward, now being guided by the draggers.

The bags sit there for a full ten minutes. Then the interior door opens. "Interior door opening," I report. "Female juvenile in the lobby. She's pulling one of the bags inside... Now she's gone."

A moment later, "Okay, the female's back. Taking the second bag inside... She's gone and the door's closed."

And that was that. Please God, I prayed, Let her come out now. Please! "CP to SERT! HNT update... Okay... They say Andrea's on her way out. Entry, stand by to receive!"

"Ready!"

The interior door opens.

"Geller to CP! Door's opening!"

And then the ultimate humiliating indignity. I press the transmit button without realizing it. "Oh God, no. You bastards!"

"CP to Geller, update!"

"It's Andrea, Vince, only, she's... She's naked!"

Trying to hold her head erect, but with tears streaming down her face, Andrea walks out. Her hands keep finding their way between her legs in a feeble attempt to preserve her dignity, but she obviously knows the effort is an exercise in futility. It is the ultimate insult. We made them promise to deliver her without injury, and they have apparently done so. But they certainly gave themselves the last word, as well as a stark reminder of who is calling the shots.

But in so doing, they have committed a serious error. Like the Japanese after Pearl Harbor, all they have really done is to wake the sleeping giant.

As I watch my beautiful Andrea being roughly grabbed and dragged from my view in a confusion of woodland camouflage, pink flesh, and a fleeting glance of raven pubic hair, I vow that I would personally kill the motherfucker who has done this.

20

TWO O'CLOCK A.M.

Something is wrong. So far, everything has gone just the way the bad guy had dictated, right up through the delivery of the money and the humiliating release of Andrea, but after that, absolutely nothing has happened. No movement, no contact, no response to HNT—nothing.

Andrea was released nearly five hours ago. We'd gotten word an hour later that she was in great spirits despite how she was treated. She was unharmed, and had not been assaulted in any way. In typical Andrea style, she had refused to go home, choosing instead to remain and feed the negotiating team vital intelligence. At the news that she hadn't been assaulted, I again uttered a silent, agnostic prayer to the great I-Don't-Know-Who in appreciation of her intact sanctity. I was certain she had been raped.

The plan had called for the suspect to count the money and then make his departure. But since Andrea had walked out, there had been no communications from the bad guy whatsoever. He had not called us, nor would he respond when we called him. The helicopter sits like a giant dead dragonfly in the parking lot, the pilot still awaiting orders to start the engine.

We are exhausted, having been here more than fifteen hours. Two hours ago, Portland SERT arrived to relieve us, but Vince wants us to finish this one ourselves, after what had happened with Andrea. To a man, we all agree.

Twice since her release, I had checked Slater's position. The first, about an hour after she came out, he was not there. The manhole cover was still off, his gun was still set up, but Slater was not visible anywhere. The second time, about an hour after that, he was lying next to the rifle, the manhole cover had been replaced, and the phone was now nowhere in sight.

Something about this bothers me far beyond his inattention on the gun, but I can't put my finger on it. With everything else going on, it is simply too mentally taxing to dwell on. All I can do is record the times I check on him, and what he is doing, in my log.

"CP to SERT. We are going to use the robot to deliver the throw-phone and have a look around in there. Geller, keep a sharp eye for any activity whatsoever as the robot goes in. He may still try for a covered pile."

"Geller, copy."

The robot, a multi-tracked futuristic looking contraption which is operated remotely by members of the explosives disposal unit, can go just about anywhere. It can negotiate stairwells, tight turns, and grades, and can carry, pick up, or deliver payloads weighing up to fifty pounds. It is equipped with lights, cameras, and microphones through which a negotiator can communicate, and could be armed with a specially adapted shotgun or pistol.

In this case, EDU will use it to deliver the phone. Once inside, it will have a look around the interior using intelligence gleaned from Andrea.

After several minutes, I hear the electronic whirring of the robot as it makes its way across the parking lot. I track its progress using peripheral vision while peering intently at the glass front and the interior door of Northwest Healing.

The robot maneuvers around the body of the fallen hostage, then crunches its way over the broken glass of the foyer. It pauses near the still-closed interior door.

A telescoping arm extends, and literally knocks on the door. There is no response, and even from this distance, I can hear a tinny voice identifying itself as the police robot, saying we want to reestablish contact. There is no response. It then announces it is going to enter the building and deliver a telephone.

The robot tries to force the door, but is unable to do so. I zero in on the thing and watched it lower a shotgun. I know from previous training it is loaded with a heavy lead bag known as an Avon round, which will take the deadbolt apart.

A tiny red dot appears where the bolt slides through the jamb, and then there is a cloud of smoke and dust. As it clears, I can see that the door is now open. The sound reaches me a moment later,

The robot's treads change angles, and it makes its way up the two stairs and into the back part of the building where I can no longer see it.

"Robot's inside," I announce over the radio.

Half an hour later, Capelko gets on the radio.

"CP to SERT, EDU reports they are unable to locate or contact the suspect. The hostages have all been able to communicate freely with the robot through locked doors which it is unable to breech. We're going to make a hot entry, so perimeter units, stand by."

I don't understand it. Northwest Healing isn't all that big, and it's my guess that the robot has been able to make a relatively decent search, yet it has turned up nothing with respect to the bad guy. Had he somehow managed to get away?

Then I remember Slater's inattention on side three. If the suspect had broken out while Slater was playing around off scope, I will see him brought up on criminal charges.

But a breakout by the suspect on side three is still unlikely, because in addition to Slater, we've had a perimeter unit stationed back there since the callout began.

No, no one had ever escaped a SERT perimeter before, and that hasn't happened today. He's still in there, perhaps so well hidden that he thinks he can wait it out until the team eventually leaves, hoping we assume he somehow escaped. But we will find him. We have dogs, X-ray scanners, and all the time in the world.

"CP to SERT, entry team moving! Side three diversion, *now!*"

A tremendous explosion from the back of the building shatters the stillness of the night. Simultaneously, a panel truck speeds from around side four to the front and crashes right through the plate glass window. The truck slides to a stop on broken glass, and the team spills out.

They make a beeline for the interior door, tossing flashbangs from the moment they step out. From my position, it sounds more like the Fourth of July than a SWAT assault on a barricaded hostage situation.

"Code red," I announce, as the team makes entry into the building. Through the open door, I see flashes and hear the concussions, which make it look as though a thunderstorm is raging inside. Over it all, I hear louder concussions, as members of EDU cross-trained to go in with SERT on hot entries, blow the steel doors to the rooms containing the hostages with detonation cord.

"Hostages secure!" comes a voice on the radio.

"Front room secure!"

"Back right, secure!"

"Back left, secure!"

"I got a crawlspace entrance in the rear closet," someone says.

"Hold for the dog!"

A canine officer and his partner are brought in from their place on the perimeter.

I can't hear them shouting for the suspect to give up or face the dog, but I knew that's what they are doing. Faintly, the dog's barking reaches my ears.

The silence on the radio tells me after only a few moments that the dog's search had been as unsuccessful as that of the team.

Hauser's voice came on. "Entry, form up in the front room! Secondary search, two-man cells. Go!"

I can see nothing through the scope. Instead, I move to look over at Slater's position, only to see that he is lying on his back, his rifle unattended, his hands clasped behind his head. There is a smile on his face.

"Geller to Slater," I say over the radio. "Do you have any movement on side three?"

Slater's only movement is his hand lazily pressing the transmit button on his lapel mike. He never moves from his back. "Negative, all locked up tight."

He's not even looking in the direction of the building. I want to say something to him, to call him on it, but I decide to save it for my report to Capelko.

A third and a fourth search prove equally fruitless. The sun comes up, and still the body of the dead man lies on the sidewalk, and the rest of the hostages remain cuffed on the floor of Northwest Healing. The team, refusing to give up their hold on the building, remains inside.

At 10:00, twenty-four hours after the callout began, the hostages are led from the building and taken under guard to Stratton PD headquarters on a bus. There, they will be debriefed by detectives from the Multnomah County Major Crimes Team.

Once they are gone, Capelko calls for the perimeter to be broken down and the snipers to come in. Though nobody wants to admit it, there is no longer any way around it. Somehow, the suspect has eluded us and seems to have made a clean getaway.

With the fifteen million dollars.

21

WE DEBRIEF FOR an hour and are then told we were free to leave. Because we have worked over twenty-four hours straight, everyone is given an administrative day off for our next shift, which meant I won't have to go to work tonight.

Most guys take off, but I elect to hang around. I go out to watch the body snatchers from the medical examiner's office pick up the dead guy. A detective is with the medical examiner, taking charge of the slain hostage's personal effects.

The detective, Carl Jostens, opens the man's wallet and removes the driver's license. He writes the information down on a tablet in his notebook.

"Was he from around here?" I ask.

"Yeah," Jostens said. "Local Stratton address. As a matter of fact, this is his place. This guy is the founder of Northwest Healing."

"No kidding? Can I see his DL?"

Jostens handed me the guy's driver's license. I take one look at it, and something clicks.

"Hey," I said excitedly. "Tim Connors. I know this guy. I contacted this dude the night of the last SERT callout, the one on Wainwood. He ran into a cop car, and before I got the chance to do field sobriety tests on him, that call came out.

"But there was something else... I remember I thought I knew him then, too, but I can't remember where. But after that Wainwood callout, I just forgot about it."

"What was he driving when you stopped him that night?" asked Jostens. "We need to match vehicles to victims, to see if we can maybe locate the suspect's car. It's a long shot, but it's something we need to do."

"It was a truck. A green truck, with a load of dirt and shovels."

"Dirt and shovels? On graveyard shift? This guy doesn't look like a gardener to me. He looks like a businessman."

"Yeah, to me, too," I muse, wondering where in the hell I had contacted him before. I speak briefly with the two uniforms who had been assigned to remain with all the detectives and crime scene people just in case the bad guy was somehow still there and comes out of hiding, then seek out Capelko, who, along with me, is one of the few remaining tactical people at the scene.

He offers to give me a ride home, which I gladly accept. We both remain silent as we pass the feeding frenzy in the media staging area

Capelko is probably trying to figure out how the bad guy made his getaway, and how that might affect him personally. I wouldn't want to be in his shoes. Unfortunately, I have another burden to lay upon his overworked shoulders.

"Vince," I say as soon as we neared my temporary trailer home, "there's some stuff you need to know about Slater on this callout."

Capelko sighs heavily. He's the type of guy who likes a tight ship, run with no bullshit and interpersonal problems. Capelko is smart enough to see that a guy like Slater can slowly poison a unit as tight as SERT from the inside, but he's also the kind of guy to lash out at those whom he views as not being able to keep family secrets in the family. I am toeing the line, but what I have to say has to be said.

"I already know that you two have been having this little personal rivalry for too damn long now," he says.

"That's not what this is about. I can handle that. Slater's an asshole, and I'm sure the feeling's mutual, but what I have to say isn't about our petty little problems. What I have to say is about something that can affect the entire team."

"I'm listening."

"Tonight, on the callout, I could see Slater's position, and you probably won't believe what I saw."

"What do you mean, you could see Slater's position? How could you do that while you were on scope? You're my primary sniper, not my primary babysitter."

"I know, Vince, but I had my reasons for checking, trust me. I only had to shift about three feet, and then I could see his position. I wasn't off scope for more than a couple of minutes total."

"A couple minutes? While a guy with a fucking machine gun was holding hostages? Was *shooting* hostages? Was holding *Andrea?*"

That, I can't take. Maybe it's just because I've been working for twenty-seven straight hours, or because of all the crap that's happened in my life over Andrea, but I snap at him, "Goddamn it, Vince, don't throw her up in my face like that. You got some real problems in this outfit, and you're too damn blind to take a look at them. Don't toss Andrea's name out at me like it's my fault for what happened to her, and if you have something to say about me and her, I'd rather you just say it than snicker like a schoolboy behind my fucking back!"

Capelko's expression is one more shock than anything else. Then he smiles, which is a rarity. I want to stay angry, but with him giving me that stupid grin, I can't. I smile back and we both shared a brief laugh.

"Okay, what did Slater do, fall asleep on the gun?"

"Worse than that, Vince. He ignored it. I checked him out long before anything really happened, and he was sitting up, talking on the phone. His rifle was set up, but he wasn't even near it."

"When?"

"About an hour or so into the callout. And it wasn't a cell phone. I mean, it looked like a regular handset, with a line that went to something behind this sewer pylon he was lying next to. I was thinking a satellite phone or something, because I've never seen one like it outside a building before."

"Is that it?"

"No, later on, he wasn't even there. I just glanced briefly at him, and his rifle was all set up, but he was nowhere to be seen."

"Are you sure, Ben? I mean, that sounds a little, uh, hard to believe. When was he not there?"

"It was two forty-five, right before the first deadline. I thought maybe he was taking a leak, but I looked all around, and he simply wasn't there. And then, afterward, when we were waiting for the money to be delivered, he was back. He disappeared during a SERT callout, when he should have been on the gun."

"Anything else?"

"Little stuff, like the way he cleared away the grass in front of his rifle. He just stood up and walked around, totally visible to the target. And for whatever reason, he pulled the manhole cover off that sewer pylon. Just you-simply-don't-do-that-kind-of-stuff-on-a-callout kind of shit. Come on, that's pretty fucking weird, Vince."

Capelko says nothing, so I continue. "Well, to me, it's unacceptable. Either Slater's gone, or I am. I won't work with a guy who does that kind of crap. So if you keep him, I go, and that can be how your primary sniper conducts himself on callouts. Sorry, but that's it. Him or me." I don't mention that I'm considering quitting the team, and maybe even the department.

"Ben, what you're saying is almost inconceivable. The guy's a professional shooter. He's a good cop. There was a fellow officer being held hostage in there. What I want to know is, why didn't you say anything at the time? I mean, you've got a side three sniper who isn't even at his gun, and you chose not to say anything?"

"I don't know, Vince. I probably should have. I thought of it, but it was the middle of a callout. I figured that if I said something, he would hear me and have time to come up with an excuse. And obviously he would be back on the gun if anyone came around to check on him. I know it sounds lame, and I probably should have, but I didn't."

"Well, you're right, you didn't. And to me, it seems you would have. I don't know. I'll talk to Slater about it."

"I'm serious, Vince. Either he's off the team, or I am. That guy's gonna get someone killed."

Capelko doesn't say anything else. He pulls up in front of the house where my friend's fifth wheel is parked, and I get out without another word.

I try calling Andrea, but all I get is a busy signal. I am too tired to go over there, so I leave her a voicemail message telling her to call me, and I go to bed.

I get up around nine in the evening. I have two messages from Andrea and one from Leah. Leah is crying, wanting to know when I am coming home.

I call Andrea first, and we talk for almost an hour. She doesn't want to see me or anyone else today, after her humiliating naked walk out of Northwest Healing. She had been given a few days off work on paid administrative leave, but is sure that she will be facing some sort of disciplinary action after going into Northwest Healing alone without backup.

She tells me that she was the first on scene, and the moment she stepped out of the car, a witness came running out of the building screaming about shots being fired. The bad guy had just disappeared inside, and the building was wide open. The witness, whose wife was still inside, literally pushed her toward the doorway, insisting that she do something. She said all she could think of was something I had taught her as a new rookie.

I had told her when she's in doubt, do *something,* even if it's the wrong thing. Indecision will get you killed more often than the wrong decision. Well, she couldn't decide what to do. Backup was coming but was still a few minutes away. She had the element of surprise. She had good communications with everybody and their brother in law enforcement. She had the advantage of training.

She confesses that winning the departmental medal of valor for rescuing Dan Hollister had influenced her, too. She felt she had an impossibly high standard to live up to. So she went in.

She was taken captive immediately. Apparently, the bad guy had been watching from the shadows, and when he saw her make her approach, he simply hid behind the door. Andrea had followed all her training on making an entry, but without backup, there was no way to cover all the angles. The moment she stepped through the inner doorway, she felt the rifle barrel behind her ear.

She'd been disarmed, searched, and locked away with the other hostages. The suspect appeared to be alone, and never removed his black ski mask. After he locked the hostages all away, she didn't see him until he came to release the teenage girl and her baby.

At three, he had come in, taken the founder of Northwest Healing, and locked the door again. Moments later, they all heard the shot, and there was no doubt among them that he'd been killed. All of them knew that any one of them might be next.

The next time they saw him was when he came for her. He took her out at gunpoint into the main warehouse area and told her to strip naked. When she wouldn't do it, he popped her in the chest with the rifle barrel, knocking her down and leaving a 7.62-mm circular bruise between her breasts. He then placed the barrel of the rifle in her mouth and screamed at her to do it or she would die. She was sure she would be raped.

She stripped. By this time, the suitcases were already in the building, and had already been opened. After she took her clothes off, he told her to get out. When she opened the door, she saw the dead hostage's body lying on the ground and was certain she'd suffer the same fate, but the shot never came.

She said she knew I was the side one sniper, and would be the first to see her. She said the walk was the longest of her life, and she wished the shot would come, but then Hauser and Pole and several other guys grabbed her and dragged her around the side of the building. There was no blanket or anything to cover her with, so Hauser dropped his vest and equipment, ripped his own shirt off, and gingerly put it around her shoulders. It was big enough to sufficiently cover her, and she was taken to the command post, where someone had produced a paper suit of the type we make prisoners wear when we confiscate their clothing as evidence.

Then, clad only in the paper suit and a jacket, she refused transport home and insisted on staying to provide intelligence to HNT.

I told her that made her a hero again, but she wouldn't hear it. The bottom line was, she'd been humiliated, but not hurt. Everything that belonged to her had been recovered, even her gun. The only thing she couldn't find was her Law Enforcement Memorial silver dollar, which must have dropped out of her pocket somewhere along the line.

She tells me she's not ready to see me yet, which I completely understand, and after a few minutes of niceties, we run out of things to say, and hang up with a promise to see one another soon.

Next, I drive home, where I am coldly received by Sharon, and warmly received by Leah, whom I wake with a light kiss and a song I often sing to her at bedtime. Leah can't stay out of my arms. She sits on my lap and we watch TV for a while, and then I put her back to bed. Sharon and I talk, but there isn't much to say. I tell her I want my family more than anything else, but after her friend saw Andrea and me in the restaurant, she doesn't believe me. I can't blame her. With nothing resolved, I go back to my little trailer.

I try to go to sleep, but I can't. What eats me is not Andrea, my family problems, or even Slater's behavior on the callout. What bothers me is that dead hostage, Tim Connors. I just cannot recall how I know the guy, apart from his crashing into an officer the night of the Bowman callout.

I recall wondering if I had arrested him before, because his name was so familiar. This bugs me so much that I drive to Stratton PD and begin looking through the old notebooks I keep in my locker to see if I could find his name.

And that's when it hit me. I *had* written his name down, but it wasn't in a police notebook. It was in the surveillance notebook I'd been keeping on Slater, to see if he was in collusion with Pammi Route on her lawsuit.

I rip open my equipment bag, and pull out that notebook. There it is, two weeks after the Route callout. A green pickup truck parked in Slater's driveway, registered to Tim Connors. I had checked up on Connors, to see if he was a lawyer, but he wasn't, and I had assumed he was a friend of Slater's and forgotten about him.

Then he rear-ended a cop the night of the Laszlo Bowman callout. In the same green pickup, only this time it had a load of dirt and shovels.

It's coincidence enough that Connors was at the accident scene, and then he next shows up as a dead hostage at Northwest Healing. It's mind-blowing that he had been visiting Bob Slater just two weeks earlier. Slater, the ex-marine loner cop, friends with Connors, the conservative-looking businessman who doubled as a midnight gardner? I don't think so. There's definitely something wrong with that.

Being a cop, I'm naturally cynical, and I don't believe in coincidences. Not of this magnitude, anyway.

I run downstairs and grab a computer terminal. I look Connors up in PPDS, and in moments, I have an arrest report in my hands from five years ago. Slater had arrested him on illegal gaming charges when Slater was a detective. It seems Connors had a gambling problem. There is no other record of him in the system.

But Connors had gone on to found Northwest Healing. And he was murdered at the grand opening. Now my radar is really pinging. This is more than just coincidence. Why was Connors out in the vicinity of Northwest Healing the night of the Bowman callout? Why was he at the home of Slater, his arresting officer from five years ago, just two weeks before?

As I sit at the terminal, the door opens, and weary detectives begin streaming through the office on their way back to the Investigations section.

"What's going on?" I ask.

"We just found out how the bad guy got out of Northwest Healing," one of them says.

22

JUST AFTER MIDNIGHT, I join the detectives at their briefing in the investigations war room. A large diagram of Northwest Healing has been superimposed over an engineering plan of the city's sewage system on the projector screen.

"The entrance was built into a shelving unit in the main warehouse area, right about here," says Detective Sergeant Phil Mahoney. "The lower section of the main shelving unit is set on hinges, which are hidden against the back wall. There's a short cable hidden behind the shelving frame that forms a loop. You have to reach around the back of the shelves, feel around for the loop, and give it a tug. That releases a catch, and then you can swing the shelf out. There's a four by four-foot tunnel entrance under the shelf that drops vertically a distance of six feet.

"From there, there's a hand-hewn tunnel, four feet high and three feet wide that runs in a southerly direction for about fifteen yards, where it bisects the city's main sewer line buried under Burnsdale Street." Mahoney uses a laser pointer to show the location of the tunnel on the diagram.

"From there, there's just about unlimited access to the entire city. The system has scores of branches, each with numerous exits, mostly to manholes in city streets. He could have an accomplice parked in an alley somewhere, pop a manhole cover, and disappear in about ten seconds. We figure no less than forty manhole exits to the system within a mile circumference of Northwest Healing."

"He couldn't have done it alone," opines a detective.

"He would have had to have had an insider at Northwest Healing," says another.

"Exactly," says Mahoney. "Enter Timothy Connors, founder of Northwest Healing, and our suspect's partner in crime. After looking at his credit card purchases, which show that he bought much of the stuff used to modify the building in preparation for the SERT callout, not to mention sewer schematics and other stuff we found at his house, it's pretty clear that

Connors was a co-conspirator. What we don't know is who the *other* accomplice is, or how many there are for that matter. But it seems pretty clear that his accomplice double-crossed him and murdered Connors in cold blood. My guess is, the plan called for Connors to be released, but the shooter murdered him to double his take of the ante. From debriefing the hostages, we know there was only one guy inside Northwest Healing, so if there wasn't anyone else on the outside, the guy who got away now has the entire fifteen million to himself."

"So, he could be anywhere," remarked one of the detectives.

"Yeah. I got MCT-B looking into the backgrounds of all the hostages. In the meantime, we're gonna break into two-man cells and start combing the sewers. We're already a day behind him, so lets hustle, people."

I leave, my head spinning. Already, I'm putting things together in my mind. Connors's little accident on the night of the Bowman callout, about two blocks from Northwest Healing. He had trouble stopping because his truck was overloaded with dirt and shovels. Why? Because he'd been digging a tunnel.

Slater and Connors' association just isn't coincidental in all this. Slater had arrested him for illegal gambling five years ago, so Slater was aware of Connors' love of money. Then there was Connors' midnight visit to Slater two weeks before Northwest Healing.

Add to this Slater's insistence that I take side one during the callout. He damn near panicked when Capelko ordered him to take side one. Why? How does that fit in with involvement with Tim Connors?

I have to put the brakes on this line of thinking. Bob Slater is a police officer. He's an asshole and, as proven by his bizarre behavior during the callout, a monumental screwup, but he's still a police officer.

His behavior on the callout... Suddenly I recall that the most bizarre thing about his behavior was the fact that he'd been monkeying around with the manhole cover on the sewer pylon. I remember thinking that those things almost too heavy to lift, and wondering why he'd be farting around with one, callout or no callout. But the bad guy had used the sewer to escape Northwest healing, and a *manhole* to escape the sewer.

A sudden image of Hogan and his heroes using a tunnel to go in and out of Stalag 13 comes to mind.

Slater must be Connors' co-conspirator.

That's why Slater nearly panicked when Capelko put him on side one. He needed to be on side three because he needed to be by that sewer pylon to get in and out of Northwest Healing during the callout, which explains both his absences, *and* the fact that the manhole cover was off.

When he was gone, he was *inside* Northwest Healing.

And that business about the telephone? The only explanation I could think of was ridiculous, but it fit. It wasn't a cell phone or a satellite phone, it was a regular landline telephone. I remember the cord disappearing somewhere beneath him. The only thing I can think of is that it ran through the sewer line, into Northwest Healing!

Tim Connors had been locked away with the hostages, so Slater wasn't talking to him. Unless there was a third co-conspirator on the inside who was talking with HNT, the only person Slater could have been talking to was... *Bo Pinter.*

And if Slater and Connors were the only ones in on it, then it had to have been *Slater* who gunned down Connors in cold blood.

I have to take a deep breath and sit back for a moment. This is ridiculous. Slater's a bad apple, yes, but a cold-blooded murderer? That's a little hard to swallow.

Then I think of his suspected collusion with Pammi Route and her lawsuit. When I had informed him that Moody was going to have us both polygraphed, what was it Slater had said?

Oh well, it won't matter by then anyway.

It's dark outside, and I head straight for Northwest Healing. Specifically, to Slater's secondary sniper position on the hillside off the three-four corner. When I get there, I go immediately to the sewer pylon.

I pop the manhole cover off and find a ladder descending about fifteen feet into the dank hole. I climb down and find myself in a pipe about six feet in diameter with a couple inches of gray, musty-smelling water at the bottom.

Everything is black in both directions, the darkness so thick it strangles the beam of my flashlight mere feet in front of me. The line runs north and south, though Northwest Healing is located to my west. I choose south.

After what I estimate is the approximate distance to Burnsdale Street, I come to a large confluence of two pipes. The new one runs roughly east and west. A right turn to my west should take me closest to Northwest Healing.

By dead reckoning, I come to a place that I think is the closest point of approach and began studying the north side of the sewer tile. Almost immediately, I come to a hasty patch job on the west side of the pipe that looks brand new.

Wishing I had stopped to bring a camera or a chisel, I retrace my steps, ever wary of running into one of the detective search teams. It is difficult, because the distances seem so different underground. Fortunately, I had been smart enough on my way in to count the manhole covers on both legs of the journey, and in moments I am back at the pylon where I started.

As I ascend the ladder, my keys fall out of my pocket and splash into the water below. I go back to get them, but they fell out again on the way up. The rungs are set so high that ascending the ladder spills my pockets every time.

This time when I go back to get them, my fingers close on something smooth and round. Like a disk.

I fish it out, and my heart nearly stops beating. "Thank you, God," I mutter, looking at a Law Enforcement Memorial silver dollar proof. Just like the one that Andrea had given me, which is tucked away in the right front pocket of my uniform pants in my locker at Stratton PD. Just like the one Andrea report missing after the suspect at Northwest Healing had made her strip.

I call the office and have the records clerk give me Capelko's home number. When I call his house, his wife tells me he's sleeping. I make her get him up.

"Vince? I got him. I finally got that son of a bitch. You're never going to believe this. Hell, I can hardly believe it myself. You ready for this? It was Slater. The Northwest Healing suspect is *Bob Slater*! I know it sounds crazy, but I can prove it."

"Geller? What the hell are you babbling about? Ben, have you been drinking?"

"Huh? No, I just came from the office. Mahoney found out how the Northwest Healing suspect escaped. It was a tunnel, dug under the building into the sewer system. The phone I told you about, the satellite phone Slater was on? It was no satellite phone, it was a regular landline, with an extension cord going through the sewer to Northwest Healing. *Slater* was negotiating with Pinter, Vince! Slater got all that money. Jesus, Vince, *Slater* shot Tim Connors!"

"Geller—"

"No, Vince, listen! When he disappeared from his rifle, he went into that sewer pylon and through the sewers into Northwest Healing. That's when he shot Connors!"

"Ben! Jesus Christ, get ahold of yourself. You're talking crazy. Dear God, it's all catching up to you. Shooting Pammi Route. The lawsuit. Getting biffed by Bowman. And now this Slater business. Look, Ben, I know you and Slater have your problems, but do you really think he's a cold-blooded killer?"

"I can prove it, Vince. The only thing Andrea is missing is a special coin she was carrying in her pocket. Well, I just found it, in the sewer under the pylon where Slater was supposed to be covering side three. When he was gone, he was down in the sewer! Vince, this isn't crazy. It all fits. Remember how he insisted on taking side three? He had to, because otherwise, he wouldn't be near the pylon and he couldn't get into the building."

"Ben, if you did go down into the sewers and found some evidence, and you took it, you just screwed up a crime scene. You know that. And you call some coin found in the sewer *evidence*? You want evidence, bring me the murder weapon. What are you, a one-year rookie? Come on, you know better than that."

"Vince, we need to arrest Slater before he gets away with the money. I've got plenty of probable cause for his arrest based on what I've seen and found. Look, Mahoney's got MCT in the sewers right now. You should have him put some people together and get eyes on Slater's place right now. I can't do this, Vince, I'm just an officer. You're a lieutenant. I need your bars to make this happen."

"Ben! Nobody's getting eyes on Slater's place. Where are you? Are you alone?"

"What's that got to do with anything? I'm in my car, heading to the office. You need to meet me there. Slater's probably gonna go down hard."

"Goddamn it, Ben, stop it. You're having a problem, and you need to get some help. Slater's not going down, hard or otherwise. I'll meet you in the office but only to get you some help."

I'm getting more frustrated by the second. I sound like a kook to him, and listening to myself, I sound like a kook to me, too. But damn it, I *know* I'm right.

"Vince, yeah, you're probably right," I force myself to say calmly. "All this has been getting to me. Forget about meeting me anywhere. Look, if for some reason I'm right, I'm sure the dicks'll get him. If not, well, maybe I should take some time off. Forget about it, okay?"

"Ben, are you sure you're okay? I mean, is there anything I can do for you?"

"No, I'm good. Thanks for bringing me back down, man. I owe you one, all right?"

"Okay, Ben. You owe me one. Look, uh, call me if you need to talk, okay? Maybe you *should* take a vacation or something."

"I'll check into it. I gotta go now, Vince. I'll talk to you later."

We hang up, and I slam my fist into the dashboard. He thinks I'm nuts, but I know Slater really did do Northwest Healing. He *had* to have.

Capelko made a damn good point about screwing up a crime scene, though. I pull a U-turn in the middle of the road, intending to go back and replace the coin as I had found it, but then I wonder what would happen if a team of detectives saw me. It'd look a hell of a lot like evidence planting. Plus, I'd already told Capelko about it, and he'd have to testify about that. So, I make another U-turn and stop.

I don't know where to go next. Mahony? Slater? I end up driving over to Slater's house, but his truck isn't here. I go down the road and park with the lights off, and pull out my department Nextel phone and direct-connect him.

"Slater, answer up. This is Geller."

"Geller, what the hell do you want?"

"You're not as smart as you think you are, Slater. I know all about Northwest Healing, Tim Connors, the money, the tunnel, the sewer, the whole damn enchilada. They're going to give you the needle, Bob."

There was enough of a pause that I know I'm right. "What the fuck are you babbling about, Geller? You been drinking tonight, or what?"

"You wouldn't say anything over the phone, that much I understand. But I just wanted you to know. I'm onto you, and now so is Vince Capelko. And, I got evidence. You were stupid enough to drop something in the sewer. Something you took from Andrea."

Thinking about Andrea walking out naked pisses me off more than anything else. "And you know what else?" I say, my anger starting to come out. "You are going to pay dearly for what you did to her, you emasculated little dickless fuck."

I'm answered with silence. He'd disconnected. That's fine by me. Now, at least, he knows that *I* know. Thirty seconds after I disconnect, my personal cell phone rings.

"Geller."

"You're about the dumbest dumb shit I ever met," says Slater. "You have no idea of the fire you're playing with. You got yourself in way over your head this time. It's not *me* that's going to wish you never fucked around in this, Geller. It's *you.*"

Before I could even respond, he hangs up.

Threats now. I have to admit, I am a little unnerved. If I'm right, Slater is a cold-blooded killer. What the hell am I doing?

Well, we've definitely gone to the next level now. I can handle this. You get someone like Slater frazzled, and he's bound to make a mistake.

I call Phil Mahoney's Nextel, with the intention of filling him in and getting him to put someone on Slater. However, it seems Lieutenant Capelko has already gotten to him. Mahoney tells me that I misunderstood some stuff I'd heard at the detective's briefing and that I am to stay away from the investigation. He says he's spoken with Chief Moody, and I am on stress leave effective immediately for an undetermined amount of time. I am to go directly home, and in the morning, someone from the department will be in touch with me. In the meantime, I can rest assured that they are doing everything in their power to find and catch the guilty party. I argue, but the saner I tried to sound, the crazier I appear.

Devastated, I hang up. My head is spinning, and I wonder if they're right. Had I misconstrued everything and created all this in my mind? Was I that messed up by everything that had happened to me?

No, in my heart of hearts, I know I'm not. But now I have an even greater obstacle in my path, and that is overcoming the department's doubt about me. About *me.* When Slater, a Stratton police officer, is a stone fucking killer, they have doubts about *my* sanity.

Capelko said they need real evidence. 'Bring me the murder weapon,' he'd said. Well, I have a pretty good idea where the murder weapon is. I am parked right down the street from it. All I have to do is go get it. The problem is, I can't do that without becoming a felon myself.

But you know, some things, you just *gotta* to do.

23

I KNOW SLATER'S house is alarmed. He's gone, but I don't know where, and he could come home at any time. The alarm company will call the police the moment they detect entry, and from that point, I will have only a few minutes to get away. But, what I need to do shouldn't take longer than that.

I open the medical kit I keep in the passenger door compartment and remove a pair of surgical gloves. I then leave my shoes in the unlocked car and go into a neighbor's backyard. I wish I had my police radio with me, but it isn't a perfect world.

I hop a low fence into Slater's yard and climb onto his deck. The door and windows are all locked, but that doesn't matter to me.

I place the point of my pocketknife against the lower right-hand corner of the kitchen window and poise the palm of my hand over it.

Point of no return, I think.

One sharp blow, and the window shatters. The noise isn't too bad, and fortunately there is no audible alarm. I literally dive through the window into the kitchen, knocking over plants and prescription bottles on the sill. I bang my knee sharply on the faucet, but then I am in the house.

So far, no alarm. I run through the kitchen and down some stairs to a sunken living room. Next to that is the den, where Slater keeps his guns.

I go directly to the far wall. I know it's a false wall, and that Slater keeps his best guns in a hidden panel behind it. He showed me once, years ago, when he was still trying to get on the team.

When I get to the panel, an audible tone tells me I have set off the motion detector. The countdown begins. I know I have only five to ten minutes of safe time before I have to worry about the police.

I can't remember how he opened the panel when he showed it to me, and I can't find any catches or releases. Knowing Slater, the release will be well camouflaged.

By thumping on the wall, I easily locate the hollow spot beneath it. I don't have time to screw around looking for little catches. Instead, I grab a dining room chair and smash my way through the wall and into the compartment behind it. Inside is a rack containing five rifles. Two are valuable Civil War relics, two are competition high-powered rifles, and the other is a cheap Chinese AK-47. The guns are secured only with a steel cable through the trigger guards, which is fastened to a metal eyebolt in the wall.

I glance at my watch. Elapsed time—three minutes. Using a heavy chair leg, I pry the eyebolt out of the wall and pass it through the trigger guards. I grab the AK-47 and the Remington sniper rifle with the Dedal NightVision scope, since I am sure these were the weapons used at Northwest Healing. I remember the sound of shot that killed Connors; there was no way it was the AK. Each weapon has a box of ammo beneath it, and I take these, too.

I close the rear slider and leave through the front door, locking it behind me. I know the police would be here in minutes, but I am pretty sure I'm still ahead of them, and that I have left no real evidence other than sock prints. If there's an investigation, this will give them nothing more than my foot size. No tread patterns to match with shoes, no fingerprints, and no blood on broken window.

Exhilarated, I make my way through the backyards to my car, load the weapons into the trunk, and simply drive away.

There, I am a felon, just like that. I know that from this point on, my testimony about seeing Slater on the phone and his being gone and opening the manhole during the callout is no longer good. The rifles won't be good evidence, either, if it ever becomes known how they were acquired. But I've already thought that through.

The Stratton Police Department will receive an anonymous tip about where the weapons used in Northwest Healing are being stored. They will be in a public place that won't require a warrant or a substantial search by responding officers, and bingo, ballistics tests will show that rounds fired from the AK-47 match those recovered from inside Northwest Healing, and rounds from Slater's .308 will match the one that killed Connors. I already know the customized Remington is registered to Slater by serial number. In addition, its serial number is on record through the National

High-Powered Rifle Competition in Ohio, since it's the rifle he used to score third place last year.

As far as the AK's registration, that might be a different story. The weapon is fully automatic, and therefore illegal, plus it wasn't part of the collection Slater showed me several years ago. My guess is the serial number is gone, and Slater had either stolen it from someone in exchange for not arresting him, or had purchased it on the black market. Anyway, it will no doubt be covered with Slater's prints, as he is too confident in himself to have wiped it down. A guy like Slater would never consider the idea of getting caught.

I head home to collect my wife and daughter. Even if Sharon doesn't want to be with me, I still want her out of the house until Slater is arrested. He's a slimy little weasel, capable of anything.

I have to pass the police station first, and I can't resist the urge to check the detective status board. It gets updated regularly, and if anyone is starting to look at Slater, I need to touch base with him.

On the way in, I phone Sharon to prepare her in advance. She answers on the second ring.

"Sharon, it's me. Listen, I really need you to do something."

"Ben, it's late. I'm sleeping, and so is Leah. What are you doing calling at this hour?"

"Listen to me very carefully, honey. I don't have time to explain. I want you to pack a bag for you and Leah, at least than a week's worth of clothes. I'll be by in about twenty minutes to pick you guys up. Okay? Do you understand?"

"Ben, it's one fifteen in the morning. Are you crazy? Are you drunk? Leah's not going anywhere at this—"

"Sharon, shut up and listen to me! Just *do* it! It's dangerous for you to be there right now. No questions, just do it. I'll be by to pick you up in a few minutes. You don't have to stay with me if you don't want to, but you do have to get out. I'll see you in a few minutes."

I hang up. She's the third person to ask me if I'm drunk tonight. Well, I'm not drunk, I know that. I don't think I'm crazy either, although I guess I'm not positive about that. One thing's for sure though. If I'm wrong, I'm screwed.

I pull into the police department parking lot and go inside. The detective division door is closed and locked. I suppose this could mean they're focusing on Slater, and don't want it going around the department. But I doubt it. Not yet.

Bypassing the main report writing room, I go to the SERT office, which is dark and locked. I let myself in and log onto the computer. The first thing I do is check on the call load for Stratton.

Two officers are at Slater's house on a burglar alarm.

That's all I needed to know. I fire off an e-mail to Chief Moody informing him I am going on voluntary stress leave until further notice, and cc my patrol sergeant, Capelko, and Phil Mahoney.

That done, I log off and call home one more time. Sharon is in tears, but says she is packing. I tell her to get Leah up and ready; I'll be in the driveway in five minutes and we're leaving immediately. My house is just over a mile from the department, and ignoring speed limits and traffic lights, I covered the distance in about two minutes.

The lights are on and the front door is open when I get there. I leave the car running and get out to help with Leah and the suitcases, but stop short, staring in disbelief as I near the door.

The frame is shattered. Parts of the jamb, splinters of wood, and the intact deadbolt are scattered across the floor of the foyer.

My hand goes reflexively to my side, but there is no pistol on my belt. That's back at the fifth wheel, with my police radio and the rest of my equipment.

With a feeling of dread spreading over me like a sodden blanket, I push the door open and enter my house. Two suitcases are packed, standing in the entranceway. Patrick, the little stuffed starfish Leah sleeps with, is on the floor next to a spilled glass of milk. Nothing else looks out of place.

Frantically, I go through the house, but Sharon and Leah are not there. Everything is in order. I search the house again, calling out their names, knowing there will be no response. And then I go into the living room, pick up a lamp, and smash it against the wall.

24

I AM UNABLE to think clearly. I consider calling the police, but what good would it do? I already know who has them.

Well, there's no longer any doubt in my mind as to whether Slater is the Northwest Healing suspect. He'd even given me a warning. He'd told me to back off, that I was in way over my head. Apparently he was right.

When I was a year out of the academy, I went to a car crash scene and held a man in my arms as he died. He drew a final breath, held it for about thirty seconds, and as it slowly escaped unmoving lips, his whole body just deflated. After that, he was still. And that is exactly what I do in my foyer while holding Leah's starfish. I deflate like the dead man.

Suddenly, none of this is exciting anymore. I had gotten caught up in the rush. I had stumbled onto something huge and unraveled it, solving Northwest Healing and implicating my nemesis all at the same time. Putting it together had been exciting and satisfying, as well as a little fun. Like being a character in an action movie. But now, I can see my mistakes. Now, as a result of my screwing it all up, my wife and child are gone—in the hands of one who has killed for personal gain, without remorse.

I've become a threat to Bob Slater. I've carelessly pushed him, and told him what I know. This I had done out of ignorance. I am a moral individual, a police officer in spirit as well as uniform. He is the proverbial wolf in sheep's clothing. I had provoked him, and it was like David challenging Goliath, only I had forgotten to bring my sling.

I've totally misjudged Slater. I've always thought of him in terms of a police officer gone bad, which has been my biggest mistake. As a police officer, there are limits to that which he can allow himself to do.

But Slater isn't a cop who'd gone bad, he's a bad guy who'd gone cop. He's a cold and calculating killer, an antisocial psychopath without a soul whom I've backed into a corner. And now he's reacted as such. I don't think there are limits to what he'd do to protect himself, a fact I can see clearly now, although it's too late. Now my six-year-old daughter and my beautiful wife, whom in my heart of hearts I love more than any other woman on earth, are in his hands.

What good will calling the police do at this point? What will I tell them—that I broke into Slater's house and stole the murder weapon, and he returned the favor by breaking into my house and stealing my family? Both Capelko and Mahoney already think I've rounded the bend. They might even think that I staged the kidnappings to further frame Slater. In any case, all Slater has to do is either report to work in the morning, looking and acting sane, or simply kill my family and disappear with his millions. I'll probably end up in the nuthouse either way.

In fact, why hasn't he already just disappeared? I can think of only two possible reasons. One, he just hasn't had enough time. I discovered what he'd done and let him know about it within twenty-four hours of the crime. Or two, he doesn't want the spotlight turned on him.

Slater's not the kind of guy who would allow himself to become a wanted fugitive. He would have thought of a way to legitimize or justify the money somehow. After that, he would quit his job and just sort of melt away. Nobody would be looking for him, and he could live as he pleased. Bob Slater was a lot of things, but stupid wasn't one of them.

Sitting on a bench in the foyer of the house I had so recently been kicked out of, I try to evaluate my options. My problem is, I can't think of any. I find myself in the awkward predicament of turning to God yet again for help, and shamelessly offer him plastic prayers for my family's safety. What else can I do?

I know of only one. I punch in Slater's Nextel phone number. Predictably, he doesn't respond. In desperation I go back to the fifth wheel and armed myself with my pistol and police radio. Then I take a drive past Slater's house, but it is dark and his car isn't there. The police cars are now gone.

I still have Slater's guns in my trunk. They may be the reason he's taken my family. I consider putting them back in Slater's house as an offering of sorts, but I realize that would leave me nothing with which I can bargain for Sharon's and Leah's lives.

As long as Slater knows I have the guns, he has a reason to bargain. I have nothing else left. I told him that Capelko knows everything, but now I can see that was a stupid thing to do. He'll be even more desperate now, thinking that a lot of people suspect him.

Switching gears, I try to think of the situation from Slater's point of view. He and Connors had meticulously planned Northwest Healing for no other reason than having rich celebrities to kidnap for ransom. They had booked Loretta Epstein, knowing that her father had millions and would be willing to put it up for her. It took some mighty big balls to rip off a guy like Pio Cantelli.

But Slater was too greedy to stop with seven and a half million dollars. He wanted it all. So, when the plan probably called for him to release Connors as a token of goodwill, he killed him in cold blood, which no doubt accomplished a couple of goals. It doubled Slater's take, it greatly shortened the duration of the callout, and perhaps most importantly, it ensured that there were no witnesses to his involvement. Unless, of course, there is still some undiscovered third party out there.

But then I come along and give him a phone call from the blue, telling him that I knew everything. Jesus, what a Boy Scout I had been.

Well, that was the old Ben Geller. It's nearly 6 a.m now, and the new, wiser Ben Geller is thinking clearly, armed, and ready to do battle. But at the moment there is no one to fight. I have no idea where Slater is. My family is with him, and I am powerless to help them. And the world around me sleeps.

I head back to my house and call Phil Mahoney on his Nextel.

"Phil, it's Ben."

"Geller? I haven't been home an hour yet. What's up now?" he asks sleepily. I don't care about the hour. I'm willing to risk sounding like an idiot. I have to do *something*.

"Look, Phil, I know you think I'm going nuts, but give me the benefit of the doubt. Phil, I've got nowhere else to turn."

"Ben, what the hell are you talking about? I told you that we're handling it. Have you been up all night?"

"Phil, just listen to me, okay? Slater did it. I swear to God on my daughter's life, Slater did it. But I don't care anymore. All I care about is my... my family..." The emotional battle sneaks up on me, and I really have to fight to hold it together, which makes me feel all the more that I am losing it.

"What?"

"My baby.... My little girl..." I lose the battle. My voice cracks, and I choke up.

"Get a hold of yourself, Ben. Calm down, it's gonna be okay. We're on it, I promise you."

"He took my family, Phil. I pushed him, stole evidence. I burg'ed his house, took his guns. Now he knows I can prove it, so he broke into my house and kidnapped my wife and little girl. Please, Phil, find Slater and bring him in. Forget about Northwest Healing. He's got my little girl..." Cursing myself, I break off and choke back a sob.

"Okay, Ben. Okay. We'll bring him in. We'll get to the bottom of all this. Relax, all right? It's gonna be okay. I promise. You go to sleep, and I'll call you myself in a few hours, when we know more. I promise I will"

He's shining me on. He thinks I'm nuts. That's okay, because at least he'll remember what I told him.

"Okay, Phil," I said, making a supreme effort to sound controlled. "I know I sound nuts, but I'm serious. Please just try to remember I said that, okay?"

"Okay, Ben. You get some sleep. I'll find Slater and your family, and I'll call you later."

He disconnects. Keeping my pistol with me, I sit down on Leah's bed, suddenly drained and exhausted, both emotionally and physically. I don't remember falling asleep, but the next thing I become aware of is the doorbell waking me up.

Glancing at Leah's clock—a puppy with a wagging tail for a pendulum and eyes that moved opposite the tail—I see that it's just past 3:00 p.m.

My God. I've been asleep for nine hours, while my family is... I don't even know.

I answer the door holding my pistol behind my back. Standing there glancing suspiciously at the broken door frame is a black man and a white woman. I don't recognize either of them.

"Are you Ben Geller?" the woman asked.

My thumb is on the hammer. "Who's asking?"

"Ben," said the man, "I'm Carl Witherspoon, and this is Karen Jones. We're from Project Respond, and we'd like to talk to you."

I close the door in their faces. Project Respond is Multnomah County's answer to a growing problem with the mentally ill. They are trained counselors and social workers who make on-site visits to mentally ill people in the field. They often have prearranged court committal papers, and take a couple of police officers with them as backup when visiting the potentially dangerous.

More banging on the door, harder this time. "Ben, it's Charlie Deaver. Come on, man, don't do this. Open up, okay?" Charlie Deaver is a day shift officer. A friend.

Charlie knocks again. "Ben, they're not here to take you away. I swear to God. They just want to check up on you. We're concerned, that's all. Five minutes. Okay? Five minutes.

I bury my weapon in the back of my pants and cover it with my shirt, then open the door.

Deaver steps inside ahead of the Project Respond people. "Five minutes, Charlie," I tell him. "If you're not here to take me away, then you all leave in five minutes."

"Swear to God, we're not." He closes the door behind them.

"Ben," says Deaver, "Man, we understand you've been under a ton of stress lately. I mean, it's got to be hard, knowing that you shot a hostage in order to save her baby's life. And suffering the loss of a brother officer, not to mention almost getting killed by a suspect in the field. And on top of it all, watching a man get shot and killed in cold blood at that last callout. Ben, we understand what all that can do to a man. It could happen to any of us. We sincerely want to help you."

"Look, I appreciate you guys' concern. But the truth of it is, you don't know the half of what I'm going through, and I'm not going to waste your time, or mine, telling you about it. I have stuff I need to do. I don't have the time to be screwing around with you guys."

They look at each other, as if silently getting one another's permission. Deaver looks pained, as if this is very difficult for him. His eyes dart to the splintered doorframe and his nod to Carl Witherspoon is barely perceptible.

"Ben, where are your wife and daughter?" Witherspoon asks in a quiet voice.

My instincts tell me to be very damn careful if I wanted to stay out of the nut house. "I don't know," I say. "I came home last night and the house was locked up. They were gone. They didn't tell me where they were going."

"How'd that happen?" asks Deaver, indicating the damaged frame.

"I didn't have my keys. Why, Charlie? You want to read me my rights?"

"Come on, Ben. I'm your friend. Cut that shit out."

"You're here with Project effing Respond, Charlie! I want to know why. Who called you?"

"That doesn't matter," answers Karen Jones. "Look, Ben, you're a cop. You've been on the other end of this a million times. We don't want to waste your time, but I just want you to know that cops have legitimate feelings and limits, just like anyone else, and that it's no sign of weakness to need some help now and then. We all do, you know."

"Ben, I gotta ask you something," said Witherspoon. "You know there are resources out there available for help. I couldn't begin to imagine what kind of stress you're under. Would you like to check into a hospital? We think you could really benefit from it, *without* any negative stigma. It's all very confidential."

"No. I know you guys have good intentions, but you don't have a clue what's *really* going on. You're so off base it's pathetic. I already know who put you up to this, so let's just roll the ball to the end of the lane here, shall we? No, I don't feel like hurting myself, killing myself, hurting anyone else, or killing anyone else. I'm not thinking of suicide, I wouldn't have a plan if I did, and I'm not self-destructive or suicidal in any way. And, I am perfectly capable of taking care of my own welfare. That about covers your job. Now, your five minutes are up, so thanks just the same, but leave."

They look at one another and get up to leave. Charlie says he's going to hang out a moment, and the others depart.

"What's going on, Ben?" he asks. "The whole office is buzzing. They're saying you've had some kind of breakdown, that all the shit that you've gone through has finally caught up to you. I heard that Mahoney wanted to have you taken on a seventy-two hour police officer's mental hold, but Vince Capelko shot that down. What's going on?"

"Nothing, Charlie. I can't talk about it, all right? Hey, let me borrow the computer in your car, okay?"

"Why? You're on leave, man. I can't do that."

"Then answer me this. Is Slater scheduled to work today?"

"No. I saw him in the office earlier. He was taking vacation time. He got special permission for unscheduled vacation."

"How long?"

"I don't know. Why? What's he got to do with this? Everyone says you're obsessed with him. Come on, Ben. Tell me what's going on."

"Look, Charlie, take off, okay? Go report back to Mahoney that I'm okay. I'm not nuts. Some serious shit is happening, but I have to work my way through it, all right?"

"I can hang out for a while if you like, Ben. It's a slow day."

"No, you need to leave. Thanks, man."

"Be careful, Ben. You didn't hear this from me, but there's an IA going on. It involves you. And Slater. Who, by the way, spent some time in Capelko's office while he was here this morning. But like I said, be careful. There's serious talk of having you committed. I don't know what the hell's up, but watch yourself. And watch Slater."

He leaves and I am stuck wondering what in God's name I'm supposed to do now.

My Nextel beeps a short time later. It's Slater. "Geller, answer up." His voice makes my flesh crawl.

"You better not hurt them or I'll kill you. I swear to God, I will kill you."

"I'll keep that in mind. Go to the phone booth at the Seven-Eleven, Crane and Division. I'm already there, watching. Be alone and no recording equipment."

I try beeping him back, but he won't respond. I go to the store and stand by the bank of phones. There are two of them. Who even uses a pay phone any more? Twenty minutes later, one of them rings.

"Geller."

"I don't want to hurt them. I need a week, maybe a few days more, and then I'm out of here. You've nearly fucked everything up for me, but if you cooperate, I can fix it and you'll get them back."

"Listen, Slater, I don't give a shit about Connors or Northwest Healing. All I want is to get my family back. I'll trade you the guns and my silence forever for them."

"I'll get my guns back, cheesedick. And your silence. And if you play by my rules, you can have back, on *my* schedule, not yours. Now listen very carefully to me. Who did you tell, and what did you tell them?"

"No! Give me back my little girl first, then I'll do everything you ask."

"Your little girl can suffocate and you'll never even know where to look for the body, you fucking dipshit! You're not in any position to bargain. Worse comes to worst, and I'll just disappear. And that would be the last you ever heard of them, so *don't fuck with me!* I told you once—you're in way,

way over your head. All you can do is dance when I tell you to dance. You have no other power; no other options. Do you understand me? You don't tell me a goddamned thing except for what I ask you. Now, who did you tell, and what did you tell them?"

"I told Capelko you were dicking off during the callout. I told him you weren't even there half the time. That's it."

"Bullshit. What else?"

"Nothing. Wait, I told him I thought you might know more about Northwest Healing. I didn't tell him why. I want them to figure it out."

"You fucking liar. Your little girl's sucking her last breath."

There's a click, and the line goes dead. I look around frantically. Slater is nearby somewhere, watching me to make sure I hadn't been followed or recorded the conversation. I am scared. He is capable of anything, and I am powerless to find him.

I go home, and out of desperation, I call Vince Capelko on my home telephone. Thankfully, I catch him at his desk at work.

"Vince, please, listen to me and don't hang up or tell me I need to go to a hospital. Please, I beg you."

"Go ahead, Ben. I'm listening."

"I know everyone thinks I'm nuts. Project Respond just paid me a visit, and I know that Mahoney wants to have me committed. Put that aside for a moment, and hear me out.

"Slater talked on the phone during the callout, on a landline phone that went through the sewer to Northwest Healing. I saw him. I also saw him with the manhole cover off. You heard him insist that I take side one. That was so he could take side three. He went through that manhole, and he and Tim Connors did Northwest Healing together. Slater double-crossed Connors and executed him so he could have all the money. Mahoney's people discovered that the bad guy went out through the sewers. I went into the sewer, and right under Slater's side three manhole, I found the only thing Slater took from Northwest Healing, which is Andrea's coin. Hell, he stripped her naked to get to *me*, because he knew I'd be watching."

"You already told me this story, Ben."

"No, wait. I… I broke into Slater's house, and I stole his competition rifle. The one he used to kill Connors. I have it. Ballistics will prove it's the same one. And I have the AK he used when he took the place over. Do you hear me, Vince? Ballistics will *prove* they're the same."

"Ben, like I told you last time we talked, you're no one-year rookie. If you did what you said, all that is fruit of the poisonous tree—tainted, unusable evidence. The only thing that would have convicted him, you just rendered useless because of an unlawful search and seizure."

"That's why I called you, Vince. It doesn't matter anymore. Slater found out I took the guns, and he kidnapped my wife and daughter. Last night." I start losing it again. "Goddamn it Vince, I have no where else to turn. I *need* your help."

"Ben, you sound as if you're losing it, but I can't really ignore what you're telling me. I'll, uh, I'll check into it."

"Vince, I just talked to Slater, not more than five minutes ago. He demanded to know what I told you, and said he was going to kill my daughter. He did Northwest Healing and killed his friend, and he knows I can prove it. Vince, he's gonna kill them. He knows I've told you, and he's not going to give them back to me."

"Ben, stay at home. Stick around by your phone. I'll call you back in an hour."

25

I DO WHAT he says, and stay by the phone. What else can I do? An hour passes, then two, then three. Still, I wait. Then, at 8:15 p.m., an unmarked detective's car pulls up in front of my house.

I watch Phil Mahoney approach my door, alone. He is carrying a bag. He wouldn't be alone if he was going to take me away against my will. So, what's going on? Am I being set up?

I open the door as he approaches, and he enters as if he knows I am waiting for him.

"Ben, I want you to listen to this," he says without preamble as he pulls a digital recorder out of the bag. He sets it up on my kitchen table and brings up a sound file from the menu.

Before he can start it, my pager goes off. "That's going to be related to this," he says. I pull the pager out and look at it.

SERT callout. Motel 6, Frontage and I-84. Possible kidnapping in progress. Command post Travel Center Truck Stop.

"What? Is that about my family?"

"Yes. We think so. About a half-hour ago, we got a call from the manager of the motel. He said a dark-skinned man with a shaved head rented room fourteen on the ground floor. He used what we have determined to be a fake ID in the name of Richard Bayer.

"After Bayer secured the room, he went back out to a van, which he pulled up to the door, and then unloaded a woman and a little girl. Both were crying, and both seemed to have their hands bound behind their backs. They seemed to have something around their eyes; the clerk thinks it was maybe a stocking. The man held his hand inside his jacket like he was carrying a gun. The suspect left after about ten minutes. Then, at seven twenty, this call came into 911."

He presses the Play button. "Nine one one, do you have an emergency?"

"Help me! My daughter and I have been kidnapped! We're in a motel somewhere. Please, I don't know—"

The line goes dead, and Mahoney shuts off the tape.

I am shocked into silence. The voice was undeniably Sharon's.

"Ben, the voice on the tape. Is it your wife?"

"Y-yes. What's going on at the motel?"

"The trace came back to room 14, Motel 6 in Salmon Creek. We've got people there now. The suspect came back shortly after that call, driving the van, which is flagged sold, last registered to a recovery yard in Bend. He went into the motel room about ten, maybe fifteen minutes ago. Right now, we've got people in front and back."

"Have we tried contacting the room?"

"Yes, patrol did. There was no answer. You're sure that's your wife's voice?"

"Goddamn it, yes! Let's get going."

We head out to Mahoney's car. As we make our way to the motel, I say, "The suspect is Slater. You know that, don't you?"

"Ben, Slater's been at the office for most of the day. The clerk at the motel described the suspect as being a dark-skinned white or Latino male, mid-fifties, with a shaved head and acne. He's also very tall, at least six four. It's not Slater. What I want you to do is tell me how they were kidnapped, and why you didn't report it when Deaver and the folks from Project Respond paid their little visit. You think they believed you kicked in your own door, for Christ's sake?"

"Come on, Phil. I don't care who's got them now, but it was Slater who took them. I *talked* to him about it this afternoon. The guy at the motel was probably Slater in disguise. *He* kicked in my door. I didn't report it because I already know what he wants and what he'll do if he finds out I dropped a dime on him. He wants the rifles I took from his house, which can prove he's the Northwest Healing suspect, and he'll merely kill them and disappear if he finds out I've come to you. He told me that himself."

Mahoney rode along in silence. My pager goes off, telling me the van was leaving the office.

"I'm taking side one," I tell him.

"The hell you are. You're on sick leave, which means you're not here. You stick with me on this one, at all times. If HNT or anyone needs you for anything, they'll get you through me. And that's a direct order."

I mull this over. It could be worse. I could be in the lockdown ward in the Emanuel Hospital psych unit.

"Look, Ben, we know that's your wife and daughter in there. You know as well as anyone that nobody is better able to deal with this than SERT. We're gonna get them out for you. I promise."

Five minutes later, we pull into the Travel Centers of America Truck Stop. Capelko and Hauser are already there, conferring with the swing shift patrol sergeant. Patrol officers are cordoning off the area in preparation for the arrival of the SERT van.

The van arrives ten minutes after we do. The back doors open like a vertical mouth, vomiting black-clad ninjas bristling with weapons. I cannot say how relieved I am to see Hank Venegall, the team's former primary sniper, get out with them.

I know that Venegall has been allowed to maintain his monthly sniper qualification since leaving the team a year and a half ago. Capelko had asked him to do so ever since Slater started showing his true colors with his attitude after I dissed him in training. It takes months to train a sniper, and if something were to happen to me, that would leave the team with only Slater, and now that he was gone, there would be none. I was supremely happy that Capelko had put the kibosh on Slater's sniper duties. It's about fucking time.

I find Capelko, who is being briefed by the team's intelligence officer, along with the HNT lead, Bo Pinter. I hate to interrupt, but I have to.

"Vince, you got a sec?"

"No, Ben, sorry, I don't. But we're going to get them out, I promise. Stick with Mahoney till I'm set, then you can join me in the van."

"Okay, but Vince, the guy in the motel room—" I didn't know how to say it was Slater without sounding paranoid.

"Ben, not now. Catch me in twenty minutes, okay?"

"Yeah. But if it's not the guy I think it is, if he responds here, you're not going to let him suit up are you?"

"Christ, Ben. I don't want to hear it. Not a word. You can stay here only if I don't hear a word about Slater, deal? So don't worry about it. But just so you know, Slater's out."

"Thanks, Vince. That's all I needed to know. I'll catch you soon."

I tune Mahoney's car radio to the Stratton tactical frequency, which is where SERT callouts usually are until the team is in a position to take it over. The air is silent.

The motel is just down the street, blocked from view by several buildings. I wish I could be there, but unfortunately there is no way they will let me go to the scene. Not with my wife and daughter being held there.

The radio sounds. "One fourteen, I have movement inside the room. The blinds just jumped, like someone was looking out. Plus, I can hear a lot of moving around."

A female dispatcher answers. "Copy, movement in the room."

"CP to Venegall. Can you identify anyone in the room?"

"Negative. I'm not sure, but what I saw might have been a cat."

"Copy. CP to Slater, any movement side three?"

"Negative, all quiet."

Slater was out there? On the gun? He'd kill them for certain. Capelko had lied to me. I couldn't believe it.

"No!" I shout, opening the car door. "No, get him off the gun! Vince!"

"Ben," Mahoney shouts, grabbing the back of my pants and holding me in the car. "Cut it out, and get back in here!"

"Phil, they put Slater out there, on the gun! He'll kill them for sure!"

"Goddamn it, Ben stop it! Slater's a police officer, for Christ's sake."

I fight him, but he is now leaning across the front seat, holding me with both hands. Mahoney is my height but nearly thirty pounds heavier. He yards me back into the car and nearly out the other side in one move.

"He lied to me, Phil. Vince told me Slater was off the team!"

Capelko has heard me and comes running up to my side of the car. I break away from Mahoney, pop out of the car, and take a swing at Capelko.

Vince used been a defensive tactics instructor, and easily sidesteps my wild swing. He brings me back to reality by bitch-slapping me in the face.

"Get ahold of yourself, Ben. You're not helping anything. How do you expect us—"

"Vince," I interrupt," You lied to me. You said Slater was already off the team."

"I did not. That's what you *heard*, because that's what you wanted to hear. I said, 'Slater's out.' As in, out there, on the gun."

"How come you put him on the gun? You know he took my wife and baby."

"I don't *know* anything. Ben, I hate to tell you this, but Slater was in the office for most of the day yesterday. And he was driving back from court in downtown Portland when this whole thing went down here today, at the motel."

"Bullshit! He's fooled you all! He took my family, Vince. So he put them in here... which means he set this up like he did Northwest Healing! Vince, he's planning something. Something bad."

"Listen to me, Ben. You're not helping anything here. Apparently, I've got a legitimate kidnapping on my hands. I have an eyewitness, the motel clerk, whom I showed a picture of Slater to not twenty minutes ago. He's a good witness, never forgets a face. It wasn't him. Ben, get this through your head. Slater is *not* the suspect. He *didn't* snatch your wife and daughter. I have my own suspicions about him in other matters, but not in the kidnapping of your family. Now, I know you're under a ton of strain, but I don't want to hear any more about it. You hear me?"

Mahoney, who has overheard my tirade, said, "Focus on this, Ben. That's your wife and daughter in there, and we're going to get them out. Just that. And the lieutenant is going to do it the best goddamn way he knows how. In order to do that, he needs a sniper on that front door. That's where Venegall comes in. Slater's on the back side of the motel, since there's a door leading to the adjoining room which opens to the three side, and that room's vacant. It wouldn't be the first time we've faced someone who has kicked a hole in a motel wall to escape."

Capelko says, "Now, I gave Slater the chance to bow out, but he wanted to do this. And I need a side-three sniper. So just try to take it easy. We'll get your family out, and then we'll sort through this whole goddamn mess." He turns toward Mahoney and said, "You keep Geller under wraps, or I'll take him into custody. That's an order, Phil."

With that, Capelko storms off.

The HNT van has arrived, and preparations are being made to contact the room. Inner perimeter units are getting set in their various locations, and the entry team forms up for a briefing. This takes place in the SERT van and lasts twenty minutes. During that time, IP reports more sounds coming from room fourteen.

Capelko takes his place in the hot seat, and everything settles down into the routine of a normal SERT callout. To me, those terms no longer apply.

Slater planned this callout the exact same way he planned Northwest Healing. But why? Why kidnap my family, and then give them back like this? To kill them like he did Tim Connors?

I can't get past the fact that Bob Slater is out there, right this minute, with a sniper rifle in his hands. I am sitting right here, in Mahoney's car at the command post. What is the biggest impediment to Slater getting away scot-free with Northwest Healing? *I* am. And he knows exactly where I am at this moment. Suddenly, I feel like a caged animal, and the urge to flee is nearly overwhelming.

But my family is out there, not a block away from me.

Or are they? I know inside me that I'm not crazy. I know damn well that Slater's snatched them and is holding them. But I can't imagine he's stupid enough to take them bound and gagged into a motel room in broad daylight. Nor is he stupid enough to work with someone who would do that, either. And if he kidnapped them and it went bad like this, he would never show up at the callout.

Which means he had to have planned it to go this way. He arranged this callout the same way he arranged Northwest Healing. Which brings me back to the original question. Why would he fake a callout with my wife and daughter as hostages?

Because he knows I told Capelko the whole story! Oh my God, I was wrong… *I'm* not Slater's biggest impediment. Capelko is. With my family in his hands, Slater can control me. It's Capelko who can prevent his clean getaway!

Now that Slater's little plot is unraveling so quickly, all he needs to do is get away, and use the fifteen million to hide out somewhere. But I told Slater that I told Capelko, and Capelko is in a position to do something about him. And even if he were to just disappear with the money, with Capelko looking for him, Slater would have to look over his shoulder every minute of every day. In addition to having SERT at his disposal, Capelko is the lieutenant in charge of Investigations, which means he has the investigative power of the Major Crimes Team to help track down Slater and the stolen ransom.

Vince Capelko is the one who can unravel Slater's neatly laid plans for a clean getaway and find him after he disappeared, not me. Therefore, Slater would have to deal with Capelko first, *before* he disappeared. My family and me, we're just incidental. Excess baggage. He can kill them, and deal with me at his leisure.

I look over at the command post. Capelko is firmly entrenched in his hot seat as he is on every callout. And Bob Slater is out there right now, on side three, on the gun. He knows exactly where Capelko is. All he has to do is get in a position to take him out.

Suddenly, I know what I have to do.

Mahoney is standing outside the car talking to HNT. None of them are looking at me. I take the opportunity to bail out of the car and disappear into the truck stop. There are several exits, and I call for a cab to meet me at one that can't be seen from the command post.

Fifteen minutes later, I am back at my temporary home. My car, with Slater's guns still locked in the trunk, is parked in the driveway. I grab my pistol and my SERT radio, and take off in the direction of Motel 6.

26

IT IS ALMOST fully dark by the time I pull up several streets away from the command post. I take a moment to study a patrol map of the area. Knowing the layout, I close my eyes and try to picture where Slater might be.

And then it comes to me. There is a hillside about a half-mile from the area Slater would be using for his side-three sniper position. The hillside is a pretty good distance from the command post, but with Slater's ability, the shot should be relatively easy. There is a large amount of new home construction in the vicinity. At this hour, the sites are all deserted. The hillside would be the perfect spot to get a shot at the command post. I'm sure it's where Slater will go to kill Capelko.

At the bottom of the hill is a creek, and then a large marshy area, from which the hillside can be easily watched. And from the marsh, I should be able to see the command post as well.

I drive as close to the marsh as I can, then park and get out. In order to get to where I'll be able to view both the hillside and the command post, I'll first have to cross about two hundred yards of wooded wetlands. But if I'm going to prevent Slater from killing Capelko, I have to do it. It's all so clear to me now.

I take out Slater's competition rifle—the same one he used to kill Tim Connors—and enter the marsh. It is muggy out, and the mosquitoes are unbearable. Despite the air temperature, the water is cold and grimy. It is knee deep in places.

Gnats try to squeeze into my eyes, and the crazy-making whine of mosquitoes in my ears makes me bat savagely at my head. I crawl over fallen logs and cross dry spots, then find myself back in the water. I wish I had taken the time to put on camouflage clothing and boots. My feet sink several inches into soft, grimy mud with every step, and the going is agonizingly slow. My leather slip-ons are instantly ruined.

My radio tells me HNT is attempting to contact the motel room. I push on, and finally come to an area devoid of blackberry tangles, but full of poison ivy. I'm sure I'll be covered with it. But the ground is dry, and it offers a great view of both the hillside where I figure Slater will end up, and the command post, which will be his target.

Capelko will be in Slater's range, but from here, Slater will be in *my* range.

This spot forms part of an unequal triangle, with the legs being my position to Slater's position, Slater's position to the Capelko's position at the command post, and the command post back to my position. I feel as if providence has led me here.

Everything is crystal clear now. Slater set up this callout for the purpose of taking Capelko out of the game. He will leave his sniper post sometime during the callout and will make his way to the construction site, where he'll have a direct, albeit long-distance, shot to Capelko at the command post. He will kill Vince, and then disappear, leaving my wife and daughter to die wherever he has hidden them. With Capelko out of the game, and me forever crippled by the loss of my wife and daughter, he and his, and his fifteen million dollars can make a clean getaway. If he feels the need to take me out, he can do that whenever he pleases.

I lay down on a patch of dry ground and set up Slater's rifle. I support the stock on a log, since the weapon lacks a forward mounted bipod. I load it with four rounds from the ammo I took with the rifle, and fashion a butt rest, then take aim at the construction site. The scope is set up for night vision, and I turn it on.

The construction site jumps out at me in crisp, green relief. Now comes the problem of scope setting. This is not my rifle, so I haven't set the zero. Obviously, I can't fire for effect and zero the scope myself, so I am forced into making my best guess as to how Slater has left it.

I consider what I know for certain. Slater is a SERT sniper. For SERT, we keep our rifles zeroed at one hundred yards. I also know that the last time this rifle had been used—when Slater shot Connors at Northwest Healing—it had been at a distance of fifty-eight yards.

I know a fair amount of ballistics that will help me make an educated guess. A bullet traveling at supersonic velocity rises from the moment it leaves the barrel before achieving its apex, at which point it begins its descent, following a mathematical trajectory called the ballistic curve. It continues dropping until it either strikes a target or falls to the ground.

Slater's rifle is a highly customized Remington 700, and the rounds I took with it are match-grade 168-grain boat-tailed hollow points. I knew the muzzle velocity is be just about 2,600 feet per second.

Putting everything together and applying the proper formulas, this weapon, firing this ammunition, will share a zero point at both fifty and one hundred yards as the bullet first rises, and then begins falling. In other words, if I am either fifty or one hundred yards away from the target, the rifle will shoot with pinpoint accuracy if I hold the target exactly at the intersection of the crosshairs.

If the rifle is set at a hundred yards. It's a guess, but an educated guess, and I am betting the farm on it. If I am right, it will be fine for what I am planning. If I am wrong, my family and I are screwed.

I figure I'm looking at just about two hundred twenty yards to the general area of the construction site, so, offering one of my now frequent wooden prayers that my guess is correct, I make the necessary scope adjustments to set it for that distance. Then I settle in to wait.

I switch my radio from the SERT net to the patrol frequency, intending to put out the info on Slater's position the moment he shows up. When he gets to the construction site, which I am certain he will, I will call Capelko and dime Slater off. At the same time, I will call it on to patrol as a man with a gun on the hillside, aiming at the SERT command post. If Slater even lays down behind his rifle, I will take him out.

I have a lot of area to scan. In order for Slater to make it to the construction site from his side-three position, he will have to scrabble down the relatively steep grade in front of me. That hillside is my best chance of seeing him, and I began scanning it intently.

Being on scope for long periods of time is hard enough on the eye, but being on a starlight scope causes even more strain. After forty-five minutes, my eye feels as if it's being pulled out of its socket.

I am idly listening to swing shift officers being dispatched to various calls, trying to ignore the strain on my eye, when I hear my name go out on the main patrol net.

"Repeating the BOLO from Stratton SERT. All units, be on the lookout for Officer Ben Geller, last seen at the command post at Travel Centers Truck Stop. Stratton PD has ordered Geller to be detained on sight.

Use caution, he is armed and suffering from PTSD. Stop and detain on Peace Officer's Mental Hold."

Jesus Christ. Now I'm *wanted*? I feel as if I'm falling into a pit from which I will be never be able to escape.

I am positive that Sharon and Leah not in that motel room. That they're locked away somewhere, dead or dying, and that the man responsible will offer himself as my target on the hillside in front of me any time now. Providence has dictated it. I am powerless to make decisions about the outcome now. All I can do is play my part, sit back, and watch how it all ends.

I've been out here for two dreadful hours. Mosquitos are devouring me alive. I have to go to the bathroom. I have the worst headache of my life. The disgusting swamp water has made my feet itchy, cold, and clammy. Ghosts, in the form of horrible thoughts of my family dead or dying, have visited me regularly the entire time. I think I might be losing my mind.

I feel myself begin to doze and shake myself awake.

Another hour passes. About fifteen minutes ago, I could swear I heard Leah calling my name.

I begin to doubt my actions. My reasoning is way off. The cops are right, and I am wrong. I begin weeping softly to myself, and grow so full of doubt that I am ready to get up and turn myself in.

Slater has not wormed his way down the hillside. He has not staged a fake SERT callout for the purpose of killing anyone. I'm not the key to this whole mess. I haven't figured anything out with respect to Northwest Healing and Bob Slater. Somehow, I've manufactured it all in my mind. I now realize how narcissistic, or even paranoid, I've been.

My mind is being pulled apart. I call into doubt everything I've taken for granted and believed earlier. Was my front door really kicked in? Did Slater really threaten my family? Are Sharon and Leah actually home sleeping safely in their beds?

Am I looking for Soviet messages in American publications like the schizophrenic in that movie? Am I suffering from delusions?

I roll off scope and look up at the stars. They are blurry with tears. A shooting star draws a silent line directly toward the hillside, then fizzles out in earsplitting silence. Is this a sign from my fair-weather God? If so, of what? My madness or my sanity?

I want this all to be over now. I'm done. I'm no good to anyone now. Especially Sharon and Leah. I need to turn myself in, but I don't have it in me to hump back through that fucking swamp.

I will give myself up. I will broadcast my location over the radio, and have a patrol unit pick me up. But how will I describe my location? In a swamp south of the hill? I don't even know where I am!

I feel the heat of poison ivy beginning to burn the skin on my arms and legs. I am hungry, thirsty, and tired. I've wet myself. I lie here in misery for several minutes, considering, then discarding the idea of suicide, and then decided to hump to the construction site. There are street signs there. Once I get there, I can call for patrol officers to meet me so I can turn myself in. I will voluntarily check in to Emanuel Hospital's psych unit. My days as a police officer are over. I'll be lucky to draw a quarter of my salary on a stress retirement.

I take a look at the ground between my position and the construction site through the night vision scope to determine the best way there. There is a small valley I will have to cross in order to get there. It consists of a downgrade in front of me, then what looks like a dry, rocky stream bed, and finally the uphill grade I've been watching for the past four hours. It won't be a hard hike…

I draw a sharp, extended intake of air, which in the still night sounds like a jet engine winding up. My head is instantly light, and my heart flutters like a wounded bird in my chest.

Right there in front of me, at the crest of the hillside, in bright green relief silhouetted against a dark, starry sky, is a man lying on the ground. He is digging around in a backpack, one that perfectly matches his woodland camo fatigues. In front of him is a sniper rifle.

I dial in the magnification, and his face becomes crystal clear. It is Bob Slater.

He withdraws his hand from the backpack, and moonlight glints off a sharp .308 round. He inserts the cartridge in the open chamber of the rifle and closes the bolt.

I watch in fascination as he nestles the gun under him, drawing it tight as a lover might in the afterglow of lovemaking. He settles his face into the scope, and I realize he is about to take a shot.

I quickly re-aim my own rifle in the direction Slater is aiming, and see exactly what he is doing. There, five hundred yards in front of him, is the command post. Specifically, the SERT van. More specifically, Vince Capelko, seated in his customary spot in the hot seat, bathed in light from the various computer terminals in front of him and red night-vision-preserving lights behind him.

I've watched Slater shoot before. Because of his background as a competitive shooter, he likes to take his time to ensure a good shot. But he's been taking aim at Vince for several seconds already, and I realize I'm just about out of time.

"Vince," I shout into the police radio, "Get out of the SERT van! Get out now, Slater's got you in his sights!"

Capelko doesn't move a muscle.

"Last unit, repeat?" says the dispatcher incredulously, as if she hadn't really heard what she'd just heard. I forgot I'd switched over to the patrol frequency.

"That was Geller, the BOLO subject," says the voice of a patrol officer.

I don't have time to change frequencies, so I ignore the radio and take aim at Slater. My scope setting is off, since I have set it for the construction site. In fact, Slater's position was a hundred yards shy of it, giving me a range of about a hundred twenty yards. There is no time to make the adjustment, so I just hold the distance off in my mind and hope that my years of training will serve me well.

Holding the crosshairs a fraction of an inch below the crown of Slater's head, I started pulling the trigger, taking what is referred to as a snap shot—a shot taken in such haste there isn't time for accurate aiming.

At the very last fraction of a second, it occurs to me that by killing Slater, I will be killing my only chance at finding my wife and daughter, but it is probably too late to stop the shot. Muscle reflex had already taken over. Instead, at the last moment, I moved my aim down along Slater's body.

27

THE SHOT RINGS out, echoing off the surrounding rocks and hillside. Hoping my aim is as good as that of my target, I robotically chamber another round as I bring the rifle back down on the log, and then take a long, hard look through the scope.

Slater has rolled off the rifle and is hunched over, cradling his shattered left lower leg. I breathe a tremendous sigh of relief. My round has damn near severed his leg below the knee. He is no longer a threat to Capelko, at least, not at this moment.

I manage to switch the radio over to the SERT frequency, where the air is crowded with voices.

"Unknown where the shot came from!"

"Entry, we are all code four."

"Venegall, I did *not* fire. Side one has not fired!"

"CP to Slater. Did you fire? Did you fire!"

I add my own voice to the cacophony. "Geller to Slater! Roll off that gun!"

Slater doesn't respond, but Capelko does. "Geller, what the hell are you doing out there? What is your position?"

"Geller to CP. Sniper shot out. Target is Bob Slater. Target is down, but not out. Five hundred yards west of the command post, on the hill above the construction— *Shit!* Slater! Roll off that fucking gun!"

Slater has crawled back to the rifle and is taking aim once again. I settle in for another shot, but he beats me to it, pulling a snap shot of his own.

I squeeze the trigger a fraction of a second after him, my shot nearly getting lost in the rolling echo of his. The shots are so close together, by the time they reverberate off the hills and the sound reaches the command post, it sounds like only one report. I fight the rifle back down to target as I simultaneously chamber a third round and reacquire Slater in my scope. He is hunched over his other leg, which is now shattered and showing bone at the knee. The blood is greenly luminescent in the ghostlight of the night scope. Slater's distant screams, audible across two hundred yards of black night, slide off my conscience like water from a duck's feathers.

"Command post hit by sniper fire!" comes a desperate radio transmission from the CP. It was not Vince Capelko on the radio. "All units, Geller is firing on the command post!"

"Negative," I shout in the radio, unsure whether anyone can hear me over the din of other voices. Slater, lying next to his weapon, is still cradling his shattered legs.

After thirty seconds, the radio traffic dies out. I know that every patrol officer in Stratton is combing the surrounding area, looking for me, thinking I am shooting at the command post. I also know that under the circumstances, they won't hesitate to take me out.

Somewhere in the back of my mind, I realize that our radio transmissions are being audio recorded, and another stupid idea forms in my mind. I seem to be full of them tonight.

I have the transmit button affixed to my left index finger as I normally do on a callout. That way, I can talk on the radio while maintaining target acquisition. I pressed it now without taking my eyes off Slater, who is now writhing on the ground, still in close proximity to a live weapon.

"Geller to Slater." There is no response.

"Geller to Slater!"

"Slater to Geller" comes his strained reply. "Fuck you."

"Bob, I once told you not to silhouette yourself against the sky. You should have listened. Now, *where is my family?*"

Slater straightens out some. Kind of into a shooting position. Almost. His hand goes to his lapel mike. "Slater to Geller," he breathes weakly. "You'll... never... see them...again."

"Geller to Slater. Wrong answer."

My rifle jumps again, the sound of the exploding gasses leaving the barrel bouncing around the rocky hillside. When I get back on scope, Slater is in the same position, but where his left thigh had been there was nothing but blown-apart ragged meat. I have completely destroyed his legs, and he is obviously in excruciating pain. I don't think he's capable of taking another shot at the command post, not that it matters. I'm sure it's been evacuated by now, anyway. I hope he hadn't shot Capelko.

"Geller to Slater."

"No more." He is crying. Good.

"Where is my family?"

"Slater to Geller... Northwest Healing... They're there... You win. No more. I did it... I did it all. Lied. About Route's gun. I didn't bring... ammo. To the Route callout... Stupid. Northwest Healing—Connors... I doubled the money. I got it all..." His voice was barely above a whisper, and apart from his dialogue, the air is as quiet as a tomb.

"The money. You can have it. The money is..." He says something unintelligible, presumably the location of the stolen money, but it comes out as little more than a mumble.

"Fuck the money, Slater. Where is my family?"

"Too late... no air..."

"Where!"

"Dead..."

The rifle jumps again. Slater may have been whispering over the radio, but he screams loudly across the canyon. This time, it is his hip. I'll be lucky if that one didn't kill him.

"Geller to Slater."

His voice is stronger now, his yelling audible enough to be broadcast in the background of my transmission. I guess dismantling a man with a .308 is a good way to wake him up. At this point, I don't give a shit about Slater or the consequences of my actions. All I care about was finding my family.

"Okay! In the tunnel... between Northwest Healing... and...and the sewer... You bastard!"

One final shot, right through the head, causing it to evaporate into a shimmering red spray, just like Connors'. Only, the image was in my mind, not in reality.

Abandoning the rifle, I jump up and head off in the direction I had come, through the swamp. I splash my way through the grimy water, and head straight for my car. As I approach the road, however, I slow and dive to the ground.

Patrol cars are everywhere. One has a spotlight on my car. Frantically, I switch over to the patrol frequency.

"...copy. K-9 six, any updates?"

The breathless voice of the dog handler answers. "Tracking north, back now, toward the car, coming from the swamp. He can't be too far ahead of me."

"One sixteen, I've found his rifle!"

"Copy. SERT says Geller is likely armed with a handgun as well. All units, use caution."

I am trapped between the dog and the roadway, which is full of cops, and I have nowhere to go. I hear the dog barking behind me, and I realize that I have only seconds before it catches up to me.

I belly crawl to the roadway and roll into the ditch. My only hope is to find a patrol car idling while the officer is out searching for me on foot. It's a long shot, but it's all I can think of.

I make my way toward a pair of red taillights, but before I go three feet, my world lights up in brilliantly blinding white light, as harsh and bright as the unfiltered sun.

"Freeze, Ben! Don't move! You're under arrest," barks a voice behind the sun.

28

"ANDREA!"

"I said, *freeze!* Ben, please, don't make me shoot!"

"Andrea, I beg you, help me out of here! He's got my family, and I know where they are!"

"Ben, I can't."

Keeping my eyes on her, I stand up.

"Ben, get down on the ground! Please!"

I reach behind my back. Through the light, I see her gun barrel rise up to the level of my chest.

"Ben, oh God, please. *Please* don't."

I withdrew my pistol from my belt.

"Ben…" Her voice cracks, and her hands tighten on her weapon.

I toss the gun aside, into the high grass. "Shoot me if that's what you have to do, Andrea. But you'll do it while I'm trying to save my family. I'm getting in your car, and I'm going to Northwest Healing."

"Ben, no. I can't…"

I start walking toward the light. Andrea doesn't move, but keeps her pistol on me as I approach. I have no idea what is going to happen.

I reach her car. Andrea seems to come to a decision. She lowers her gun and snaps it into her holster.

"Damn it Ben. I'm driving," she says.

I get in the passenger side and toss her gear into the backseat while she gets in and closes the door. Apparently, nobody's seen us.

"Everyone in the county is looking for you. They think you're taking potshots at the command post and at SERT members. Tell me it isn't true, Ben. Tell me, and I'll believe you."

I fill her in on what is happening until we pul into the Northwest Healing parking lot. I hit the release switch on the Unitrol that opens the magnetic shotgun lock, and pull the 870 pump gun from its rack.

Together, we go to where the front doors of Northwest Healing used to be. The area is now covered with plywood sheets fashioned into makeshift doors. They are secured with a metal padlock and have yellow "Police Line—Do Not Cross" tape across them.

I level the shotgun at the lock and pulled the trigger. When the smoke clears, the lock is gone. Using the butt of the weapon, I pound my way through the door and head to the main storeroom. There is a huge rack of steel shelving covering the entire back wall. I feel around the back of the shelving, against the wall in the right-side corner. In twenty seconds, I hook my finger through a loop of steel cable, and pull.

There is gentle resistance, and then the cable yields. A section of shelving swings open on a hinge, revealing a black rectangle beneath it. There is a hiss, and I feel cool air rushing past me into the tunnel. A crude ladder descends into the darkness, and without hesitation, I climb down.

"Sharon? Leah? *Sharon! Leah!*" I call frantically. There is no response.

The air is dank in the tunnel, and so thin I can't breathe. Sucking air that isn't really there, I feel myself get lightheaded, but I continue, feeling my way along the narrow corridor with the shotgun in my right hand, and my open left palm on the rough-hewn wall. There is an electric line overhead with naked bulbs every few feet, but is dark and I can't figure out how to turn it on.

A bright light snaps on behind me. Andrea hands me her patrol flashlight. I make my way farther into the tunnel, rushing headlong, my lips and lungs working like the gills of a landed fish.

I nearly trip over the form of my little girl, lying on the cold ground, her nightie soiled with her own urine and feces. Her eyes are closed. In the harsh light of the flashlight, she has no color whatsoever, and she looks dead. Sharon lays nearby, her eyes open and pleading. Both are gagged and bound with duct tape.

As I bend to Leah, there is a loud blast several feet in front of me. Concrete chips shower us all with sharp insect-like bites. Another bright light fills the chamber as officers rush in from the now broken main sewer line.

The cavalry has arrived. My head begins to swim, and my knees go weak. Suddenly, I think I am going to pass out. If I do, that's okay. It is over.

I look at the officers pouring through the hole in the main sewer line, but am horrified to see that, rather than rushing to Leah's aid, they are instead pointing guns at me.

"Drop the weapon, Ben!"

"You asshole," I wheeze, "can't you see she needs hel—"

Before I can complete the sentence, the nearest weapon to me, a shotgun like the one in my hand, erupts in a pillar of flame, and a sledgehammer smashes me squarely in the chest. I fall backward, and that's the last I remember of the underground chamber.

29

I WAKE UP sometime later in a hospital. A searing pain in the back of my head escorts me into consciousness from a dream in which I am helplessly struggling to stay afloat in a raging whitewater river. In the dream, people on the riverbank watch me rush by them, and I think how sad it was that I am going to die in front of so many people who either cannot or will not help me.

My eyes open, and the first thing I see is the lovely face of my wife, Sharon. The second is a patrol lieutenant named Jered Scott.

I try to get up, and that's when I discover that my right hand is shackled to the bed rail by means of a locked leather restraint.

"Ben," Sharon yells, obviously relieved to see me awake.

"Sharon." Just saying her name brings twin flames of pain to life, one in my chest, the other in my head. "Where am I? What hospital?"

"Emanuel," she says. "They shot you with a beanbag, and you hit your head on a chunk of concrete and passed out."

The tunnel comes back to me slowly, scene by scene in disjointed pieces. Darkness. Stuffiness. Airlessness. Panic. Dread.

Then I remember Leah, bound with duct tape and gagged, lying like a tiny rag doll on the dirt and rocks of the tunnel floor. I see again the sewer opening up, and officers entering the chamber. A shotgun pointed at me.

"Leah," I croak. "Where's Leah?"

Sharon's eyes fill. "She's here, Ben, in Emanuel. In intensive care. She still... hasn't woken up. They say her brain was oxygen starved, and they won't know whether any permanent damage has been done until she wakes up."

Desperately, I yank on the restraint binding me to the bed. "Jered," I yell, "get this goddamn thing off me. I want to see my daughter!"

"I can't do that, Ben. I wish I could, but I'm under orders from the Chief. You're to remain in your room, under guard. Uh, you've been placed under arrest, Ben. I'm sorry."

Well, why not? Had I not made it clear to everybody and their mother that I burglarized Slater's house? And I *had* taken Slater apart with my rifle, on a recorded radio network. I knew even then that amounted to torture. Hell, I probably killed him. It makes no difference to me that I am looking at some serious time. In fact, I don't give a shit. My career is over and I know it. All I care about right now is seeing my baby girl.

"Come on, Jered, then frickin' guard me. You think I'm going to run away? I'm buck naked, for Christ's sake, except for this stupid gown. I'm covered with poison ivy. What do you think, I'm gonna escape?"

"Come on, Ben, I can't. Give me a break."

"Jered, you and Sarah have a kid, don't you? Abigail, right? My daughter's name is Leah. Come on, man, take me to see my baby."

Jered thinks for about two seconds, and then, without hesitation, he unlocks my wrist, leaving the restraint and its little padlock hanging on the bed rail. "You try running away, I'm gonna clobber you in the face with a shovel," he says.

"Been there and done that," I retort, standing. The moment I get my feet under me, though, I swoon and nearly fall to the floor. Sharon and Jered guide me into a wheelchair.

Once I recover enough to continue, Nurse Ratched flies in directly from the set of *The Cuckoo's Nest* and begins yelling at all of us. "What do you think you're doing? That man has a closed head injury!"

"Police emergency," Jered says as he pushes me past her. Sharon leads the way, and we leave the sputtering woman behind.

"How long have I been in here," I ask Sharon, who I now notice for the first time is also clad in a hospital gown.

"About five hours," she said.

"Are you okay?"

"I'm fine. They have me in for observation. I'll be out of here in a day or two."

Hesitantly, I take my wife's hand. At first it is cold, a dead fish, but after just a brief moment, she squeezed it warmly. "Ben, we'd have died if you hadn't shown up."

I almost cry, but I fight it back and asked, "Is Slater here?"

Jered answered for her. "No. Uh, Ben, Slater's dead."

Though I try not to show any reaction, my world dims, and I am glad I'm sitting down. No wonder I had been restrained and under guard. I supposed I'll be charged with murder.

But it really doesn't matter, not as long as my family is alive. I close my eyes and offered a sincere prayer for Leah. I'd been praying a hell of a lot lately. Right now, I am desperate enough to believe in the tooth fairy if I thought she could help.

Jered sees my reaction and says, "You didn't kill him, Ben. After he told you where they were, he pulled his pistol and shot himself in the mouth."

"Waste of a good bullet," I hear myself saying. But my body betrays my arrogance, and I start hyperventilating. I actually begin to go into respiratory distress, until Sharon runs for help. Nurse Ratched joins us, handing me a paper bag and telling me to breathe into it. She grudgingly accompanies us to intensive care, where I dock my wheelchair at Leah's bedside.

"Her signs are all stable," said the nurse, her tone much more human than anything I'd heard from her to this point. "She's suffering from what they call anoxic-ischemic encephalopathy, or brain damage due to oxygen deprivation. They don't know the extent of the brain damage, but this much I'll tell you, it happens within minutes. From the time the brain is denied oxygen, you have five to seven minutes before the damage is irreparable. If you hadn't found her for another two or three minutes, she wouldn't be here right now."

I am strong enough to get out of my chair and kiss Leah on the forehead. I whisper to her, telling her that I love her, and that we were all going to live together as a family again, but there is no sign that she can hear me. She lies unmoving in the bed, looking as peaceful as she does every night with her arms wrapped around her starfish as she sleeps in her bed. Monitors keep a metronomic vigil over her.

To see her like this is heartbreaking. For all I've done, I feel cheated that Slater shot himself. Gazing down at Leah, I wish more than anything that I'd put one right through his fucked-up little head.

They wheel me back to my room, where I voluntarily manacle my wrist to the bed. Jered, not bothering to close the little padlock, offers to guard me from outside my room, leaving Sharon by my side.

"Honey, tell me what happened," I say when we're alone.

"Oh, Ben, I was so mad at you, after, you know… I still am. You *bastard! Why* did you have to keep seeing her? I thought you loved me! I thought you wanted to stay with us, and be a *family.* Jesus Christ, Ben, we *needed* you. Look at everything that's happened, and you weren't there." She breaks down, sobbing. This is more than my betrayal. This is for the kidnapping, her fear, Leah, everything. I don't argue with her. She needs to get it out. Besides, what can I say? Every word she's saying is true.

She is sitting on my bed, her head in her hands. I place my arms around her, and she yields to me for a moment, then begins beating her fists against my chest.

She nails me repeatedly right where the beanbag round had turned my entire right pec to black and blue mush. I relish the pain. I deserve it.

After a few blows, she notices the way I wince and falls all over herself apologizing.

I tell her it's okay, that she has every right to hurt me after what I've done to her. This seems to take the wind out of her sails for the moment. She settles down, and then continues her story. But I know we have more talking to do on that first topic. A lot more talking.

"I thought you were crazy when you called and told me to pack a bag," she tells me after pulling herself together. "But there was something in your voice that made me do it anyway. Then you called and said you were five minutes out. A couple of minutes later, I heard a car pull into the driveway. I thought it was you, and I opened the door, but it wasn't you. It was a man, wearing a ski mask. He was running up the sidewalk. I slammed the door, but he kicked it back open. Leah was right there in the foyer. He… He pushed me away and grabbed her. He put a gun to her head and told me to go to his car. Oh my God, she was so frightened. She didn't move or say anything. She just opened her mouth, but nothing came out. Ben, what could I do? I did it. I marched right out to the car. He had Leah, with a gun pointed—"

"Honey, it's okay," I assured her. "You did the right thing. He was desperate. Enough to hurt her. I'm *glad* you went with him. You probably saved both your lives."

"Anyway, he put us in this van and taped us up. He gagged us so we could hardly breathe. Ben, Leah still didn't cry. She made little noises is all. That's what scared me the most. I think she was in shock.

"Anyway, he drove us somewhere, I don't know where, and parked. I thought he was going to rape us. I had a nightmare in my mind that he was going to rape Leah and make me watch."

Unable to relive this, Sharon breaks down again. This time, she clings to me without beating me as I hug her. After a few minutes of my comforting her, she continues.

"But he… he didn't. He left and was gone for a long time. Then, later, he came back and drove us to Motel 6. He made us get out, then took us into the room and left again. He came back and climbed in through the bathroom window, made me call 911, then threw Leah out the window. He just *threw* her, like she was a sack of garbage. I heard the wind go out of her when she landed. From that time on, she wouldn't open her eyes, and *there was nothing I could do for her!* Oh Ben, she still hasn't opened them."

"She's going to be okay, baby. I promise. She comes from good stock. She'll recover and probably won't even remember anything about it."

"You really think so?"

"Of course. I've seen it happen. In that kid who drowned in the pool a few years ago, remember?"

The child is a vegetable today, but she doesn't know that. The lie doesn't sound convincing, even to me, but I think Sharon buys it for the moment. She seems to relax some.

"He made me go out through the window, too, then put us back in the van. He drove to Northwest Healing and took us down into that tunnel.

"God, Ben, Leah was terrified, I could see it in her eyes. You know how she hates the dark. He threw us on the ground, and we couldn't move. There was no light, and then he just left us there. We've been there ever since.

"I couldn't tell if Leah was alive or not. But at some point, she got sick and started gagging and having diarrhea. I remember the air getting thinner and thinner. It got harder and harder to breathe. I don't even know when Leah lost consciousness. I was in and out for hours myself."

She dissolves into tears again. Her story is so vivid, and Leah looks so pitiful in her big hospital bed, I am crying right along with her. I'm glad Jered left the room.

"Ben, I didn't think we were going to get out of there. All I could think of was us; how I didn't want to die like this, with us being separated and all. I—I was so *mad* at you. But at the same time, I knew that I loved you and that you loved me. I prayed that we would be rescued, but I didn't think we would be. I knew the air was running out. There just wasn't enough. After a while, I couldn't hear Leah breathing anymore, and I thought she was dead. So, I gave up myself, and just waited to die, too. I *wanted* to die, to be with her. And then you came in.

"I thought I was dreaming when I saw you. But just as you came in, there was more air, and I knew it was for real. It was cool, and it filled my lungs. I was so relieved! Then the wall broke open, and more cops came in, and I was sure I wasn't dreaming. I just hoped Leah was still alive. I remember thinking that we were all together again, that somehow, everything would be all right. And then, they shot you and I thought you were dead.

"It had to be a dream, but it wasn't."

30

THE NEXT SEVERAL weeks pass in a hazy blur. The doctors tell me Leah might be able to make a full, or at least close to full, recovery from cerebral anoxia. But then again, her recovery may only be partial. Effects of anoxic brain damage can include amnesia, dementia, Parkinsonism, visual agnosia, which is failing to recognize common objects or shapes, or paroxysmal choreoathetosis, a condition in which she could suffer attacks of involuntary movements of the limbs, trunk, and facial muscles. These prognoses terrify me. Probably the worst part is that we won't know if she will develop any symptoms until she develops them. If she makes a normal recovery, we'll never really know for certain.

Five days after being freed from her entombment, Leah opens her eyes and asks for a glass of water. I've already been remanded to house arrest, with an electronic monitor on my ankle to record my comings and goings, an incredibly liberal gesture given the gravity of my charges. I am allowed daily supervised visits to the hospital.

I am home trying to sleep when I get the call from the hospital telling me she is awake and asking for water. Despite the hour—4:34 a.m.—I am in her hospital room in twenty-five minutes, my police escort agreeing to meet me in the hospital lobby.

All along the way, I enjoy fantasies of Leah leaping into my arms and me tickling her to the ground in the way she loves so much. When I think of her waking in a strange bed in a hospital, alone without Sharon or me to comfort her, I drive faster. This is the first night that Sharon, exhausted, has allowed herself to come home and get a full night's sleep since being released herself.

I've created a fully alive and vibrant image of her, when all I had been told was that she was awake and thirsty. Imagine my disappointment when I find her as mentally and physically diminished as a severely developmentally disabled child.

I stand over her bed, staring into her filmy blue eyes, devastated to see no recognition reflected back to me. She falls asleep shortly after I arrive, and I climb into her bed with her. More than any time in my life, I wish I would die. I simply cannot stand seeing my baby girl like this.

Over the next several days, Leah regains recognition of Sharon and me. According to her attending physicians, this is a good indicator that her recovery would be fairly complete. But as the days pass, her body simply doesn't change. She seems to have lost about twenty percent of her voluntary muscle control. Unpredictable spasms cause her to flail her arms as if shadow boxing imaginary opponents, or to jerk her head violently to the left.

Every day I berate myself for allowing Slater to live after he disclosed their location. His suicide has robbed me of the vengeance I feel I deserve. I am already facing the probability of spending the majority of my remaining days in custody; so to add Slater's murder really wouldn't have made that much of a difference.

The police department has had plenty to keep them busy while my family and I try to pick up the pieces of our shattered lives. Slater had some of the Northwest Healing money with him, but the majority still hasn't been found yet. Two weeks after the incident, there is word of a shattering new development. Nobody will talk about it, but Mahoney lets it slip that they've developed information that leads them to believe there is another, so far unidentified, co-conspirator. That's all I know, and it's little more than rumor.

I hear through the grapevine that there is some new, bizarre, sexual-type twist to the whole thing. I really don't care about the steamy, sexy side of Bob Slater, or the Northwest Healing money for that matter. I am far too preoccupied working on regaining the trust of my wife, and being there for my daughter when she needs me to worry about anything else.

Things in the family department are finally begin to shape up, I'm happy to say. Leah is beginning to show real progress. Sharon and I are living together and getting along better than we have in a long time. After getting out of the hospital, I started sleeping in Leah's room, but one night, I awoke from a terrible nightmare, crying into her pillow, and Sharon came in. She got in bed with me and held me until I fell back asleep. After that, I moved back into our room. Now we are at least sleeping in the same bed again.

I remember how she was after I shot Pammi Route, and once again, it is that same tender, nurturing side of her that makes me love her more than ever. There is no awkwardness about sex; neither of us want it, and for the moment we are satisfied to just be with one another.

I am not made of stone, however, but I choose to bear the pain of my lust with stoic patience, waiting for Sharon to make the first move. Then, two months after the kidnapping, she takes me with the wild abandon of a first-time lover, and I won't speak further of that. All I have to say on the subject is that when a person truly repents, and genuine heartfelt forgiveness is issued, the renewed love can be more intense than the original.

During this time, I have no direct contact with Andrea whatsoever. I enjoy the support of the police department from the chief to the newest rookie, and many of my brethren on the force have given me her third-party support. But Andrea herself is prudent enough to see what's happening with Sharon and Leah and me, and she stays completely out of it. I can only assume that she is quietly bowing out, and for that, I am grateful.

Officially, I am on unpaid leave from the force, pending termination. The city tried to fire me outright, but the union grieved it, and the negotiated result was unpaid leave. Once I am either convicted or found to be in violation of department policies, I will be fired.

Because I wasn't terminated outright, I am able to remain on stress disability for several weeks at full pay, but once that runs out, I'll have to draw from my sick leave, vacation, holiday, and compensatory banks. In total, that ought to give me another twelve weeks. Leave bank donations from other officers should add another week or so, but when that runs out, I'll be on my own.

Sharon and I have some pretty good investments, and Leah has a substantial college fund from which we can draw, but without my paycheck, we will have no more than nine month's income at our current standard of living.

As Leah improves, the case against me progresses. On the day she begins talking in complete sentences, the Multnomah County District Attorney's office presents the grand jury with my torture/attempted murder case. Testimony takes two and a half days. This time, I elect *not* to testify, knowing that I will be indicted. In the end, of course, I am. The charges are attempted aggravated murder, aggravated assault in the first degree with a firearm, and coercion.

In the state of Oregon, there is no more serious crime than aggravated murder. Had any of my shots killed Slater, I would have been charged with that. As it was, he took his own life, but Jessica Perez, Multnomah County's first female district attorney, makes no bones about the fact that Slater's autopsy revealed that I had severed his left femoral artery, and that given his location, medical help probably would not have arrived in time to save him from bleeding out. "Probably" is the operative word.

But he did shoot himself, and that's why the charge was reduced to attempted aggravated murder. The addition of the word *attempted* meant a one-stage reduction in the maximum penalty, which in this case, would have been death by lethal injection. So I am looking at life without the possibility of parole. Period.

The other charges merely enhance the sentencing power of the judge. The aggravated assault charge carries a minimum of seventy-two months, and there are no minimum guidelines for the charge of coercion, a mere class C felony. Coercion is when a person compels or induces another to engage in conduct from which the other person has a legal right to abstain, by instilling fear of bodily harm.

D.A. Perez and I have a serious disagreement about that one. As if Bob Slater had a right to abstain from telling me where my dying family was. My attorney, Randy Bulger says that what Perez really means is *any* person has the legal right to abstain from a forced confession of an alleged crime.

So, as my daughter struggles to hold a straw in her mouth with half-dead lips because of Slater, I face the possibility of spending the rest of my life in an isolation cell, eagerly hoping for a peek at the sun on my weekly one-hour walk in a tiny outdoor cage.

In my decade and a half with the department, I have always been somewhat of a nonentity, known mostly for my sardonic sense of humor and entertaining banter. But since the Route shooting, I've rocketed to departmental fame. Now everyone in the department seems to be trying to outdo one another in showing me support.

Officers donate time from their leave banks for me. Collections are taken up. The Stratton Police Officer's Association coordinates things like keeping my house clean and yard mowed while I stay with Leah in the hospital. Everyone I run into has nothing but good words to say to me.

There are no hushed conversations that suddenly quiet when I walk in the room. And finally, the piéce de résistance: Though I am suspended from duty, I am called to the Chief's office and given the Departmental Medal of Valor with two lifesaving clusters, in absentia. My photo, with Sharon pinning the medal to my uniform shirt (which I am holding, since I am suspended from duty), appears in the newspaper. In it, my nose is leaking and my eyes are wet. That photo hangs framed in my living room to this day.

But if the limelight from within the law enforcement community is overwhelming to me, I am in no way prepared for the support I receive from the general public after what quickly becomes known simply as Northwest Healing. Primarily, it comes in the form of cash donations for my legal defense. The fund quickly grows to the point I think it just might cover all my lawyer bills and then some.

I spend the majority of those days in the hospital with Sharon and Leah. Leah still can't get out of bed, but she's staying awake for periods of hours at a time now, and moving around a lot. She seems to be fully aware of everything going on around her, and is clearly frustrated at her body for not doing what she commands it to do.

She does, however, show steady, albeit painfully slow, improvement; something for which I thank my fair-weather God every day.

Within two weeks of opening her eyes, she has regained some control of her arms and legs, and her attempts to smile begin to register elsewhere on her face than just in her eyes. Her slow but steady improvements are the only thing that keep me going.

Four months after the incident, two significant things happen. Leah takes her first steps with a walker, and five days after that, my trial begins.

31

AS HARD AS they try, the prosecution is unable to seat a jury devoid of parents and married people. With the exception of an elderly widow and a twenty-year-old young woman with a fourteen-month-old infant, all are married. All have children. If I was the assistant DA trying the case, I would have probably thrown in the towel and dropped the charges after the first day of *voir dire* hearings.

The trial gets under way with several motions to suppress by the prosecution. They want to suppress everything related to Northwest Healing, particularly with respect to "the victim's" involvement, since, in their opinion, it is completely separate to that with which the defendant—me—is being charged. Hearing them refer to Slater as the victim and me as the defendant takes a lot of getting used to, and I can't seem to come to grips with it. At any rate, the judge shoots that down. Northwest Healing could be brought up all we want.

They want to suppress the warrant to search Slater's house and car and all the evidence that we have as a result, and that motion falls by the wayside as well. All of that can be used in my defense.

They want to suppress any evidence as to Slater's involvement in the callout at Motel 6, particularly Slater's sniper location at the time of his death, as not being relevant to the matter at hand, which was nothing more than my "torture of the victim in retaliation for perceived wrongdoing on the part of the defendant." Not just no, but hell no.

Finally, the prosecution moves to disallow medical evidence and testimony as to "the physical condition of defendant's spouse and minor child after the alleged mistreatment of same and with regard to the alleged involvement of the victim." Denied!

Good guys four, bad guys zero.

In making his ruling, Judge John Jelderks, a former deputy sheriff turned lawyer turned His Honor, rules that the defense is allowed to present "all necessary evidence supporting any reasons he may have had for undertaking any actions he may have undertaken."

On top of everything else, the normal roles of witnesses in a criminal trial are juxtaposed in this case. In my case, as in nearly every criminal trial, police officers, forensic crime scene investigators, and detectives are the state's primary witnesses. However, these witnesses, though they are technically on the side of the state, are all hostile to the prosecution and sympathetic to the defense. Not a common trait in a major criminal trial, to be sure.

Media coverage goes national on the opening day of *The State of Oregon v. Benjamin M. Geller.* Mention of it is made on the *Today* show, which my mother promises to videotape for me in Florida.

Though things do appear to be slanted in my favor, I am nevertheless terrified as to the outcome of the trial. No matter how you say it, I had still used a deadly weapon to systematically torture a confession from a man who ended up committing suicide as a result. And Bob Slater was, at the time, a police officer, although he was arguably not at the time of his death engaged in the performance of his lawful duties. It is a gamble with the highest stakes—my very freedom—and I've always been a two-dollar table man.

Opening arguments run long and predictable. The assistant DA, my old friend from the Route grand jury, Rebecca Allison, says I am a vengeful man who's had it in for Slater for years. Perhaps I'm jealous of his superior shooting abilities. Maybe I've been afraid of losing my coveted position as primary sniper. It could be that because of recent traumatic events in my life, I'd gone temporarily insane. Who knows? But, she says, even the defense won't be challenging the facts of the case.

And those facts aren't pretty, she adds dramatically. They're not going to be easy to hear. With callous and cold disregard for the value of human life, I intentionally tortured, maimed, and attempted to murder a police officer who was on-duty and working a barricaded hostage standoff with a kidnapper and his victims. Let the defense try to explain *that* away. In so doing, she adds, I coerced him into saying things he otherwise wouldn't have said. Things he was constitutionally protected from saying due to a little court case known as Miranda vs. Arizona. And it would be my very own voice, she says, played in this courtroom from recorded police tactical radio transmissions, that will bear out my intent and my guilt.

In trying to weasel their way out of charges, Allison opines, the defense will likely try to take the focus off the shooter and put it on the victim; to try *him* in this court for actions they are *not* here to judge or consider. Actions that nobody can ever put him on trial for because he, the victim, is dead after having been shot numerous times by me, the defendant. Allison admits that she knows I had been under extreme emotional distress, and says she feels supremely sorry for me. But unfortunate as it may be, duress has never been a justification for any crime, let alone one as heinous as torture and attempted aggravated murder. We've seen that, she says, at the highest government levels, and most would agree that utterly destroying a human by shooting him to pieces is more torturous than waterboarding.

Even I have to admit that, without knowing the facts of the case, she makes me sound pretty bad. But that's only one side.

According to my lawyer, Randy Bulger, it will be proven that, not only am I not guilty, but the wrong party is on trial. Had he not opted to avoid prosecution by taking his own life, the "victim" (I have to smile, as do many members of the jury, at the exaggerated finger quotes Randy makes in the air to establish his disdain at calling Slater the victim) would be on trial for numerous counts that would include, among other things, first degree burglary, first degree kidnapping, aggravated murder, and attempted aggravated murder. It is, in fact, only due to my heroic actions above and beyond the call of duty, my tremendous personal sacrifice, and my devotion to my family and my job, that the terrible truth of this officer-gone-bad story could be exposed. Alone, I had managed to not only solve the most notorious hostage-for-ransom case in the history of the Pacific Northwest, but more importantly, effect the last-second rescue of my wife and daughter from certain death after they had been kidnapped and cruelly entombed alive at the hands of the alleged (and here his finger quotes were stabbing and brutal) *victim*. And the police department, though they felt they had to suspend me because of the way the rescue of my family went down, still felt compelled to recognize me with their highest honor after I had heroically rescued them; the Medal of Valor with two lifesaving clusters.

Several spectators and two jurors actually applaud at the venom in his voice, and Judge Jelderks bangs his gavel for order. The response of the people in the courtroom gives me much-needed strength.

The opening statements, the highlights of which I am only briefly touching upon, take an entire day and a half to complete. By the time they are done, my team and I are psyched and ready to do battle.

The prosecution's strategy is to make me look as though I had it in for Slater from the beginning. Allison calls Chief Moody to testify about the state of hostility between Slater and me and how it affected our work. Moody is made to testify that Slater and I had come to blows over the Route callout after Dan Hollister's funeral, and that he'd ended up ordering us both not to have contact with each other. Allison makes him go through the department's general orders with regards to internal affairs matters, and has him testify that the proper procedure would have been for the complaining party in an IA matter, that is, my complaint against Slater, to go to the detective sergeant to file an initial complaint.

Allison then calls Detective Sergeant Phil Mahoney to testify to the fact that neither Capelko nor I notified him about our suspicions regarding Slater's involvement in Northwest Healing. She gets him to admit that the failure to report a crime such as the one of which we supposedly suspected Slater, was unheard of. She forces him to say, despite the fact that he is obviously on my side, that prior to my shooting Slater, there existed no tangible evidence to indicate Slater may have been involved in any crimes. She has him run through the proper procedure for the reporting of a potential internal affairs and/or criminal matter concerning a member of the department, and wonders aloud why those procedures weren't followed. Her line of questioning amounts to nothing more than speculation and innuendo; a lawyerly version of the old magician's smoke-and-mirror illusion, but it is nonetheless effective, and stands a good chance of having some influence with them.

Through Allison's clever maneuvering, Capelko admits that the results of any forensic examination of the rifle I had used to shoot Slater—which is the same rifle he'd used to kill Connors—would have constituted what is known as "the fruit of the poisonous tree" if there had been any prosecution of Bob Slater for his alleged crimes. She gets him to explain that the evidence would be inadmissible, since the manner in which it was collected (me burglarizing Slater's house to get it) was illegal. Therefore, it and anything it may have eventually led to, could not be used in any court.

Randy Bulger declines to cross-examine Mahoney, instead reserving the opportunity to recall him as a witness for the defense. Of course, this is allowed by Judge Jelderks.

Allison begins calling the members of the SERT team to testify that they knew of the existing animosity between Slater and me, and that they heard me "question" him over the radio, shooting him for (in my own words) "wrong answers." After the first two, Randy concedes they will all testify to the same thing, which was recorded on audiotape anyway. This concession saves a great deal of time.

The prosecution's case is relatively short, since the majority of the evidence consists of the defense's strategy of arguing that the end justified the means. Allison finishes with her strongest evidence, my own voice on tape from the radio transmissions.

At this point, she calls Lieutenant Capelko to the stand. She spends an hour establishing his credentials as a court-recognized expert in police tactical applications and standardized interrogation techniques. Once that is done, she says, "Now, Lieutenant, I am going to play portions of a tape recorded by the Bureau of Emergency Communications, or the 911 operations center, for you. These portions were taken from the tactical SERT incident at the Motel Six in Stratton on July twenty-fourth of this year. Bear in mind these are only portions of the entire tape, which has been marked State's Exhibit ten."

Capelko acknowledges. As I listen to my own words from that night, I see much of the sympathy dissipate from the faces in the jury box. How can I blame them? My own face drains of color as the sound takes me back to that horrible night.

Allison tells Capelko, "Immediately prior to this first segment, I mean only seconds before, Ben Geller shot Bob Slater in the leg. Then there were two quick shots, at least one of them from fired by Geller which struck Slater a second time. The other, possibly fired by Slater, struck the command post, is that right?"

"The shot that struck the command post did come from Slater," Capelko said. "I know. I supervised the investigation."

"Thank you. Now, please listen." She presses the Play button.

"Command post hit by sniper fire!" a desperate voice shouts above a din of confusion on the radio. "All units, Geller is firing on the command post!"

My reply is lost in static. I know I had said "negative," but even I could barely discern it on the tape. There are thirty seconds or so of confusion, which dwindles down to an eerie radio silence, and then, my voice.

"Geller to Slater." A pause. "Geller to Slater!"

After a moment with no response, Slater's voice, "Slater to Geller. Fuck you."

And then me. The sarcasm dripping from every word is not lost on the jury. "Bob, I once told you not to silhouette yourself against the sky. You should have listened. Now, *where is my family?*"

"Slater to Geller" came his weak reply "You'll… never…see them… again."

"Geller to Slater. Wrong answer."

Allison says, "This is where the defendant took his third shot on the victim, Bob Slater. You were there, Lieutenant. What was happening at the command post at this time?"

"We had already evacuated it."

"And, where were you?"

"I was with everyone else. Under cover."

"Were you in a position of safety from the incoming fire?"

"Yes."

"What does the phrase 'wrong answer' mean to you, Lieutenant Capelko, as it was said in the context of this recording, being immediately followed by another sniper shot from the accused to the victim's thighs?"

"It sounds like Ben didn't believe him."

"'It sounds like Ben didn't believe him,'" she echoes. "So, it would appear that if Ben Geller thought you were lying to him, and he really wanted you to tell the truth, he would shoot you until you did. Is that what happened here?"

"Objection, Your Honor," shouts Randy, standing. "She's being deliberately argumentative. And does the assistant district attorney actually want this witness to testify to the state of mind of another man, who by the very nature of the inquiry is under extreme emotional duress?"

"I object to that objection, Your Honor," said Allison without missing a beat. "Defense counsel is now presenting testimony himself as to the defendant's state of mind!"

"Enough! Try to remember that you are attorneys, not children fighting over toys in a sandbox," Jelderks admonishes. "Your objection is overruled, Mr. Bulger. And as for yours, Ms. Allison, I, er... I'm not even going to entertain sensationalism. And, Mr. Bulger, please restrict your objections to the proper format. Now, Lieutenant Capelko, answer the question."

"Yes," Capelko says, gritting his teeth. "That's what it sounds like. Of course, I can't—"

"Thank you, Lieutenant, that will suffice. Now, I'm going to wind the tape forward just a bit, and I'd like you to listen to this portion." There is a brief Chipmunks-sounding babble, and then she slows the tape down. Again, my voice booming out with authority and confidence, and Slater's, sounding weak and pitiful.

"Fuck the money, Slater, where is my family?"

"You'll... never... see them... again."

"And this, Lieutenant, is when Geller fired his fourth and final shot, is it not?"

"Yes."

She restarts the tape. My voice saying, "Geller to Slater." In the background you can hear his screaming. It was chilling.

"In the tunnel... between Northwest Healing... and...and the sewer... You bastard!"

"Now, Lieutenant, as an expert in the area of police tactical applications and interrogations, would you say that inflicting nonlethal gunshot wounds on a man in order to obtain information from him is a standard sniper maneuver?"

"Well, I supposed, it could be construed as that, in a certain light, ma'am."

I nearly crack my neck doing a double take. So do most people in the courtroom, Allison included. She recovers fast, though, the mark of a damn good lawyer.

"Really? Please explain."

"Well, a sniper is trained to make what we call surgically precise shots. The standard is known as 'sub-minute-of-angle.' A minute-of-angle loosely translates to within the diameter of an inch for every hundred yards. So, a shot at a pinhead at the distance of a football field would be minute-of-angle if it were within a one-inch circle of the pinhead. At three hundred yards, it would be within a three-inch circle, and so on. A *sub*-minute-of-angle would be half, or even a quarter, of that. My snipers are all quarter-minute-of-angle shooters.

"Therefore, this indicates that Geller intended to do Slater as little harm as possible. This falls into generalized police doctrine with regard to the application of force, which is using the least amount of force necessary."

"I see," said Allison thoughtfully. "So, you've cross-designated your snipers as inquisitors who are trained to cause as little damage as possible when questioning people with firearms—"

"Objection! Your Honor…"

"Sustained. Miss Allison!"

"Sorry, Judge. Lieutenant Capelko, aren't snipers trained to shoot to kill?"

"No, ma'am. They're trained to shoot to *stop*. Too often, that means to kill. But a sniper wouldn't shoot to kill if it meant the destruction of another life. Say for example, the sniper was presented only with a profile shot of the suspect's head; no other part of his body was available except his leg, behind which the background was clear. Say it was a shot of opportunity situation, where he was ordered to fire upon the suspect. Say the suspect had surrounded himself with hostages, all lined up with his own head. Now, if the sniper had to shoot the suspect, the chances of a through-and-through shot to the head killing a hostage are very high. Unacceptably high. He would shoot the suspect in the leg in order to save the lives of the surrounding hostages. The sniper, like all police, will take only the least destructive means necessary to stop the threat."

"I see."

"Another example would be, say the sniper's family was being held hostage, and the target was the only person alive who knew where—"

"Uh, thank you, Lieutenant, that's quite enough. Lieutenant Capelko, as an expert in police interrogations, have you ever been trained in the use of torture?"

"What he did didn't constitute—"

"A yes or a no will do, sir."

"No."

"Have you ever seen other officers torture a person to glean information, however important it might be?"

Capelko looks right into my eyes and said, "Not in this country I haven't."

"Have you *ever* seen men tortured, Lieutenant?"

"Yes, ma'am. In southeast Asia."

"Can you be more specific?"

Capelko's grip tightens on the handle of the witness stand. "In Hoa Lo prison, Hanoi, Republic of Vietnam, 1971," he said through gritted teeth.

"And when you saw men tortured in Hoa Lo prison in Vietnam in 1971, how did those men react?"

Capelko, his face compacted into a truculent scowl and his teeth grinding together, looks to Randy Bulger for help. His knuckles were white on the dark wood of the stand.

"Objection," shouts Bulger. "I don't even know which objection is most pertinent. Relevancy, foundation, badgering the witness, they all apply."

"Not so fast, Mr. Bulger. Ms. Allison?"

"I think you'll see in just a moment how relevant the question is if you let me continue, Your Honor."

"Can you wrap this up in a few short questions?"

"One more question will suffice, Your Honor."

"Then I'll allow it. Lieutenant, please answer the question."

"They screamed," Vince said quietly.

I know what her next question will be, and I'm sure Vince does too. Allison rewinds the tape for a fraction of a second and poises her finger over the play button.

"And when those men being tortured in Hoa Lo prison in 1971 screamed, did it sound anything like this?"

Down goes the finger. Click goes the recorder.

"Geller to Slater." In the background, but clearly audible, is Slater screaming hideously in what has to be sheer agony. She shuts the tape off. "Lieutenant?"

Capelko, purple with rage, stands up and walks out of the room. Neither Judge Jelderks nor Rebecca Allison try to stop him.

"No further questions."

32

IN OREGON, AS in every other state, the burden of proof lies with the prosecution. They've presented their case well. If I were a juror in this case, going strictly by the letter of the law, after hearing the prosecution's case, I would at this point want to convict at least for aggravated assault charge, but not attempted aggravated murder. Coercion wouldn't even figure in, as far as I was concerned.

Having said that, I'll now say this. Any cop, district attorney, or defense attorney will tell you that the letter of the law, or the right and wrong of an issue, rarely plays much of a factor in deciding a case such as this. American jurisprudence grants us the right to a trial by a jury of our peers. Peers are people, however similar or dissimilar they are to us. And people have emotions, and emotions usually decide issues. Especially issues such as this.

A defendant like me is under no obligation to prove his innocence in court. In fact, the opposite holds true. It is the burden of the prosecution to prove the defendant's guilt. More often than not, it is wiser to allow the prosecution the opportunity to *not* fully prove their case, then throw in one or two elements on the defensive that plant a seed of doubt in the jury's collective   mind, and hope for a verdict of not guilty.

The question I want to raise to the jury in my case, however, has nothing to do with whether I repeatedly inflicted nonfatal gunshot wounds on Bob Slater with the intent of torturing him into disclosing the location of my family. The prosecution has already proven I did that beyond any reasonable doubt. What I want—need—the jury to ask themselves is this: Was doing so *justifiable* under the circumstances? What would *they* have done if their families had been kidnapped and buried alive? Emotions, not facts, are going to save me in this trial.

Judge Jelderks has already ruled that all of the facts and circumstances surrounding Slater's involvement in the Route callout and Northwest Healing can be brought out in this trial, which is the key to my strategy. His ruling was been based primarily on two factors. One, because Bob Slater referred to both incidents on the tape, and two, so my defense team can lay the foundation of the animosity that existed between us.

This effectively allows us to try Slater posthumously for murder, kidnapping, and extortion in the Northwest Healing incident. And as an added bonus, it should serve to clear my name in the Pammi Route shooting, thereby eliminating her chances for a successful lawsuit.

Randy and I have gone over my testimony so many times in the past couple of weeks that I practically have it memorized. Most importantly, he doesn't want me to appear vindictive toward Slater. The jury has to know about the underlying animosity between us, but I have to come off to them as a victim. They have to believe that I hated to do what I did; that I had no other possible recourse. That should be easy. I hadn't.

He doesn't want it to appear that the animosity between us was mutual. The jury can't think I had been stalking Slater. They need to perceive the animosity as coming from Slater to me, and not the other way around. Throughout all the years he hated me, it can't appear to them that I hated him back. If the jury were to think I did, then it would be too easy for them to construe that I gleaned some sort of enjoyment from shooting him, or worse, that my shooting of him was a personal vendetta. Once they thought that, Randy said, it would be all over. After all, I *had* tortured him. Absent a clear, almost holy motivation for doing so, I would be found guilty.

Randy coaches me on how to sound contrite and sorrowful about Slater's suffering, particularly after hearing his agonized screams over the radio. I am not to use words like "after I shot Slater," but to couch my actions in terms such as "after what happened to Bob."

Being a police officer, I've never cared much for defense attorneys, and this is the reason why. He is teaching me to be manipulative and unduly influential, to toe the line between the whole truth and nothing but the truth, and an exaggerated, skewered version of the truth. I can approach the line, maybe even stand on it, but never quite step over it. I don't like it now any more than I had any other time I saw a sleazy defense attorney pull this kind of stunt when some scrote was charged with a righteous crime. However, this time it's *my* ass on the line, so I don't have much choice.

I retaliate by telling Randy my favorite lawyer joke, how a drunk proclaims to the entire bar, "All defense attorneys are assholes." Another drunk approaches him and says, "I heard what you said, and I take exception to that remark, sir," at which point the first drunk says, "Why? Are you a defense attorney?" The second drunk replies, "No, I'm an asshole!"

Randy doesn't find it as funny as I do. Go figure.

He begins his defense by calling Detective Sergeant Mahoney to the stand. If I thought Allison was good at leading her witnesses, Randy is even better. Mahoney makes an excellent witness for me. Randy leads him through a rundown of the animosity between Slater and me. He leads him through the mechanics of the Route standoff, specifically the shooting reconstruction and the conclusions that had been drawn from it.

Mahoney testifies that the reconstruction made it clear that there existed a great deal of doubt as to Slater's version that Route had not had a gun in his hand when I shot him. He admits that though the results are inconclusive, the consensus among the investigators was that I pretty much had to be telling the truth, and that Slater was lying. He goes so far as to testify that he decided to polygraph the only three people who were in a position to see Route's hand—me, Bob Slater, and Pammi Route, something that is almost never done in such a situation. He said that my willingness to do so, and the refusal of Pammi and Slater, caused him to believe there may have been some other motivation for their stories.

When Randy asks him what motivation he thought they might have had for lying about it, Allison objects, and Judge Jelderks sustains her objection. It doesn't matter; now the jury knows that investigators sided with me.

Randy then asks Mahoney if he knows of anything else that might have fueled animosity between Slater and me, leading him right into the Northwest Healing investigation.

Mahoney talks freely about how Lieutenant Capelko had called him the night after the standoff had ended, and told him that I might be in touch concerning my suspicion that Slater was involved.

"At the time," he says, "we just thought the stress of shooting Pammi Route, and her pending lawsuit, coupled with the fact that Ben's friend Andrea Fellotino had been taken hostage and humiliated, was getting to him. Ben called me shortly after Capelko's call and told me he was convinced that Slater had somehow gone into Northwest Healing during the callout while he was supposed to be the side-three sniper and actually negotiated with our hostage negotiators. He said it was Bob Slater who had shot Tim Connors, and that Slater had made Andrea strip naked when she was released just to get at him, because they are close friends."

"And how did this sound to you?" Randy asks.

"It sounded ridiculous. I told him so, and told him that I would see to it that he would take some stress leave whether he wanted to or not. I thought he was either trying to get back at Slater for supposedly lying about whether or not Route had the gun and the fight they'd had, or that he was either psychotic or delusional. In any case, I dismissed his suspicions entirely."

"And did your theory about his motivations prove to be true?"

Mahoney shakes his head and says, "Absolutely not. Quite the opposite, in fact."

"Can you tell us what you mean by that?"

"Of course. We found out that Bob Slater *was* in fact responsible for Northwest Healing."

At this point, Rebecca Allison objects and requests a sidebar consultation. She and Randy approach the bench and spend a minute and a half speaking to the judge. He speaks sternly back to Allison, shaking his head the whole time. A moment later the lawyers return to their separate tables, and Judge Jelderks has the trial resume. Obviously, Allison's objection had been shot down, because Randy continues questioning Mahoney without missing a beat.

"Sergeant Mahoney, you stated that you found out Bob Slater was responsible for Northwest Healing. Would you give the court some background on that incident, and then explain how you found out Slater was responsible?"

"Certainly. Northwest Healing was ostensibly a charitable organization designed to provide food, blankets, and the like to the homeless. It consisted of an office, a main warehouse, and several storerooms—approximately eight thousand square feet of space.

"At the grand opening celebration, several local celebrities and one internationally acclaimed movie star were there to make speeches. Just prior to the opening, a man armed with a fully automatic weapon entered the building and began shooting at the ceiling. This man, who was described as anywhere between five feet seven inches and six feet two inches tall, was wearing a black ski mask to conceal his identity. He locked up all the hostages in two separate storerooms.

"The first officer on the scene, Andrea Fellotino, entered the building alone, and was immediately taken hostage. She was imprisoned unhurt with half the hostages in one of the storerooms. A standoff ensued with SERT, which lasted for twenty-four hours. At one point during this standoff, the suspect gave negotiators a deadline. When that deadline passed, nothing happened."

He pauses, as if to collect his thoughts. The courtroom is riveted by his account.

"Shortly thereafter," he says, "the suspect ostensibly negotiated the release of a hostage. As the hostage was walking out, the suspect shot and killed him, and then extended the deadline. We later learned that this dead hostage was the founder of Northwest Healing, Timothy Connors."

I hear several murmured comments among the spectators in the courtroom. After a moment's pause, Mahoney continues, "The suspect, using cell phones we couldn't disable, contacted members of the wealthy hostages' families and made arrangements with them to provide a fifteen-million-dollar ransom. He arranged with negotiators to have an Oregon State Police helicopter provided to transport him, or *them* as the case may be, and several hostages to an unknown location.

"The money was delivered at nine p.m., which is when Officer Fellotino was released. The plan had called for the suspect to count the money, and then escape aboard helicopter, which was waiting on scene. Yet, after the delivery of the money and the release of Officer Fellotino, nothing happened.

"SERT waited for five full hours and then sent in the EDU robot. The robot searched the entire building, calling out for the suspect, but there was no sign of him. Only then did the team make entry. Several searches were made without finding any trace of the suspect or the ransom money. It was felt that he was hiding among the hostages, who were all unhurt, but to a person, their backgrounds all checked out, and they all said nobody had joined them other than Officer Fellotino after the incident began."

"How did you resolve this issue of the missing suspect?" Randy asks.

"Ultimately, the hostages were taken under guard to the police station for debriefing, while SERT systematically dismantled anyplace large enough for the suspect to hide inside the building. There was no trace of him. At ten a.m., after the entire building had been repeatedly searched as thoroughly as possible, the team secured it, leaving patrol units and detectives on scene.

"Obviously, we had people working around the clock at the scene. Our SERT team had assured us that they were positive that no suspects escaped the perimeter during the incident. At eight p.m., we discovered the method of escape. A tunnel, prepared in advance and concealed under the shelving units in the storeroom, was used to evacuate the suspect to the city's main sewer line.

"This tunnel led approximately fifteen yards feet due east, where it bisected the city's main sewer system. It broke into a line running north and south, which intersected with numerous other lines, providing hundreds of avenues of escape.

"This information was disseminated to detectives at the Stratton police station during late evening the day the siege ended. Present at that briefing was Officer Geller. I thought nothing of his presence and didn't see him once the briefing ended."

"Wasn't anyone concerned with Geller's whereabouts?"

"Not really. I mean, he was a police officer, and everyone trusted him. Plus, we were obviously plenty busy, and I forgot all about him. But early the next morning, not more than an hour after I got home after working twenty-four straight hours, he called me at my house."

"And what did he say?"

To his credit, Mahoney's face displays a lot of emotion, as if in retrospect, he was sorry he hadn't listened to me. His eyebrows are arched, and he conveys a look of sadness. I glance at the jury, and see that to a person, they are intently focused on him and his story.

"He was crying, and he sounded drunk. He kept saying Slater did Northwest Healing and had kidnapped his family. He was nearly incomprehensible. This was not the first such conversation he'd had with me. I took another call like it not long before, in which case Ben had told me he'd recovered a coin that belonged to Andrea Fellotino from the sewer that Slater was hiding behind during the Northwest Healing SERT callout. I thought Geller was plain nuts at that point, and I put no stock into it at all. In fact, Lieutenant Capelko had already briefed me on his condition, so I basically shined him on in this second phone call, too, telling him he misunderstood things he'd heard at the briefing and the like. I wish now I hadn't."

"Can you tell us the gist of this second conversation?" Randy prodded.

"Yeah, basically I told him that Moody—the chief of police—was putting him on leave of absence, and that we would get to the bottom of everything, and then I hung up on him."

Sympathetic heads shake in silent admonition among the jury. Seeing this, I offer up silent thanks to my fair weather god.

"Did you follow up on the call?"

"Well, I called Project Respond, which is a service that makes house calls to mentally ill people. I knew Geller was on leave, so this was about the most I could do. Project Respond always takes an officer with them when they do house visits. I didn't want to do this, but I felt I had no choice. I hoped Geller was only drunk, but in my heart, I thought he was having some sort of delusional breakdown."

"And what happened next?"

"Well, then we found out just how wrong about Geller and his wild accusations we really had been. A clerk from the Motel Six on Frontage Road called in a possible kidnapping. He'd seen a man lead a woman and a little girl into a motel room. He'd seen a gun and thought the woman's and child's hands were bound in back."

Mahoney's voice echoes the self-punishment evident on his face at his failure to believe me. I feel sorry for him, and if he weren't testifying, I would have told him to forget about it.

"As officers were talking to the motel clerk over the phone," he continued, "911 got a call from the motel, from the same room the man had taken the woman and child to. The caller was a woman who said she and her daughter had been kidnapped. The first thing I thought of was what Ben had said. I talked to Vince Capelko, who told me that Ben had called him up and told him the same thing. Capelko told me Geller told him that he, Geller, had stolen the weapons Slater had used at Northwest Healing, and in retaliation, Slater had kidnapped his family."

"Please continue."

"I immediately secured a copy of the tape from Motel Six while patrol units surrounded the motel. I sent a detective to interview the clerk, and I took the tape directly to Ben Geller's house.

"Geller identified his wife's voice. It seems that what he said about his family being kidnapped was true. But the physical description of the man who led his family in the motel room was so radically different from Slater, we knew it wasn't him. Or at least, that's what we thought at the time."

"So, even as you were investigating that incident at Motel Six, you didn't believe that the suspect was Bob Slater?"

"That's right. This guy was at least four inches taller than Slater and had a very dark complexion, as well as a shaved head, facial hair and other differences. But we obviously did believe that Ben's wife and daughter had been kidnapped."

"And what was the response at the motel?"

"We called out SERT. I took Ben with me to the scene."

"And was Slater allowed to respond with the SERT team?"

"Yes."

"Why was that?"

"Because we had no reason not to let him. True, he and Ben had their difficulties, but there was as yet no reason to think Slater had anything to do with Northwest Healing or the kidnapping of Ben's family. We just thought that because of everything that had happened, Ben was fixating on Slater."

"Okay, so what was the time frame between these two callouts, Northwest Healing and Motel Six?"

"Northwest Healing ended on the morning of August fifth. We spent all that day investigating inside the building, and discovered the tunnel late that evening around eight. Then, I was there all night until about five a.m. on the sixth, at which time I went home. Ben called me around six a.m. with that phone call I described earlier to you in which he was hysterical, telling me his wife and daughter had been kidnapped and he had the rifles Slater used in the shooting.

"Later that day, around three thirty p.m., I got another call from Lieutenant Capelko telling me that Ben had called him and sounded much more rational, but was still sticking to that story about breaking into Slater's house and stealing weapons. I began to wonder if he may actually have done so, so I called Slater to ask him."

"And what did Slater say?"

"Slater said Geller was going crazy. He said Geller had called him no less than ten times that day accusing him of kidnapping his family. He said Geller told him he was going to notify the FBI and that he had friends in

the White House. Geller told him if necessary, he had friends in the United
Nations that could sway the president.

"Slater said Geller sounded mentally ill, and that he had intended to
call Chief Moody to let him know what was happening. I asked him if his
house had been broken into, and he said no. I told him what Geller had said
about stealing rifles, and Slater said he was very concerned about Geller's
mental health. He reiterated that there had been no burglary, and that all
his rifles were locked away in his safe as they always had been. He sounded
sincere. He said everyone knows he and Geller weren't friends, but now he
felt responsible in a way for Geller's downfall."

"And did you believe him?"

"Of course I did. Hell, I wish I didn't, but Slater sounded very sincere.
If his house had been broken into, I felt he would have said something. Ben
Geller's mental state, on the other hand, had been declining since the Route
incident, and we felt that it had been a mistake to keep him on the gun for
Northwest Healing. Obviously, we thought watching that hostage get shot
had sent Ben over the edge."

"So, Slater was your sniper on the Motel Six callout."

"Yes, our side-three sniper. We used another qualified sniper on side
one. At the time, there was no real reason not to put Slater on the gun and
every reason to do so."

"And what happened on that callout?"

"Well, Ben was with me in my car, but when our hostage negotiating
unit arrived, I took a moment to confer with the team leader. When I
turned around, I saw that Ben was no longer in my car. I knew he was upset
after finding out that Slater was on the call, and I notified our patrol division
to keep an eye out for him. We put the word to the cops on the street to pick
him up if they found him, and we broadcast a description of his car. After
that, there wasn't much to do."

"And did anyone locate Ben?"

"Yes. A couple of hours later, we heard a rifle shot that came from
somewhere near the incident at Motel Six. Nobody knew exactly where it
had come from. We immediately began asking officers if they had taken
shot, and taking roll to insure that none of our people were hurt. It turned
out to be Geller's first shot at Bob Slater."

"Ben Geller, who had left the command post, returned two hours later
and began shooting at your sniper, Slater?"

"Yes."

"Please continue."

I take a moment to look around. Mahoney's testimony has captured the attention of everyone in the court from the judge, to the jury, to every spectator present.

"As it turns out, Geller *had* broken into Slater's house and stolen two rifles, both of which later proved to have been used at Northwest Healing. It was later proven to be the truth that Slater was, in fact, responsible for committing the terrible crimes at Northwest Healing, all the while pretending to maintain his position as the side three sniper. One of Slater's guns, the sniper rifle with which Slater shot hostage and partner in crime Tim Connors—"

"Objection," shouts Rebecca Allison.

"Overruled," answers the judge immediately. "The witness will continue."

Allison sits down heavily and Mahoney continues, not having missed more than an intake of breath.

"—was the one Geller was using now, to counter-snipe Bob Slater. Geller knew that nobody believed him that Slater had kidnapped his family. But he knew it to be the truth, and he also knew that Lieutenant Capelko was suspicious of Slater as well. Ben figured out that Slater had somehow disguised himself and arranged this callout at Motel Six for the purposes of eliminating witnesses. Knowing what he knows about sniper tactics, Ben was able accurately determine where Slater would have to go in order to get a good shot at the command post, specifically, at Vince Capelko."

Randy says, "So, what you're saying is that Ben, now armed with an extremely accurate high-powered sniper rifle, went to a location from which he could observe the area from which Slater would likely try taking a shot at Capelko. Did Ben try warning anyone? When he saw that Slater actually was going to attempt a shot at Capelko?"

"Yes, he had his standard-issue police radio with him, and he tried to give a warning. But the radio was tuned to the patrol frequency, and though his warning was broadcast over the main patrol net, it did not reach the SERT team in time."

At this point, Randy introduces the patrol tape taken from the 911 dispatching center of my frantic broadcast on the patrol net. The tape is received as evidence, and played for the court. On it, my voice sounds panicked.

"Vince! Get out of the SERT van! Get out now, Slater's got you in his sights!"

"Last unit, repeat?" the dispatcher says, her voice registering her failure to understand what was going on.

"That was Geller, the BOLO subject," another officer says. There follows a brief segment in which it was determined that I must have been referring to Vince Capelko at the SERT incident at Motel Six, and the dispatcher said she was switching frequencies to notify them that Geller was asking for Lieutenant Capelko.

"Before the dispatcher got on our frequency, Geller did. He informed us that he had shot Slater, but that Slater was still alive. Moments later, as everyone was trying to figure out what had happened and how we were going to find Ben, he yelled into the radio for Slater to get away from his gun. We knew what was happening, but we didn't know *where*. At that time, we still thought Ben was emotionally disturbed and that he was firing on Slater out of some paranoid-type delusion. But after a very short time, we discovered that everything Ben had been saying about Slater was true."

"And how exactly did you determine that?"

"Because Ben questioned him over the radio."

"Using the rifle as a backup to his questions?"

"Yes."

"But how could you possibly rely on such answers as being truthful? Wouldn't a man confess to anything under such physical duress?"

Phil doesn't answer for a moment, and I wonder how he would field this one. When he next speaks, it is with confidence in his voice.

"Yes, many men would. However, there was only one man alive who knew the location of Ben's family, and that was the kidnapper. And Ben eventually got that location from him. From the kidnapper. From Slater."

33

THE COURTROOM ERUPTS, and Judge Jelderks pounds his gavel to restore order. Once things quiet down, Randy goes on to introduce the rest of the tape of the SERT communications for the Motel 6 callout as evidence, and plays it for the court.

Bulger approaches an easel set up in the front of the courtroom. On it is displayed an aerial photograph of the Motel 6 and its surrounding terrain. "Sergeant Mahoney, referring to this aerial photograph, can you show us exactly where Bob Slater's assigned sniper position was at Motel Six?"

"Of course." Mahoney approaches the photograph, on which major landmarks are labeled. Using a laser pointer he picks up from the chalk tray on the easel, he says, "Slater was assigned a position on the number three side, which is here. He advised he was about one hundred yards south of room twenty-six, which would have placed him right here, under these trees."

"And can you point out the command post? Specifically, the SERT van."

"Right here."

"Where was his assigned sniper rifle recovered?"

"From his side three position, where he said it was."

"And, where was Slater's body recovered?"

"All the way over here." Even to a layman not familiar with the terrain, it must appear clear that Slater couldn't possibly have been attending to his sniper duties from where he had ended up.

"Did Slater ever advise he was changing his position?"

"No. Nor would he have had any reason to. And if he wanted to change position for a better shot or because he was afraid he'd been spotted, he wouldn't have gone where he ended up. He was completely out of view of the target where he ended up."

"Can you tell us what position his body was in?"

"He was in a prone sniper position, essentially lying behind a high-powered scoped rifle that belonged to his personal collection. The rifle was loaded, the safety was off, and there was a round in the chamber."

"Was this rifle aimed at anything specific?"

"Yes. It was aimed at the SERT van, here, parked at the command post. Specifically, it was aimed directly at the right side of the front windshield, at the area known as the hot seat."

"Was the hot seat occupied at the time of these radio transmissions and shots?"

"Yes. By Vince Capelko."

Randy says, "I will now play the remainder of the audio tape of SERT radio transmissions." He hits the Play button on the recorder, and the final words, Slater's confession, plays out.

"Geller to Slater!"

"Slater to Geller. Fuck you."

"Slater, I told you not to silhouette yourself against the sky. You should have listened. Now, *where is my family?*"

Slater's voice was weak and pitiful. "Slater to Geller, You'll... never... see them... again."

"Geller to Slater. Wrong answer."

This is when I took the next shot. My voice, when next heard on the tape, is incredibly cold and cruel.

"Geller to Slater."

"No more." Slater was crying as he said it.

"Where is my family?"

"Slater to Geller... Northwest Healing... They're there... You win. No more. I did it... I did it all. Lied. About Route's gun. I didn't bring... ammo. To the Route callout... Stupid. Northwest Healing—Connors... I doubled the money. I got it all..." Here he trailed off, mumbling unintelligibly.

"Fuck the money, Slater, where is my family?"

"Too late... no air..."

"Where!"

"Dead... "

Slater's mike remains open, but his voice trails off into silence. From his radio, you can hear my final shot.

"In the tunnel... between Northwest Healing... and...and the sewer... You bastard!" His voice is stronger now.

Randy switches off the recorder. "What happened next?"

"I switched radio frequencies to the patrol net and had officers head toward Northwest Healing. I also started paramedics and fire that way, just in case."

"So you believed what you'd heard Slater say? Despite having a witness who said that Geller's family was inside the motel?"

Mahoney looks directly into Randy's eyes. "Yes, absolutely," he says without hesitation.

"Why? I mean, given the manner in which this confession was given."

"Because Slater volunteered everything Ben had suspected him of, without his asking. All Ben asked him about was the location of his family. But Slater confessed to seeing the gun at the Route callout, doing Northwest Healing, killing Connors, and stealing the ransom money. And he gave the location of Ben's family." Mahoney's tone was that of patient adult stating the obvious to a particularly thickheaded child.

"And it was the proper location, was it not?"

"Yes, it was. Immediately after the confession, Ben went to that location. I had sent patrol officers, and they arrived shortly after Ben discovered and rescued his family."

"Is there any conceivable way that your investigative team could come up with to explain Slater's knowledge of all that, *apart* from his complicity and guilt?"

"None whatsoever."

"Thank you, Sergeant Mahoney. Incidentally, what did the SERT team find when they finally did make entry into the motel room?"

"Nothing. A ground squirrel had been released in the room, probably for the purposes of making noise and showing movement of the blinds."

"A ground squirrel. But no Sharon or Leah Geller?"

"Correct."

"Thank you. Now I'd like to switch gears for a moment, and go somewhere else. After the Motel Six callout was over, and it was determined that Bob Slater had left his assigned position and had attempted to kill Lieutenant Capelko at the command post, what direction did the investigation take?"

"Well, many directions. We tested the rifle Ben had used to shoot Slater, and it was determined it was indeed the same rifle that had been used in Northwest Healing to kill Tim Connors. Tim Connors' fingerprints were found extensively in the tunnel, and a partial palmprint of Bob Slater's was recovered from the underside of the shelving that concealed the tunnel entrance. Slater's fingerprints were also found in two places inside Northwest Healing.

"In addition, we acquired and executed a search warrant at Bob Slater's residence and found a plethora of evidence there."

"Would you please give us a rundown of what was found there?"

Mahoney draws a deep breath and says, "Okay. We were able to follow the paper trail showing how Slater contributed to the financing of the Northwest Healing operation by second-mortgaging his home and liquidating his assets. We also found several documents relating to the planning and execution of the incident. Among those were lease agreements for the building in Connors's name, Stratton city sewer schematics, and rental agreements for excavation equipment. There were numerous hand-drawn diagrams showing the sewer system and potential tunnel locations, as well as notes for the probable locations of all SERT inner perimeter and sniper locations. We even found scripted notes for potential dialogue with hostage negotiation personnel.

"Probably the most damning evidence taken from Slater's house though, was nearly two hundred thousand dollars in cash that came from the Northwest Healing ransom money."

Randy then introduces photocopies of bills that had been delivered to Northwest Healing as part of the ransom money provided by Pio Cantelli, the father of actress Loretta Epstein, the richest hostage. The only intact bundle, one of fifty hundred-dollar bills, matched serial number for serial number.

"Was the rest of the ransom money ever located?"

"No. Exactly one hundred and ninety-one thousand, two hundred and fifty dollars of Northwest Healing money was recovered, which included a thousand dollars in Slater's pocket. The rest remains completely unaccounted for."

"So what you're saying is, fourteen million, eight hundred and eight thousand, seven hundred and fifty dollars of that ransom money is still out there somewhere?"

"Well, I can't do the math that quickly in my head, but yes, I believe that's right."

"Is the investigation complete?"

"No. The case is still classified as open, and will remain so until we can account for the rest of that money. There still remains the possibility of another, unidentified third party out there somewhere who was a silent partner of sorts, who may have ended up with it."

"But you don't think so."

"No, personally I think, from what we found in Slater's and Connors's homes, that it was just the two of them, and that when Slater killed Connors, he was the only remaining conspirator. There are, however, those in our office who think otherwise. Handwritten correspondence in a third, unknown person's script with what could be perceived as incriminating statements was located in Slater's house. Some of it may well have been related to Northwest Healing, but much of this correspondence was of a bizarre, uh, sexual nature, and may not have been related to the case at all. It indicated that Slater was a closet homo—"

Allison is on her feet before Mahoney could finish his sentence. "Objection! Foundation, your honor, and is it really necessary to further rub this man's reputation into the dirt on gossip and heresay?"

"Watch your wording, Miss Allison! You don't get to render judgements in my court on what is heresay evidence. However, I agree with you, and your objection is sustained."

A heated buzz goes up from all directions in the courtroom, and Judge Jelderks had to bang his gavel yet again to quiet the room down.

"The question is withdrawn," said Bulger. "Sergeant, what is your conjecture about the rest of the Northwest Healing money?"

"Personally, I think he stashed the money somewhere and it will remain hidden until discovered by a lucky disinterested party. Or perhaps, forever, if he secured it remotely enough."

"Wow, that leaves a lot of food for thought. But I don't think anyone stumbling on nearly fifteen million dollars in cold, hard cash would remain disinterested for very long."

Mahoney remains silent, and after a moment, Randy says, "I have no further questions."

Judge Jelderks looks at Rebecca Allison. "Cross-examination, Ms. Allison?"

"I have no questions for this witness," she says dejectedly.

"You may step down, Sergeant."

"And now," announces Randy Bulger with a grandiose flourish, "I would like to call Stratton Police Officer Benjamin Geller."

My turn. A muted buzz goes up from the spectators as I walk to the stand. I raise my right hand, and with utter solemnity, swear or affirm to tell the truth, the whole truth, and nothing but the truth.

That won't be a problem. I'd been doing it continuously since the Route callout.

Epilogue

I HELP LEAH negotiate the tight aisle of the 767 as people stretch to vie for their turn at the overhead luggage compartment. The flight was five hours, and our connection in Atlanta was delayed for three hours. But we made it, and she is having a tough time in the crowded narrow aisle.

It's been two weeks since the trial ended, and after a week of hell reliving all that crap in the courtroom, I have given myself a vacation.

My mother will be waiting for me in the terminal at the bottom of the escalators. Even here in Daytona Beach, probably the smallest international airport I've ever seen, waiting relatives cannot greet their loved ones at the gate.

Sharon is not with us, although she was supposed to come. She canceled at the last minute because last night, she entered the den while I was on the phone, and I cut the conversation short with an "I'll see you tomorrow, Ma," and then went to the store.

The moment I left, she pressed redial, and Andrea Fellotino answered.

I think I am perhaps the stupidest man alive. Not because I forgot to hit zero after I hung up, but because I cannot seem to let her go even though I want more than anything to be an intact nuclear family with Leah and Sharon. I only wanted to make sure Andrea was okay, but of course, that has led to big trouble in the past. Anyway, I now realize such a family and the happiness that goes with it is something I do not I deserve.

Leah and I finally make it to the jetway. I constantly have to overcome the urge to pick her up and carry her, but it is a matter of great importance to her to do this herself. I am very proud of her. There are huge blank spots in her memory, and she sounds much like a deaf person who has recently learned to speak, but physically, she is making steady progress. Her recovery is slow but the doctors say the prognosis is good. Another year, perhaps two, and if everything goes well, she should be near the way she was before the incident. Of course, progress could cease without warning anywhere along the line.

"Look, Leah, it's Big Mama!" Nobody is quite sure how this five-foot-nothing mother of mine, whom I have labeled a giant among midgets, acquired that nickname, but it rooted immediately and is now very much a part of her personality.

Leah's face lights up. No amount of brain damage can mask the adulation in her eyes at the sight of her beloved grandmother.

My mother has not seen us yet, though she studies the disembarking crowd intently. She looks small, but not fragile. The recent death of my father has taken a tremendous toll on her, but has failed to break the spirit of the woman who has always been the cast-iron apple of my eye.

Her eyes widen briefly when they take in the way her granddaughter shambles like an old woman, but she recovers quickly and gracefully.

Leah doesn't mind Big Mama picking her up and allows herself to be swung in circles before issuing a ladylike request to be set down.

"Where's Sharon?" my mother asks suspiciously.

"It's a long story," I tell her. This won't suffice for long. I know I must either try to lie to her or suffer her indignation. I have no desire to do either and have never been very good at the former. I haven't been very good at the latter, either if I think about it.

Mom makes chitchat with Leah all the way home. The kitchen is spread with kosher salami and homemade Italian wedding soup, which makes me smile. I once told Mom it was a difficult recipe to find, but the dish was a favorite of mine. She found the recipe immediately and has made it for me ever since. Leave it to Mom.

Our internal clocks are scrambled and Leah conks out after only a few bites.

"So, why isn't Sharon with you? It had to cost a fortune to change the tickets," she says.

"She's furious with me."

"I gathered. Why? Or do I not want to know?"

I look at her and say, "I promised her I was getting off SERT like she wanted. Last night, I told her I changed my mind and was staying on the team. We had a major fight, and she said she wasn't coming."

This is a half-truth. We had that fight last week, and it was a really good one. I hold my breath to see if Mom buys it.

"I don't blame her," she says. But it's what she leaves unsaid, and the way she doesn't say it, that tells me she knows I'm not telling the truth, the whole truth, and nothing but the truth, so help me God.

When I was a child, I used to love the *Captain Kangaroo* show. Bob Keeshan used to end the show with the saying, "Now, remember, kids, you can fool some of the people all of the time, and all of the people some of the time, but you *can't fool Mom*." I swear he must have met my mother at some point.

"So, they're going to let you stay on as a sniper, are they?" she asks.

"Yeah. That's what the chief tells me. I'm supposed to start working again when I get back next week, assuming I pass the psychological eval."

"I hope you don't. I hope they see how dumb you really are for wanting to go back to that no-good job. And after spending a fortune on law school, too."

Mom hasn't stopped harping on that since the day I became a cop. And she always hated the fact that I joined SERT. It seems that in her book, bespectacled Jewish lawyers aren't supposed to go around shooting people.

"So that's a reason for her not to come out and visit? Far be it from me to get involved, but you better listen to me on this one. Don't blow the one thing you've got going for you, which is family. Don't do that, Ben. So, enough about that. Tell me about court. How'd you get your own lawyer so mad at you?"

"Not much to tell. He wanted me to tell the jury how difficult it was for me to shoot Slater. He wanted it to seem like I hated doing it and I was really sorry. He felt that if I didn't seem contrite, the jury would think I was vindictive."

"So?"

"So, I couldn't do that. It wasn't true, and it would have looked like a lie if I'd tried it."

"What did you say?"

"He asked how I felt about the shooting. It took me a long time to answer him, but I finally told him that it felt good. I thought he was going to pass out, he looked so shocked."

"Why would you say that? A lawyer, and you said it felt good to shoot him?"

"Yeah, Ma, because it *did*. The jurors gasped, even the judge did a double take at me. I thought my lawyer, was going to have a coronary. But it seemed to be the right tack, so I pushed it. I told them Slater had kidnapped my family, and that even though I didn't know it at the time, Leah was lying in that little chamber, dying. So shooting him felt good, and I told them so. Randy asked if I felt sorry. I said yes. I was sorry I didn't kill Slater myself. I said that every time I look at my little girl's frustration because nobody can understand what she's saying, I'm sorry. Every time I remember her climbing the tree in the backyard and now she can barely walk, I'm sorry. About Slater, I could care less.

"The prosecuting attorney, this young hotshot gal just itching to put a cop away, jumped all over it. She tried getting me to tell the jury how I *wanted* to shoot Slater after what he did. I testified that as a father and a husband, I would have loved to kill Slater, but as a human being and a police officer, I couldn't do that. But I'd have given up anything, my job, my conscience, *anything,* to save my wife and baby. So, shooting Slater, while it felt good, was simply the last possible way to find them. Not to mention the fact that the shooting started because Slater was aiming to gun Capelko down."

"How do you think the jury took it?"

"I don't know, Ma. I suppose, we'll never know."

"I think they would have found you innocent."

"There is no innocent finding, Ma. Not guilty is how they find you. There's a technical difference. Anyway, I agree with you. I think they'd have found me not guilty."

"That prosecutor, Miss Hot shot Allison, who looks Jewish I might add, was all over the news screaming for a new trial, saying how crazy the police department is for taking you back."

"Well, I think I always had the support of the police department. They had to take me to trial over this, but I think they always hoped I would be found not guilty, and Chief Moody even told me during the trial that my job was waiting for me if they did."

"But won't they try you again?"

"Nope. The DA's office says that in light of overwhelming community support and in view of the evidence presented at the trial, they no longer feel that they have a prosecutable case. After the judge declared a mistrial, they dropped the charges, so there can be no more prosecution."

"And that was because someone tried to buy off the jury."

"Right. One juror was caught taking a bribe, and five others admitted they were approached anonymously, by a party offering a hundred thousand apiece for a 'guilty' verdict. They think he approached every one of them, but only five were willing to admit it. The others were probably going to take it."

"Tell me honestly, and don't lie to your mother. Is there some other guy out there this Slater was working with, who got all that money? Someone with a vendetta against you, willing to spend a million dollars to see you go to prison?"

"No way, Ma. It was a kook. A publicity stunt by some rich mamzer who wants to screw things up. That money is probably buried in the ground under a cabin in the woods or wired into some Swiss bank account, never to be seen again. Slater was alone after he shot his partner. There was nobody else, and even if there was, why would they want to get to me?"

Mom nods her head and visibly relaxes. Either Captain Kangaroo was wrong, or my mother *wants* to believe the lie. The fact that some of the bills in the jurors' possession matched the recorded serial numbers of the ransom has not been made public, and they tell me it never will be. But eventually, it will leak out.

My week passes without incident. I gain five pounds and wish I could stay here forever. When I get back to Stratton, I pass my psychological review board with flying colors. I'm not surprised; I've slept like a baby since taking Slater apart with that rifle.

And now, its all over. I futz around the house and get ready for bed. I want to get a good night's sleep. Tomorrow, I go back to day shift patrol. I wanted to work nights, but the department thinks they should keep their eye on me for a while. So, it's day shift patrol, when all the brass and suits are on duty to baby-sit me. Okay, I can handle that; it's better than twenty-five to life in the pen.

I check all the windows and doors, then release Schmeisser, the German shepherd the police department retired early and gave me for protection after the trial. He will let me know if anyone comes into the yard. Unless, of course, they bring a steak. Schmeisser loves steak.

It is Sharon's first night back from her own vacation to her mother's house ten blocks away, and she has asked me to sleep in the den. I can live with that. I'm just glad she came back.

I check my e-mail one last time before bed. Yesterday, I got a request from the man who ghostwrote the story of that California Highway Patrol officer who was kidnapped and held for ransom last year. The book is due out this fall, and I hear it is supposed to sell well. Who knows, maybe I can write about what happened to me.

Today, there are three messages. The first is junk mail telling me how to extend the length of my penis without any painful suction devices. The second is from the *New York Times,* requesting an interview. How they got my e-mail address I don't know. The police department has asked me to forward all such requests to the public information officer.

The last e-mail is from watchinu@hotmail.com. It is entitled "Bob Slater." Hesitantly, I open it.

There is a lot I can do with $14,708,750. You cannot hide and cannot run. Bob Slater lives on through me. Expect to see me when you don't expect to see me. Have a nice day. :)
    Yours,
    Watchin U

I forward this to Phil Mahoney, then delete it from my computer. Looking at the door to my bedroom, I wish to God it was not so tightly closed against me, and I lie down on the couch and turn off the light.

RETURN FIRE, the stand-alone sequel to Barry W. Ozeroff's SNIPER SHOT, picks up Ben Geller's story two years after his epic confrontation with fellow sniper Bob Slater, in which Geller thwarted Slater's staged hostage-for-ransom siege at Northwest Healing.

The fifteen-million-dollar ransom ended up in the possession of a heretofore unknown co-conspirator of Slater's, who then began threatening that he would use it against Geller to avenge the death of Slater.

When Geller is finally at a point in his life where he is getting comfortable with his family, his life erupts again with ghosts of the past. It's never a good time to have your world turned upside-down...

RETURN FIRE

SWAT sniper Ben Geller and his family have a lot on their plate. They were victims of a recent hostage siege, their debts far outweigh their earnings, and they're trying to adopt a troubled young African-American boy. So the last thing they need is to be stalked by a madman with a grudge, a creative imagination, and fifteen million dollars.

Ben has other problems as well. Of the three ladies in his life, the only faithful one is his eight-year-old daughter. The other two—the wife he thought he knew, and the badge-wielding girlfriend who thinks she owns him—are both full of surprises. When the stress gets to him, and his job is threatened by an excessive force complaint, Ben realizes he's lost all control of his life.

Then things begin to change for the better, leaving Ben back in full control. But better isn't always what its cracked up to be, and control isn't just something Ben's lost... It's something he never had.

read more...

RETURN FIRE EXCERPT

I STARE AT the computer in disbelief, wishing I had never decided to check my email. Nearly three months have passed since I got one of these, and I had begun to think it might be over.

But clearly, it is not. Jesus.

"Ben! Come on!" shouts my wife. I hear her put on Christmas music in the living room, and I am beginning to smell the first batch of cookies. Glancing at the screen again, I try to decide if I should show it to her.

Just as I'm about to call her in, the sound of sirens in the distance gives me pause. My ear, trained by nineteen years on the job, picks the sounds apart and identifies them individually. Two, maybe three, police cars, an ambulance, and the old-school mechanical windup of a firetruck, all going somewhere fast. Idly, I wonder what has ruined someone else's holiday. But as the sirens fade to the west, toward the tracks and their inevitable other side, I dismiss them. Not my problem, right?

Some questions are better left unasked.

"Ben?"

"Hang on, Sharon, I'll be right there," I yell. She has every right to know about the email. It is my responsibility to tell her, but on the other hand, I don't want to do that to her. I especially don't want anything to ruin tonight. Sharon wouldn't be able to hide the fact that something's wrong, and Leah, our eight-year-old, would pick up on it immediately.

No. Can't do it. I delete the email, close the program, and hit the power button. Not tonight. Not on Christmas Eve.

I go to the living room and pause, looking, before I enter. I am the worst kind of schmuck, and I do not deserve this, but here it is, and it's mine. Looking around the room, I take a mental picture of it all. Not just of the sights, but of the sounds and scents, too. It's as if I have an instinctual knowledge that all this might change, and I want to preserve it forever in my mind as it is now.

Having already experienced just that, I tend to follow such instincts.

The lights of the tree cast a soft red and green glow about the living room, which smells strongly of natural pine. Beautifully wrapped presents are piled a little too high for a family of only three. Sharon has put on the *CHARLIE BROWN* Christmas CD, and we listen to their version of the traditional carols. Seeing me at the door, Leah begins dancing the silly dance of the *PEANUTS* characters to the tune of *LINUS AND LUCY*, and we all laugh.

Like roughly a third of American Jews, the Geller family celebrates Christmas, minus the Christ part. I just can't bring myself to deny Leah the experience of it all. It's Christmas Eve 2007, and all seems right with the world. Welcome to this side of Stratton, Oregon's proverbial tracks, where white, middle-class working stiffs thrive.

I am Officer Benjamin Geller, a veteran of the Stratton police department; a former corporate tax attorney who left the good life to fulfill a boyhood dream of becoming a police officer; one who has learned that we all live by the choices we make.

I am also a SWAT sniper. Originally, the Stratton SWAT team was known as SERT, or Special Emergency Response Team, but after a little incident involving me, the team was disbanded for a year, and when they brought it back six months ago, it came with the name change. Out with the old, and in with the new, I guess.

I don't like to think about that little segment of my life, and though I am sure I'll have to recount it at some point, for now all I will say is that about a year-and-a-half ago, I shot another cop during a SWAT incident. He was a fellow sniper, and I nailed him a total of four times with my .308 sniper rifle from a distance of about 120 yards, smashing his legs and hips like dry twigs. I guess I can't say it was an accidental discharge. He was my partner, and he shot himself in the mouth after I was done with him. 'Nuff said.

It is raining outside, and the forecast calls for snow. Snow is a rare treat in Stratton, which is only about fifteen miles east of Portland, but a white Christmas... Well, that's almost unheard of.

I am lucky to have the holiday off. My normal days off are Sunday and Monday, and Christmas happens to fall on Monday this year. This means I will also get New Year's Eve off.

It is going on ten thirty p.m., and Leah is fading fast. She doesn't believe in Santa Claus, or anything she can't see, touch, or otherwise experience; a characteristic she has learned from me. Nevertheless, she has made it a goal to stay up until midnight, just in case, but she will not make it.

Sharon is baking cookies. Not Christmas sugar cookies, but real, gooey chocolate chip ones. Is there another kind? The first batch is due out of the oven in four minutes.

And then, as if preordained by The Great Destroyer of Holiday Cheer, my department Nextel phone goes off, and I roll my eyes. Guys with families like to be with them on holidays, so there's almost always a last-minute outbreak of the flu on Christmas. The department has to maintain minimum shift staffing even on the major holidays, so when I happen to be off duty on Christmas, I get called first, because I'm the Stratton Police Department's token Jew, which is supposed to mean I won't mind coming in. Well, tonight they will be surely disappointed.

Sharon's eyes plead with me, and she says, "Ben, you're going to tell them no, aren't you?"

"Of course I am, honey," I say, opening the phone and revealing the little color screen.

But it's not a sergeant's pleading text for overtime. Not just my Christmas, but that of about twenty-five or thirty other families, has just been ruined. I look at the words and wish they simply weren't there. Not tonight.

SWAT CALLOUT. DOMESTIC HOSTAGE/BARRICADED SUSPECT. ATTEMPTED MURDER/KIDNAP/ASSAULT. COMMAND POST ROCKLEDGE PIZZA HUT. SAFE APPROACH FROM THE SOUTH.

"Christ," I mutter.

Sharon, who knows I'm not much of a praying man, looks at me and says, "Is it a SWAT callout?"

I can tell what's coming. Still, I can't just not go, simply because it's Christmas.

"Yes."

"Ben, it's—"

"Shar," I interrupt, cutting her off. "There are seventeen other guys on the team who really *DO* celebrate this holiday. They have to leave their families and go, just like me. It's not like I have a choice."

Sharon slams the oven door open and proclaims, "You do have a choice, Ben. You can choose your family over your job."

I'm not doing this. I really don't want to do this. "Come on, Sharon. You know someone has to do it. You never complain about the overtime or the extra ten percent I get for being on SWAT."

"Yeah, but it's *CHRISTMAS* Ben. Can't you just say you've been drinking? Paulson does it all the time!"

"Shar, you know I can't do that. I've got to go. You *KNOW* this."

"But think of Leah. What about *HER* holiday?"

"Sharon, do you really want me to say it?"

"Say what, Ben?" she retorts, the challenge plainly evident in her voice.

So I say it. "When you and Leah were being held hostage, what was I doing? Was I out there doing what I had to, or did I call in sick?" I start getting ready to leave, using exaggerated movements to let her know I mean business.

Sharon glares at me with an expression that looks capable of freezing water. "Well, I guess I should be thankful you weren't in what's-her-face's apartment getting laid! At least not that night."

I stop what I'm doing, and turn to confront her face-to-face. I'm so pissed, my body is as tense as steel, and for a moment, I consider slapping her. Instead, I grab her face roughly and kiss her, hard. "Sharon, I love you. It's *OVER* with Andrea. I think I've more than made up for that, don't you? Now let me get out of here, 'cause the sooner I leave, the sooner I'll be back, okay?"

She wipes a tear and exclaims, "Merry friggin' Christmas, world!" This is real profanity for her, a sign she is truly angry. It's also a compromise, and a temporary end to the hostilities.

It's too late, though. Leah is in tears now. She cries whenever Sharon and I fight, because the memory of when I moved out, back when *IT* was going on, is so fresh.

"Daddy, are you going away again?" she asks. Before I can answer, her head jerks violently to the right, narrowly missing the wall.

She still suffers from residual effects of anoxic-ischemic encephalopathy—a form of brain damage—and undergoes occasional random spasmodic muscle contractions that make her jerk like a marionette at the hands of a drugged-out puppeteer. This, along with occasional holes in her memory, are the only reminders of the time when she and Sharon were kidnapped and buried alive without sufficient oxygen, and I had to use my .308 to torture their location out of the renegade officer who had kidnapped them. But as I said before, I really don't feel like talking about that.

"Yeah, baby, Daddy has to take off for a while."

I belatedly realize she interprets this as me going away to live in a trailer, which I did when her mother caught me screwing Andrea Fellotino, another Stratton cop, just before the aforementioned incident, and I hastily add, "But I'll be back before you get up in the morning, Princess, and we'll open all the presents together. I'm not moving out again."

She visibly relaxes, and I go into the bedroom to change. I keep a pair of camouflage BDUs and some cold-weather gear at home. Because I live close to the police station, I am usually among the first to arrive at the SWAT van when the team gets called out.

Ten minutes later, bearing a Tupperware container of steaming cookies for the team, I am racing toward the Stratton police station. There is no traffic, and I am able to make the two-mile trip in record time. After all, 'tis the night before Christmas, and all through the city, not a creature is stirring, except for a Rockledge shitbag who is holding his family hostage. Hell, that's not that big a deal for that part of town; around the precinct, we usually refer to it as Rockledge foreplay.

I arrive to find the parking lot empty and quiet. Buzzing myself into the portion of the building housing the fire department, I open the fourth bay, revealing the big, midnight blue SWAT van. I unplug the 220 umbilical, toss it into an exterior cabinet, and climb aboard. Removing the key from the ashtray, I start the big Caterpillar diesel and pull the rig out onto the tarmac. I then start the generator, and turn on the night vision-preserving red interior lighting. Next, I light up the rig's various computer systems, then go to the back and begin gathering my gear.

Within moments, my teammates begin to arrive. Carlos "Backflip" Vega is first, smelling a little like beer, which I pretend not to notice. Hugh "Baby Hughie" Wilkes is next, wearing a Santa cap, which he will likely try to wear in his place in the entry team "conga line." Next is Ray "Oy Vey" Schmeer, my new sniper partner. We are close friends, unlike my last sniper partner, Bob Slater, whom I shot to pieces.

"Happy Chanukah, Helen," says Ray.

"Sieg heil!" I bark in return. He knows I hate the nickname Helen, which stems from a day I shot so poorly someone remarked that my target looked as if Helen Keller had shot it. Helen Geller, get it? Ray's team-issued nickname is Pap—Pap Schmeer—but I call him Oy Vey, because coupled with his last name, it fit so closely to the Yiddish expression "Oy vey iz mir," which means, "woe is me." There is nothing remotely Jewish about Ray, who is a Teutonic blond-haired, blue-eyed German. I tell everyone we meet that he is Jewish, which used to piss him off, but now he just finds it funny.

He clicks his heels together, stands ramrod straight, and spews in flawless German, *"KUCHEN MEINER MUTTIS SIND IMMER AUSGEZEICHNET!"* The way he delivers it, it sounds like a phrase recorded from one of Hitler's speeches, but in fact means 'My mommy's cake always taste great,' and is the only thing he knows how to say in that guttural language.

It is team practice that the van will leave when the first five to respond are dressed out and fully prepared. That way, we have a ready-made IRT, or immediate reaction team, to conduct whatever type of immediate operation that might be called for—downed officer rescue, hostage extraction, emergency hot entry, or anything else that may be required. Even we snipers are cross-trained for such a possibility.

Most of the men (or the woman, as in the case of Ellen "Hairdo" Fitzsimons, Stratton's first female SWAT member), keep their equipment in the van so they can respond from home and prepare while en-route to the scene. Quickly, the initial responders join me, and start getting ready.

Several folks show up, and Ellen Fitzsimmons is the last to arrive before we pull out. Not one to worry about modesty, she doffs her uniform and dons her BDUs without regard for being seen in her underwear. Too bad she's built like a Russian Olympian, but frankly, I'm glad of it. Not a month ago, I was attacked by a man whose wife I had just arrested for beating him up, and Ellen was my cover officer. She damn near wiped the floor with the guy. Not only is she willing to give one hundred percent in a fight, but she is more capable of laying a major hurtin' on someone than half the men in this outfit.

Fourteen minutes after my arrival, it is time to get under way. Carlos Vega gets on the computer and sends a page that the van is leaving. Hugh Wilkes, who has been our driver since he joined SWAT two years ago, gets the van rolling. Team leader Stan "Housing Authority" Hauser and Fitzsimmons drive the chase cars, one in front, and one behind the van. As we roll out the back gate, we slow briefly, and I extend an arm, hooking Brian "Armpit" Pole, the assistant team leader, into the van.

Surfing the floor against the motion of the van, I make my way to the weapons locker and carefully extract my rifle. It is a highly customized Remington 700 with a beautiful Dedal DayVision/NightVision interchangeable starlight scope. This rifle was once used to score third place in the National High-powered shooting competition at Camp Perry, Ohio. Its previous owner and the holder of that title was Bob Slater, my late former partner, of whom I spoke earlier.

After the matter of my little disagreement with Slater over the kidnapping of my family was adjudicated to my favor in court, Slater's parents donated the rifle to the police department for use on the SWAT team. Being the primary sniper, it fell to me. We share some significant history, this rifle and I, and we have grown rather fond of one another.

Lovingly, I load three .308 cartridges into the magazine. The second one is in case I have two bad guys to kill, and the third is in case one of the first two is a dud. It doesn't take more than one round to kill a man with this baby. Unless, of course, you're only torturing him.

Gustavo "Mini Me" Oronco, who has just comes from the scene, fills us in on the call. Oronco is a jovial five-foot, three-inch Hispanic entry team member who is bald as a cue ball and is considered by all to be one of one toughest hombres on SWAT. He tells us that it is the Hicks family, and that Delray has stabbed his wife. He said the ambulance crew told him it doesn't look as if she's going to be celebrating Christmas this year, or ever again, for that matter.

I am well acquainted with Delray Hicks, his wife Denise, and their kids, as is just about every officer in Stratton. We have been dealing with them for years. They have two children, a teenage girl and a younger boy, neither of whom stand a chance of making it in the real world. Delray is a big, strapping man, but his wife is a whale, standing at least five-ten and weighing in at nearly four bucks.

Oronco tells us Christmas Eve got underway in the Hicks' trailer when, during an argument, Delray beat all but Jesus out of Denise in front of the children, and she returned the favor by smashing a beer bottle over his head. Either the nasty cut he received, the loss of the beer, or both, pissed him off, and he sank a ten-inch butcher knife into her right kidney

When the cops showed up, Delray answered through the door, threatening to "gut the first honkey-ass muthafucka'" who tries to take him out of there. Fortunately for us, Delray is more of a knife guy than a gun guy.

This is exactly the sort of thing our hostage negotiators live for. HNT, or the hostage negotiating team, loves to listen to the bad guy, kiss his ass, offer him milk and cookies or maybe a hug, then have him come out once they gain his trust. It generally works, but it can go on for hours, which doesn't bother them at all. Of course, HNT doesn't have to sit outside in thirty-five degree pouring rain, either.

I paint my face a frightening combination of green and black, hoping for a Navy-SEAL-in-a-foreign-jungle look. I hate the paint, but I like the look. I put on my fleece-lined Gore-Tex green jacket and my dirty, floppy boonie hat. Over my long underwear is a pair of lightweight rain pants, over which my BDU pants go. The idea is that my BDUs can get soaked, but my legs will stay dry. It rarely works like that.

After pulling on a pair of camouflage green hunting gloves with a slit for my trigger finger, my ensemble is complete. I attach a remote transmit button to the outside of my left index finger by means of a Velcro strip and don my radio headset. Switching over to the proper frequency on my portable, I do a radio check. Finally, I jump up and down, and hearing no jingling or other unusual noises, I pronounce myself fully prepared.

I have a backpack containing water, energy bars, fresh gloves, binoculars, wire cutters, waterproof waxed paper notepad, space pen that can write on the moon, and a host of other equipment, which I throw across my back. I place my rifle into a woodland camo Gore-Tex drag bag, and wait for the van to stop rolling.

I know this trailer park well; particularly number eighteen, the Hicks' trailer. The park itself is situated on a main road, but number eighteen is in the back and faces railroad tracks, a wastewater treatment plant that smells suspiciously like a wastewater treatment plant, and a large, tree-covered hillside.

Ever since he got out of prison, we've all known that there would be a callout here. I first arrested Delray twelve years ago, when he was nineteen, for beating a neighbor with a metal pipe. The DA dropped the Assault I charge in exchange for his pleading guilty to an Assault IV with a minimum of six months, and which he did locally. He was just smalltime then. His last stint was seventy-eight months for manslaughter. Delray Hicks has spent over half his adult life in either prison or jail.

Stan Hauser goes to a filing cabinet and removes a file marked "Hicks." It is a site survey of Hicks' trailer—a detailed plan for rapid deployment of the team if there is a callout there. It covers most of the logistical aspects of deployment and operation, such as the best routes of approach, the best staging areas for the command post and hostage negotiation team, and suggested locations for inner perimeter team members and snipers. Also covered in the site survey are detailed drawings and measurements of the trailer and its interior, evacuation routes, the gas plans, entry plans, LifeFlight landing zones, medical staging areas, the nearest schools, etc. There are similar plans for every hospital, school, government building, and trouble spot in our area of operations, which includes all of Multnomah County except the city of Portland, which has its own SERT team. Included in the packet are photographs of the entire family, and I take one of Delray for target identification. We update this file regularly, whenever new potential trouble spots are identified.

Studying the plan, I see that if I choose the predetermined side one primary sniper location, I will have the cover of heavy brush, and a straight 105-yard shot into Hicks' front door and living room window. My partner will be lucky; his best position is from a neighbor's trailer directly behind Hicks'. While I'm freezing my ass off lying in a puddle and getting rained on, some old lady will be serving Ray Schmeer coffee and cake while bending his ear about her grandchildren. *OY VEY.*

The van slows, and the siren is silenced. As the cacophony around me quiets, it is time again to wonder if I will have to kill a man tonight. This time, though, my thoughts differ from before I joined the exclusive club whose members have taken human life. I still wonder if I will have to do it again; only I no longer experience dread at the thought. I have already bloodied my hands in this job, and whereas I don't *WANT* to do it again, I know that I can if I have to. Sometimes I am amazed at how I can so flippantly consider the very real prospect of killing again.

One thing that makes it easier in this case is that it is what we refer to as an "AVA NHI" situation, as are any problems between Delray Hicks and his wife. AVA NHI is copspeak for asshole versus asshole, no humans involved. The only potential humans involved are the kids, maybe. At least, the youngest one. As shallow as that seems, it really does make considering his death much easier to stomach.

The van comes to a complete stop, and I throw the pack across my back and grab the drag bag containing my rifle. Shouldering past everyone, I position myself at the rear door, where I am joined by Ray. Since we're the first to be deployed, we like to be the first out of the van.

Our job is not so much to shoot the bad guy as it is to make detailed observations of everything going on at the target location, filter that information, and report it and its meaning to the command post. Our roles on the team are commonly referred to as primary and secondary sniper (primary on side one, or the front of the target location, and secondary on side three—the rear; the sides being numbered clockwise from the front of the building), but technically we are sniper/observers. Observing is by far the majority of what we do.

It was *ALL* we did until May 24, 2005. That was the night Hugo Route tried to kill his infant daughter, and I was forced to take him out as he placed a .357 Magnum to the baby's neck. My shot, which should have been taken by my then-partner Slater, passed through his wife's bicep on the way, severing her brachial artery and nearly causing her to bleed out. The wife, Pammi, later conspired with Slater to lie in her testimony to say her husband was not holding a gun at the time of the shooting. She was caught in her lie, but the police department still had to pay her thirty-thousand dollars in an out-of-court settlement.

The ruling in favor of Pammi Route was not because I took the shot and she got hit, but rather because Slater *HADN'T* taken the shot when he should have, which forced me to shoot from an impossible angle. The original ruling was for sixty-thousand, but the jury ordered that thirty-thousand of it had to be donated back to the police department, earmarked specifically for sniper training.

Because of that donation, I went to a Special Forces Advanced Urban Sniper School in Maryland. Additionally, the money allowed for a secondary sniper, and they brought Ray on the team, sending him to the beginner, intermediate, and advanced sniper schools within six months of each other. The deal basically hosed Pammi Route, considering that her lawyer bills were about ten grand, leaving her with approximately twenty-thousand dollars when the dust settled. I heard she bought a new car and went to Vegas with her share. Drive safely, Mrs. Route.

The van comes to a stop, and Ray and I jump out the back, ready to do Christmas battle.

For sales, editorial information, subsidiary rights
information or a catalog, please write or phone or email

ibooks
1230 Park Avenue, 9a
New York, NY 10128, US
Sales: 1-800-68-BRICK
Tel: 212-427-7139
www.ibooksinc.com
email: bricktower@aol.com.

www.Ingram.com

www.ingramcontent.com/pod-product-compliance
Lightning Source LLC
Chambersburg PA
CBHW071832020726
47502CB00004B/1326